Agatha

or a narrative of recent events

Elizabeth Jervis

(later Elizabeth Pipe Wolferstan)

Second Edition

Edited with introduction by John Goss

To my good friend Malcolm whose loyal support over many years for my humble literary efforts is greatly valued -

John

**Grosvenor House
Publishing Limited**

First edition published privately by the author in 1796 and sold by C. Dilly,
Hookham & Carpenter, and Allen & West, all of London.

This book is published by
Grosvenor House Publishing Ltd
28-30 High Street, Guildford, Surrey, GU1 3HY.
www.grosvenorhousepublishing.co.uk

First edition 1796.
Second edition 2010.

Cover illustration from a miniature of Elizabeth Pipe-Wolferstan thought to be by
George Engleheart.
Vignettes by Thomas Stophard, R.A. from the first edition.
Statfold Hall engraved by T. Donaldson from Stebbing Shaw's *History of Staffordshire*.

A CIP record for this book
is available from the British Library

ISBN 978-1-907652-02-8

Preface

I discovered the author of *Agatha* while working on my thesis about the social concerns of English novelist Robert Bage and considered it to be such an important literary discovery that even if it proved detrimental to my thesis I was determined to place this scarce novel before the public eye as soon as possible in an attempt to rescue its author from hitherto obscurity. Elizabeth Jervis deserves to be credited and recognised, even if more than two centuries have passed, for a first novel which contains some lovely turns of phrase, and some dramatic incidents. She was a spinster when she wrote it but did not remain so for long. The story behind her marriage and the courtship prior to it is as intriguing in many ways as the novel itself. An introductory chapter shares details of this remarkable love story. To balance the way it is presented I have consulted the diaries of Samuel Pipe Wolferstan as well as some of the poems of Elizabeth, especially *Three Years After Marriage*, which is particularly revealing because of the way in which it presents a very different aspect of their lives together from that of her husband.

From an editorial viewpoint I have taken liberties in changing some archaisms and old spellings including *increase* for *encrease*, *truly* for *truely*, *basin* for *bason*, *impolite* for *unpolite*, *condemn* for *contemn*, *satin* for *sattin*, *carpeted* for *carpetted*, *burden* for *burthen*, *chase* for *chace*, *complete* for *compleat*, *portray* for *pourtray* and many others. I have also taken out some of the long dashes and exclamation marks, even changing some of these to question marks when the sentence is clearly a question. Although this decision may be at odds with accepted practice the purpose was to try to make the novel more appealing to modern readers. Despite these editorial intrusions and corrections in punctuation, the content of the work is very little changed from the original 1796 version.

I dictated the whole novel using voice-recognition software and have endeavoured to eradicate a few minor errors found in the original, without adding too many of my own. I persuaded my brother, Charles, and my musical friend and composer, Daniel Rodger, to proofread the text and I have been pleased with, and thankful for, the errors they found, that I had earlier missed, and the suggestions they made to improve the narrative. I am indebted too to Isobel Grundy for reading the introductory chapter and her helpful comments. Members of staff at Stafford Record Office deserve my thanks for their dedicated service and help. In particular I am indebted to subscribers who have each played a part in bringing the second edition to fruition and helping to establish the reputation of an accomplished woman writer who might otherwise have remained unknown. My thanks go too to Major Wolferstan for allowing me to photograph family possessions. Finally, my wife, Barbara deserves special thanks for tolerating my eccentricities in pleading the cases and causes of neglected Midland novelists; namely Elizabeth Jervis and Robert Bage.

March, 2010.

Agatha – a remarkable love story

The author of *Agatha* bore the same maiden name as the more feted, and oft-ridiculed widow, who late in life married young Samuel Johnson; his much-lamented "Tetty". Like Johnson's wife, Elizabeth Jervis emanated from Leicestershire (though born in London), and she too married a Samuel; landowner, lawyer, antiquarian, campaigner against the slave-trade and meticulous diarist. Samuel Pipe Wolferstan had a formidable estate at Statfold near Tamworth and after his marriage to Elizabeth would four years later acquire another at Pipe, not far from Lichfield. He proposed to her on 1 September 1796 and their marriage took place on her thirty-third birthday just over a month later.

1796 was an eventful year for Elizabeth, as it was for Samuel. Six months before their big event her first novel *Agatha; or, a narrative of recent events* had been privately published for the author and sold by C. Dilly of London. Elizabeth's father was Philip Jervis, a long-time family friend of Samuel's who had made his wealth in the London silk industry at Spitalfields. He also had one hundred acres of land at his country seat in Nether Seale, Leicestershire. Jervis held out high hopes for the success of his daughter's novel, demonstrating a parent's devoted enthusiasm, strong enough to cause Wolferstan to note how he was "mightily pleased" his daughter had not sold the copyright. The reviewers did not see *Agatha's* future in quite the same light. The *Critical Review*, called the story "tedious and improbable", and the characters "insipid or out of nature", while Arthur Aikin, in the *Monthly Review*, drew the conclusion it had been written by a man. He censured that when "a novelist assumes the grave and important character of an historian, it is incumbent on him to adduce his proofs and cite his authorities."

Entering the world as an author and getting married were high events of the year for Elizabeth but these achievements must have been toned down by the bitter reviews, and further tempered by the failing health of her father who would die in February of the following year. There were uniting elements in the lives of Samuel and Elizabeth, including a long family friendship. One of these was a love of literature. An avid reader of fiction in his early years, Wolferstan had been a member of the Lichfield book-club until 1787, and he went along periodically to the Tamworth book club. He later played a part on the committee of Tamworth library. Early friendships boasted a number of the Staffordshire literati including Erasmus Darwin, who before moving to Derby in 1782 had been his family doctor, and Anna Seward. Thomas Gisborne, another author and also a friend of Darwin's, called on Wolferstan's services in helping to coordinate the Staffordshire campaign against the slave-trade. Other literary notables Wolferstan entertained at Statfold were John Allcock, doctor of music, novelist, and former organist at Lichfield cathedral, then later organist at Sutton and Tamworth; he was also familiar with Robert Bage, the popular Elford and Tamworth novelist and paper-mill owner, whose best-known novel *Hermsprong; or Man as he is not* was published the same year as *Agatha*.

From a literary viewpoint the political writings and involvements of Robert Bage and Samuel Pipe Wolferstan were aimed at seeking constitutional reform of the monarchy whereas *Agatha* is a novel supportive of the old order, at least as it existed in France before the revolution. Determining Elizabeth's real politics is quite hard to assess, for she changed as she grew older. Over the years she did much work on behalf of clothing the poor and like Samuel, was opposed to the slave-trade. Freedom of speech was becoming commonplace before the French revolution and in south Staffordshire and Derbyshire there were lively and healthy debates among the propertied classes which quite quickly gave way to fervent nationalism shortly after the revolution. It sometimes divided families. In December 1794, at Darley, "W. [probably William Wray] made an affronting speech" on Wolferstan's "French politics". Two years later the Statfold lawyer was reading a novel by his future wife that ought to have found favour with the anti-Jacobin school. It seems, however, to have been overlooked by that canon of criticism.

Five days after Samuel first learned her novel was due to appear he ordered four copies of the expensive edition; a limited number being printed on fine paper. At that time Elizabeth had hardly been considered a nubile prospect by one who would soon become her husband, though there was an occasion when he briefly speculated about the possibility. He started reading *Agatha* in early May, and was quick to display strong reservations about her debut into the world of fiction, commenting how it "begins rather improbably" then a fortnight later pronouncing that if he had seen the manuscript before publication he could have saved her "some criticisms" regarding "several slips of language" and "some inconsistence in character". His only positive comment amounted to "some pretty verses". This lack of support may have been crucial in determining Elizabeth's future as an author since no other known novel of hers was published and it was not until after Samuel's death in 1820 that she ventured back into print – this time publishing several volumes of "pretty verses" under her married name. How much Wolferstan's criticisms were influenced by the reviews, if at all, is difficult to gauge, but it is worth the observation that before reading *Agatha* he had shown only a passing inclination towards seeking the hand of his friends' daughter, even though he had been looking for a matrimonial partner for almost a decade following the death of his first wife in 1786.

Wolferstan was an Anglican by birth but he was very much influenced by dissenters, especially when in London, and in 1790 frustratingly commented "between Presbyterians and Church folk, where am I to get a wife?" Over the years he made occasional favourable remarks about Elizabeth, for example he enjoyed having her as a partner at whist, but there were unfavourable ones too. He showed disapproval of her choice of dress on one occasion. On another he even noted how she had lost her youthful glow: "Elizabeth not very attractive – one would fancy the plumpness, the vivacity of youth all faded".

If Samuel was concerned about where he might get a wife, Elizabeth must have been just as concerned as to where she might get a husband, at least a husband with whom she could find contentment and a freedom of expression that her intellectual leanings warranted. Having a respectable family fortune there would have been no shortage of prospective suitors. As she wrote:

Where Beauty, Youth, and Fortune join,
Love will a world of hearts purloin;

Indeed it was her wealth that finally won over Samuel. Yet wealth was anything but the theme of *Agatha* a novel more concerned about overcoming worldly pursuits and coming to terms with a self-imposed, almost solitary life, even if this was to be spent amid the company of friends. Agatha's calling as a nun was not very far from Elizabeth's real mode of life at the time she was writing the novel. The story of how her heart was won is fascinating, almost unbelievable, and contains many of the ingredients of a good period drama.

She was no longer young as Wolferstan so candidly observed on a visit to the Jervises with his son Stanley. Almost three years before their marriage, in late December 1793, at Nether Seale, he heard a rather cutting remark which strongly hinted at Elizabeth remaining a spinster which by chance was precipitated by one of his son's drawings. Samuel had gone to distribute some of the boy's pencil sketches, "a single rose bud falling to Elizabeth Jervis' share". At this portentous sign a female friend in the company observed it was an "emblem of living and dying in single blessedness" or words to that effect. But the observation turned out to be a long way from the mark. Less than three years later Elizabeth would walk down the aisle with a man who spent his leisure-time researching local history, campaigning for the abolition of the African slave-trade, supporting the rights of young chimney-sweeps and making donations to other philanthropic causes. Superstition, in the form of a rose-bud, might have its place in poetry, of which both were fond, but Elizabeth was not destined to live and die in "single blessedness", even if her fictional Agatha may have done. On her first visit to the monastery the heroine of her novel consoles herself.

> If in the thorny paths of adversity one comfort raised its kindly head, she saw and cherished it, nor disregarded its sweets on account of the baleful weeds by which she was surrounded; and if every rose had its thorn, and every joy its allay of sorrow, or in the fragrance of the flower she endeavoured to forget its prickles, in gratitude for the blessing, to lose sight of its attendant uneasiness.

In July 1796 Samuel, who was not the most confident of lovers, made a much more accurate prediction about Elizabeth's future which was based on his own resolute determination to get a wife and a mother for his children before winter set in. When he caught her eye and that of her neighbour Mary Gresley on the same night at the same gathering he resolved to "get one of these or the others lately suggested". And there had been, and were, plenty of others, including Lord Stafford's daughters and sisters, Mary Ann and Lucy Wray.

At the time of his marriage to Elizabeth he had two children from his first marriage to Margaret Biddulph; a daughter, also called Margaret, 17, and son Stanley, 11. There can be very little doubt that Elizabeth would have been excluded from his intentions if Samuel could have persuaded the children's aunt to marry him. Ann Maria Biddulph took on the responsibility of bringing up the children after the death of her sister Margaret. For years Samuel pestered her to marry him and less than a month before Elizabeth accepted his proposal he made one last attempt to win her over, though how much of this was in earnest is not easy to determine from the diaries. His relationship with Ann Maria Biddulph was often tempestuous and Samuel, with his usual honesty and legal turn of mind and phrase, took down many of the high points of events and conversations verbatim. The final rift in this stormy affair came in October 1788 when he tried to get her to commit to an engagement. She shilly-shallied which caused him to resort to profanity. The outburst so shocked her that she quickly declared "I am afraid of you". Wolferstan's response was: "And I of you proving an unaffectionate mother-in-law and a madwoman". In the coolness of reflection when he wrote down the conversation he realised madwoman was a "fatal word". Samuel made several attempts to heal the rift. He even used Robert Bage's expertise as a miller to help her brother Simon restore to better working order some corn-mills in his possession which were not operating at full efficiency. Bage assisted him, but told the lawyer, he was only giving his time out of respect for Samuel's first wife. When Ann Maria learned about this unsolicited attempt to win her favour it had the opposite effect to that intended and caused even more problems between her and Samuel. Eventually the relationship fizzled out into friendship. She got herself a new man, Richard Hergest, who had sailed with Captain Cook, but who was unfortunately killed at Oahu in May, 1792, on another expedition. After Hergest's death early the next year Ann Maria requested her letters back, sending Samuel hers.

The Biddulphs and Jervises moved in similar circles as did another family, the Gresleys, who were near neighbours of the Jervises at Nether Seale in Leicestershire. Only slightly younger than Elizabeth was Mary Gresley and Samuel found her much to his taste, though this fondness was barely, if at all, reciprocated. The Jervises were well aware of Samuel's penchant for Mary Gresley, but probably equally aware that it would be a fruitless pursuit for him. On the same evening that Elizabeth received her rose-bud sketch, Samuel played a couple of rubbers of whist with her as his partner, thinking her a "good girl", but it was in another room when he was discussing taking fellow antiquarian and architect, Thomas Blore to see the Gresleys, that Jervis commented "Then will be your time for Miss Gresley". For a further two years he deliberated, rehearsing and modifying a marriage proposal speech, but he never seemed to get the right opportunity to use it, or even a variation of it. It did not stop him from proposing to others. There was Mary Anne Wray of Darley, who refused him, her sister Lucy Wray, who accepted him but would later send back his letters, if not the £40 watch or bracelet he bought her. And Betty Stafford refused him too. Throughout these encounters Elizabeth was waiting in the wings. On one occasion in 1795 when the Jervises could not provide him with a bed because Elizabeth's mother was "still quite lame" her father let it be known that he was aware Wolferstan was 'said to be marrying a young lady in Derbyshire' which silenced the lawyer. Just over a month later at a disappointing lecture on astronomy in Measham, Elizabeth strongly hinted at her interest in Samuel, by asking "Will you go home with me?" He accompanied her to Nether Seale but then rode on to Statfold with other company.

When he went to see a theatrical production in Tamworth called the "Jew and my Grandmother" he sat next to Robert Bage but only "near enough" to bow to Miss Gresley who seemed to "answer very slightly". In his various courtships there is a strong sense that Samuel, even after a previous marriage, and all his experience on the law circuit, was still diffident in the presence of women and this was demonstrated two months later in mid-July when he found himself alone with Mary Gresley in a bay window at her house. Instead of proposing, which was his intention, it was she who "chattered" while for him the occasion turned into a bit of a "predicament" and he almost forgot what he called her assumed shyness at the Tamworth play. Afterwards he reproached himself for his weakness. Word must have got out about this aborted attempt because others reproached him too.

When it was asked shortly afterwards by one of the local gentry, Gache, if there was no woman who could keep Wolferstan at home, John Meacham, another man of property, at whose house the company was gathered, put forward the name of Mary Gresley. Mary's sister, Elizabeth Gresley, had died in 1792, and Gache believed that when there were two Gresley sisters they were after something better than a "private gentleman". Mrs. Lyon, wife of one of the Tamworth doctors with whom Robert Bage's son Edward was in partnership, thought such talk was damaging but Measham added that he had heard Miss Gresley say she thought Mr. Wolferstan "ought to have a widow" and that he was "too timid" by half. Wolferstan laughed off this ribbing but inwardly kept imagining himself in the "bow window last Saturday".

It determined him to take action. When he did pluck up sufficient courage to propose to Mary he began by outlining his worth and ancestry. She confessed she was "obliged for the honour done, but must beg to hear no more of this subject" adding she was happy to see him as a friend of her brother. While his inept courtship of Mary Gresley was ongoing Samuel finished reading *Agatha* and thanked Elizabeth for the "entertainment from her pen". Events moved quickly after that. He still fancied a more "ardent attack" on Mary but the next time he rode over to Nether Seale the Gresleys were out visiting Sir Nigel at the pottery and it would not have been appropriate for him to attend the women alone. So he popped into the Jervis household and there heard something which would quickly change the whole direction of his courtship, though not with instant effect.

Mrs. Mary Jervis, Elizabeth's mother, started to tell him at dinner about the family fortunes of the Jervises. This information ought to have registered something in his mind since it was only three days earlier he had found himself advertising his own family history and personal wealth to Mary Gresley. It is almost certain that Mary and Elizabeth were confidantes. Elizabeth had been present on the evening Wolferstan proposed to Mary. What is more the two women were of the same age-group and close neighbours which might be why Mrs. Jervis, after explaining that there was a good £10,000 for all the children irrespective of her husband's personal wealth of £23,000 to £24,000, added the proviso: "You'll be good enough not to say a word to anyones". On the same day a short time after his future mother-in-law made this fascinating disclosure Samuel would join Elizabeth and her younger brothers and sisters in Acres Field going by Gorey Lane, and when the others got "together in a party … I was not quite sure whether she did or didn't make a move toward a view from the corner in lane, which might have left us alone together". Procrastination seems to have been Samuel's own worst enemy, but perhaps also, in the long term, his best friend. Elizabeth Jervis had been fond of Samuel for many years even going so far as to show him her garters when she was only twenty and he a young married man of thirty-three. Nearly a decade later he still recalled the incident and pondered if "that exciting girl who could cause emotion" might have the same effect were she to show him her garters then. His observations regarding Elizabeth were mixed; occasionally favourable, more often the opposite.

Normally an early riser the next day he overslept, missing the alarm, and began to reflect on Mrs. Jervis' "unexpected information" worrying about miscalculations but believing if her arithmetic was right there would be "nothing against this good girl but lack of brains", a comment he appears to have borrowed from Thomas Gresley. This is incongruous with information he received at dinner the previous evening when Mrs. Jervis informed him that Mary Gresley and her brother, Thomas, extolled the virtues not just of Elizabeth but also of her novel *Agatha*. Troubled by doubt his next concern was whether Elizabeth "may be entirely ignorant of her mother's intimations" but decided to take the initiative anyway. At this time too Philip Jervis was diagnosed by Erasmus Darwin as having a large abscess and his case was pronounced "hazardous", a euphemism for terminal. Burton-upon-Trent was recommended for Philip the next day, followed by Matlock. When Samuel received confirmation that Elizabeth would accompany her father he arranged to meet up with them when he went to Chesterfield.

> The carriage built, the cakes bespoke,
> While Lawyer's clerks their quills invoke.

As the various legal representatives were getting together to iron out the financial details of this proposed union Samuel breakfasted with Ann Maria Biddulph, and as she entered from the chamber, he approached her, kissed her, squeezed hands and the conversation, as recorded by Wolferstan, went like this.

"Do these kisses and squeezes mean anything Nellie?"

"Nothing particular" (smiling up at me).

I threw my arms round her and with a loud sigh of thorough emotion said (pressing her) "Durst you begin again with me?"

"Not for the world," still smiling.

"Are you quite resolved?"

"Yes."

"Could you bear to see me embrace another?"

"Yes, I believe so."

"Then I'll not disturb you."

We sat ...

"I have very great regard for you."

"I do believe you have".

Three days later they were together in Derbyshire and Ann Maria Biddulph again squeezed his hand saying with a smile, "You'll remember in future this (pressure) is only from a sister to a brother". She told him it was impossible that they could marry for she could never be easy afterward. The probable cause of her uneasiness was ecclesiastical law. To marry the sister of a late wife was regarded by the church as incestuous, though Matthew Boulton married siblings from Staffordshire as did Richard Lovell Edgeworth. Ann Maria, who was far from well and short of money, remained resolute in her continued rejection. She had heard through various sources of his being refused by Fanny Stafford, but did not give it full credit till she heard it from Samuel himself. Wolferstan seemed a little disappointed that nobody had thought of him and Betty Stafford. When he talked of his approaches towards Elizabeth Jervis "she hoped in that case, (still smiling and laughing, good creature) to have credit of match maker". He then visited Philip Jervis who was said to be feeling better and the next day it was back to scrutinising the finances.

With the maid coming in and out to remove tea things, Mary Jervis and Samuel discussed Mr. Jervis's apportionments for his daughters. Some of the sums mentioned would have been enough to have widened, if not popped, the maid's eyes, could she have overheard them. Spitalfields market, where Philip Jervis had his silk interests, sold for £28,000 and immediately let for £2,000, and although there had been a lull in profits, Samuel, with his own income from property of £1000 to £1500 per annum, found what he heard much to his liking. He thus confirmed to her mother that he was "very happy to pay his addresses to Miss Jervis". A pause took place in which he expected an objection but Mrs. Jervis simply stated: "Why all I can say is that a more worthy creature does not live". Samuel "knew that perfectly, had known it long" quickly forgetting his other love pursuits and some of the less delicate comments he had subscribed to on previous occasions.

Philip Jervis was deteriorating further and was of major concern. On the last day of August Samuel walked with Elizabeth on a terrace with a fancy for addressing her "in pathetic style" but it was not until the following day that he actually marshalled the courage to go through with the proposal. When Samuel crossed his left hand to her right hand saying "I have no doubt that I shall make you happy", Elizabeth responded with "and I hope I shall make your children happy". "If you don't," said Samuel, "I do not know what woman will" and the next day she freely let his fingers press hers when on a canal towpath which was too narrow for three of them. The third person would have been a chaperone, probably one of Elizabeth's sisters. A week later her birthday was suggested for the wedding and the plans were set in motion.

There can be fewer more detailed or more openly-written accounts of the progress of a courtship, but Samuel would never lose the image of his first wife. Less than two years prior to his engagement he confided to his diary that the changes of this mortal life would probably make him forget his poor Margaret, "dear faithful mother of my children." On the contrary; with less than a month to go before his wedding day he placed "portraits of himself and his former wife on Elizabeth's wrists". Elizabeth, took no offence, and kindly penned a few lines to her memory, the last of these Samuel decided to edit, for which she again courteously thanked him. By then he was "in full possession" of Elizabeth's "lips and arms". She added to the verses making her own alterations and their time together quickly blossomed, so much so that her mother feared gossip in the neighbourhood from them "sitting up" together. Worrying about Elizabeth's "fair character" she gave her daughter a lecture. Elizabeth defended herself claiming her main objective now must be to please Samuel. "Yes, I see it is, and that I've lost a daughter" said her mother. Her father was not as overtly concerned and with a wry sense of humour said: "Why, Mr. Wolferstan seems very fond of our old one Betty; what a strange taste". The wedding took place:

> Six weeks from that eventful day
> Which saw them first, in formal way,
> Bow, curtsey, smile, then bow again
> The day was fix'd and all *en traine* –

It was not an extravagant event like his first and afterwards there was not much of a honeymoon, probably due to Philip's poor health. The newlyweds did however get to see some of the sights of Derbyshire including Chatsworth Park with a visit to Arkwright and Wilkinson. In her poem, *Three Years After Marriage*, Elizabeth alludes to the trip, transforming herself into the persona of Matilda, while Samuel is portrayed as Julius.

> Not with less grace and fearless speed
> Matilda rode her beauteous steed
> Where Willersley's proud turrets vie
> With Cromford's lovely scenery.

Willersley Castle was Arkwright's home on the hill above Cromford village. It overlooked the valley in which he had his famous mills.

Four months after the wedding Elizabeth's father was dead. Mary Gresley's brother, Thomas, officiated at the funeral, at which Samuel found the lead coffin to be "very cumbrous". He was then faced with sorting out the legal affairs. It had been exactly eleven months to the day Philip Jervis died from when he first informed Samuel of the publication of his daughter's novel for which he had such high hopes.

Agatha; or, a narrative of recent events is not nearly as bad as contemporary critics tried to make out and had it been published at a time when fiction had undergone some of its later metamorphoses might even have been considered a precursor to novels of the absurd, though it probably fits best into the Gothic genre. The plot is sound and at least one character, Mr. Craggs, is unique to fiction of the day. The reader comes across him early in the novel. Agatha, who has mixed Anglo-French ancestry is left with her only friend, Miss Hammond, when her father and mother are called abroad to look after family and business affairs. When Miss Hammond suddenly loses her life to a "baffling fever", Agatha, who has seen less of the world than *Evelina*, is invited to Milson Hall by her new acquaintance, Miss Milson. It is at Milson Hall where she encounters in mixed company, the extraordinary Mr. Craggs. A fanciful hypochondriac he is described as a little emaciated figure of about forty who has "lavished his fortune on empirics" and carries with him a pail of water to counter a discovery he has made that one half of his body is heavier than the other.

Wolferstan encouraged science and philosophy in females as well as males but this diversion into Newtonian physics was too much for him and he made an exclamation in his diary about carrying a pail of water and 'in company!' He further wondered why her father and brother, Swynfen, had not picked up on such a rare piece of fictional absurdity because he thought he could have saved Elizabeth potential embarrassment from the critics. His censure is somewhat unjust. Craggs is quite an endearing character, as long as he remains a product of fiction. Another of his eccentricities is to pass frequent electric currents through one hand to promote a quickening of the circulation, with a nitre poultice on the other to impede it. When brought to task about his oddities Craggs defends himself, "if it is a crime to take poison to shorten our lives it is a crime not to take any possible means to preserve them." Inconsistency in character is not a criticism that can be levelled at Mr. Craggs who makes appearances in the first and third volumes. To describe any fictional characters as being "out of nature" indicts a large proportion of authors of fiction, since one of the novel's purposes is to entertain, and to be entertaining it needs to have an element of the extraordinary and uncommon. *Agatha* has plenty of entertainment.

There is some justification in calling the novel "improbable" but readers of that other improbable novel, *The Female Quixote* by Charlotte Lennox, might find compatible and comparable elements of humour in this which might be lost on other readers, reviewers and, it would appear, even by the man who would become her husband. Two thirds of the way through the first volume, when Agatha has fallen for Edward Hammond, brother of her late lamented friend, her parents return rather hurriedly from France, and whisk her back home with them. It is then learnt that Agatha's grandmother, who employed assassins to waylay and murder her adulterous husband, extracted on her deathbed a solemn promise that her daughter, or failing that, any daughter her daughter might have, would atone for the sin of which the grandmother was guilty by devoting herself to a life of chastity and charity as a nun. The black humour is excruciating, it being too late for her mother to pay for her grandmother's cardinal sin. Agatha's mother, also Agatha, has already fallen in love and married, so when Agatha unexpectedly comes along the penance falls on her, who is, as might be expected, none too pleased with the prospect. Dutifully abandoning any ideas of unity with Hammond she accompanies her parents to France where, after a lot of soul-searching and wavering, commits herself to the convent at Issoire.

The year of Agatha's self-imposed committal is 1788 giving rise to the alternative title of the novel, *a narrative of recent events*. It covers the period of revolution, but more strikingly and starkly the period immediately before 'the terror'. It captures an atmosphere of mistrust and fear, where peasants of the revolution, formerly reliant on the church for charity, now fear for their lives and seek to dispose of members of the aristocracy and supporters of the Catholic Church in compliance with new government policies. No favour is shown to nuns or priests, which is largely how it was in reality. Figures for executions in France up to the end of the 'terror' vary from 17,000 to 40,000 which prompts the question: what angered the English critics? It is true the novel is somewhat one-sided. There are few attempts, and none by the main characters, to criticise the Church as an institution even though its wealth was built on contributions from poor peasant workers. Criticism against the church and the aristocracy is confined to occasional rants from disenchanted minor characters all portrayed in a bad light. In reality the church was the biggest pre-revolution property-owner in France. However, the early period of French history after the revolution was both bleak and bloody in the extreme. It may be, in his criticism about Elizabeth not citing sources, that Aikin was more concerned about a lack of historical evidence about what happened at Issoire, the site of Agatha's convent, and whether it suffered any worse than other religious institutions in the country, if it suffered at all. It is questionable whether the story was actually passed on to the author, a claim made on the last page of the last volume.

In the novel, Madame St. Clermont, a sort of liberal mother superior or abbess, prays that God grants her "countrymen make good use of the liberty their Monarch has so generously given them." At the time of publication every reader would have been aware that the monarch in question, Louis XVI, had already been guillotined, something at which most free-minded English people were appalled, including Tom Paine, whose writings had helped bring about the revolution. Strict laws were in force in France with capital punishment being the penalty for anyone found harbouring aristocrats or members of the church – Agatha was both. This wisdom after the event is a little irksome, somewhat one-sided, unjust towards the peasantry and perhaps deliberately tailored to suit the personal views of the author at the time she wrote it. It fails to mention that Louis XVI was obliged by changing circumstances to give his countrymen their liberty rather than being a generous and philanthropic benefactor of his throne and power, as he is drawn by the Mother of the convent. However Madame St. Clermont cannot be criticised for holding views that may not be approved by historians and radical factions, any more than can minor characters who oppose them. After all she is just a character in a book, and despite what the *Critical Review* claimed, constant in her beliefs and actions.

The only characters who vacillate in their views and actions are Agatha, until her confinement, and her mother, and these vacillations are sustained. The personality of her mother is worthy of closer study. She sympathises with Agatha and shares her soul-searching over committing herself to a religious institution but at the same time discourages her daughter from becoming involved in the social affairs of the world or with friends she made while her parents were in France. Preparation had been made for the seclusion mapped out for her before she was even born.

In Agatha's attempt to escape from France one poor family, that of St. Valorie, at its own risk takes her in. Unsurprisingly St. Valorie is also from an aristocratic family even though the family fortunes are no more. When knowledge of Agatha's presence at St. Valorie's becomes known to the village she hides, in true Gothic style and tradition, behind a panel which another family had formerly used for smuggling salt. St. Valorie is told his fate will be prison and death if he does not hand her over. He refuses to admit she is there and the stand-off seems to be going quite well until, in a moment which almost suspends belief, Agatha reveals both herself and the smuggling panel. She does not quite say "Here I am!" but surprises of this nature make it an uncommonly entertaining and, for me, a humorous novel. Royal academician, Thomas

Stophard, captured this scene in his vignette for the third volume cover page. Further elements of the Gothic are found in secret and subterranean passages within the convent and ruined chateaus which too frequently enable various escapes. When imprisoned Agatha shares a cell with the corpse of a baby; and when her parents try to flee her father discovers a torture chamber in the house in which they are seeking refuge.

Separated from other nuns, and from her parents, Agatha tries to make her way back to England but the peasants to whom she had formerly been so charitable show her no, or very little, charity themselves out of fear for their own lives. On the point of starvation, and on the point of becoming the victim of rape, Hammond unexpectedly turns up to rescue her. Together they make their way back to a disused convent, to the secret underground cave of Father Albert, and eventually to England.

Apart from these commonplace adventures little of the stereotype is found in *Agatha,* making it a refreshing read. Against the tide of anti-Semitism one character, Israeli, who had been protected against abuse and discrimination at school by Hammond, turns out to be a true and loyal friend, coming to Hammond's aid more than once, whereas in standard literature from Shakespeare to Dickens, particularly through the characters of Fagin and Shylock, Jews are portrayed on the whole as despicable rogues and usurious moneylenders. It is further credit to Elizabeth's liberal-mindedness that she herself was an Anglican whereas anyone reading the novel might well be convinced it had been written by a Roman Catholic, an observation which may account for why critics in England were opposed to it while French critics endorsed it.

On the first day of February 1798, Samuel Pipe Wolferstan's journal notes that a French edition of his wife's novel in four volumes was advertised in the London papers. There is some reason to believe this was the second French edition because a three-volume edition of 1797 was previously advertised though no copies of this seem to have survived. It was translated by Madame de Guibert as *Agatha, ou la Religieuse anglaise* and published in Paris at the house of Maradan. Using this French edition as a text there followed a three volume Dutch translation *Agatha, of de Engelsche non: eene hedenaagsche Fransche kloostergeschiedenis* in 1802.

Agatha's love for Hammond and the church intermingled with filial duty, which is depicted as being as heart-rending for her mother as for Agatha, allows for the kind of in-depth psychological soul-searching present in Samuel Richardson's novels, but because the novels are of a different nature, they cannot be compared as like for like. The main uniting factor is virtue, and the rewards virtue is said to bring. Richardson's

Clarissa remains virtuous by refusing to marry despite family pressure and rape, whereas *Pamela* is rewarded with marriage for her virtue. For *Agatha* the rewards are of a heavenly nature. A twentieth century critic of the French edition noticed elements of Richardson, as well as Goldsmith, Young (presumably from the verses) and Rousseau. Far from the negative press it received in England the French edition was presented favourably and compared to Diderot's *The Nun*, which like *Agatha* was first published in 1796, though written years earlier. In Diderot's novel the nun is confined against her wishes, a circumstance lending itself to a critical comparison with the flippant Sister Frances, another memorable and consistent character from *Agatha*, who through family pressure takes vows against her disposition and who can hardly wait for the unfolding events to make good her escape in order that she may marry. The revolution enables her to achieve this ambition even if her husband, a sickly artist to the French nobility, may not have been the man of every woman's dreams, not even the dreams of Sister Frances herself. The artist, Monsieur La Rive, may have been based on a real French artist Bruno Hamel, whose parents were guillotined, and who escaped to England dressed as a fisherman before settling in Tamworth after marrying a Birmingham girl, Elizabeth Hunter. Wolferstan met him in 1793 when he "sat an hour together with Hamel the new emigrant French teacher, and a good scholar ... but poor man could share little in our talk which was chiefly on the wrong side for his politics ...".

There was, perhaps, quite a lot of Agatha in her creator Elizabeth. When Miss Hammond died Agatha resolved "until the last sad duties were paid to her departed friend, she would not quit her remains". Other deaths also find her, and others, hanging around corpses in what even then might have been considered macabre. When Elizabeth's father died Wolferstan recalls how he took his wife in for a last time before the coffin was soldered: "I and Swynfen [her brother] could not get her out of chamber again – at last she found resolution to kiss the corpse twice, and Anne [her sister] followed her".

Like her fictional heroine Elizabeth was not over-enamoured with social life and when the Tamworth Yearly Hop came round in January 1798 she excused herself even though her sister Catherine (who had not been well for a week) was well enough to go along with Wolferstan and his daughter, Margaret, and they all stayed late. Others saw Agatha in Elizabeth too and when one of Samuel's old tutors from Repton School, William Bagshaw Stevens, another diarist, came to dinner at Statfold he recorded "dined at Wolferston's. Agatha a pleasing woman. Margaret warmhearted." There was, of course, no Agatha at Statfold so it is almost certain he meant Elizabeth.

Statfold Hall from the South East in 1798.

Elizabeth seemed quite content with reading, clothing committees and Sunday School. Surprisingly she worked alongside the teacher and curate, Richard Davies, who preached a charity sermon early in 1803 to raise funds, in this instance £34, for her clothing repository. Judging from the political tone of her novel this working partnership would hardly at the time *Agatha* was written have been conceivable since Davies was a liberal clergyman and Mrs. Wolferstan in the early days of her marriage could not "bear him" especially when he talked politics. Davies, who was also a tutor to Stanley Pipe Wolferstan, had angered some of the Tamworth congregation back in 1793 by preaching on Christmas Day from "Peace on Earth". Although this was quite in harmony with the Christian message it was less than twelve months after the start of the war with France; a likely cause of such anger. The politics of Davies are made quite clear in a letter from Robert Bage to fellow-novelist William Godwin in which he describes the clergyman – whom Godwin had actually met at Bage's – as having learning and talent but being deficient in political orthodoxy which had "rather incurred suspicion than certainty, of his tendency to opinions held in abhorrence by every good member of Church and State". Five years of marriage to Wolferstan coupled with the influence of his associates may have tempered Elizabeth's political opinions and the family friendship with Davies continued even after he got a post at Leicester School. He tended to visit his old pupils and friends during the Christmas period and on

New Year's Day, 1809, Elizabeth chose not to go to church because of the snow preferring Davies to officiate upstairs. Elizabeth, like Agatha in the novel, threw herself into charitable works "bestowing benefit and easing sufferings, a source of the purest delight and highest satisfaction."

As can be seen from the last sentence hyperbole is an ever-present ingredient of style and superlatives reign supreme throughout the descriptive text and narrative. Yet it remains an entertaining, readable tale, darkly humorous and constantly in breach of reader expectations. If it is read, as the early reviewers seem to have done, as a straight narrative, then the irony is lost. There are many "out of this world" incidents and other improbabilities, but few authors can survive without creating moments of tension, drama, originality and escapism. Elizabeth also showed a talent for portraying conflicts of interests within domestic scenes. The vast majority of readers would align themselves with the sentiments of the servant-girl who tries to save Agatha from the plans of her parents to get her to a nunnery, by encouraging her to disobey their wishes and elope with either of two potential suitors rather than spend the rest of her days incarcerated in an ecclesiastical prison. As well as the constant overstatement through exaggerated description the first edition contains an excess of exclamation marks and long dashes, which do nothing to improve the reading fluency and much to reduce the impact that would have been created with less frequent usage. In this edition many of these excesses have been removed.

In order to increase the tempo when action is involved one common device adopted by Elizabeth is a shortening of sentences, nearly all of which by today's standards would be considered far too long. Despite their length, however, they remain comprehensible. Modification in style shows literary competence and since shortening sentences gives dramatic impetus it demonstrates that Elizabeth Jervis was well-acquainted with writing technique. Richard Brinsley Sheridan's play *The Rivals* had been popular for twenty years, and the character Mrs. Malaprop must have made a strong impression on her mind. Not only does she get a mention through the voice of Mrs. Herbert; '... now, as Mrs. Malaprop says, all our retrospections shall be to the future' but two of her own characters, the maid servant, Hannah, and the self-important Sir John Milson, are vulnerable to the snares of this figure of speech.

Her husband saw her poetry as having merit, which it did, and still does. *The Enchanted Flute with other poems and Fables from La Fontaine* provides a well-maintained sense of metre, and without the knowledge she had a novel to her credit, she is already recognised as one of England's minor poets. Yet there are bad poems as well as good ones in *Agatha* and the poor lines are generally reserved for characters most deserving of them. As Mrs. Herbert, the second female to Agatha, says of William Milson, who is infatuated with the young widow and keeps writing verses for her:

> By shortening or lengthening his lines occasionally, he often takes liberties, perhaps not licensed by the rules of poetry; but where the heart is deeply affected, our feelings are apt to run away with us; and it is difficult to confine our metre within its just limits.

The prose shows poetical content too as in Mr. Crawford's sober view of marriage once the honeymoon period is over.

> By giving us one to share the pains and pleasures incident to human life, it diminishes the one and increases the other; and for happiness equally exquisite and durable we must look beyond an existence which hangs but by a thread, and all whose gayest colours, like the vivid hues that paint the air-blown bubble, may vanish in a moment, destroyed by the very breath which created them.

Elizabeth had no first-hand experience of married life when she wrote this. Wisely she leaves any judgment to her readers as to whether married life diminishes the 'pain' or the 'pleasure' but she remains well aware that the brightly-coloured bubble of life can burst at any moment. When she did try out married life herself there is reason to conclude that she and Samuel had problems, especially in the early years. Samuel still had an eye for a pretty woman. In September 1797 he went to hear Wilberforce preach a "dreadful sermon" at Shepshed and described the politician as looking "like a drowned rat himself" while Wilberforce's new wife was "an excellent looking creature with lovely eyes – and after service presented her – I wish I could have seen more of her and of others..." Elizabeth was certainly unhappy with his absences at Statfold and Seale and the earlier cynicism about married life was hardly quelled by her experience of it.

> There is a Moon made all of Honey,
> Which couples newly married eat,
> And find it a delicious treat;
> But when 'tis gone are glad to seize
> One manufactured of Green Cheese,
> Which disagrees in ev'ry way,
> Brings heart-burn, bile, et cetera.
> And this they tell you is the reason
> Why marriage has a Winter Season,
> When all looks blank, and cold, and drear,
> And *Sir* and *Ma'am* succeed to *Dear*.

The flippant comment made by Philip Jervis about Wolferstan having "strange taste" in being fond of his eldest child may have concealed a worry about the suitability of the match, and her father's forebodings were seemingly realised in the early months of their marriage.

> His child's distress he must deplore;
> He pitied, but could do no more –
> Where folly and imprudence reign
> A kingdom's wealth were giv'n in vain.
> Some pangs he felt of wounded pride –
> But stifled them – and so he died.

The poem from which the above and other extracts come is from *The Enchanted Flute* and is called *Three Years After Marriage*. In it Samuel becomes Julius, possibly after Caesar, and Elizabeth becomes Matilda, possibly after the Conqueror's wife, Matilda of Flanders. In her preface to the volume Elizabeth informs the reader that some of the verses were written many years earlier. The poem covers, over four cantos, a considerably longer period than three years, and must have been added to over time. Although it is known that Wolferstan was friendly with the Jervises from his early twenties it seems the relationship went back much further for she writes: "Playmates in childhood, friends in youth, our intimacy called for truth."

As the years passed their married life became more stress-free and each got involved in individual interests, for him still mostly of an antiquarian nature, for her through charity work and various committees. As John Money has noted Samuel became more business-like following his

Elizabeth Pipe Wolferstan and Samuel Pipe Wolferstan.

marriage to Elizabeth, and this can be witnessed, among other improvements, by "the greater energy and method which from now on began to mark his management of his estates and his dealings with his tenants". He had always been "a man of his word", but became "a hard bargainer and a shrewd judge of personality."

Elizabeth craved children of her own. She had played a part in the upbringing of Samuel's two children and was devoted to her brother Swynfen's daughter, another Elizabeth, who she often took to school with her. It is probable that she was teaching at a day-school of her own by 1805. Thirty years later she would publish a small volume on education called *Fructus Experientiæ or Conversations on Early Education*, which sold for two shillings and sixpence and went into a second edition in 1837. Aimed at educators of the very young it is a three-way conversation between a lady whose daughter, Georgiana, is in need of scholarly improvement; a Mrs. Grant, who has heard that four is the age to start a child's education, and Mrs. Bentley, the pillar of educational wisdom. The book's message is that children develop at their own rate and should be encouraged but not pushed beyond basic reading until they show an inclination themselves. Forcing them could generate an aversion. Georgiana, who goes to school with poor children, has an ear for music, so Mrs. Bentley suggests encouraging this gift, with an arguable claim that "music is to a girl, what mathematics are to a boy – by forcing the mind to fix steadily on one subject, it gives the power to dwell on others." Several neat little anecdotes like that of the rich girl, Emma, who would be happy to give a poor little beggar-girl with no frock her Duncan plaid, which she did not like, but not her muslin, which was a favourite. There are appendices; a reading list, a Latin word list, and at a time when scholars were still majoring in Greats, *Latin to amuse very young children*. A few verses mixing Latin and English are presented in this manner.

> Sua filia, His daughter
> cecedit, fell
> in aquam, into the water.
> Filia, The daughter
> ejus, of him
> incepit, began
> nare, to swim.

Elizabeth was herself a Latin scholar and in 1827 translated into verse Ovid's *The Fable of Phaëton*. She was also a French scholar. There can be little doubt that the author of Agatha wrote all the works attributed to her in this introduction. However, during the course of the 19th century there were two other Elizabeth Pipe Wolferstans. The first was daughter of Elizabeth's brother, who as a girl Elizabeth took to school and whose maiden name, like her aunt's, was Elizabeth Jervis. Further confusion arises from Stanley marrying Elizabeth Steele Perkins in 1861 after the death of his first wife. She was another talented poet who had published under her maiden name a horticultural poem *Flora and Pomona's Fête*, which by 1838 had gone into eight editions and would later be published under her married name, Elizabeth Pipe Wolferstan.

The last known portrait of *Agatha's* Elizabeth was painted in 1834, and shows her, aged 71, with a young child on her knee, reading from, it may be assumed judging by the red binding and its size, *The Enchanted Flute*. Sadly, like her fictional nun, Elizabeth would remain childless. On New Year's Eve, 1807, the Wolferstan's were both hoping for God's will to be done with the "possibility of a pregnancy" but a week later Elizabeth came down in tears. Samuel comforted her in his belief that everything was ordered for the best. She was then forty two.

Elizabeth was an educated and talented woman with diverse interests. Despite suggestions to the contrary women took a wider notice in the developments of science than has sometimes been observed. Wolferstan escorted his first wife to lectures given by John Warltire (1738/9 – 1810) in Derby and he regularly went to Darwin's lectures while the famous physician was still living in Lichfield. Elizabeth knew Erasmus Darwin too since he was the family doctor before her marriage to Samuel. From the ludicrous examples of applied science through her character Scraggs, it can be seen she knew more than just the bare rudiments, and as mentioned, she invited Samuel to escort her back home from an astronomy lecture. After marriage she continued to keep her knowledge up to date and accompanied her husband to a series of scientific lectures given by Dr. Stancliffe which went on for more than a week. Electrical and chemical experiments were demonstrated at these events and members of the audience were encouraged to sample some of the results, including those produced by nitrous oxide. After hearing of the "extraordinary accounts of medical good effects" of this mixture those present were invited to partake and it caused "pretty considerable laughter" from two Quaker wives (Lakon and Bourn). Samuel preferred to "remain well". At another lecture Elizabeth's ears were "disordered" long afterwards following the explosion of an "inflammable air bubble".

Though Elizabeth and Samuel wrote and edited pre-nuptial verses together, and Samuel had long before presented some of his own poems to the impressive Lichfield Book Society, his interest had dwindled by 1787. He was an avid reader of novels until his antiquarian interests took over, after which he helped Stebbing Shaw compile the weighty *History of Staffordshire* which understandably has a section on Statfold, the Pipe-

Wolferstan estate. Nevertheless as a family they continued to buy books at annual book society sell-offs and Samuel reluctantly got himself elected to the committee of the Tamworth library in 1809, but fiction no longer held the magnetism it once had for him. Elizabeth tried to get him interested in the works of Robert Burns but these simply set her husband "dozing". His former love of literature did not entirely die and when they were on a bathing holiday in Hoylake in 1811 she managed to persuade him to read Oliver Goldsmith's tale of suffering *The Vicar of Wakefield*. For all Samuel's pretensions, and continued annotations of Shaw's *Staffordshire*, it was Elizabeth who retained the literary leanings – although his diaries are of phenomenal historical importance. As far as is known she never attempted another novel but, as well as the aforementioned educational book for infants, she went on to publish several volumes of poetry under her married name after Samuel's death.

There was a period just before she became a widow when hardship was a major factor for the couple. Harding's bank crashed due to a sustained run in 1819 and it seems the Wolferstans suffered with many of the other residents of Tamworth and surrounding districts. *Three Years After Marriage* suggests that they reduced the number of house servants to two footmen and a maid, ate with steel forks from white plates and no longer sampled exotic fruit from the West Indies. But they had property, and tenants, so recovery was better assured than for most. Their marriage, despite earlier misgivings, had grown in warmth until:

> To Julius and Matilda seem
> Their former lives a fever'd dream.
> Years have gone by and seen them blest,
> Their spirits calm, their minds at rest.
> Of former envied good bereft,
> They praise their God for blessings left.

Earlier the household had been thronging with servants and the servants' personal lives were sometimes the topic of conversation and gossip, as when a somewhat innocent and "valued dairy girl ... had confided to a married woman that J. Saunders had (inter alia) put hand up etc". The maid confessed to liking Saunders, who may have been a blacksmith, although there was "little conception he thought not of marrying". An implied double negative here leaves the reader bewildered, but the dairy girl promised to avoid being alone with him and "acquaint of all proceedings". Servants in the Wolferstan household were treated as part of the extended family especially in Samuel's younger years. If a servant was ill the doctor was called and the servant's master duly paid for any treatment.

Samuel died in 1820 and in 1822 Elizabeth produced her versified translation of *The Enchanted Flute with other poems and fables from La Fontaine.* It was much different from her novel and in the preface it seems she had resigned herself to the notion that the world had passed judgment on *Agatha.* While not mentioning it by name she may well have had her romance in mind when she wrote.

> *The world then can alone decide for us, and its decision is generally just... ultimately, it is probable, every work finds its true level. Let but one view, one motive influence us, and then, whether what we publish shall live, or, wanting literary merit, sink into deserved oblivion, we shall have no cause to regret the trial made: may we write,*

> *"As ever in our great Task-master's eye."*

She did, however, make one last attempt to sell off the remaining copies of her novel when her next volume of poetry, *Eugenia,* appeared in 1824. Other volumes followed including *Fairy Tales: in verse,* in 1830 and *Golden Rules,* 1841. The latter contains a series of rhyming proverbs, mostly couplets, which make references and acknowledgements to celebrities of her lifetime, including Maria Edgeworth, William Wilberforce, William Cowper and Hannah More. Some of these personalities she would have met. A couplet suggests a change in political opinion with a revealing acknowledgment to Mary Wollstonecraft.

> Advancing years will tempers guard
> When reason tunes the strings that jarred.

The more radical leanings of her husband, marriage itself, and the influence of liberal-minded reformers like Richard Davies must have tempered the establishment-views she held before marriage, those she espoused at the time she was writing *Agatha,* and perhaps the wisdom of seniority had revealed a more expressive need for the reform in the rights and education of women. Her last collection was *Old stories versified* which was published in 1842. She died an old lady in 1845. From the publication of the first edition of *Agatha* to this, the second edition, there has been a span of 214 years.

Bibliography

PRIMARY SOURCES

Manuscript

Diaries of Samuel Pipe Wolferstan, Stafford Record Office, D1527/1-45 (1776-1820).

Letter to William Godwin from Robert *Bage*, (Bodleian Library, Abinger Collection). When this was accessed the collection was being re-catalogued hence no reference available.

Typescript

Diaries of Samuel Pipe Wolferstan, Stafford Record Office, (1776-1812 with summaries for 1813-1820, on temporary loan).

Literary works consulted

Jervis, Elizabeth, (see also Pipe Wolferstan, Elizabeth), *Agatha – or a narrative of recent events*, printed for the author and sold by C. Dilly, Poultry, Hookham & Carpenter, Bond Street & Allen & West, Paternoster Row, London, 1796.

Pipe Wolferstan, Elizabeth, *Fructus Experientiæ or Conversations on Early Education*, Baldwin and Craddock, London, 1835.

– *Conversations on Early Education*, R. Hastings, London, 2nd ed., 1839.

– *The Enchanted Flute with other poems and Fables from La Fontaine*, Longman, Hurst, Rees, Orme and Brown, London, 1822.

– *Golden Rules*, R. Hastings, London, 1841. Googlebooks.

SECONDARY SOURCES

Articles and advertisements

Chinard, Gilbert, <u>Agatha et le vœ fatal d'atala</u>, in *Modern Language Notes*, Vol. 46, February 1931, John Hopkins University Press.

Edinburgh Review, List of New Publications, 1836, p. 256.

Gibbons, Ian, *Portrait of An Artist, Etienne Bruno Hamel*, Tamworth Heritage Trust. URL: <u>http://homepage.ntlworld.com/greenhall/tht/history/Hamel.htm</u>

London Literary Gazette and Journal of Belles Lettres, Arts, Sciences, etc., 1824 (advertisement on page 240 for *Eugenia*).

Money, John, <u>Provincialism and The English "Ancien Regime": Samuel Pipe-Wolferstan and "The Confessional State," 1776–1820</u>, in *Albion: A Quarterly Journal Concerned with British Studies*, Vol. 21, No. 3 (Autumn, 1989) pp. 389-425. Stable URL: <u>http://www.jstor.org/stable/4050087</u>

Historical

Bagshaw Stevens, William, *The Journal of The Reverend Bagshaw Stevens*, ed. Georgina Galbraith, Clarendon Press, Oxford, 1965.

Shaw, Stebbing, *The History and Antiquities of Staffordshire*, printed by and for J. Nicholls, Fleet Street, London, 1798.

Bibliographical

Raven, James, and Antonia Forster, *The English Novel 1770-1829: A Bibliographical Survey of Prose Fiction Published in the British Isles, vol 1: 1770-1799*, Oxford University Press, Oxford, 2000.

Chronology

4 October 1763	Elizabeth born in London, the daughter of silk-throwster, Philip Jervis and Mary (née Dove). Baptised at Spitalfields, 31 October 1763.
1776	Samuel Pipe Wolferstan diaries begin containing references to his association with the Jervis family.
1796	*Agatha – or a narrative of recent events* privately printed and sold by Dilly, Hookham and Carpenter, and Allen & West. Samuel orders four deluxe copies.
1796	Wolferstan proposes to Elizabeth and they are married on her birthday. They honeymoon in Derbyshire where her father lies critically ill.
1797	Philip Jervis dies.
1798	French translation: *Agatha, ou la Religieuse anglaise*.
1801	Dutch translation: *Agatha, of de Engelsche non: eene hedenaagsche Fransche kloostergeschiedenis*.
1804	Miniature portrait of Elizabeth painted by George Engleheart.
c1805	Elizabeth is teaching at her own school.
1817	Samuel's son, Stanley Pipe Wolferstan, marries Elizabeth's niece, Swynfen Jervis's daughter, also called Elizabeth.
1819	A run on Hardings bank in Tamworth causes family hardship for the Wolferstans.
1820	Samuel Pipe Wolferstan dies.
1822	*The Enchanted Flute with other poems and Fables from La Fontaine*, Longman, Hurst, Rees, Orme and Brown.
1824	*Eugenia, a poem*, Longman, Hurst, Rees, Orme and Brown.
1827	Translation in verse of Ovid's *The Fable of Phaëton*.
1828	*The Fable of Phaëton*, with Latin text.

1828 Portrait of Elizabeth seated and wearing a lace bonnet.

1829 First publication of *Fairy Tales in verse*, Lichfield, 1829.

1834 Portrait of Elizabeth reading to a child sat on her knee.

1835 First edition of *Fructus Experientiæ or Conversations on Early Education*, Baldwin and Craddock, London.

1837 Second edition of *Conversations on Early Education*, R. Hastings, London.

1841 *Golden Rules*, R. Hastings, London.

1842 *Old stories versified*, London.

1845 The year Elizabeth Pipe Wolferstan died.

Agatha

or a narrative of recent events

Elizabeth Jervis

(later Elizabeth Pipe Wolferstan)

Chapter 1

The following narrative affords an instance of one, who, endued by nature with the most tender and susceptible of hearts, was nevertheless mistress of herself – of her reason – and triumphed over every propensity not warranted by the strictest, and in her case, by the cruellest duty. If these volumes should fall into the hands of those who possess ingenuous hearts, and who, with the warm feelings of youth, are yet open to conviction, let them read them, and learn to triumph likewise: for others they are not written. No! Let those who determine madly to swim down the stream of passion, sink in the dreadful vortex which it will inevitably carry them! To such the friendly hand is in vain held out – the friendly warning in vain offered – neither precept nor example can teach us to conquer what we are determined to believe unconquerable.

Sir Charles and Lady Belmont had long lived happy in each other, and equally loved and esteemed by all who surrounded them. Their ample fortune afforded means for the indulgence of every luxury, but what they esteemed the greatest, was the power it afforded them for dispensing comfort to others. Their hospitable table was open to everyone whose merit as well as rank entitled them to regard; while the crumbs which fell from it were a daily supply to numbers of their poor neighbours, whose prayers and blessings followed them wherever they went.

Twelve years had elapsed since Sir Charles, who fell in love with and ran away with Lady Belmont on his travels, had been married, and he had yet no prospect of an heir to his ample possessions. For many years he had appeared to desire such a blessing with the most anxious solicitude; and Lady Belmont, a sharer in all his wishes, viewed frequently with tears, and almost with envy, the ruddy offspring of the peasants around them; while their cottages seemed to possess greater felicity than her splendid mansion, since they contained that for which alone she sighed. But, whether from a resignation taught her by her mother in her last and only visit to her in France, or from whatever other cause, Lady Belmont as well as Sir Charles had for the last three years appeared to dread an event which they had before considered as so necessary to their happiness; and they were heard to thank Heaven that there was no probability of their adding one to the long list of those, who, born with apparent prospects of comfort, were nevertheless destined to pass their days in unavailing sorrow.

At length, however, contrary to all expectation, and now, it appeared, contrary to her wishes, Lady Belmont became the mother of a daughter, whose infant beauty, and her mother's sorrow were equally the wonder of all her friends. She would gaze upon the child wistfully as it lay on her lap, and then, bursting into a flood of tears, give it to the nurse to convey out of her sight.

The little Agatha, for so she was called after her mother, evinced, as early as the marks of disposition were discoverable, every sign of a warm and benevolent heart, a sweet and serene temper, and a soul exquisitely susceptible. Her mother surprised her one day, when about three years old, wiping with her frock the tears from the cheeks of a little beggar girl, and emptying her pocket of all her little treasures to give her; and as Lady Belmont approached, looking up in her face, yet scarcely able to speak for the feelings which agitated her infant breast, she said, "Poor girl cry, Mama, Agatha heart break!" This is but one of a thousand instances of early benevolence remembered and related by those who knew her in her childhood.

Studious to make her parents happy, if her penetrating eye discovered a mark of dejection on either of their countenances she would throw aside every toy that had before seemed to delight her, and prattle for an hour till her repeated efforts had dispersed the gloom. Nor did she possess the qualities of the heart alone. Her mind was susceptible of and anxious for improvement; and as she grew older, she excelled in every solid as well as ornamental accomplishment. Her parents encouraged her application, and were delighted, though, apparently, not without a mixture of sorrow at all her attainments.

Lady Belmont would often say to her, "Endeavour, my Agatha, to excel in everything; but chiefly I recommend to your attention those accomplishments which are resources to us when deprived of society; which make us not alone even when alone, and which may render even a life of seclusion a life of pleasure. To depend on others for amusement is to build our happiness on a sandy foundation, which every wind that blows may destroy in a moment. A thousand inevitable circumstances may separate us from the world and from all we prize in it. Let us not, therefore, leave ourselves friendless. A book, a pen or a pencil, are sure and faithful friends.

These will attend us when deprived of all others, and prove a source of unvarying delight. The world is replete with instances of folly and ingratitude; the comforts it affords are transitory and futile; repentance treads upon the heels of pleasure; and there is no real happiness to be found but in retirement and solitary amusements.

Imagine not," she would continue, "that the gay and dissipated are ever happy. After a night passed in forced mirth and dancing, they arise at noon languid, haggard, and dispirited; not with the glow of health, not with the cheerful serenity depicted on my Agatha's countenance when she arises to the duties of the day.

Love, perhaps the purest of worldly pleasures, since, if genuine, it includes benevolence, is productive of sorrows for which its vaunted blessings are inadequate to atone: if it meets with obstacles it is misery! If it finds none, it either creates them, or languishes through very indulgence: then jealousy, the most agonizing of human sufferings, is its constant attendant.

Marriage, honourably as it is spoken of, and, happy state as it is represented, is replete with troubles. For one pair who find comfort in each other, as your father and I have done, there are thousands who curse the day that united them. If love be the inducement to marry, our happiness must experience a diminution; for even its votaries, and warmest advocates acknowledge that love is transitory. A marriage from mercenary views has no chance of happiness. Friendship is the only allowable motive: and for friendship why should they marry who may be friends without."

These were the lessons Lady Belmont constantly inculcated, and this the picture she incessantly drew of the world. Agatha listened with respectful attention; yet could not forbear thinking that her mother reasoned too severely: and with the ardour of youthful hopes, she still fancied that the world, bad as it was, might afford her some happiness: and that when the time should arrive that she was permitted to enter it, thus guarded by caution, she should be able to discriminate; to separate the bad from the good; to make a moderate use of pleasures; to dance without fatigue, love without much jealousy, and be one of the favoured few who married happily like her parents.

At sixteen, Agatha, beautiful and accomplished, formed the subject of conversation throughout the neighbourhood. The few who had seen and conversed with her dwelt so continually on her praises that many, even of her own sex, walked frequently near her house to catch a view of her; which was perhaps the more desired as it was obtained with difficulty.

One person only was treated by Sir Charles and Lady Belmont with any degree of intimacy, all their other acquaintance, as their daughter grew up, they had dropped by degrees; till at last a few ceremonious visits were all they paid or received. Miss Hammond alone they received and acknowledged as a friend, and with her only was Agatha permitted to associate. Miss Hammond was an amiable and uncommonly sensible woman, and was universally beloved and respected. Though considerably turned of thirty, she had every requisite to render her the companion of youth: she was lively, entertaining, and studious to please; and possessed a happy talent of creating, as it were, amusements. With her

Agatha passed some of her most delightful hours; and, while she looked up to her for instruction in her graver moments, in her gayer ones she regarded her as a sister. To her she laid open every thought of her innocent heart, which a severity in Lady Belmont's manner forbad her to do to her. Miss Hammond, nevertheless, inculcated the same dread of the world, the same wish for solitude; but the tints in her picture were softened by benevolence, and Agatha listened without reluctance. To Miss Hammond she was indeed indebted for the most valuable lesson of her life; to her precepts she owed that conquest of herself, that command of her feelings which rendered her truly estimable, and her character perfect.

"Our feelings, my beloved friend," Miss Hammond would say, "were given us for the noblest of purposes. Heaven endued us with sensibility that we might be alive to religion, pity, charity, and friendship. And while that sensibility is directed by our reason to its proper channel, it is our richest ornament! But when our feelings, our passions, get the better of ourselves; when, because we have such and such wishes, such and such propensities, we feebly yield to them, we are no longer free agents: we are under the dominion of those passions which while they are suffered to govern us will infallibly render us wretched; but which if, on the other hand, we governed them, would only serve to make us happy, and give a zest to our enjoyments."

Agatha's life had thus passed in study, retirement and conversation, when an immediate summons to France on account of Lady Belmont's fortune, obliged her parents to leave England for a short time. Agatha, but recently recovered from a severe illness, was too weak to bear the journey; and they left her, not without uneasiness, under the care and protection of Miss Hammond, at whose house she was to pass the short period of their absence.

A new scene now presented itself to her view. She had never passed a night under any roof but her father's, had scarcely ever entered another door, and to spend a few weeks with Miss Hammond in her house, see, perhaps, some of her friends, was a prospect of delight, small indeed to many, but to her most enchanting. She could not sleep for some nights in her new abode. "The novelty of the situation, my dear Miss Hammond," she said, "keeps me awake."

Among the few who called upon Miss Hammond on her return home, (for to most of her friends she had written to say that Lady Belmont wished her daughter to be seen as little as possible at present), was the eldest daughter of Sir John Milson, a neighbouring baronet. Miss Milson possessed a tolerably good understanding, which she had so far cultivated as to render herself esteemed sensible by many of her acquaintance.

Indeed she concealed no part of the knowledge she had acquired, and eagerly made a display of it upon every occasion. She had read a little history, a little poetry, and an abundance of novels. In the first branch of knowledge, she was mistress of some of the leading events, and most of the common-place anecdotes relative to our own country: talked of Julius Caesar's invasion, was familiar with the names of Hengist and Horsa, and perfectly acquainted with William the Conqueror's illegitimacy. In poetry she was no less an adept, dwelt perpetually on Pope's delightful flow of versification; was absolutely enamoured, as she styled it, of the sublimity of Milton, from the first book of whose *Paradise Lost* she daily quoted some lines, beyond which, it had been supposed, she had never read. She possessed from nature some sensibility, and from art infinitely more. She would watch for whole hours a few flies imprisoned in a ditch; and delight her feeling heart by snatching them from their watery grave, and restoring them one by one to life and liberty. But the chief of her perfections, and that for which Lady Milson most prided herself in her daughter, was her skill in planning and executing beautiful little ornamental boxes, purses &c.; and in her taste, superior to everything that ever was seen in working trimmings; her roses as large as life, and heartsease so naturally coloured that no one could mistake them for anything else, were the admiration of all her acquaintance. Such was Miss Milson, and such her perfections. Agatha possessed sufficient discernment to remark her foibles, but had too graceful a heart to feel insensible of the attention paid her.

"This, your lovely inmate, dear Miss Hammond," said Miss Milson, "reminds me of Milton's beautiful lines,

Grace was in all her steps –[1]

for there is something in her beyond all our imagination can paint of a Clarissa[2] or Cecilia![3] Her society must render your little habitation infinitely interesting."

"I consider it indeed," said Miss Hammond, "as one of my greatest felicities; and only regret," continued she sighing, "that I may be soon deprived of it."

"Ah! Miss Hammond," said Agatha, "you forget the precept you have so frequently taught me: never to embitter present comforts by a dread of losing them. But I will not forget your lessons; and will not suffer myself to think that I shall ever lose the happiness I now enjoy."

---

[1]John Milton, *Paradise Lost*, Book 8, line 488.
[2]*Clarissa* is the eponymous heroine of a novel by Samuel Richardson.
[3]*Cecilia* is the eponymous heroine of a novel by Frances Burney.

"A very just reproof!" said Miss Milson. "Hope, rather than fear, is a divinity whom we ought to worship eternally. When Julius Caesar landed in Britain," (How thought Agatha can Julius Caesar have any connection with the present subject?) "When he landed, had he not indulged hope, instead of fear for the future consequences of his temerity, we might never have owned the Romans as masters."

"Possibly so;" said Miss Hammond, "yet neither you nor I should have been great losers if such an event had not taken place."

"Doubtless not," returned Miss Milson, "I speak, principally, with reference to him. Yet the Romans introduced luxury; and luxury, by enervating our forefathers, obliged them to have recourse to Hengist and Horsa for assistance; and from the Saxons we inherit many of those virtues which adorn a Sir Charles Grandison.[4] Thus, you see, the event has in reality, an intimate connection with ourselves."

This was reasoning too deep to be controverted, and Miss Hammond gave a nod of assent.

When Miss Milson took her leave, she gave Agatha a pressing invitation to visit her at Milson Hall. "Such as our mansion is, Miss Belmont," she said "it will delightfully receive you. You shall visit my summer-house, my *Cassetta*, as I term it. You understand Italian?[5] A lady, who was perfect mistress of the language, taught me that name for my little rural retreat. It is placed on the summit of a mount of honeysuckles. My father will receive you with pleasure; and though I must apologise for the coarse rusticity of the reception you may meet with from him, be assured he will think his table gladdened by your presence."

When Miss Milson was gone, Agatha entreated with so much earnestness to be permitted to accept her invitation that Miss Hammond, at length, promised to accompany her thither.

But a far different scene – a scene of misery awaited Agatha, and nipped all her fairy prospects in the bud! Miss Hammond, the friend of her heart, her companion from infancy, to whose precepts she owed her virtues, to whose friendship she was indebted for most of the hours of happiness she had known, was seized with a violent fever; and though every possible assistance was procured immediately, the disorder baffled medicine; a delirium ensued, and she expired in the arms of her distracted friend.

Agatha remained during several hours in a state of stupefaction; and when she, at length, recovered her senses, awaking but to anguish, she

---

[4]The eponymous hero of Samuel Richardson's seven volume novel, *The History of Sir Charles Grandison*.
[5]*Cassetta* is a diminutive of *cassa* and means a little box. The diminutive of *casa* is *casino* and means summerhouse.

was seized with fits which threatened her life; or, if that was preserved, at least her reason. Miss Hammond's servants treated her with every possible attention; and by their assistance, added to the benevolent exertions of her physician, she was at length restored to some degree of calmness and composure. But she, who a few days before had felt herself the happiest of human beings, was now the most miserable! She seemed alone upon the earth. Beside Miss Hammond she had never had a friend, never a companion for even a day. To her own servants she had never been permitted to speak; and her parents far distant, there seemed not a being in the world to whom she had the least relation, or on whose regard she had the smallest claim. And when to this melancholy reflection was added her anguish for the loss of the kindest of friends, imagination can hardly draw a more distressing picture.

By the advice of the physician she determined to return to her own house, and await there the return of her parents, to whom she wrote, as soon as she had the power to write, to inform them of the melancholy event: but until the last sad duties were paid to her departed friend, she would not quit her remains, and determined, on the day after, to affix, as Dr. Harley had proposed, her seal on everything, and quit the house.

Chapter 2

The melancholy day was now arrived. Agatha had shut herself up in the back parlour, that she might avoid a prospect of the sad procession. She had thrown herself into a chair, and was indulging those tears from which alone she hoped for or obtained relief, when the door opened, and a young man entered, on whose countenance were depicted the strongest marks of agony and horror. Agatha started up, and attempted to quit the room: but her trembling limbs refused to support her, and she sunk again into her chair. The young man at first seemed not to remark that she was present: totally absorbed in misery, he appeared insensible of everything. Agatha, whose gentle heart for a moment almost forgot her own sorrows in the sufferings of the stranger, again offered to rise, and said, "Shall I fetch you anything?"

"Nothing, nothing on earth! No, there is not a being who can give me comfort now!" Then covering his face with his hands, he leaned against the wall without having the power to utter another word.

Agatha, again assuming strength to speak, in the hope that by divulging his sorrows they might be softened, "You are some friend," she said, "of the dear friend?" She could say no more. He made no reply. At length, going up to him, with a strength inspired by terror, "Sir, Sir," she said, "whoever you are, recollect yourself, recover your senses for God's sake! I am ill able to administer comfort who so greatly stand in need of it myself: but I will strive to forget my own sorrows to offer consolation to you. Speak, speak to me, I conjure you! Who are you? What can I do for you?"

The stranger who had seemed insensible of everything before, now turned round, and looked at Agatha with a mixture of wildness and astonishment. At length, putting his hand to his forehead, and forcing himself to speak, "Oh," he said, "wonder not at my agony! Wonder rather, that I have seen what I saw, and live! I met – just Heaven. I met my dear, my only sister carried –" He was unable to speak. After a pause, endeavouring to recollect himself, he continued. "Many, many years had we been separated; at length, released from captivity, I returned, I flew to meet her – Good God how –"

"Amazement!" said Agatha. "And are you the brother whom she so long believed dead, whom she lamented?"

"Lamented!" he replied. "Oh that I had never lived to lament her!"

His agony by degrees began to subside into a settled sorrow which found relief from dwelling on the subject of his grief. "Oh," he said, "had you known her kindness, her sweetness! Oh! She was sister, friend, mother, everything to me!"

"Alas," said Agatha, "I know but too well the kindness of her heart; for though bound by no ties of blood, she was all those to me!"

"And what kind of angel are you" said Mr. Hammond, "who, thus miserable, could forget your own distresses, to give compassion to a stranger?"

"Alas!" said Agatha, "I too am a stranger in the world! My parents are in France. They left me under the protection of the best of friends. She is taken from me; and I have none to fly to."

Agatha again burst into a flood of tears.

"Forgive me, Oh, forgive me," said Mr. Hammond, "that I thus cruelly recalled the remembrance of your grief. Oh let me not be such a wretch as to add to your sorrows who have so kindly poured balm to mine!"

"Say no more," said Agatha, "we will both strive to be comforted, indeed we will. We will apply to Heaven for resignation, and seek for alleviation to our sorrows where only it is to be found. But since you are so kind as to accept the poor consolations a sharer in calamity can offer, will you permit me to fetch you any refreshment?"

"Generous, kind as you are," said he, "how can I ever be sufficiently grateful! But may I not ask the name of one to whom I am so greatly obliged?"

"Agatha Belmont."

"Agatha Belmont!" he repeated. "Never, shall it be forgotten – never will I cease to acknowledge to whom I owe a restoration of reason, to a calm I never conceived it possible again to have felt."

Agatha now left the room to order refreshments, and retired for some minutes to her own, in order to recover by reflection her almost exhausted spirits. Yet far different were her sensations on returning to her chamber to those she had felt in quitting it half an hour before. She was still wretched; she had yet lost the friend she lamented, and was sensible she should eternally lament; but she was no longer alone in the world, no longer the only sufferer it contained. In the yet more poignant distresses of Mr. Hammond, her own appeared to lessen, and in him she had found one to whom she could unbosom them; one who from his own would pity hers, and the hope of mitigating whose anguish promised comfort: and she thanked Heaven that had thus given her, in the bitter moments of separation from one friend, another who might, in some measure, supply her place.

The sad remainder of the evening was spent in mutual sorrow, and mutual tears; but sensible of comfort from each other's society, they parted at a late hour.

Agatha had before purposed to return home on the day following; but studiously kept ignorant of the customs of the world, she knew not that there was the smallest impropriety in her remaining with Mr. Hammond; and receiving comfort from him, and conscious that she bestowed in return, she determined for a few days at least to remain with him. But whatever consolation Mr. Hammond received from her society, he determined to seize the first opportunity of hinting to her the necessity of her leaving him. He soon discovered how much she was a stranger to the world, and he had too much generosity to purchase a moment's comfort at the expense of the character of one, of whose purity and sweetness he was every moment convinced. But the opportunity he sought never seemed to arrive. The task was most painful and almost savoured of ingratitude. Yet, on the other hand, the ingratitude of suffering her to sully her fame for his sake appeared far greater: and he determined at length, whatever he might suffer, to assume courage, and introduce the subject the next hour they passed together.

"Miss Belmont," said Hammond, as they walked in the evening, "appears to have seen very little of the world!"

"Very little, indeed," said Agatha, "and I have been taught to dread it; but the few persons I have known contradict those ungenerous sentiments. I have met with seven or eight persons, and never yet knew an instance of ingratitude, or experienced a mark of unkindness from any of them. Miss Milson, though a stranger, was very kind to me; your sister was all my heart could wish, and you appear to resemble her."

"It shall be equally my study and my pride to merit your esteem," replied Mr. Hammond; "and I would rather inflict the severest punishment on myself than deserve to forfeit it."

"You never will, I am assured," said Agatha, interrupting him. "I have been deceived, I am convinced. Of the world, of which so dreadful a picture has been drawn to me, you, and all I have known, form a part; and are all so many evidences of the falsehood, or, at least, of the mistakes of the system of distrust I have been taught."

"Certainly," replied Mr. Hammond, "the world deserves not all the censures you have heard. Yet there are many who, under the semblance of a regard for propriety, cruelly, barbarously condemn the innocent."

"Ah!" said Agatha, smiling, "this is but a repetition of my mother's lessons. But perhaps it is thus with everyone. Society may resemble what I have read of life itself, which, though all condemn as replete with troubles, all court a continuance of, and all fear to lose."

Mr. Hammond had now made two attempts to introduce the subject, which Agatha's artless interruptions had as often frustrated; and he was meditating another, when a servant came to inform Agatha that a lady enquired for her; and she went into the house, promising Hammond to return to him as soon as possible.

She was met at the parlour door by Miss Milson, who, taking her hand, said, in her usual style, "After the severe loss you have sustained, sweet Miss Belmont, in the death of our much valued friend, I have come to say how sincerely my heart sympathizes in your affliction."

This introduction was more than Agatha could support, and she burst into tears. Her lost friend had been the perpetual theme of Mr. Hammond and herself; and to talk of her with him had now become familiar and even a consolation to her; but the subject thus injudiciously mentioned by another revived in a moment every painful reflection, and probed too deeply a wound yet unhealed.

"Sweet sensibility!" said Miss Milson. "How these feelings elevate you in my esteem! Ah! Let others boast of their apathy, and delight in the want of all that is endearing or lovely; I would not forego the painful luxury of sensibility for the wealth of worlds. My heart bleeds for the sufferings of even an animal, an insect: and it is my glory that it does."

Perhaps the moments in which we really feel, are of all others the least suited to a dissertation on sensibility; and Agatha was incapable of replying, or indeed attending to this elaborate harangue.

After a minute's pause, Miss Milson proceeded, "I am come, likewise, to solicit my dear Miss Belmont's presence at Milson Hall, to entreat you to accompany me thither this evening. Sir John and Lady Milson having heard you still continued with Miss Hammond, and reflecting on the injury you might sustain from it, have requested me to add their entreaties to my own."

"They and you are very kind," said Agatha; "but," continued she, misunderstanding the injury alluded to, "far from receiving any injury from Mr. Hammond's grief, his distresses, strange as it may seem, have been a means of lessening my own. The fear of adding to his sorrows has forced me to combat mine, and I am convinced his society has given me a relief I could not have found elsewhere."

Miss Milson smiled at Agatha's misapprehension; but without explaining her meaning, renewed her entreaties to accompany her home.

"Everything," she said, "shall be done to amuse and delight your mind. We will together explore the fairy region of romance, turn over together the page of history. Pope's melodious numbers shall harmonize our souls, and the sublimity of Milton lift us out of ourselves; while our needles shall create an ever-blooming garden."

Agatha repeated her thanks; but requested permission to consult with Mr. Hammond before she determined on leaving him; to which Miss Milson, not without evident marks of surprise, assented.

When Agatha returned to Mr. Hammond she informed him of Miss Milson's invitation; but added, that she had many doubts whether she could or ought to accept of it, and was come to advise with him,

"Since Miss Belmont does me the honour to appeal to me," said Mr. Hammond, "I must, however I may suffer by the loss I shall sustain, entreat her not to refuse a proposal every way so eligible; where new scenes and new society will chase the painful remembrances this melancholy spot excites."

"I know not that," said Agatha, "yet did my inclination plead with me to leave you there is a monitor within my own breast which would forbid me. That tells me that to forsake the afflicted to whom my presence may afford consolation, to forsake them for those to whom many comforts I could give no increase, would be contrary to that duty which I hope to make the constant rule of my conduct. No, Mr. Hammond, Miss Milson is happy and wants me not; you are unhappy and I ought not to leave you."

"Kind, sweet Miss Belmont! What words can express my gratitude!" replied Mr. Hammond. "But, be assured, there are no means by which I can receive a comfort equal to the consciousness of your happiness."

"Ah," said Agatha, "there was a time when to have gone to Miss Milson's would have made me happy! But my heart is no longer turned to gaiety; and to wander alone with you, mingle my tears with yours – to dwell on the loved idea of one dear, O, how dear to us both, affords more real comfort, nay pleasure than any society on earth could bestow."

"Dear, dear Miss Belmont!" said Hammond taking her hand, and pressing it involuntarily between both his, "this is too much!" Then appearing to recollect himself, he loosed her hand.

"Why this?" said Agatha. "I do not, you see I do not refuse on your account. No, it is chiefly on my own; for how could I bear the idle jests of the thoughtlessly happy, when my own heart was sinking within me!"

"My dear Miss Belmont," said Hammond, "never, not even in the first sad moments of our meeting, when your sweetness recalled me to life and reason, never did you appear so amiable as to me at this moment. Yet believe me when I assure you that you must accompany Miss Milson. To lose you, to part from you is a trial only less severe than that your presence enabled me to sustain. But there are reasons why your continuance with me would be highly improper."

"Highly improper!" repeated Agatha. "You astonish me,"

"The world," resumed Mr. Hammond, "contains few hearts as pure as yours; and those who are incapable of benevolence themselves impute the actions it inspires to motives like those which govern their own conduct. Thus ungenerous, they might condemn your continuance with me."

"And to what motives could they impute it," said Agatha, "for what reasons condemn it?"

Mr. Hammond hesitated, and Agatha repeated her question.

"To motives," said Mr. Hammond, "farthest from the purity of your heart. Yet deign to receive from me the assurance of perpetual gratitude, of an esteem amounting to veneration. O Miss Belmont! You are – you are an angel!"

Miss Milson now coming to them prevented any farther conversation; and Agatha informed her that she meant to profit by her kind offer; but that she could not yet dispel her anxiety at the thought of leaving Mr. Hammond thus alone, friendless, and a prey to sorrow.

"If Mr. Hammond will sometimes stay at our abode," said Miss Milson, "he will be received with the welcome of a friend."

To this invitation Mr. Hammond replied with politeness, and Agatha heard it with evident pleasure. Then turning to him, and laying her hand upon his arm, she conjured him, with a countenance expressive of the most anxious solicitude, to endeavour to support his spirits. "O, Mr. Hammond," she said, "think of me; and if ever you are inclined to indulge in grief, remember, O, remember Agatha Belmont!"

Hammond, who had scarcely power to reply, and who feared in the presence of Miss Milson, to utter, as Agatha had artlessly done, all that he felt, replied, after a moment's hesitation, "Yes, Miss Belmont, never shall your unmerited anxiety for a stranger be forgotten. I were unworthy such generous injunctions should I not endeavour to obey them."

The coach, which had been in waiting, was now ordered to the door; and Agatha went to her chamber to make the few preparations necessary for leaving a house which she had entered with far different sensations.

When Agatha had left the room, Hammond gave Miss Milson a short description of their first melancholy interview; and to the benevolence of a heart unpractised in the world, and which felt for everyone that was unhappy, he said he was indebted for the kind solicitude she had just witnessed. His explanation, added to her own observance of Agatha's ingenuousness, removed in a great measure the doubts she had at first entertained of her conduct being actuated by more tender motives.

Agatha returned to them in tears, and with a heart almost broken. The remembrance of the friend she had lost, and whose habitation she was now perhaps quitting for the last time, rendered her unable to speak; and Hammond, little less affected, could only bid Heaven bless her, as he put her into the carriage: while their mutual distress opened ample field for Miss Milson's powers of elocution; and she was uttering another pathetic dissertation on the charms of sensibility, when the coach drove from the door. Agatha put her head out of the window, waved her hand to Mr. Hammond; and when both he and the house were out of sight, burst into an agony of tears, which all Miss Milson's efforts and eloquence were unable to restrain. Milson Hall was a few miles distant; and with difficulty could she recover her spirits sufficiently to enable her to speak with any degree of composure before they arrived there.

Chapter 3

Milson Hall was a venerable structure, which had remained in the possession of the family whose name it bore, for many generations. It owed more alteration than embellishment to the taste of its present possessor; who, to the ancient gothic edifice of stone, had added a wing of brick in a modern style; and who had cut down two venerable rows of elms which formed an avenue to the house, to make a sweep for carriages in front round a plot of grass, in the centre of which was planted agreeable to Lady Milson's taste, one tall fir tree; and around it, half a dozen rose trees, in compliance with her daughter's. A new walled garden on one side, and superb coach-house and stabling on the other, effectually precluded any prospects which might have opened upon the house when the elms were taken away. Sir John, notwithstanding, esteemed himself a man of very great taste; and indeed all his family laid claim to the same merit in some respect or other.

Sir John was the youngest son of the youngest branch of the family of the Milsons; who, from the improbability of his ever inheriting the family title and estate, and from his father's inability to give to his sons sufficient fortunes to live independent of trade, had been brought up a hosier. In business he was esteemed a shrewd, wary prudent man; and had he never been exalted to a rank for which neither nature nor education designed him, he might have passed through life with a tolerable share of respectability. In person he was short and sturdy; and on his face the marks of low cunning were so legibly written, that less than the skill of a Lavater[6] was necessary to trace the outlines of his character. His little grey eyes, sunk deep in their sockets, "twinkled rather than shone"; while his complexion, which was universally red with a tinge of purple, bespoke the clover, as he termed it, of his own table. Imagining himself wonderfully facetious, he delighted in his own jests; though the diversion they afforded were chiefly confined to himself; her Ladyship's excellent appetite, his daughter's sensibility, with now and then a story of his contriving to give a kiss to a pretty girl, were the most frequent subjects of his mirth. In short, his wit was coarse vulgarity, his sense mean cunning; his piety, charity, and hospitality, were each ostentation.

---

[6]Johann Kaspar Lavater (1741-1801), famed for his treatise on physiognomy: *Physiognomische Fragmente der Menschenkenntnis und Menschenliebe* (1775-1778).

Lady Milson was tall and somewhat awkward; but her face still retained the marks of beauty, for which in her youth she had been eminently distinguished, and which she still regarded as her highest perfection. Her understanding was rather below the common level; but, considering it had received no advantage from education, disgraced as little as could be expected her present station. She was good-natured and obliging to her friends; and had she been married to a man of a liberal turn of mind, instead of one whose meannesses she had early learned to contract, she would probably have been a respectable member of society. A professed votary of taste, her dressing room was filled with pictures, vases, and numberless other ornaments; which, though they bore no mark of the correct taste of the painters or sculptors of antiquity, were, nevertheless, highly commended by her Ladyship, and their various beauties pointed out to her acquaintance. She had a summer-house in the garden fitted up entirely in her own taste; the only opening of which was to a south brick wall. But the want of prospect from without, was amply supplied by that within, the walls being entirely covered with landscapes.

The family of Sir John Milson consisted of himself, his Lady, two sons, two daughters and ten servants. His house was besides generally filled with company, as he prided himself on his hospitality.

Miss Cassandra, the youngest daughter, was the exact counterpart of her mother, whose darling she had been from her infancy; she moderately wise, very handsome, and very good-humoured.

Mr. Valentine Milson, the eldest son, had been married for some years to a woman of sense and refinement. But though possessing much goodness of heart and disposition, he was proof that mere good-nature, unattended by some share of sensibility, and wanting absolutely the polish of a gentleman, is incapable of making a woman of feeling and discernment happy. Mrs. Milson had married him, partly at the insistences of her friends, who were unwilling she should reject an offer so advantageous, and partly because she felt the gratitude natural in a young mind on being distinguished as the object of attachment by a handsome, and generally esteemed young man; she mistook, as is frequently the case, that gratitude for love.

Mr. William Milson was a character totally opposite to his brother. Like his eldest sister he was vain of and exulted in his sensibility; and his romantic attachment to a young widow in the neighbourhood was the theme of every tongue. Sonnets and pastorals were found in every path he frequented; and, shunning society, his whole time was spent in a little retirement sacred to himself at the end of a grove; the style and taste of which differed entirely from those fitted up by his mother and sister. It was built in the form of a cottage, and thatched; while a

16

"Wicket opening with a latch" [7]

led to it, at the distance of a few paces.

Such was the family to which Agatha was now to be introduced.

She was met at the door by Sir John himself, who, as he handed her out of the carriage, declared that she was such a nice young woman that if Valentine was not married, and William desperately smitten already, he should like her for a daughter most monstrously, upon his credit. "But you are welcome here," he continued, "heartily welcome, Miss. It has never been said by anyone, I believe, that anybody of any sort of rank, especially the daughter of one who is a baronet like myself, is not welcome to Sir John Milson's."

Agatha had scarcely time to return thanks for this extraordinary civility, before he interrupted her by saying. "And as for your continuing there with that young fellow, Miss, do you see I thought it was as well let alone. As for an old man like me, why I may steal a pair of gloves perhaps; but what of that? The world won't talk. Now a young fellow is quite another thing."

Agatha coloured, and felt a sensation of uneasiness entirely new to her. She was now sensible of the truth of Mr. Hammond's assertions, and of the kindness and generosity which had prompted him to urge her departure; and she began, for the first time, to believe that the world is sometimes what he and others had represented it.

Sir John, observing her confusion, said, "Come, come, Miss, don't blush, and we'll say no more. Upon my credit and honour as a gentleman, I did not mean to distress you. Come, what say you?– If I had a son to dispose of, what should you think of Sir John Milson as a father?– Egad, I don't know, if my old Lady would but tip off, what I might say to you myself!– Hay?– You are as pretty a lass as I've seen these forty years."

Agatha, who knew not how to reply to this farrago of folly and vulgarity, was silent. But Sir John repeated his question, and declared he would be answered. "Indeed, Sir," said Agatha, "I am quite a stranger to the world and its customs; and know not how to reply to the compliments paid me."

"I wish, Sir John," said Miss Milson, "that you would not thus torment my lovely friend immediately on her arrival."

"Torment her, Miss Sophy!" replied Sir John. "No, no – nothing like it. Show me the woman that's tormented when you talk to her of a husband!"

"I could show you a hundred," said Miss Milson. "To a mind refined like Miss Belmont's the idea of a husband unconnected with

---

[7] Oliver Goldsmith (1728-1774), from *The Hermit*.

every romantic tenderness of the most ardent passion would be dreadful. To a heart like hers even an exclusive preference would be insufficient."

"Exclusive fiddlestick!" said Sir John. "My poor dear Miss Sophy when you once get into these flights the Lord have mercy upon those that hear you. I tell you, you'll all take the first man that offers; and have always done from grandmother Eve down to my Lady Milson. Indeed if Eve had been so mighty nice, I wonder where we should all have been."

Thus saying, and laughing heartily at his own wit, he left them, to Agatha's great relief; who, disgusted at the specimen she had already seen, almost dreaded to meet the rest of the family; and felt more reason than ever to regret the society she had just quitted. She was now introduced to Lady Milson, whose kind reception and frank good nature made her feel immediately at ease in her company; and, disposed as she was to be pleased with those she met, almost, she thought, atoned, for the coarse manners she was obliged to bear with Sir John.

Lady Milson led her into the drawing room, which was filled with company, most of whom were making visits of some weeks to the family. The first of the party to whom she introduced her was the honourable Mr. Craggs, he being a person of the highest rank and most consequence. Mr. Craggs set down the pail of water he usually carried, and rising slowly, made a gentle inclination of the head.

Mr. Craggs was a little emaciated figure, about forty; who, born to affluence and independence, and blest by nature with an excellent constitution, had lavished his fortune on empirics, and ruined his health by fantastic endeavours to preserve it. Without having from nature one real ailment, he fancied a hundred; to remove which he frequently employed means which occasioned real ones. His darling, and, for many years past, his only studies, were medicine and philosophy as it concerns the human frame. By these means, what his physicians failed to accomplish was completed by his own prescriptions; and long before he was thirty, he had every appearance of one standing on the brink of the grave. He had discovered very early in life, that the pulse of one hand beat, by two in an hour, at least, faster than that of the other; and convinced that an equal circulation was necessary to preserve life and health, by passing frequent electric shocks through one hand he endeavoured to promote and quicken the circulation, and by a poultice of nitre to impede it on the other. But, unfortunately, a severe frost setting in soon after, the nitre too effectually answered the end proposed; and by that means brought on a mortification from which he was with difficulty recovered.

He had lately discovered that one half of his body was considerably heavier than the other; and of this he was convinced by an inclination he felt to lean to one side in preference to the other. To remedy this inconvenience, and to produce an equipoise, he constantly carried a pail of water on the lightest side. A slight and gradual inclination of the head was the only species of bow he suffered himself to make. He was no stranger to the dreadful consequences of the slightest injury to the spinal marrow; and he conceived it possible that every bend of the back, by forcing the vertebræ out of their natural, upright positions, might be a means of weakening the spine, and injuring at the same time that marrow which had so intimate a connection with life itself. He therefore avoided a bow with as much caution as he would the plague.

Whenever the sun shone he wore a large hat in the form of an umbrella to preserve his eyes from its beams. If, as he would observe, light consists, as Newton has proved, of matter, be that matter ever so fine, be its particles ever so minute, it must endanger the sight on which it darts, since its force is in proportion to its velocity calculated at the amazing rate of a hundred and fifty thousand miles in a second. Besides, he observed, the contraction of the pupil in a strong light seems to point out to us from nature and instinct the fatal effects it experiences from it; or why should that organ which has supposed to be constructed for no other purpose than to profit by the light, by a natural impulse contract, and, as it were, shrink and retreat from its rays. And this was, he observed, the reason why the owl, a bird which discovers no other mark of especial sagacity, has nevertheless, from the instinctive prudence of closing its eyes in the light, been termed the bird of wisdom. With these, and other arguments of a similar texture, Mr. Craggs entertained his friends, when he condescended to speak; which, however, was not very frequently, as his mind was generally engrossed by the contemplation of his own complaints.

Mrs. Craggs, who accompanied him whithersoever he went, was the best of wives; and, perhaps, the only woman who could have borne with his caprices without making a sacrifice of her own peace. But she was blessed with an even, cheerful temper; and cherishing the idea of every merit she discovered in her husband, made it a subject of self congratulation. His foibles she smiled at, when his umbrella concealed her smiles from his view, combated when it was prudent, and humoured when she found it necessary.

The rest of the company consisted of Mr. Ormistace, his niece, Mrs. Herbert, a young and beautiful widow, the object of Mr. William Milson's unsuccessful passion, Mr. Crawford, Mr. and Mrs. Valentine Milson, and the rest of Sir John's family.

Mr. Ormistace was a character, which though not absolutely singular, is rarely met with; and it is, perhaps, happy for the world that it is. He was an extraordinary mixture of virtue and foibles, genius and folly – kindness and cruelty; and formed a striking proof that, the warmest and most generous of hearts, actions impelled by the most romantic virtue, are incapable of making ourselves and those around us happy, when not regulated by the standard of prudence, when not conformable to the dictates of cool sense and reason.

Liberal and profuse to an excess, if Mr. Ormistace heard of an object of distress, he would have beggared himself and every friend he had, to succour and relieve them. Yet his charities were too indiscriminate to afford real service. Acting by the impulse of the moment, it was enough that a pretty woman in distress, a man whose countenance interested him, or any other circumstance as trifling, worked upon his feelings: before he had given himself time to weigh the merits of their case, every resource was ransacked to supply them with all and more than they asked; while every remonstrance of his niece, or any other friend, who saw the circumstances through the clearer mediums of prudence and reason, were condemned, and themselves probably upbraided, and threatened with an eternal forfeiture of his regard. Passionately attached to all for whom he professed a friendship, he would have sacrificed his fortune and his life at any moment, to preserve them from distress; yet on the slightest grounds, a tale fabricated by falsehood or malevolence, he would despise and discard them. This feature in his character will be best illustrated by the relation of a circumstance that occasioned the termination of a friendship, which, from extreme youth till the period when it arrived, had constituted his chief felicity.

Mr. Saville had been the companion of his childish sports, the associate of his studies; and as at school they began, so at the university they finished together their education. A diversity of sentiments and cast of character was no bar to their friendship. Saville, more volatile, and thinking more like the rest of the world, did not the less admire the heroic generosity which dignified his friend; and except a few slight disputes which had never amounted to an actual quarrel, they had continued friends and companions during twenty years; when Mr. Ormistace's misplaced charity, and the irritability of his generosity (if the expression may be allowed) occasioned their final separation.

A young woman beautiful in person, and interesting in her manner, called at Mr. Ormistace's lodgings, and requested immediate admittance. Struck with her appearance, he conjured her to inform him by what means he could serve her.

"Alas! Sir," she said, "long though, I trust, not deservedly so, a stranger to kindness, to find it thus in a stranger excites a gratitude I feel better than I can express. My parents, though born to prospects of affluence, are now sunk in poverty and want; and the labour of my hands is insufficient to maintain them. I have a brother, who left us many years since to enlist as a soldier. We have been informed of his return to his country; and in search of him, from the vague information given me by an acquaintance, I have wandered from town to town, till wearied with my fruitless attempts to discover him, and my little stock of money exhausted, I was advised to apply to you, whose generosity merits the praises I heard bestowed on it."

"Excellent young woman!" said Mr. Ormistace, "how much will suffice you?"

"A trifle, Sir, – a few pounds."

"Here are fifty. And have you applied to no one else?"

"Only to Mr. Saville, Sir."

"And what did my friend offer you?"

"Alas! Nothing, Sir."

"Nothing! Good God!"

"He disbelieved my sad tale, and refused to assist me."

"Mean distrustful wretch! The man who could act thus is no longer a friend of mine – from this moment I discard him – renounce him forever."

"O, Sir! Let me not be the means of dividing you from your friend, or I shall be miserable that I applied to you. The world is filled with deceit, and he may have experienced but too many proofs of it already."

"Excellent creature! And you plead for the wretch that has insulted you by taxing you with the grossest falsehoods! Saville my friend! I blush that I ever called him so! But you shall not return on foot to your parents – my servants and horses shall attend you."

"Ten thousand blessings light on you, kind, generous Mr. Ormistace! Let me but leave you to indulge the fullness of my heart."

"Do. And return an hour hence; and my servants shall be ready to attend you."

Scarcely was she gone, never to return again – since her brother, and, in short, her whole tale never had existence but in her own fertile imagination: Mr. Ormistace's known character producing many such ideal adventures – when Mr. Saville called, and was denied admittance. Astonished at the refusal, and convinced that his friend was at home, he rushed in, in spite of the efforts of the servant.

On his entrance, "Saville," said Ormistace "we meet now contrary to my inclination; but it is for the last time."

"Dear Ormistace," said Saville, "to what strange caprice am I indebted for this polite reception?"

"Saville, I am serious. We meet no more. He who could insult injured and suffering innocence is no friend of mine."

"O, I understand you now, perfectly. The suffering innocence you allude to, is the artful tale invented by the excellent actress who has honoured us both with a visit."

"Mean, suspicious wretch! I have done with you. Who that saw her tears, her distress, could have withheld their bounty?"

"Those who know the whole to be a fiction. But if I could borrow a pair of bright eyes, and were to put on petticoats myself, I could impose on your credulity at any hour."

"Saville, I will not be ridiculed with impunity. I will have satisfaction."

"Most certainly you will very shortly – of your own folly."

"Do not affect to misunderstand me. The satisfaction of a gentleman. We will meet again; but it shall be –"

"To fight!"

"Yes – to fight!"

"Ormistace, I have sincere regard for you, but I have some likewise for my own life: and since it seems impossible to preserve that, while I am destined to be the victim of your passion and caprice, we will meet no more. But I will do justice to your character, and if I am asked my opinion of you, I will say, Jack Ormistace is an honest, credulous, passionate, and worthy fellow as ever existed!"

Thus saying, he left him; and meeting accidentally with a party going to Rome, he accompanied them, rejoiced to leave a country where the man he most valued had renounced him, and not without hopes that his friend's eyes would soon be opened, that he would see and acknowledge his error, and seek to meet him on his return with as much eagerness as he had sought to part.

Mr. Ormistace did see his error. He was shortly convinced that the whole tale was a forgery; and, in spite of his self-love, which was somewhat wounded by the concession, would gladly have flown to implore forgiveness of the man he had unjustly accused. But he was no longer within reach; and a few days after his arrival in Rome, before a conciliatory letter from Ormistace could reach him, he was seized with a fever and died. Mr. Ormistace never ceased to regret the loss of his friend; yet his own character remained unchanged: rash and capricious prepossession still governed his conduct, and repeated convictions of their injustice were insufficient to prevent them. He doted on Mrs. Herbert, yet made her life miserable.

Married at sixteen to a man whom she rather esteemed than loved, Mrs. Herbert had never known what it was to be happy. She had accepted him by the advice of her uncle, who encouraged an alliance which had every prospect of aggrandizing his niece. But adverse circumstances injuring Mr. Herbert's fortune, at the time he died he was possessed of so small a property as to necessitate his widow to accept the asylum Mr. Ormistace eagerly, and with the most unbounded kindness offered her. With him she had continued ever since; one hour admiring his liberality, the next suffering from his caprices. In short, she had daily reason to acknowledge, that a mere common character, destitute of genius or feeling, yet endued with that prudence which retains their conduct in the beaten track of common sense, must inevitably render those around them, if not more happy, certainly far less miserable, than the wild actions of the votary of ungoverned passion, though that passion be prompted by virtue, and its aim be benevolence.

Far different from Mr. Ormistace was the worthy and excellent Mr. Crawford. He had all the sensibility necessary to render him kind and indulgent to the happy family around him; yet unaccompanied by those starts of passionate affection, those sudden gusts of tenderness, which rather pain than make us happy. Calm, unruffled, and serene, his mind was like the still lake – every object discoverable in it was just and beautiful. He sought out the afflicted, he pitied, and, as far as prudence would permit, relieved them. The widow and the orphan found a husband and a father in him; while his munificence to others endeared him to that wife and those children whom he considered having the first and chiefest claim on his charity, which, in St. Paul's excellent definition of it, "suffereth long, and is kind;"[8] and without which, though he had given all to the poor, it "had profited him nothing." Mild and benignant, a smile, the smile of conscious rectitude, and the self-complacency of habitual virtue, sat on his face, and seemed in earnest of that peace which awaited him hereafter. There is something in the image of a truly good man which few can behold unmoved: we see him in the path which leads to Heaven, and our imagination already paints him enjoying the happiness prepared for the virtuous.

A silence of some minutes ensued when Agatha was seated, which was interrupted by Mr. Valentine Milson addressing Mr. Craggs. "If it is not impertinent, Sir, may I ask the reason of the little nod of the head you gave that young lady just now. I know I have heard that you have reason for that as well as all the rest of your oddities."

"My oddities, Sir!" said Mr. Craggs, somewhat piqued. "If it be a crime to take poison to shorten our lives, it is a crime not to take every possible means to preserve them."

"Especially where they are so useful to the community," returned Mr. Valentine laughing, and winking at the rest of the company. "But how may that little nod preserve your life?"

"It may preserve that on which my life depends. Homer was aware of this; for, speaking of the death of one of his characters, he says,

"*He broke his spinal joint, and wak'd in Hell.*"[9]

---

[8] I Corinthians 13, v. 4.
[9] Alexander Pope (1688-1744), *Homer's Odyssey*, Book X, l. 688. The actual quote refers to a Elpenor, a youth who half asleep from drunkenness missed his step when descending from a turret.

"And you are afraid of waking there too, perhaps?"

"You must be little acquainted with ancients," said Mr. Craggs angrily, "if you are ignorant that hell was their term for the places of reward, as well as punishment in the other world."

"I have not read any of them since I left school, I confess", said Mr. Milson, "but I read enough to last me my life."

"But if you read none else, Galen, and Hippocrates are surely worth your study."

"I do not recollect ever being introduced to those gentlemen. What may they treat of, pray?"

"Of medicine."

"Medicine! O, horrid! I hate the very name. A basin of camomile tea, and, in very desperate cases, a little grated ginger, is all the medicine I take, or ever was acquainted with."

"Pitiful pride of ignorance!" said Mr. Craggs, contemptuously; then returning to the reverie from which he had been awaked, he appeared in a moment lost to everything but his own reflections.

"Mr. Valentine Milson," said Sir John, who observed that Mr. Craggs had taken offence at his son's ridicule, "I am amazed that you talk in this free way to a man of Mr. Cragg's rank and consequence. Mr. Craggs is the *honourable* Mr. Craggs, you know; and may be more – he may be a lord, some time. Upon my honour and credit, therefore, as a gentleman and baronet, I must say, you behave very uncivil and impolite."

"With regard to politeness," said Mr. Valentine, "I don't pique myself upon it; for I hate outside. But with regard to civility, plain English civility, yes, and plain English politeness too, I have enough of both in conscience. What say you Nance?" addressing Mrs. Milson.

"I say," answered Mrs. Milson, "that if you had no other good quality in a greater degree than you possess politeness, you would not be so estimable as I think you,"

"Fie Nance," said he, "that's not the answer I wanted. Mr. Ormistace do you speak for me: you are often my advocate."

"Politeness," said Mr. Ormistace, "I despise – 'tis the borrowed polish with which insincerity is varnished over, and beneath the notice of a man of worth. One generous action, springing from the heart, is superior in real value to the frivolity of a whole life spent in external civility – in affected courtesy."

"Yet do those generous actions you allude to, preclude the practice of politeness?" asked Mr. Crawford.

"Yes," said Mr. Ormistace, "for when great actions employ and animate our minds, trifles are condemned."

"I beg your pardon," said Mr. Crawford; "but it is not a trifle to contribute to the innocent pleasure of those around us. Many days must pass over our heads in which we have it not in our power to snatch a suffering family from want, to sacrifice our own to the dearer interests of our friends. Yet we need not, like the excellent Titus, lament the loss of a day, when we may make even strangers pleased with us, and contented with themselves by urbanity and courtesy, not affected but real, not springing from the lips but from the heart. Is not every man a brother? Shall we then think it beneath our notice to give them pleasure?"

"To me there is no pleasure," said Mr. Ormistace, "in frothy compliments; and when a stranger is uncommonly civil to me, I conclude that he is instigated by artifice, or at least by vanity, hoping for the same treatment in return."

"Frothy compliments," said Mr. Crawford, "are indeed the offspring of a little mind; but polite and just praise is neither beneath a man of sense to bestow nor to receive. 'Tis a commerce of good will, where each party is a gainer. And, with regard to civility to strangers – he must be narrow-minded and suspicious who imagines everyone he meets undeserving civility till time has convinced him of their worth: rather let us believe everyone merits it, till time convinces us to the contrary; which, for the honour of human nature, will be, I trust, but rarely the case. And if, when our hearts are touched, we cannot withhold our bounty from a stranger, why should we deny those who want not money, that civility which is due to all, and from bestowing which we receive no diminution of our stock."

"I have heard," said Miss Milson, "that Charles the Second, from the superior grace of his address, frequently gave more satisfaction and pleasure while he denied, than his father while he granted a favour."

"The remark is apposite," said Mr. Crawford, "and proves the influence of politeness."

"Yes," said Mr. Ormistace, "but its influence is no proof of its worth. Did not Charles the Second make use of that very politeness you contend for, to deceive, and to pay off those who asked his favours in the cheapest coin? And was he not in every respect a contemptible character?"

"I grant it;" said Mr. Crawford, "yet it was his licentiousness, not his politeness, which rendered him such; and if to the glaring vices he possessed, he had added the brutality of ill-manners, he would not have been a whit more respectable. But genuine politeness is one of the brightest ornaments to a man of real worth and integrity. It renders virtue itself more amiable, and, from dressing it in the most fascinating garb, gains many a proselyte to its cause. It is well known that Nelson, as he was one of the most moral and pious of men, studied to be likewise one of the politest."[10]

"Virtue," said Mr. Ormistace, "should be loved and imitated for its own sake, not for the tinsel with which it is covered in order to recommend it to our view; such glitter can add no more to its intrinsic value, than the gilding on a piece of wood, which is still wood, however ornamented."

"Miss Belmont, I observe," said Mr. Crawford, "has been paying much attention to our arguments: she shall decide the contest."

"Aye, aye," said Sir John, "I dare say Miss can speak as prettily as she looks. What say you to it, Miss?"

"I have been endeavouring to profit from what I have heard," said Agatha.

"But whose arguments agree with your own sentiments?" asked Mr. Crawford. "I have the vanity to think that from your countenance during the last remark, you will be an advocate on my side."

"I was wishing," said Agatha, "instead of wood, rather to have compared virtue to silver, which, if it receives no additional value from the polish given to it, loses none, and acquires a beauty which recommends it to those who are ignorant of, or careless concerning its genuine worth."

"My lovely friend has charmingly decided," said Miss Milson; "and had Edgar, who is equally famous for clearing his country of wolves, and marrying the beautiful Elfrida, seen and conversed with Miss Belmont, Ethelwald might have continued in peaceable possession of the wife and mistress of his soul."

A summons to supper terminated the conversation; and Agatha, though she yet regretted the loss of Mr. Hammond's society, which, in her present frame of mind, was more congenial to her heart than any other, yet rejoiced to find that all she met with were not like Sir John, and that there were some among the guests from whose conversation she might derive both pleasure and instruction.

The family retired to rest at an early hour, agreeable to Sir John's request, who thought it a good old English custom to be in bed before the clock struck ten.

Miss Milson accompanied Agatha to her apartment, which she informed her Mrs. Herbert had obligingly resigned to her, and had taken herself a remote one in the new building, in order that Agatha, in a house both new and strange to her, might not be removed to a distance from

---

[10]Nelson was still alive and it is curious why the past tense is used here. Nelson's superior, Admiral Sir John Jervis, was the nephew of Elizabeth Jervis's grandfather. He took harsh measures to prevent mutiny and "licentiousness" even hanging sailors for sodomy.

the rest of the family. This apartment and her own adjoining it, Miss Milson informed her, had been finished agreeably to her taste, and had obtained much admiration from all who were so happy as to possess minds susceptible of romantic beauties.

Festoons of artificial flowers were hung around the room, tied together occasionally with pale blue satin ribbons. Round the posts of the bed, which were made to represent marble pillars, were entwined wreaths of myrtle.

The bed itself was in the form of an alcove, and covered entirely with flowers, except a large oval medallion of white satin in the centre of the tester, on which was painted a Venus descending from her chariot, and bearing in her own hands an alabaster vase, filled with some celestial liquid to refresh her weary doves; emblematic, as Miss Milson observed, "of that sensibility, and tender compassion which are the loveliest embellishments of beauty." The dressing table, placed in a recess, and covered with spars and shells, was made to resemble a small grotto. The floor, carpeted with green velvet was intended to imitate a grass plot, and small benches in lieu of chairs, covered with the same to represent hillocks; while the ceiling, painted in imitation of an evening sky, completed the "romantic beauties" of the apartment.

When Miss Milson had retired, Agatha, little disposed to sleep, her mind now with the contemplation of the novel objects around her, and now dwelling on the friend she had lost, and friend she had left, took out her pencil and wrote the following lines.

Sweet were the scenes my fancy drew
As life just opened to my view;
While sage experience vainly strove
To bid fair fancy cease to rove.
And is that fancy false as fair?
And life's gay visions lost in air?
Alas, too soon this truth I know!
The sweetest flowers of hope fade ere they blow.
Maria! Sister of my heart!
I met, – but only met to part –
To part – O agonising pain!
Never on earth to meet again.
One other friend, how justly dear!
With whom to mix the sorrowing tear,
Was bliss more soothing to my heart
Than giddy mirth can e'er impart.
I met – I saw – my soul approv'd,
His sorrows wept, his virtues lov'd.

In him 'twas sweet – how sweet to trace
The semblance of Maria's face!
And still, as friendship lent her balm,
By gentle hearts his grief to calm,
To hush his many cares to rest,
And blest! Blest talk! To make him blest.
From him, alas, ordained to part,
Who now can cheer my drooping heart?
Condemn'd this fatal truth to know,
The fairest flowers of hope fade ere they blow.

In youth especially, there is something soothing to the heart when it is under the influence of any distress, either not in its nature too violent to admit of such relief, or softened by time till it is enabled to bear it, in expressing our feelings in poetry: requiring some little reflection in the choice and arrangement of words, it calls our attention in some measure from the subject next our heart, at the very moment we seem to indulge in it; and Agatha's heart felt lightened of a part of its burdens when she had thus indulged herself in expressing them. Not intending the effusions of her solitary hours for the perusal of anyone, and considering what she had written of no farther value than as it served to amuse her mind and chase the painful reflections which oppressed it, she put it carefully into her pocket, and was preparing to undress, when she was startled by a voice under her window. She was alarmed at first; but recollecting herself, and reflecting that she might probably have no cause for terror, she went to the window and softly opened it to listen, when she heard a man's voice repeating some verses in a tremulous tone. She listened more attentively and as the same few lines were frequently repeated, could distinguish the following.

He, in whose wretched hut chill want prevails,
In dreams, each luxury of wealth may gain;
And the wan victim whom disease assails
Enjoys in sleep, a short relief from pain.
No blessings light on my devoted head,
For Emma frowns – and hope, and sleep are fled!

The voice ceased; and the person, after heaving a profound sigh, walked with hasty steps towards another part of the garden. "Alas," said Agatha, "I then am not the only person who wakes at this hour to utter their complaints and bewail their sorrows! But what are mine compared to the despair expressed by this unhappy being? Yes – this must be love. Thus it was that my mother painted that fatal passion; and her colouring

28

was but too just. Heaven be praised my heart is a stranger to it, and will ever, I trust, remain so. In my bosom friendship has filled the space too often occupied by love. In friendship all my wishes are centred – all my hopes might be completed and divided for ever from my first friend, could I but enjoy the society of her brother, my heart would bear every other privation with resignation – happy in him who only can supply his sister's place in my affection."

Agatha now shut the window; and having commended herself to the protection of Heaven went to rest, with a heart, if not happy, at least free from that anguish, which any the least failure in our duty occasions; and which is perhaps the most poignant of human afflictions.

Chapter 4

Sleeping rather later than ordinary in the morning she was awakened by Miss Milson and Mrs. Herbert who came with much kindness to enquire how she had rested. She informed them of the verses she had heard repeated under her window.

"Ah," said Miss Milson, "the ill-fated writer and repeater of those verses was my poor brother William, whose attachment to this cruel lady is too well known for any proofs he may give of it to excite surprise."

"I wish," said Agatha, "that Mrs. Herbert pitied him as much as I do; and though he dared not hope to be beloved, that, at least, would be a consolation."

"If my pity could console or make him happy," said Mrs. Herbert, "there would not be at this moment a happier being upon earth. My heart bleeds for his distress; and scarcely does he suffer more severely than I do from his unfortunate partiality. Did not daily experience convince us of their existence, I could not believe it possible there could be such a being in nature as a coquette: a woman who finds pleasure in exciting a love she neither can nor is desirous to return."

"Certainly," said Miss Milson, "malice itself can accuse you of no fault concerning my brother, for you have never given the smallest encouragement to his hopes."

"Never," said Mrs. Herbert, "and I should despise myself if I had. I have even forced myself to suppress the gratitude and esteem I felt, lest he should give them a more tender interpretation. Yet in spite of every effort of mine to destroy it, his passion continues; and but yesterday I found in my work-box a fragment of his writing."

"Poor William," said Miss Milson, "the fictitious sorrows of a Werter are nothing compared to his real ones, Henry the eighth did not love Anne Boleyn with a passion so ardent, and finding his only consolation in poetry, as the elegant Pope has expressed it:

His heart still dictates, and his hand obeys.[11]

"May I ask to see the verses you mentioned," said Agatha; "my heart feels an interest in his distresses."

"Surely," said Mrs. Herbert, "nor do I give you any proof of confidence by communicating them; since others, equally tender, are

---

[11]Alexander Pope, *Eloisa to Abelard*, l. 16, "Her heart still dictates, and her hand obeys."

found and read by every servant about the house. He was at Oxford, where, in hopes of amusing his mind, his friends had persuaded him to spend a few weeks; and hearing by accident that I was expected at Milson Hall, he set off immediately, though it was then eleven at night, and arrived here the day before I came, I mention this, as it explains the journey to which he alludes in the lines you wished to read. By shortening or lengthening his lines occasionally, he often takes liberties, perhaps not licensed by the rules of poetry; but where the heart is deeply affected, our feelings are apt to run away with us; and it is difficult to confine our metre within its just limits."

Mrs. Herbert then gave to Agatha the following lines.

FRAGMENT

And then – when borne upon my bier
Say, will not Emma shed one tear?
Yes – she will then my fate deplore!
And fame shall tell my tale the village o'er.
Then haply as some rural maid
Shall hear, beneath yon pensive shade,
Some friend my ill-starred love relate,
Shall ask while weeping o'er my fate–
"And did he journey many a mile
To steal one look – to catch one smile?"
"Alas! He did."
"And did he love so long, so true,
Without one cheering hope in view?"
"Alas! He did."
"And did he such a love relate?
And could she after prove ingrate?"
"Alas! She did."
She'll pause – and heave a pitying sigh,
And then forswear all cruelty.
And thus my hapless fate shall prove
A blessing to another's love.

"His unfortunate passion interests me extremely," said Agatha; "and these artless lines, which appear to have been written in the moments of real anguish, without effort or study, affect me yet more than the melancholy ones I heard last night. How bitter are the agonies of love!"

"You speak feelingly, my dear," said Mrs. Herbert.

"Not from my own feelings, indeed," said Agatha; "for I am an utter stranger to it; and friendship has hitherto proved so delightful, that

I shall never sigh to exchange it for what I believe the most dreadful of sufferings."

"Certainly," said Mrs. Herbert, "where love, as in the present unfortunate instance, cannot be requited, its sufferings are dreadful; but where it meets no obstacle, where it is returned with equal tenderness, it forms perhaps the happiest state of human existence: it enhances every blessing, softens every pain, and opens a little Heaven of happiness to our view. To all that was before pleasing it gives additional charms; even the fair face of nature appears fairer when viewed in the presence of those we love. It gives a thousand innocent and artless sources of delight unknown before – gives value to a thousand before indifferent things: to select flowers, gather fruit, perform innumerable otherwise insignificant offices for those we love, is infinitely sweet; while every trifle they have possessed or prized becomes a treasure. Then, selfishness, the most degrading of human failings, is annihilated by love: since every idea of self-gratification is despised when put in competition with the wishes or happiness of the object of our affection."

"You amaze me," said Agatha. "How unlike is this to my mother's dreadful delineations on the same subject! But then jealousy is its inseparable companion; and jealousy is dreadful."

"Jealousy is so far from being the inseparable companion of love," said Mrs. Herbert, "that I much doubt whether they ever inhabited the same bosom. Jealousy supposes a mistrust of the sincerity of those we love; and that want of sincerity implies art and dissimulation (failings incompatible with virtue) and we can only truly love what we believe at least to be virtuous. I speak of real, pure, disinterested love – of love too that is requited; for then only can it make us happy, then only can it be free from jealousy."

"And why," said Agatha, "have I been thus deceived? For what end can I have been taught to dread, what, from your charming description, appears the sweetest source of human felicity?"

"Probably," said Mrs. Herbert, "Lady Belmont observed the natural tenderness of your disposition; and, knowing that love and duty are sometimes at variance, feared that, in a heart susceptible as yours appears to be, love, if indulged, might prove the conqueror."

"Ah!" said Agatha, "how little then did she know my heart! How little know the principles firmly and immovably implanted in it by the best and dearest of friends! In every circumstance, in every trial of my life, nothing shall tempt me to a breach of duty. And were I to love with all the tenderness you have portrayed, and did my love promise a life of the most enchanting happiness, yet, while that and my duty pointed different ways, duty should be my constant guide; and I am firmly resolved that no consideration of self-felicity shall ever prompt me to forsake it for a moment"

"Charmingly said!" said Miss Milson. "Spoken with the energy of a Clementina, and the courage of a Philippa."

Heaven forbid," said Mrs. Herbert, that you should ever be put to the trial. No—I hope I shall one day see you, your love, wherever it is fixed, authorized and approved by your parents, and yourself blest and blessing! And little as I have hitherto known you, I need not hesitate to foretell that "happy will be the man who shall make you his wife, and happy the child who shall call you mother."

Agatha received Mrs. Herbert's praises with equal gratitude and pleasure; and after exchanging mutual wishes that an acquaintance thus sweetly as Agatha termed it, commenced, might improve into the most tender and most lasting of friendships, she felt herself happier than the evening before she had imagined it possible to have felt; deprived by death of one friend, and by absence of another.

When Agatha was dressed, Mrs. Herbert, Miss Milson, and herself went together into the breakfast room. The company were all assembled, and Lady Milson already seated at the head of the table.

"Come in Ladies— come in," said Sir John; and the more haste you make the better; for my Lady Milson there has already swallowed two plates full of hot toast and butter."

"I am amazed, Sir John," said Lady Milson, "when you know the extreme badness of my appetite, that you will always be talking thus. You ought rather to rejoice when I can get down a little bit."

"Well, for certain," said Sir John, "though I am sorry to say it for my own sake, but for certain Lady Milson was never in love; for love, they say, takes away the appetite, and I never knew hers leave her for an hour. There's poor William now, could not get down a mouthful if you'd make him a lord or a baronet for it."

Mr. William Milson, who dreaded being ridiculed on the subject of his passion, made no reply; but walked leisurely out of the room, apparently inattentive to what was said. As he went out, happening to take out his handkerchief, he dropped a paper from his pocket, which Sir John observing as soon as he was gone, took up, and declared he would read aloud for the edification of the company. Mrs. Herbert looking uneasy, Miss Milson requested him to give it to her; but he was the more determined to keep it and declared, that the pretty little widow, whose coyness had occasioned its being written, should be punished by hearing it read to the company. Everyone present unanimously refused to hear it, and Sir John was obliged to desist; declaring, however, that he would take a sly peep at it himself – when, to his utter surprise, and Mrs. Herbert's great relief, the paper was a blank one. He then said, that to make amends for the loss of their entertainment he would tell them a story.

"You must know ladies and gentlemen," he began, "that I was once desperately in love with my lady there; for she really was a very pretty woman –"

"Yes, Sir John," interrupted Lady Milson, "you never had any beauty in your family till I came into it."

"None the worse for that neither my lady," said Sir John, "for if we were not a handsome, we were always a prudent money-getting family; and I don't know anything that's so pretty to look at as King George's head upon a guinea: it beats your Ladyship's all to nothing – pretty as you might be. But I was going to say, that I had a mind to give my lady some verses; and never having tried at anything of the sort myself, I thought it best to get some ready made; and so, meeting with a ballad with something about blue eyes in it, I thought that bid fair to suit as well as anything, and bought it for her. Now I was determined to get it at a bargain; and as the wench asked me a penny for it I tumbled a bad halfpenny that had hung a hand a long time, into the dirt; and when it was all covered with mud that it could not be distinguished from a good one, picked it up, and gave it to her, declaring that it was the sight of her bright eyes that made me drop it. This put her in good humour; and as she was really a pretty girl, I stole a kiss of her. And so, I bought a verse to please my Lady, passed off a bad halfpenny and got a kiss of a pretty lass, and all at one stroke. And now, upon my honour and credit as a gentleman and a baronet, I don't think it was amiss."

"The plan and execution were both admirable," said Mrs. Herbert, "and well worthy of Sir John Milson; and I do not believe there is another gentleman in the country who could boast of such an exploit, and then vouch for its merit upon his honour."

"I don't believe there is indeed," said Sir John, interpreting what had been said as a compliment. "But come now Mrs. Herbert, do show us some of those lovesick ditties."

"Had I any to show to you," said Mrs. Herbert, "I should imagine it would be neither to your honour nor credit as a gentleman and a baronet, to make either your son or your guest an object of ridicule."

"Why that's no how ..." said Sir John.

"Come," said Mr. Crawford, "excuse Mrs. Herbert's communicating what would give her pain; and since one poem may perhaps be as amusing as another, I will repeat some lines which were sent to Miss Lydia Travers, a maiden lady with whom I was once acquainted. She had been left early in life at her own disposal, with some beauty, some accomplishments, and an ample fortune. It was probable that, possessed of so many recommendations, she would have many admirers; but, for different reasons, none of them happening to meet with her approbation, she saw herself at five and forty, Miss Lydia Travers still. She then began to think it was time to settle in the world, and hinted as much to some of her acquaintance; which being circulated abroad, induced a Mr. Nichols, a young man who had dissipated his fortune by gaming and extravagance, to determine upon proposing to her as the easiest means of repairing it. He therefore became very assiduous, and had reason to believe he was not disagreeable to the lady; but remarking that she had rather a romantic turn, and imagining that an elegant poem would complete the conquest, already more than begun, he applied to Mr. Moreland, a distant relation of Miss Travers's, who during many years had procured a precarious subsistence by his pen, to write one in his name, having no skill in composition himself. Mr. Moreland had, in his youth, been a sincere admirer of his cousin, and would have solicited her hand, but that, from the scorn with which his attentions were received, he was convinced it would be to no purpose. Considering his passion hopeless, and fearing to augment it, he very prudently shunned every place where he had any prospect of meeting her, till time had totally effaced her image from his heart. Calamities, equally unforeseen and unmerited, having deprived him of his small paternal inheritance, writing was at last become his only resource. When Mr. Nichols made the application to him, he enquired if he felt himself greatly attached to Miss Travers."

"Attached to her," said Nichols, "what the devil do you mean? Why she's five and forty!"

"Then what can induce you to pursue with so much earnestness a woman whose age renders her contemptible in your eyes?"

"What induce me! Why what always does induce a young man to take an old woman? Want — Sir — want."

"Good God! And would you marry her merely to support you?"

"Merely! Matrimony is a devilish hard pill to swallow; but when it is well covered with gold, it is better than a bullet — and one or t'other I must have."

"Well, be satisfied," said Moreland, "you shall have the verses. You would have them written I suppose as if addressed to a young person?"

"By all means," said Nichols; as complimentary and as sublime too as possible.

"Mr. Moreland accordingly wrote these lines which he bought to Nichols for his approbation."

Yes Lydia — Thou an Angel art
In form, in face, in mind, in heart,
All that a poet could desire
To animate a muse of fire.

Such charms no painter's art could reach,
No sage's skill such wisdom teach –
Prudence with gaiety combined
Strong sense with melting softness joined.
Thy beauty might a stoic move,
And warm his frozen soul to love!
Yet love still checked by all that fear
Which seems to speak an Angel near,
Till one kind smile dispelled the pain,
And showed the woman once again.
Give but one hope thou may'st be mine
All else with transport I'll resign –
Each thought by day, each dream by night
Shall own this source of dear delight,
Prized as the miser's darling pelf,
Cherished as hopes of Heaven itself!
Lydia – you blush – look pleased, and smile –
Vain fool! I'm laughing at you all the while.

Mr. Nichols took the lines, and having read to

Prudence with gaiety combined

exclaimed eagerly, "enough – enough. This will do the business; I need read no farther. Here – take and fold it up."

This was instantly done; and it was sealed, superscribed, and sent to the lady immediately. But how great was Nichols's astonishment, when at his next visit he was denied admission. Fearing that the lady had detected the imposition, and was apprized that the poem was not actually of his own writing, he sent her the next morning a very polite note, assuring her, that however report might have belied him, the verses were every line his own composition; when, to his utter confusion, this letter was returned to him, after being opened, enclosed in a blank cover. After this, hopeless of success, he abandoned the scheme as fruitless, and endeavoured, by other means, equally justifiable, to support himself. Mr. Moreland, in the mean time, who had no selfish views in writing the verses in question, and only hoped by this means to preserve a woman he had once loved, and whose remembrance was still dear to him, from misery and ruin, met her accidentally at the house of a friend. Time, which had greatly injured her beauty, had not yet entirely destroyed it, and had left remains enough to remind Moreland of what she had once been, and what he had once felt; and, in his idea, her mind had gained all that her face had lost. Miss Travers, who saw him at a moment when she was animated by pique towards another, was disposed to be pleased with him, and by her manner easily induced him to make the offer he had not dared to venture upon twenty years before. He was accepted, and the remainder of his days were terminated in the ease and competence he deserved, while his conduct towards his wife gave her every reason to rejoice in the choice she had made. Nichols, whom she had thus fortunately escaped, did not break his heart in consequence of his disappointment; yet, believing that the verses gained the lady, lamented bitterly that "the Gods had not made him poetical."

"The story is whimsical," said Mr. Ormistace, "but tells very little to the credit of either of the parties. Mr. Moreland's conduct in deceiving the man who employed and paid him is unjustifiable; and instead of praises, his duplicity entitles him to contempt."

"You are certainly right," said Mr. Crawford, "no benefit expected to be the result, can justify deceit. Yet though the end may not absolutely excuse the means, his motives were surely laudable. Certain that advice in such cases, even when asked, is rarely followed, he took the only method by which he could preserve the lady from the misery which awaited her; and not till he was convinced that Nichols's views were merely mercenary, did he wish or intend to impose upon him. So far from it – I am convinced from his known character, that had he discovered his professions of regard to be sincere, and had imagined there was a probability of his rendering her happy, he would rather have promoted than impeded the match."

" You say," said Mrs. Milson, "that nothing can justify deceit; yet are there not particular situations besides the one just related, where we may use it with advantage and without a crime—where it can do no injury and may afford much service?"

"None—none," said Mr. Ormistace.

"It is always dangerous," said Mr. Crawford, "and may be often hurtful; and since, if we allow that it can ever with propriety be used, everyone may imagine their own situation to be the precise one which admits it, it will be both wiser and better to proscribe it entirely."

After breakfast the party separated till dinner. Miss Milson, her sister, Mrs. Herbert, and Agatha, went to Miss Milson's *Cassetta*, Mrs. Milson to the nursery, her Ladyship to her household management, and the gentlemen to their various amusements.

When dinner had assembled them all again, a ceremony took place, which, if made less public, would have raised Sir John in Agatha's estimation. Before the company began their dinner, several large plum puddings were brought in and placed on a side table, with as many jugs of ale. Sir John himself went to the table, and began to fill several plates with the pudding, and to pour ale into several mugs which were brought him — at the same time calling to the servants "Bring me Stephen Martin's plate and his mug — are these them?"

"Yes Sir."

"And now Thomas Bayley's. Is this his plate, and his mug?"

"Yes Sir."

"There, now bring me Betty and Jemima Simmonds's."

Lady Milson, in the mean time, took this opportunity of informing her visitors, that there were a great number of poor people in their village, who would not know how to live but for Sir John's charity; and that he made it a rule whatever company he might have, never to omit sending them some pudding and ale at least seven or eight times in a year; and that Betty and Jemima Simmonds, who he had now been so kind as to add to the number, had been very unfortunate of late; that poor Betty had lost entirely the use of her limbs for some years; and that Jemima, her grand-daughter, because she would not leave her, had refused to marry a young man she liked, who had since enlisted in the army, and the poor girl was believed to be in a consumption.

"How amiable would be any acts of this kind," said Agatha, low to Mrs. Herbert, "were they done more privately: but I have always been taught that charity, when purposely displayed, loses its reward."

"This does not," said Mrs. Herbert, "for our host has every reward he desires, when his charity obtains the knowledge, and, as he imagines, the consequent approbation of his guests — for he is a stranger to the pure rewards which flow from the sweet consciousness of secret benevolence, and the approbation of Him by whom alone our charities should be seen. His conduct, however, affords many excellent lessons; and I never quit this house without feeling armed against the failings of its inhabitants. We meet here with some characters, which, if they serve not as examples, are yet of use as beacons to warn us of our own danger; and from witnessing their odiousness in others, we learn to despise ostentation, meanness, and the contemptible pride of the little great man."

A silence on the part of the rest of the company obliged Mrs. Herbert to terminate her remarks; much to Agatha's regret, who listened to her with unfeigned pleasure.

Nothing remarkable occurred during the remainder of the day; but Agatha, whom the rough sketch Lady Milson had drawn of Jemima Simmonds, had interested extremely, determined to rise early the next morning to endeavour to discover her little abode, and to visit, relieve, and comfort her if possible.

Her mind impressed with this idea, she awoke early in the morning, dressed herself hastily, and went downstairs, intending to enquire of some of the servants the road to the cottage. For this purpose, she went into the breakfast room, thinking it probable she might find someone there, when to her equal surprise and delight, she was met by Mr. Hammond.

"Mr. Hammond," said Agatha, holding out her hand to him with an expression of the most ingenuous joy, "how happy am I to meet you! Thus unexpectedly too — it heightens the pleasure! And are you well? — and have you obeyed all my injunctions?"

"Dear — dear Miss Belmont!" said Hammond, "to have you thus interested for me, surely I must be the happiest of beings!"

"I would you were!" said Agatha. "But are you indeed happier, more composed than when I left you?"

"At this moment," said Hammond, catching her hand, forgetful of everything, "at this moment there is not …" Then recollecting himself he loosed her hand as hastily as he had taken it.

"I fear, O I fear," said Agatha, "from this manner, this impetuous manner, that you are not yet yourself; that your spirits, when deprived of the consolation of the friend whom Providence threw in your way, have returned to the state of agitation and misery from which her efforts recovered them. But O, let me conjure you to be comforted! Be assured that there is not on earth a friend more sincerely attached to another, and that you cannot be unhappy without rendering me so."

"Dear — dear Agatha — Miss Belmont — Angel! What shall I, can I say to such unexampled proofs of kindness!" exclaimed Hammond. "Yes, far — very far from being unhappy at this moment — this sweet moment — the generous interest you take in my behalf, makes me insensible of sorrow — insensible of everything but the blessing of being thus regarded by the loveliest — dearest of women — of friends!"

Agatha coloured she knew not why, and felt a momentary embarrassment for which she knew not how to account, from the warmth and energy of his expressions. After a short pause, during which her mind recovered its serenity, she determined to change the subject; imagining that her ill-judged reference to a distress, which had perhaps grown upon him during her absence, had occasioned emotion she had just witnessed. She then spoke of her new friend Mrs. Herbert, of the pleasure she received from her society, and that of the excellent Mr. Crawford, whom she equally esteemed; and Hammond gave her a letter from Lady Belmont which had arrived late the evening before; and which, though he came purposely to bring, in the first impulse of pleasure at meeting her, and the emotion of her artless expressions of tenderness had excited, he had totally forgotten. The letter was written before the news of Miss Hammond's death had reached Lady Belmont, and contained nothing more than expressions of anxiety concerning her health, an assurance that she would return to England as soon as their business was completed, and a wish that Agatha would profit as little as possible by any indulgence Miss Hammond might give her of mixing with a society from which she might contract much evil, could derive no benefit, and which, however fair in its exterior, was a source of constant uneasiness to all who were weak enough to mingle with it.

Agatha gave the letter to Mr. Hammond to read, expressing, at the same time, her surprise that her mother should never yet have been undeceived concerning the world of which she had formed so erroneous an opinion, and she pitied the prejudice which had doubtless abridged her of many of the pleasures of life.

Mrs. Herbert, whom the same project had occupied as Agatha, who had learned from nature all that the factitious ceremonies of politeness enjoin, introduced her to Mr. Hammond, and Hammond to her, with an expression of infinite pleasure. Mrs. Herbert's intention being now frustrated for the present as well as Agatha's, and thinking that she could not in politeness leave them immediately, she determined to defer her benevolent visit till the next morning.

After a short conversation, during which Mrs. Herbert's penetrating eye easily remarked the pleasure which sparkled in Agatha's, the family assembled, and Miss Milson introduced Mr. Hammond to Sir John, who met him with a kind of formal half-civility. Miss Milson, who was much interested in his favour, and who knew from long experience, the only road to her father's approbation, observed, that she had heard her late good friend Miss Hammond remark that there was a baronet of the name and family of Hammond, and that the title was not very far distant from her brother had he been living, which she then knew not that he was.

"Indeed!" said Sir John, "why that's a pretty thing! Pray Mr. Hammond, Sir, (I am sure I am very happy to see you here) is it far distant?"

"O yes Sir," said Hammond, "a distant cousin, I believe — indeed I scarcely know."

"But has he any sons?" asked Sir John hastily.

"Upon my word, I don't know — I believe not —"

"You believe not? Then very likely you'll have it; and if you settle in the neighbourhood, I hope we shall be very good friends. Sir John Milson will always be happy to see Sir — What is your name, pray — Hammond?"

"Edward. But indeed Sir John I have not the most distant idea."

"O, Sir Edward Hammond," said Sir John, interrupting him, "Sir Edward Hammond. And very well it sounds. But before that arrives, I shall always be happy, very happy to see you; and as your house must be dull at present, I must insist upon your coming to me for some time. The sight of these pretty ladies will do you good."

Mr. Hammond excused himself; but Sir John would take no denial; and Hammond, who could not but rejoice in the opportunity it afforded him of enjoying the sweet, though, he began to fear, dangerous indulgence of Agatha's society, at length consented to remain with him a few days.

Chapter 5

The party divided for the pursuits of the morning nearly as they had done the day before; Hammond, at Miss Milson's request, joining the ladies in the *Cassetta*, and being appointed by her to turn over, as she termed it, "the storied page for their amusement; while their needles or pencils would delineate fairy scenes, not less beautiful than those of the poet or novelist."

Mrs. Herbert and Agatha happening to walk a small distance before the rest, — "You know not," said Agatha to Mrs. Herbert, "how elated my heart feels this morning."

"I can partly imagine it," said Mrs. Herbert, archly.

"To meet," resumed Agatha, "thus unexpectedly too, a friend after so long an absence –"

"So long an absence, my dear?" said Mrs. Herbert . "Surely you are one of those whom time creeps withal! If I am not mistaken, you parted from Mr. Hammond no longer ago than the day before yesterday?"

"That is true," said Agatha, "yet a day appears long when divided from a friend."

"Certainly it does — when divided from a friend!" said Mrs. Herbert, significantly.

Agatha, who understood Mrs. Herbert as literally as she herself had spoken, paid little regard to her manner, and continued. "When time shall have a little matured our friendship, my dear Mrs. Herbert, I shall feel equal sorrow at parting from, and equal pleasure at meeting you."

"That you will feel some pain at parting from, and some pleasure at meeting me, I firmly believe," said Mrs. Herbert, "but whether you will feel as much pain, and as much pleasure as you have now experienced is a doubt with me — or rather, is no doubt at all."

Miss Milson, Miss Cassandra, and Hammond overtaking them, the conversation was changed to other subjects.

When they arrived at the *Cassetta*, it was some time before the book to be read could be decided upon: Miss Milson descanting so long upon the various beauties of Pope and Milton, and the edification and delight to be derived from historical study, that it was impossible to determine on which she would at last fix her choice; when Mrs. Herbert took down from the shelves a volume of Shakespeare, who, she said, was equally the pride and darling of every English breast; and opening to the Tempest — "Here," Mr. Hammond, she said, "read this. I have lately met with two

41

characters resembling as I fancied, Miranda, and Ferdinand; and I wish from hearing them again to decide whether the likeness was real or imaginary."

Hammond read as desired, and Agatha listened with the most attentive pleasure. She felt every sentiment as it was uttered; and though she had repeatedly read the play, and had always been delighted with it, she declared, when he had done, that she never was before so sensible of its many beauties; and that she was now convinced of what she had always believed, that a play, when read aloud, if any attention be paid to varying the voices of its characters, gives much more pleasure than when read alone.

"Certainly," said Mrs. Herbert, "and a comedy especially. Laughter is not a solitary amusement; and when anything excites it, we wish to have sharers in our mirth. Mr. Hammond has besides done ample justice to his task; and I can assure him that, like Miss Belmont, I have discovered beauties which I wonder I should have overlooked before."

"I think," said Miss Cassandra, "that the prettiest part of all was the scene between Stephano and Trinculo."

"I was most delighted with that charming though well-known speech of Prospero's," said Miss Milson, "that the globe and all which it inherit shall dissolve."

"It is equally sublime and beautiful," said Mrs. Herbert, "and, like many other of Shakespeare's images, rather gains than loses by repetition. Which is your favourite speech, Miss Belmont?"

"I scarcely know how to decide," said Agatha, "where I have found so many that have charmed me; yet Ferdinand's address to Miranda,

> — I do beseech you
> (Chiefly that I might set it in my prayers)
> What is your name?

is, I think, most strikingly beautiful. In a few words it speaks the purity and sincerity of his heart. He wishes to know her name that he may implore every blessing for her."

"You have exactly my sentiments, in this respect," said Mrs. Herbert, "and there cannot be a tender of affection where every idea of self is more completely renounced."

"Friendship, love, and every generous affection of the human soul," said Hammond, "were implanted by Heaven, and to Heaven they assist in leading us, prompt our virtues, and increase our devotions. He, whose cold heart never knew an object of tenderness, never felt a wish which had another's happiness in view, can be little sensible of that holy ardour which inspires us, when, at the Throne of Omnipotence, we implore blessings on those who are dear to us — dearer than ourselves!"

"Can that be?" said Miss Cassandra. "Is there anybody one can love better than oneself?"

"Many," said Hammond, "and everyone whose heart is capable of attachment, prizes the object of that attachment beyond himself; would on every occasion prefer the other's happiness to his own, nor hesitate were it necessary to sacrifice his life for the other's. Those who are incapable of this, are incapable of true affection. 'For none of us liveth to himself."[12]

"Eleonora, Queen to Edward the First, surnamed Long-shanks, was an instance of this," said Miss Milson.

"And many are the instances which every day presents," said Hammond. "How many mothers to their children's health sacrifice their own! How many fathers for the support of the family whose prosperity is dearer to them than their own ease and comfort, toil incessantly. These are general; but of partial instances I could cite thousands; several from my own knowledge; to one of which I am indeed indebted for the blessing of returning to my country, and of quitting a state of the most abject slavery."

Everyone present requested a relation of the circumstance alluded to. To this Hammond willingly consented; but it was already late, it was proposed to defer the recital till the next morning, during which time he promised to endeavour to recollect any other occurrence of his life capable of amusing, if not of interesting them.

The remainder of the day was spent nearly as usual, and little difference remarked in it by anyone except Agatha; to whom everything appeared to wear another face: the conversation in her idea assumed a new turn; and even Sir John appeared in support,[13] when there were so many present whose merits counterbalanced his failings. But the pleasure she received from the welcome addition to her society, did not banish from her mind the remembrance of Jemima Simmonds, nor of her own intention to visit her, and administer all the relief in her power; and she determined, if possible, to put her benevolent designs in practice the next morning.

When the morning arrived, Agatha, with a heart lighter than it had almost ever felt arose early, and scarcely allowed herself time to dress, lest her design should be impeded by finding some of the family already up. After wandering about the house for some time, she at length met with a servant who was just come downstairs, and inquiring of her was directed the road to Jemima's habitation.

---

[12]Romans 14, v. 7.
[13]Original has "supportable".

The cottage was at some distance from the rest of the village; and as the house and its situation were remarkable, she easily found it from the directions given her. It was white, and built on the declivity of a hill, the greatest part of which had been converted into a hanging wood for the benefit of the prospect from one of the rooms at Milson Hall; the view was, however, at present intercepted by the coach-house.

Around the cottage was a little rustic garden, enclosed in a paling covered with currants, and, here and there, a rose tree trained in the same simple manner. Everything bore the stamp of neatness and simplicity, and prejudiced in favour of the owner. Through a little white gate she entered the garden, and from thence along a narrow sand walk, arriving at the door of the cottage, which on her knocking gently, was opened by a beautiful girl of a figure more interesting than she had ever beheld. She appeared to be little more than eighteen, was tall, and elegantly formed. Her face was pale, and bore the strongest marks of sorrow; yet of a sorrow tempered with resignation, and which spoke the calm submission of a mild and gentle spirit, which had early learned to 'bear and forbear.' The languor of ill-health a smile of patient sufferance seemed to endeavour to conceal; and with a faint blush, and a humble curtsy, she requested Agatha to be seated, and thanked her for the honour she did them. Agatha expressed her fears that she intruded on her, and entreated her to excuse the liberty she had taken in coming thus; but the description Lady Milson had given of her, had interested her extremely, and made her anxious to see one, from the example of whose filial piety she hoped to profit.

"Dear Madam," said Jemima, "You are very kind so to speak of me; yet I have done nothing to deserve such praises. I fear, indeed, have not always behaved right; but it is my comfort that God will pardon our faults when they are not wilful."

"Surely he will," said Agatha, "and it is only when we act knowingly and intentionally wrong, that his mercy is withheld from us. But I am hurt to see you look so indifferent — I fear your health has suffered from uneasiness."

"That would be nothing, Madam," said Jemima, "did it not give me the sad, sad prospect of leaving my aged parent without a child or friend. That breaks my heart, and makes me quite unhappy when I think I shall not recover."

"You must not despair, indeed you must not," said Agatha, "but support your spirits, and your health will I hope return. Have you any physician?"

"Dear no, Madam," said Jemima, "and could we afford it, he could do me little good. My illness has been brought on I fear, by grief; and yet I have done all I could against it: indeed I have."

"I fear to be impertinent," said Agatha, "yet perhaps by unbosoming your sorrows you might find relief. And I would speak to my parents for you, do everything in my power to serve you."

"How kind you are," said Jemima, "yet, alas, there is little in my story that deserves to be spoken of. It is true I am unhappy, but who is not? — And then I could not bear, Madam, O I could not –"

At that moment someone knocked at the door, Jemima opened it, and Mrs. Herbert entered. Mrs. Herbert accosted Jemima in a tone of equal respect and tenderness. After which turning to Agatha, she said — "I am pleased but not surprised to find you here. In your countenance when this good girl was mentioned, I read every emotion that passed in your heart, and I knew that sooner or later you would visit one in whose fate I saw you so deeply interested."

"How can I ever be grateful enough for such goodness;" said Jemima, "but, alas, I do not deserve this condescension!"

"If you are not one of the best of girls," said Mrs. Herbert, "your face is very deceitful; for never have I seen goodness of heart so strongly depicted on a countenance. I wish I durst ask you to tell us all your griefs; but I fear it may renew them — and I will not ask it."

"Ah!" said Agatha, "it may indeed; and I will not again ask it. I am hurt that I should have been so inconsiderate as to desire a communication which would revive and increase instead of softening your troubles."

"O no, Madam — it is not for that; — but only –"

"Only what, my dear," said Mrs. Herbert.

"Only I should be ashamed to tell you all my foolishness. O, I durst not indeed, Madam!"

"Be not ashamed, my good girl," said Mrs. Herbert, "there is nothing in virtuous affection which anyone need blush to own."

"O Madam! But ladies who are great and learned, and who, like you, have had an education, cannot know what it is to feel, and — to love –" said she, hanging down her head, "like a poor girl."

"Education," said Mrs. Herbert, "does not destroy our feelings; it only teaches us to subdue them when they are adverse to reason and duty."

"Fear not," said Agatha, "to tell us everything. No one is faultless; and when those who are blessed with education sometimes deviate from the path of rectitude, how much more ought we to excuse it in those who have had no tutors but nature and their own hearts."

"And they are often the best," said Mrs. Herbert. "At least, where they do not instinctively lead us right, education, great as its influence, will find it a hard, and often impracticable task to make us virtuous." Then turning to Jemima she said, "You are an only child, I think?"

"Yes, Madam; and an orphan. My father and mother both died while I was in my cradle, and left me in the wide world with no friend but my grandmother; but she was everything to me — reared me from infancy by her own hard labour, and worked night and day as I grew older that she might put me to school, and give me all the little learning she could. O, she is the best of parents; and I should deserve the greatest punishment if I could have forsaken her in her old age that never forsook me while I was young and helpless. A dreadful cold and fever took from her the use of her limbs, it is now four years ago, and has confined her to her bed ever since. She has nobody to help her but me. — And now, could I leave her Madam?"

"Certainly not," said Mrs. Herbert, "but the young man who I was told was attached to you, you might still have married, without quitting your aged parent; and if he was good, and deserving, he would only have loved you the better for the time and attention you bestowed on her."

"Ah Madam! So I thought; and though I was sadly afraid that I could not do quite so much for her, if I should marry and have a family to look to, still, as his heart was set upon it, and I could not bear to see him unhappy, and as my dear grandmother too talked to me and wanted me to have him, I had consented. Poor, poor Harry! Had you seen ladies the joy that shone in his eyes when at last I consented to become his wife! How he blessed me – how he said that every labour would seem light and pleasant when it was for me that he worked!"

"Poor fellow!" said Agatha. "And what at last, what cruel accident parted you?"

"O Madam! An accident that seemed at the time to promise us greatest happiness. An old gentleman that had stood godfather to Harry, and had often been kind to him, died, and left him in his will an estate of almost sixty pounds a year in land. But it was in a distant country, many, many miles from here, and he was to go to live there, and I could not leave my grandmother. Here began our troubles."

"Could she not have been taken thither by some easy conveyance?" said Agatha.

"Alas, it was impossible, Madam. She has never, as I said, left her bed for four years, and the motion would have killed her. But old Mrs. Arnold, and all Harry's friends, would have him to go to settle on his farm, and so he begged me to go with him. I could not, you see, go, and what could I do? – And to ask him to go to leave his property to the care of others, was what I could not bear neither – and so, I told him I feared we must part; but that I should always love him and pray for him, and would never love nor think of anybody else. He did not make me any answer, but went away; and the next morning – how shall I tell you? O Madam, the next sad, sad morning he enlisted for a soldier, and I have never seen him since. His sisters are very angry with me, and their cruelty goes nigh to break my heart. They call me a bold, proud girl, and say I tried all I could to win their brother, and then refused to have him, to show everybody how he loved me, and what he would do when I slighted him; and they say if he should be killed they shall call me his murderer. O Madam! Can I bear this? It cuts me to the heart! And I want not their cruelty to increase my sorrow; for if he should die I am sure I shall never look up again. Poor, poor Harry! See ladies – but I'm ashamed to show you all my foolishness – only you are so good to me."

"Fear to show us nothing, my dear girl," said Mrs. Herbert. "What was it you meant?"

"Only this little bit of green satin – poor Harry gave it me – the housekeeper at his Godfather's gave it him as a plaything when he was a child; and he found it, and gave it me with a lock of his hair once. And see, I have worked, as well as I could, the letters of his name upon it, and wear it always next to my heart; and you know not how it comforts me! And I talk to it, and cry over it, many and many an hour: and those hours are the happiest I have now."

"And your grandmother, is not she distressed for you?" said Mrs. Herbert.

"O, I make it all appear well to her; and when my work is done, I read to her, and talk to her, and seem as happy as if nothing had happened. And she never suspects me, nor why poor Harry left me."

"Excellent girl!" said Mrs. Herbert, "how different a fate do you deserve!"

"Dear, dear Jemima!" said Agatha, bursting into tears, "my heart bleeds for you. But where is he?"

"Far, far away, I doubt," said Jemima, "for I have seen nor heard nothing of him since, and he has no doubt left this country – perhaps gone on shipboard, God knows where! Perhaps – O Madam! What shall I do! – But I forget myself, forget how I have resolved to cheer up my spirits, and keep myself well if I can – not for my own sake, for then I should not care, and I should be happy to die when it should please God to take me, but for the sake of my dear parent."

"Then you have not the least idea," said Agatha, "whither he is gone?"

"Not in the least Madam."

"Can point out no clue by which he could be traced if he has not yet left the kingdom?" said Mrs. Herbert.

"None at all, Madam. If anybody knows it is his sisters, but they would not tell me, though I have asked them many times. And they call me bold, and say, now he won't have me I want to have him, and follow him. But indeed, indeed I never was bold. I loved him dearly, it is true; and when he loved me, it was natural, you know, to love him again; and

I would have done anything to please him that had not gone against my conscience or my duty."

"May we see your grandmother?" said Agatha, whose feeling heart could support this scene no longer.

"She is not yet awake," said Jemima, "she never wakes so early; and I am almost afraid to disturb her."

"Do not, by any means," said Agatha, "and we will call again when we can see her."

Mrs. Herbert and Agatha, after the tenderest expressions of pity and anxiety, and an assurance of every assistance in their power, took their leave; Agatha putting, as she went out, five guineas into Jemima's hand.

"Indeed, indeed, Madam!" – said Jemima, "pray excuse me. We are in no want, indeed we are not, and have wherewithal, thank God, to live."

"You will oblige me greatly," said Agatha, "if you accept such a trifle from me. Wine or medicine may be necessary for you."

Jemima burst into a flood of tears, and Agatha, weeping with her, and taking her hand, besought her, in the tenderest manner, to support her spirits, and promised to call again very soon.

Chapter 6

Mrs. Herbert and Agatha had walked some distance from the cottage before either of them had power to speak. Agatha, at length, in a faltering voice, enquired of Mrs.[14] Herbert if it were not possible to discover poor Harry, and restore him to Jemima.

"I have been thinking of it," said Mrs. Herbert, "and, if he has not left the kingdom it may be possible, though at some expense, by an application to the commanding officer, to buy him off."

"O, expense would be nothing!" said Agatha. "My mother would gladly defray the charges whatever they were, I am convinced; and I would sell everything I possess to do it. The jewels on my crucifix[15] alone are worth some hundred pounds; and a plain one would be as acceptable in the sight of Heaven, when for such a purpose the jewels had been taken from it."

"There is one, I know," said Mrs. Herbert, "to whom I could apply, and from whom we could receive immediate assistance: my uncle. But to him I fear to have recourse. It is singular, but the romantic tendency of his benevolence frequently prevents my applying to him, in such a case; convinced that, when his feelings were once interested, he would ransack the universe, nor leave a stone unturned till he had accomplished his designs, though they robbed him of even the means of subsistence."

At length after some further consultation, they determined to apply to Mr. Hammond and Mr. Crawford, and if they thought it practicable, to send a messenger to overtake Harry, to purchase for him an exemption from the service, and assuring him of Jemima's attachment, to persuade him to return to her; when they hoped to enable them to maintain themselves with comfort without going to his farm, in which they proposed to place some of his relations, unless, on consideration, some better method could be adopted.

Pleased with this prospect of restoring peace where it was so justly merited, they returned impatiently; and Mrs. Herbert meeting Mr. Crawford as she entered, requested him to join the *Cassetta* party

---

[14]Original has "Mr." instead of "Mrs".
[15]**Author's note.** Agatha had been brought up by Lady Belmont in her own, the Roman Catholic religion, but without a tincture of bigotry; for she had always been taught, that every other faith, when sincere, and enjoining the practice of moral virtue, was equally acceptable to God.

that morning, and she told him they had a plan to communicate in which they wished for his advice and assistance.

In the breakfast room they found the family assembled, and waiting for them.

"Upon my honour and credit," said Sir John as they entered, "but those ladies look prettier than ever. They have been painting themselves with the morning air, the best paint in nature – is not it Mr. Hammond? Don't they look nicely?"

"You must either imagine us immoderately vain," said Mrs. Herbert, "that the praises of one person are not enough to satisfy us, or else believe your own veracity doubtful, that you call another witness to support your assertions."

"Why this is no how," said Sir John. "Whenever one talks to you, Mrs. Herbert, you answer one in such a roundabout manner, that a plain sensible man, though he may be a gentleman and a baronet into the bargain, perhaps, can't understand what you mean."

"I am sorry, indeed," said Mrs. Herbert, "and for the future I will endeavour to adapt my language to the comprehension of gentlemen and baronets."

"That's right," said Sir John, "and it will but serve your own turn better too; for no woman can get many sweethearts that shows herself fit for a school mistress to half the men she meets. Men hate a woman that understands geography and grammar, and things of that sort."

"Very true, Sir John," said Lady Milson, "who would like a wife that was a Mackereltician?"

"Mathewmatician you mean, my Lady," said Sir John.

At this moment two persons on horseback passing by the window on full gallop, attracted the attention of everyone; and Mr. Ormistace, his eyes sparkling with transport, rather flew than ran out of the room. He returned in a few minutes, and going to the window, beckoned Mrs. Herbert to him. When she approached, he said, in a low voice, "Emma, are you disposed for a feast this morning?"

"Of the eyes or the mind," said Mrs. Herbert.

"Of both," said he, "for I can bestow upon you the highest luxury."

"The species of luxury to which you allude you well know I always share with delight," said Mrs. Herbert.

"Well then, you recollect the mention of Jemima Simmonds, her situation and distress?"

"Surely I do."

"Harry Arnold is returned!"

"Is returned?" said Mrs. Herbert. "I am delighted. Miss Belmont come hither this moment, I entreat you."

Mrs. Herbert then communicated to Agatha the welcome tidings of Harry's return, who heard it with tears of delight. Some of the party observing the pleasure evident in the countenances of Agatha, Mrs. Herbert, and Mr. Ormistace, requested to know the cause of their joy, that they might share it; and a servant coming in at that moment, and saying eagerly that Harry Arnold was returned, the rejoicing became general. Mrs. Milson enquired if it was not to the benevolent exertions of Mr. Ormistace that they were all indebted for the pleasure of this event.

"My exertions have been trifling," said Mr. Ormistace. "Immediately after Lady Milson's affecting detail of poor Jemima's situation, I ordered one of my servants to make the necessary enquiries, and, if it was within the limits of possibility, to discover Arnold and bring him back. My servant is active and intelligent: he has pursued and found him, and obtained his discharge, and has this moment brought him back in transport to his faithful Jemima."

"Kind, good, noble Mr. Ormistace!" said Agatha, who could neither conceal nor silence her transports.

"Have a care of your heart, my dear," said Mrs. Herbert, "for a few more such actions as this would infallibly run away with it."

"If anything could add to my pleasure at this moment," said Mr. Ormistace, "it would be the approbation of a heart like Miss Belmont's."

"We are all sharers in the joy," said Mr. Crawford, "and shall be yet more so, if Mr. Ormistace will permit us to make cause general by sharing the expense attending it. His are the exertions, and therefore the greatest pleasure; but this, by permitting us to become, in some measure, principals in the affair, will give us consequence and complete our satisfaction."

"By no means," said Mr. Ormistace, "the expense is trifling, very trifling – nothing compared to the pleasure received! A luxury very cheaply purchased! Of one piece of cruelty I have been guilty for my own gratification. I have forbid Arnold's return to Jemima till I am present to witness their meeting."

Almost everyone present joining in an earnest request to be permitted to be spectators of the moving scene, Mr. Ormistace consented, assuring that he had not as yet even seen Jemima, being determined not to see her, till he could behold her happy.

"Excellent Mr. Ormistace!" said Agatha low to Mrs. Herbert, "bestower of such felicity – how do I envy his feelings!"

"If that moving index of yours tells true," said Mrs. Herbert, "and I am sure it never spoke falsely yet, his felicity, if it equal, cannot exceed your own."

Mrs. Herbert then proposed that they should no longer delay the happiness in their reach, nor detain the impatient Harry from the mistress of his heart. Mr. Ormistace, therefore, left the room for a few minutes to prepare Arnold for the interview, and to request him to permit a few friends who anxiously wished it, to be partakers of his happiness by witnessing it. Arnold, whose heart filled with gratitude, joy, and love, scarcely allowed him the use of his reason, required no entreaties to induce him to consent without hesitation to whatever his benefactor proposed; and the whole party, immediately on Mr. Ormistace's return to them, joined the happy lover, and proceeded with him to Jemima's cottage.

Harry Arnold was tall, and of a figure, for a person in his station, uncommonly elegant. On his rough, manly features a look of openness and integrity bespoke his genuine worth; while the warmth and ardour of youthful impetuosity were checked by a smile of placid tenderness as the sweet image of his Jemima presented itself to his enraptured thoughts.

Mrs. Herbert proposed that herself and Agatha should go a few minutes before the rest to prepare Jemima for the interview, which in her present weak state of health and spirits, she feared might otherwise be more than she could sustain. This request was instantly approved by everyone; and the rest remained at a small distance from her house while Mrs. Herbert and Agatha advanced.

Jemima, whose depression and languor had been rather increased than lessened by the dangerous indulgence of dwelling on her sorrows to them, had scarcely power to speak or stand as she opened the door to them. "This is kind indeed," was all she could say, as they entered.

"Nothing new, I hope, has arrived to distress you, my dear Jemima?" said Mrs. Herbert, observing her dejection.

Jemima put her finger to her lips, and looked towards the bed where her grandmother lay, in token of silence; then going nearer to the door, and speaking low, she assured her she had no cause for uneasiness. "But alas!" continued Jemima, "I cannot control my grief! There is a sinking at my heart, Madam."

"Which shall be removed," said Agatha, "and you shall be as happy —"

Mrs. Herbert pressed Agatha's hand, in order to caution her to break it to Jemima more gently; then turning to Jemima, she said, "We know not what happiness Heaven may have in store for us when we act so as to deserve its favours. In the moments of our greatest distress, the clouds of sorrow break on a sudden, and the sun of happiness shines upon us, and gilds all our future prospects."

"Ah Madam!" said Jemima, "but it is the fate of some to be born beneath a winter sky, when the clouds never break."

"That will not be yours, I am well assured," said Agatha. "I can foresee such happiness in store for you! What would my dear, my sweet Jemima think, if —"

Then recollecting herself Agatha looked at Mrs. Herbert; who remarking that Jemima's colour changed from the observance of Agatha's manner, "Arm yourself, my good girl," she said, "that as you have with fortitude borne the weight of severe affliction, you may not be overcome by too exquisite a happiness. Promise me to be calm and composed, and we will keep you no longer in suspense concerning the blessings you are on the point of sharing."

"I see, I see, I know it all," said Jemima, "he is come, he is here! I know he is –"

"He is, indeed," said Mrs. Herbert.

"He is, he is!" said Agatha.

"Let me run to meet him!" Then stopping herself, she fell to her knees, and raising her clasped hands to Heaven. "Thank Heaven, thank Heaven!" she exclaimed. "And O, forgive me, good God, that I have grieved, sinner that I am, at thy will, thy just will." She then attempted to rise, but her feeble efforts were insufficient without Mrs. Herbert's and Agatha's assistance. The moment she had risen, forgetful of them, of everything but her love, she sprang from them, and flew like lightning she knew not whither.

Harry, who with difficulty had been restrained from approaching the house sooner, sprang to meet her, and in a moment they were in each other's arms.

"Jemima! My love! My darling! Forgive me," said Harry. "And do I meet thee again?"

"O, forgive me!" said Jemima, "'twas I that drove you – But O, my Harry! Nothing but –"

"No reflections on what is past, dearest, dearest girl!" said Harry. "We are happy now, and shall never part! I will never leave you, nor your dear, good grandmother. Everything has been done for us by the best of gentlemen."

This reflection reminding Harry of the many who were present, which in the first moments of meeting Jemima he had totally forgotten, he loosed her from his arms; and Jemima, who, in the first transports of beholding him again, had not even seen that any other was near them, now looked around, and coloured extremely, on observing so many witnesses of her tenderness; when Harry, with the grace which the noblest feelings of nature inspired, led Jemima to Mr. Ormistace.

"Here, Jemima! Here, my love!" he said, "is our generous benefactor – here is the noble gentleman to whom we owe all our happiness. Join with me in blessing him."

They then both in one moment dropped on their knees at his feet; and Mr. Ormistace raising them, his heart big, and his eyes filled with tears, said, in a faltering voice, "I have done nothing – or if

I had, your happiness – this sweet moment, would repay me a hundredfold!"

Mr. Craggs, who had accompanied the rest of the party, and who had paid, apparently, much attention to the scene before him, now advanced towards Jemima, and with a look which implied an interest in her welfare and a desire of serving her, "I have observed," he said, "that you have shed many tears."

"Forgive me, Sir," said Jemima, "but I did not see how many gentlemen were by, and it was a relief to me."

"A temporary one, it might be," said Mr. Craggs, "but be assured from me, that tears, though they may sometimes give a momentary relief, are, in the end, injurious to the constitution, destroy its energy, and impair its vigour."

Jemima listened in silent astonishment, and Mr. Craggs proceeded: "Tears, young woman, though you may not perhaps have studied their composition, consist, as I can inform you, of aqueous and saline particles. Now the best way to prevent them is to abstain from everything which may occasion a redundancy of either of these in our constitution. I had myself an unfortunate, and, as I am now clear, a dangerous habit of shedding tears at times; but by denying myself everything which has much of either salt or water in its composition, I have lost the propensity entirely."

"Then I pity you from my soul," said Mr. Ormistace, "for the tears this sweet girl shed at that moment were the most voluptuous of gratifications: sweeter than honey and the honeycomb."

Mr. Craggs returned a contemptuous stare to this remark, and then withdrew from the company, who, except Mr. and Mrs. Craggs, entered immediately Betty Simmonds's cottage.

The old woman, who could distinguish nothing but confused expressions of joy from voices new and strange to her, was at a loss to account for what was passing, and waited Jemima's return with anxious impatience.

Jemima requested everyone to wait without, while she herself broke to her grandmother the welcome news of Harry's return, who, however, knew not the cause of his absence though she had often lamented it. Jemima then told her in a few words all that had passed, concealing nothing but her rejection of Harry, and imputing his enlisting as a soldier to some cause of offence she had unknowingly given him. The venerable old woman sat up in bed, and with a feeble voice blessed them both a hundred times, and prayed that if ever Jemima should be a mother she might have a child like herself.

The party now prepared to leave the cottage, Mr. Ormistace having first desired that the nuptials might be solemnised the next day, and Sir John promising to give them a wedding dinner.

Agatha, her eyes swimming in tears, and her steps tottering from the emotions by which she had been agitated, thankfully accepted the arm which Hammond, who had gazed upon her in silent delight for some minutes, offered, to support her home.

"Mr. Hammond, I am certain," said Agatha, "has not been an unmoved spectator of the scene which has just passed!"

"Far, far from it," said Hammond, "and could I have remained untouched by objects so interesting as those which have called us hither, the dear, the sweet emotions of that best and kindest of hearts would have awakened every feeling of mine."

"I would give anything," said Agatha, "that you had seen as I did poor Jemima's previous sorrow, to be enabled the more perfectly to enjoy the delightful reverse of happiness now displayed. Yet that you have witnessed this scene is a pleasure to me; and how do I pity those, if such there are, who know not what it is to have a friend: since even the pure joys of benevolence are heightened by the possession of a friend to share them."

"Blest, most blest am I," said Hammond, "to be, this once at least, the happy partner of your joys! Would, O, would that mine were indeed the delightful lot to share them ever; and not only to share, but to increase them!"

"You always will," said Agatha, "I am convinced. The place your beloved sister possessed in my heart is wholly yours."

"O, that that heart were all, *all*. Yet what would I say? Thus esteemed, deemed worthy of such friendship, it were ungrateful to repine; yet happy, happy he to whom that heart –"

"What do you mean?" said Agatha. "What would you say? Your manner and mysterious words alarm me. Do you doubt my sincerity?"

"I doubt nothing but myself," said Hammond, "nothing but my own resolution, which is too weak to bear such repeated trials."

"What trials?" said Agatha. "I do not comprehend you. Is there anything I can say to make you more at ease?"

"Nothing, nothing! Only hate me, despise me, do anything but call me thus your friend."

"But call you my friend!" said Agatha. "Surely I thought, I hoped, the title was dear to you?"

"Dear!" interrupted he. "Yes, dearer than life itself!"

"Then why am I forbid it, unkind Mr. Hammond? I had hoped that the place your sister possessed in my regard, should have been supplied by her brother, who for her sake, nay, for his own, was dear to me! But since you thus reject my professed friendship, I call it back; I will not force on anyone –"

"Miserable that I am" exclaimed Hammond. "What have I said? What have I done? – Dear, sweet Miss Belmont, forgive my impetuosity – forgive the frantic starts of a man whose mind is at war with itself; whom nothing but the fear of distressing you could restrain from declaring every sentiment of his soul. But say you forgive me, and will call me again your friend, and I will strive to be more master of myself, if possible: only forgive me."

"I do, I do," said Agatha, "say no more, Mr. Hammond – my friend!"

"My friend!" repeated Hammond! "My all! My – then you have quite forgiven me what has passed?"

"I said I had."

"Give me then your hand – this once give it me!"

"Here, – and with it receive the assurance of the sincerest regard."

Hammond had not courage to speak again; and pressing her hand to his lips, walked on in a silence which Agatha endeavoured, but often ineffectually, to interrupt. He gave short and vague answers to everything she said. At last, she lamented the necessity they should be under of postponing the recital he had promised them till the next morning, since it was already time to dress for dinner. Hammond replied, that he was thankful it was too late: his mind being agitated, and his thoughts confused, he felt himself incapable of reciting anything clearly; but that he would study for composure, and by the next morning he trusted should obtain it.

"Heaven grant it," said Agatha, "for to see you thus distresses me greatly."

Agatha, her spirits agitated by her interest in Jemima's fate, and afterwards by Hammond's, to her, unaccountable wildness, had not power to overtake the rest of the party, who had walked some paces first; and she did not arrive with Hammond till they were entered, and gone to dress. She, therefore, left him immediately on her return, and retired to her chamber; her mind sensible of an oppression, for which she could not account, unless from the anxiety she was conscious she felt at seeing Hammond thus strange, and unhappy she knew not why. He had said that nothing but the fear of distressing her prevented his declaring everything that passed in his soul: surely then, she thought, he is in possession of some fatal secret relative to me, and fears to reveal it. My mother, my father perhaps ill! Yet, on recollection, she thought that impossible; since Lady Belmont's letter, so lately received, had nothing in it mysterious or alarming. What then could it be? To know the worst, she fancied, would be a relief; yet she durst not ask him – durst not revert to a scene from which he had apparently suffered so greatly; and she determined, however painful her suspense, to say nothing which might renew in him feelings that had equally distressed and alarmed her.

Chapter 7

In the evening, Miss Milson, who confessed herself "enamoured of the harmony of sweet sounds," desired that they might have a little musical treat. In this wish she was joined by several others, and the rest of the day was chiefly devoted to music. Agatha, who had early attained to perfection in the charming art, made one of the principal performers, and her voice and manner were equally applauded. After she had sung several pathetic airs with feeling and taste, Mr. William Milson brought the following song which he gave to Agatha, saying, he had lately met with it, that it pleased him greatly, and he therefore would entreat her to sing and play it, certain that her performance would do it more than justice.

Dans votre lit, my charming maid!
May not a care thy soul invade;
But soft and sweet thy slumbers be,
Where hov'ring angels watch o'er thee!
Dans votre lit.

My fancy, in thy dreams, portray
The actions of thy spotless day;
Each deed of sacred charity,
In blest review retrac'd to thee!
Dans votre lit.

Should sickness come (which Heaven forsend!)
Still may that bosom own a friend,
Whose tender cares the balm shall be,
To bring returning health to thee!
Dans votre lit.

O! if a wife ordain'd to prove,
May some dear pledges bless thy love,
Who smiles with transport thou shalt see,
Their infant arms then circling thee!
Dans votre lit.

And when thy gentle spirit flies,
To join at last its kindred skies,
Then may Religion – Piety!
Smooth every path 'twixt Heaven and thee!
　　　　Dans votre lit.

"If I did not believe the author of that song actually present," said Mr. Crawford, "I should lament his absence, since he never could hear it with so much pleasure, or to so much advantage as thus sung."

Mr. William Milson coloured, and went out of the room without speaking.

"It is unpleasant to detect those we would love in crimes," said Mrs. Herbert, low to Agatha; "but I fear all my heart can plead in your behalf will not exculpate you."

"What have I done?" said Agatha, somewhat alarmed by the seriousness of her manner.

"Stolen a heart that has been long devoted to your friend," said Mrs. Herbert, "and I much mistake if my faithful Strephon has not found another Delia at whose feet to lay his bays."

"Not me, surely?" said Agatha,

"Yes, you! Very surely," said Mrs. Herbert. "I only hope that his second flame may prove more propitious than his first. But if he were to be slighted by her too, I might as well have the honour of employing his muse as another."

"If what you say were true," said Agatha, "he would be peculiarly unfortunate, since he would, if I have the least knowledge of my own heart, find the same ungenerous requital a second time."

"I wish," said Mrs. Herbert, repeating Agatha's former words, "that Miss Belmont pitied him as much as I do, he would then be less unhappy at least." Then turning to Hammond she said: "everyone has thanked Miss Belmont for her charming performance but you Mr. Hammond."

"But me!" said Hammond, startled at the unexpected remark, "I am sure I think – I am sure I felt – and sure I never heard —"

"Nor did I ever hear," said Mrs. Herbert, "thanks expressed in so clear and graceful a manner."

"If I did not thank Miss Belmont before," said Hammond, recollecting himself, "it was not that I was not delighted with her performance; for that were impossible: but there were so many others who claimed to be heard, that I did not intrude my voice."

"There are some certain occasions," said Mrs. Herbert in a lower tone, and which, from others speaking at the same time, was only audible to the person to whom it was addressed, "there are some occasions where permitting the claims of others to be heard in preference to your own, may not ensure you success. You perhaps understand me?"

"Indeed, I do not," said Hammond.

"Then time, and a little further acquaintance with Miss Belmont, will elucidate my meaning," said Mrs. Herbert.

Hammond, who perceived that Mrs. Herbert suspected him of an attachment to Agatha, and who wished at all events to drop the subject, requested any one of the ladies to sing another song, and offered to accompany the singer, whomever it might be, on the flute.

"Accept the proposal, some lady, by all means," said Mrs. Herbert; "I'm convinced that at this moment Mr. Hammond will play delightfully."

"And so he will," said Sir John. "Mrs. Herbert is always joking somebody in her manner without any respect to their present or future rank; and upon my honour and credit it's not fair."

"But you know as I seldom speak intelligibly, Sir John," said Mrs. Herbert, "my jests are of little importance: and it is not a minute since Mr. Hammond himself owned that he did not understand me."

Hammond, determined to silence Mrs. Herbert, without waiting for anyone else, took up the flute, and began to play; and Miss Milson went immediately to the pianoforte and accompanied him. The short remainder of the evening was spent in general conversation.

When Agatha went to rest, she felt herself little disposed to sleep. Hammond's extraordinary manner was a perpetual source of surprise and uneasiness; while the coolness she imagined she remarked in his behaviour to her at times, distressed her greatly; and she wearied herself in conjectures concerning its cause. Morning arrived before she had closed her eyes; and the morning brought with it the same anxiety – an anxiety different from all she had before experienced. At length, she dropped asleep; but waking soon, after uneasy dreams, she determined to arise, and seek, in the refreshment of a morning walk, a revival of her spirits, and an oblivion of the doubts and reflections which had disturbed her repose.

With this view, she went to the *Cassetta*, and when there, took down a book, determined to read. But scarcely had she read a page when Hammond entered. She started, coloured, and offered, she knew not why, to go.

"Surely I have not offended Miss Belmont," said Hammond, "that she prepares thus to leave me?"

"Not in the least," said Agatha; "indeed you have not – but –"

"But what, my dear Miss Belmont?"

"I thought you might have come here expecting to find no one, and might wish to read or write."

"That I came hither expecting to find no one, is, indeed true; but what reading, or what writing should I not exchange with pleasure for your society!"

Agatha, who observed with delight the tranquillity of his manner, so opposite to what it had been the whole day preceding, sat down again with pleasure; and presenting to him the book she was reading, asked his opinion of the author's merit. He gave his sentiments; but after a few minutes' conversation, relapsed into an absence, from which she in vain endeavoured to divert him. He put a letter he held in his hand into his pocket, and walked to the window, where he remained in silence for some time.

Agatha at length said, "I fear, nay, I am sure I interrupt you; and though your politeness detained me, you have studies which require solitude. I will go to the house, and when you have done reading, you shall come to me."

"Indeed, indeed, I have no letter to write," said Hammond. "I was, it is true, reading one – one which affected me; but which it would be now too late to answer."

"The loss of some friend, I fear you lament," said Agatha.

"Yes," replied Hammond, "a friend whose loss is irreparable; who would have advised me, consoled me, supported my feeble efforts."

"I did indeed fear," said Agatha, "that some new distress had arisen. And is the fatal loss recent?"

"Recent! – Dear Miss Belmont, what friend can I ever lament as the one so dear, so justly dear to us both? She still is, must be ever the object of my eternal regret; and the more, as every day I am but the more sensible of her loss."

"Alas!" said Agatha, "what can I say to comfort you! But tell me all you feel, impart all your sufferings to me, and if my friendship cannot cure, it may alleviate them. That letter was from her then?"

"Yes, several years since, while I was a student at college, it was written to me: it contains the best and most valuable of counsel, and nothing should have torn it from me. In bondage and captivity it has been my companion and friend; in sickness and sorrow my best comforter."

"I know not if I ought to ask to read it," said Agatha.

"You are all kindness," said Hammond; "yet I fear to communicate it – I fear to distress the most tender and best of hearts."

"Fear nothing," said Agatha, "if it will be any relief to you. We will read it together; and perhaps, though it may affect you deeply at the time, the indulgence of your grief may, in the end, soften it, and restore your peace."

Hammond attempted to speak his thanks; but his voice faltered, and he stopped. After a moment's pause, he took out the letter, and gave it to

Agatha; who, drawing her chair nearer to his, and placing the letter on a table which stood before them, read it with him.

Blagrove, March the 26th.

Separated from my beloved Edward, I have no resource but in writing to him; and the pleasure that affords is trifling compared to the delight of exchanging our ideas in conversation. Yet some advantages result from letters which are denied to conversation: we have leisure to think ere we speak, to arrange our thoughts with more clearness and precision, and then interrupted by the occasional remarks of others, can pursue our subject without any link being broken in the chain of our ideas. We can, besides, say on paper what we fear to speak, can offer advice, when we have leisure to adjust the language in which it is conveyed, with less danger of offence, and can write what, from feeling too sensibly, we are unable to speak. These ideas have induced me to venture to address the brother whom the heaviest of losses has placed under my care, with offers of advice for the regulation of that conduct, on which depends his honour, with passions strong, though, I trust, controllable, and a temper warm and ardent though not irascible, you are preparing to enter life; to mix with a world, where vice under a thousand alluring forms will attract, and virtue, in spite of all her internal graces, in as many forbidding ones repel your pursuit. Thus circumstanced it is not enough to say, "hold to the one, and despise the other," but shun, as you would vice itself, every approach towards it, however remote; whether in company, conversation, or books.

Women have many advantages denied to men: their life domestic and retired, and even when otherwise, their dissipation rarely leading to any criminal pursuit, they have not the temptations, which men initiated almost from their infancy in the schools of vice, are condemned to encounter. Yet, on the other hand, men are supposed to be framed with minds as well as bodies superior to ours in strength, and therefore more capable of resisting temptation when placed within its reach.

From pernicious precepts, from the contagion of ill example, and from the yet more dangerous shafts of ridicule launched perpetually by the weak and vicious against those who dare, in opposition to them, to be wise and virtuous, I tremble lest you should be led to relinquish the duties you now hold most sacred, the principles your native virtues would otherwise forbid you to violate. As the safest and surest armour against such attacks, form to yourself one regular plan of conduct, comfortable to your own ideas of propriety and rectitude; and to this invariably adhere upon every occasion as well trivial as important.

The inheritance you derive from our parents, my beloved Edward, is, I am happy to find, considerable enough to afford you an ample provision without the necessity of recurring either to a trade or profession to increase it; and, as your constitution is delicate, it is, as you know, my earnest wish that you should have no one decided pursuit. Yet, while I propose this, imagine not that I wish your life to pass in supineness and sloth: far from it. No! Let there never be a moment not devoted to some pleasing and even useful employment: and these, while you lay the foundation of sciences in your youth, can never be wanting.

If you study more earnestly than those with whom you associate, it is more than probable that you may be dignified with the fashionable appellation of a Quiz. Perhaps, likewise, if you refuse to reduce your understanding to the level of a brute by wine, or resist their expostulations to join in any other favourite vice, you may on such occasions likewise, be called a Quiz. But condemn their ridicule; and be assured, that every title given to us by the votaries of vice and folly because we persist in shunning their paths, is a title in which we may glory, and adds a dignity to our character more splendid than a coronet could confer!

By a thousand acts of kindness to all with whom you have hitherto associated, you have shown yourself capable of friendship, and have evinced a heart open to its sacred influence. It is the most valuable tendency of human nature, and I wish to cherish it. But be careful on whom you fix. "Be kind to many, but have one councillor of a thousand," for it is but too just, that by the insidious arts of some of their own sex, rather than the other, are men as well as women generally betrayed into vice. When you have indeed found a friend, and are convinced of his worth, prize the inestimable treasure as your life! Yet this I need not urge: the honour and sincerity of your disposition render such a charge unnecessary.

There is another, more tender, and, because ratified by the most solemn of vows, yet more sacred connection, which you may one day form; and which, from the natural susceptibility of your heart, it is improbable you should not. In this, as in friendship, seek to be master of yourself; seek to remain unguided by the impulse of the moment; not let caprice dictate an attachment on which your future happiness depends. There are many whom from the elegance of their persons or manners you may be led to admire, and, in consequence of that admiration to treat with greater attention than others. But of this be cautious: nor by a marked assiduity give any woman reason to suppose you feel that preference which a further acquaintance with her disposition or foibles may destroy. It is possible that you may thus lose the opportunity of impressing a heart capable of rendering you happy, in your favour, which another less generous admirer may, in the meantime, make his own. Yet, to an ingenuous mind, the pain of a disappointment, where the affection has not been suffered to take too deep root, is infinitely preferable to the humiliating consciousness of a deviation from prudence or propriety: and it is noble to hazard our own happiness rather than to trifle with or endanger that of another.

May heaven preserve you, my Edward, from every sorrow incident to human nature! Bless every pursuit of your life, every attachment of your heart, and shield you from the heart-rending anguish your sister has been destined to experience; an anguish which nothing but the consciousness of its being unmerited, and not the consequence of an imprudent partiality indulged in contradiction to duty or propriety could have enabled me to sustain: especially, at that early period of my life, before reason had obtained its due sway, and enabled me to command my feelings.

A person whose name I have long since forbidden myself to write or speak, had known and loved me almost from infancy, my heart was sensible of his worth and returned his affection; our parents who had been friends long and justly dear to each other, saw and encouraged our attachment. No wonder then, that in a heart like mine, love authorised by duty should make a deep impression. I yielded to its delightful influence, gave the reins to my fond hopes and ardent imagination, and blessed in his undoubted affection, and in the sacred sanction of parental approbation, looked forward with a delight impossible to be described, to the moment that should forever unite me to one in whom every hope, every wish, every joy, was centred. Too fatal indulgence! Too sweet illusion! Hope, false, flattering hope, raises meteors of bliss which dance before our deluded sight – we behold, we grasp at, and lose them forever! The fairer are our prospects of felicity, the more they are fleeting – in the bloom of youth, with a heart formed to bless her on whom it was bestowed, with every excellent disposition to endear him to society, was snatched from this transitory happiness he had promised himself in this life, to a "far more exceeding and eternal weight of glory" in another. But who shall paint your poor Maria's sufferings, my Edward! Religion alone has been my consolation and support: for we are not eternally divided – we shall meet again never to part! In those regions of endless bliss, how pure the delight to behold all who are dear to us, to see them partakers of the same eternal, and, till then, inconceivable felicity! This image robs death of every sting, and enables me to view the moment of my departure from this fragile existence, with hope, exultation, and joy.

One only tie attaches me to life. Heaven is my witness how dear you are to me! And to see you blest as this world can render you would be the consummation of my earthly wishes; to behold you as a friend, as husband, and as father, beloved, respected, and happy. Such, I trust, I pray may be your lot, my Edward! Yet who dares say that I shall live *to see it! Your constitution weak and delicate, your life seems to hang but by a thread, mine strong and unailing, promises a length of years. Yet how deceitful are such promises! How often do we behold those whose ruddy health seemed an earnest of many days to come, and threatened to bid defiance to disease or death, followed to the grave by their sickly yet surviving friends! Yes: ten thousand accidents, impossible to be foreseen or prevented, may snatch me from this world before you. Yet still if it be permitted by Heaven, and I love to cherish the hope that it will, still may I see and watch over you – still may my departed spirit hover around him, whose memory only could call it back to earth. Already does my imagination transport me to the regions of the blessed. Already do I look down upon you, as you run, with persevering piety, "the race that is set before you."*[16] *Methinks I see you at this moment – she, whose virtues have fixed and united every tender affection of your soul, the sharer and heightener of your joys, the soother and mitigator of your sorrows, the friend as well as mistress of your heart, seated beside you. I see you gaze upon her with unutterable tenderness – I hear you repeat with transport the vows which have inseparably united you – I hear you say, you are happy; – and, did but poor Maria live to witness it, should have no wish ungratified. I see a smiling infant approach his parents – I hear him lisp my name – I hear him say, that had I lived I should have loved him! – I see you catch him to your heart with tears of agonising tenderness! – Edward! The picture is too affecting – I cannot go on –*

Agatha burst into tears; and, with a motion as innocent as it was involuntary, dropped her head upon Hammond's shoulder. In all little troubles of her childhood, and when older, in every emotion excited by the perusal of fictitious distress, she had been accustomed thus to seek refuge in the bosom of his sister: that sister now present to her imagination – her image actually before her eyes – in her idea every other was lost for a moment; while her heart, softened beyond what she could support by the affecting picture just drawn, sought its comforter in Hammond. He pressed her to his heart, unable to speak, and kissed with impassioned tenderness her cheek as it reposed on him

Agatha started, and rose: a recollection of an impropriety, a consciousness that something more than friendship, both in her own and Hammond's heart, occasioned the emotions she felt, struck her mind instantaneously; and terrified, confused, and distressed, she attempted to open the door. Hammond detained her; and catching hold of her hand, and pressing it between both his, "Whither, whither would you

---

[16]Hebrews 12 v. 1.

go? My all! My dearest Miss Belmont," he exclaimed. "Why quit me at this moment? – the sweetest of my life! – Hear me first confess every feeling of this heart – this heart that –"

"Detain me not, Mr. Hammond," interrupted Agatha; "for I must, I will go."

"Say first then you forgive me my presumption."

"Let me go now, I entreat, I conjure you!"

"O, I have offended you! And can I part from you till you have forgiven me? You are angry with me."

"I am; but I am still more so with myself. I never felt so miserable as at this moment; and I have forfeited your esteem as well as my own."

"Forfeited my esteem! Good God! Never, never, Miss Belmont, dearest, best-beloved of my heart! Never did I esteem you as at this moment – never were you so truly estimable! Suffer me only to tell you all that has passed in my soul –"

"Mr. Hammond – another time – perhaps – but for the present suffer me to leave you, nor take it ill that I do, for my spirits are unequal to the task of supporting a further conversation at present."

"For worlds I would not distress you, nor urge what would give a moment's pain to one whose happiness is infinitely dearer to me than my own. It would only be a satisfaction – nay, the greatest of blessings, would you but deign to say you forgive me my presumption, pardon the ungenerous advantage I dared to take of the sweet though involuntary instance of the most tender friendship."

"Say no more," said Agatha; "nor recall to my mind what I would wish to forget forever. We will return to the house now; and, if possible, recover our spirits from the depression that has hung upon them."

Hammond tremblingly offered her his arm; and Agatha, though she had never hesitated to accept it before, was preparing to refuse it; but after a moment's pause, feeling herself unable to walk without support, she took it without speaking.

They had walked but a few steps from the *Cassetta*, when they were met by Mrs. Herbert and Miss Cassandra. Agatha coloured at meeting them, and Mrs. Herbert observing it, said, "You are an excellent riser, Miss Belmont; and the glow on your cheeks proves the benefit of the custom, and will ensure you a compliment from Sir John."

Agatha said she had found herself unable to sleep, which had occasioned her rising earlier than usual.

"There were some others probably in the same predicament," said Mrs. Herbert. "How did you sleep, Mr. Hammond?"

"O, Mr. Hammond was up before Miss Belmont," said Miss Cassandra; "for I heard his room door open two hours ago."

"You came from the *Cassetta*, if I mistake not?" said Mrs. Herbert. "'tis a delightful room, and admirably calculated for the society of a friend: and now I have no doubt that this morning every flower scattered unusual fragrance."

"It's always a pleasant place," said Miss Cassandra; "and I tell my sister that whenever I get an admirer she shall lend it me to be courted in. Don't you think it would do nicely for such a purpose, Mrs. Herbert?"

"I should think it would," said Mrs. Herbert; "but Miss Belmont's the best judge – you had better apply to her."

"What do you think, Miss Belmont?" said Miss Cassandra. "Would it not be a charming courting room?"

Agatha coloured extremely, and replied, hardly conscious of what she said, "It would indeed; – I should think – I don't know, I am sure –"

Hammond, who had watched every turn of Agatha's countenance, observed, in a moment after she had spoken, that the colour had entirely forsaken her cheeks: her spirits, before agitated, were incapable of supporting this unseasonable raillery, and she complained of feeling very ill. Mrs. Herbert, looking at her, was no less alarmed than Hammond; she begged Miss Cassandra to run immediately to the house for a glass of water, and desired Hammond to fetch a bench from another part of the garden.

When they were gone, "My dear girl!" said Mrs. Herbert, "I could kill myself for having thus distressed you! Had I the least idea I should have given you a moment's serious pain, I would not have behaved thus for the world. Pray forgive me! Yet I shall never forgive myself; to receive pleasure from wantonly giving a sensation of uneasiness to anyone is a barbarous habit; and from this moment I disclaim it. You shall tell me all that passes in your heart, if it will be the smallest relief to you; if not, you shall not say a word on the subject, and I will never start it more."

Agatha, as yet unable to reply, pressed her hand, in token of forgiveness and friendship.

Miss Cassandra, who had run as fast as possible, now returned with the water, and Hammond, at the same moment, arrived with the bench. Mrs. Herbert placed Agatha upon it, and Miss Cassandra held the glass to her lips, inquiring every minute, with much good-natured solicitude, if she was better; while Hammond, alarmed and uneasy, angry with himself, and still more so with Mrs. Herbert, leaned over her with looks of the tenderest anxiety. She soon revived, and attributing her illness to want of sleep and the fatigue of rising too early, entreated them not to mention to anyone a trifling ailment which had already left her.

When she was sufficiently recovered to walk, they went into the house, and Agatha going to her chamber to take off her cloak, and to endeavour to regain her spirits before she joined the company, Miss Cassandra followed her and took this opportunity of saying, "I hope, sure, my dear Miss Belmont, it was not my calling the *Cassetta* a courting room that made you ill; if it was, I should be very sorry. I did not mean at all to say that Mr. Hammond had been courting you. I am sure I never thought of such a thing."

Agatha assured her that her illness proceeded merely from fatigue and want of rest.

"I am sure," said Miss Cassandra, "I am very glad to hear you say so, for I would not have vexed you for the world. Not that I mean to say that Mr. Hammond don't like you, for I can see he does: and indeed everybody likes you that sees you; and my brother is much deeper in love with you now than with Mrs. Herbert, for I overheard him telling my sister so. But perhaps I ought not to tell you this, and so, for fear they should be angry with me, you had better not repeat it: however, if you do, don't say that I told you."

Agatha assured her that she should not think of repeating it to anyone, and, Mrs. Herbert now joining them, they entered the breakfast-room together.

When they were going to their accustomed amusements in the *Cassetta*, Miss Milson reminded Hammond of his promise, and Mr. Crawford asked permission to join them. Mr. Crawford's society was equally acceptable to the young and old, the grave and the gay, and from the natural complacency of his disposition, disposed to be pleased with all who strove to please, his presence was everywhere courted and prized. His request, therefore, was granted with pleasure, and attended by him, they proceeded as usual to the *Cassetta*.

As they entered it, Agatha trembled and turned pale. Hammond, who had walked by her side, and whom nothing could have induced to quit her for a moment, remarked the change in her countenance, and pressing her hand gently, while the attention of the rest was engaged by a favourite myrtle Miss Milson had called them to admire, whispered, "Dear object of all my hopes and wishes! Whom beyond everyone on earth I prize, adore, esteem – how dear is this spot to me! Dearer than even you imagine. There is a reason why, since you quitted it, it has blessed me beyond all –"

The rest now returning prevented his proceeding; and Agatha, though this address had served to add to her embarrassment and confusion, felt an emotion of pleasure as new as it was delightful. The mystery in his last words, though it surprised and perplexed, did not alarm her; and she wished the myrtle had grown a little farther off – only

– that she might have heard them explained. If what she felt were indeed love, as she now more than suspected, she found that it differed greatly from Mrs. Herbert's description, and bore still less resemblance to her mother's; it was neither so delightful as the one, nor so dreadful as the other. Its sweets and its bitters were so intimately blended that it seemed impossible to separate them. The pleasure she now felt was alloyed with a confused sensation of uneasiness, as the pain she had felt two hours before was tempered with some portion of pleasure.

Chapter 8

Everyone being seated round the table, Hammond requested their indulgence on the subject of the little narration he had promised, to which, he said, he was unable to add any graces of diction, and which would have no other recommendation than being "a round unvarnished tale" of an action that did honour to human nature. Mrs. Herbert reminded him that he had promised to relate any other circumstances which might interest them, besides the one to which he particularly alluded; and Miss Milson added her entreaties that he would "become a biographer, and not merely the reciter of an anecdote, and begin his relation from the commencement of his life."

"The commencement of my life," said Hammond, "had little in it which deserves to be repeated, all which differed from the common events befalling others. My parents dying while I was at school, the care of my education devolved on a sister whose memory I am bound to revere, and whose virtues I shall in vain endeavour to imitate. Ten years older than myself, with a mind richly cultivated, and a natural understanding superior to most others, she was every way qualified for the task she was destined to perform. In every period of my youth, her attention and care were unremitting; and she never lost an opportunity of inculcating the duties enforced by her own example. If I have a virtue or a merit, I owe it to her."

"You have many of both," said Mr. Crawford; "and this generous and grateful acknowledgment is not the least of them."

Agatha looked at Mr. Crawford with a smile of pleasure; she had always beheld him with regard, and even with affection, but he had never appeared so amiable in her eyes as at that moment.

After expressing his thanks for the flattering opinion Mr. Crawford entertained of him, Hammond proceeded. "When I quitted school, before I went to the University, I spent some months with my sister; and those were the happiest as well as most instructive of my life: not that an hour passed in which I did not derive some benefit from the lessons she inculcated. At length, to my regret, I left her to finish my education at Oxford. Attached to study as well from inclination as from the duty I conceived imposed upon me of profiting by the opportunity afforded me of improvement, I devoted my whole time to it, till, by too intense application, my health materially suffered: a cause of illness perhaps not very common at either university."

Mr. Crawford smiled; and Mrs. Herbert said, "Very far from it, I believe. Of the young men of fortune who are sent to the university as the finishing stroke of their learning, there is not, upon a moderate calculation, above one in ten who does not to go thither a dunce and return a rake or a coxcomb: and perhaps both. I do not mean to include in my censure those who are sent to qualify themselves for any profession: study is necessary for them, and I believe they pursue it."

"That there are many who fail to profit by the advantages there afforded them of instruction, is, I fear, too true," said Mr. Crawford; "yet to say, that only one in ten makes a due use of his time is perhaps too severe."

"Say one in five then," replied Mrs. Herbert; "and I am certain you will be within the mark. But I cannot resist the temptation of proving my assertion, by a recent example which accident brought within my own knowledge. My Uncle being absent one day, it fell to my share to entertain two young men who had just quitted the university. They had the character of men of fashion, and, with regard to their understandings, as report said nothing to the contrary, they were supposed passable, at least. When they had paid me the trivial attentions which politeness enjoined, I had the pleasure of hearing their conversation with each other. After ringing the usual changes of a pretty college, good apartments, excellent wine, the best horse in England, and a new gig, one of them observed to the other, that he had taken three trips to London and back again in four and twenty hours each, since the other left college, and declared that he had been ten times in London, and had never yet seen it by daylight. For my part, returned the other, that is a kind of pleasure for which I never had any relish. A snug room and a sofa were all I cared for when I was at college. I lounged and slept upon mine from morning till night, and should have been the most comfortable and happiest man in Oxford, if it had not been for the confounded noise of a fellow just over my head, that played most execrably on the hautboy,[17] and another at a very little distance, who employed himself in nursing half a dozen pointer puppies that tormented me with their continual yelping. I think," continued Mrs. Herbert, "that from the confession of these gentlemen there were four who did not employ their time to the best possible advantage; will it not, therefore, be indulgent to suppose that the fifth belonged to the order of Mr. Hammond?"

"I wish," said Mr. Crawford, "that those who are proof against the serious admonitions of their friends, could hear Mrs. Herbert expose their conduct as it deserves; that as the dread of ridicule leads many into vice it might retrieve its character by conducting others to virtue.

---

[17]Archaic name for oboe.

But by interrupting Mr. Hammond thus, we delay and suspend our own pleasure."

Hammond, at the united request of everyone, now proceeded in his narration.

"My illness threatening to terminate in a consumption, obliged me to leave Oxford; and, attended by my sister, I went immediately to Bristol, where all the tenderness and care that ever the most beloved of husbands experienced from the most tender of wives, could not exceed what I received from her. Never absent from my sight a moment, she appeared to have no thought, no wish but my recovery; while the efforts she made to overcome the depression of her own spirits for my sake – to talk cheerfully, to smile when her heart was sinking within her, were but so many additional sources of endearment to my heart. At length her prayers were heard: my health returned, and with it that sweet and natural serenity which always distinguished her countenance. Never shall I forget when first my appetite and strength returned, the sweet tears of delight which sparkled in her eyes: from prudence and affection till then restrained, they at last, found vent; and she wept more at my recovery than she had done during my illness."

Hammond paused for a moment; the memory of his sister pressed too strongly on his mind, and affected him too deeply to suffer him to go on. Agatha wept; and everyone else was too sensibly moved to interrupt the melancholy silence. At length, making an effort to recover himself, he proceeded.

"When my recovery was all but perfected, a friend with whom I formed an intimacy at Bristol, was preparing to make a voyage to Gibraltar, and as it was believed likely to re-establish my health entirely, I consented to accompany him. My sister, convinced of the efficacy of a sea voyage, and seeing me well enough to require no farther attendance, consented without reluctance to what she believed would infallibly restore my constitution and prevent any danger of a relapse; and we parted alas, never to meet again! Before we arrived at Gibraltar our vessel was attacked by a Moorish pirate, and, in spite of our utmost resistance, obliged to yield. We were taken prisoners, and carried into Algiers.

The captain, to whose lot I fell, weary of his piratical life, and satisfied with the booty he had obtained in his several excursions, determined to reside for the future at a house he had lately purchased, which though bearing no appearance of splendour in the eyes of a European, was constructed and decorated in the highest style of Moorish magnificence. The garden it was my task together with some negro slaves to cultivate. Treated with caprice and tyranny, and obliged to toil incessantly, had I had motives less powerful than those which induced me to long impatiently to return to my country, I should yet have used every possible means to affect my escape; yet some years passed before an opportunity offered of attempting it with any probability of success. At length, I determined, as my only resource, to apply to a Portuguese renegado, who was sometimes consulted by my master on the subject of his improvements, and who frequently, therefore directed my labours.

As he spoke a little French, I explained to him my situation, I assured him of an ample reward, and entreated him either to apply to the English consul to have me liberated, or to furnish me with some means of escape without. He made very liberal offers of service, and promised to lose no time in his application to the consul. In a few days he returned and assured me his endeavours for my release had been unsuccessful, and that he had no means of serving me but by favouring my escape, and putting me on board a little vessel which he would hire for the purpose, and in which I might be conducted to some European port. I accepted his offer with transport, and it was agreed that late in the evening of the next day, I should repair to a gate, the key of which he would, under some pretext, procure and did leave under the leaf of a date tree near it; and that I should find the vessel in waiting for me. I followed his instructions, found the key as specified, and opening the gate with trembling impatience, proceeded by the directions he had given me towards the sea shore. It was now almost dark, and I went forward as quickly yet as silently as possible, wishing, and at the same time, dreading to hear the sound of voices, lest, instead of my deliverers, I should be met by enemies. At length I distinguished footsteps, and a moment after, heard the renegado in a low tone of voice, calling to me in French. I replied immediately; but scarcely had I spoken, when I was surrounded by several men, seized, bound, and carried to a dungeon, where I remained all night in an agony not to be described, which was increased by the severe reverse of my fortune, from the height of hope and expected liberty, plunged into the gulf of misery, and embittered yet more by the reflection of its being the consequence of my own imprudent and misplaced confidence.

When the morning arrived, I was taken from my dungeon, and conveyed again to the garden from whence I had endeavoured to escape, with no other addition to my misery than that of being more narrowly watched than before. The renegado, who had thus treacherously and cruelly betrayed me, for no purpose, that I could conceive, but to ingratiate himself with my master, since they are generally hated and suspected by the Moors, I saw with a disgust and aversion easy to be conceived. Reproaches were futile, and could only have served to increase my own distresses; I therefore never spoke to, and avoided as much as possible, one, the frequent sight of whom was now become one of my bitterest torments: and to add to my distress, his visits were more frequent than formerly, and himself apparently treated with more confidence and regard.

Deprived now of all hopes of escape, my slavery became every day more irksome and painful. Had I enjoyed the most distant prospect of freedom, I could have supported my sufferings with patience – but I had lost all, and had no hope but in the termination of an existence now become a burden to me.

After some time, I remarked that the Portuguese discontinued his visits. I saw him no more, and his place was supplied by a Spaniard, in whose countenance I imagined the marks of benignity were too strong to be deceitful. Yet, once deceived, I dared not again place confidence in appearances: and though the Spaniard repeatedly endeavoured to engage my attention, and to induce me to speak to him, I appeared for some time inattentive to his overtures, dreading the repetition of an artifice designed to plunge me yet deeper, if possible, in calamity. At length, however, reflecting that my situation could not be more miserable, that death would be my greatest blessing, and that an increase of hardships would only accelerate its arrival, I determined to profit by the next favourable opportunity of addressing him, and to endeavour once more, by his assistance to procure my emancipation.

Some days elapsed after I had formed this resolution before I saw him again; and the dread of his coming no more, had begun to alarm and torture my mind: I imagined I had lost the only chance of freedom I ever might possess, and cursed my own folly in neglecting to court his assistance while it was in my reach. At length he came; and as he looked over my work, and directed me by signs as usual, I addressed him in French and Italian; but to no purpose: we could not understand each other. By signs, however, I made him comprehend the distress I endured, and he shook his head in token of condolence and pity. He pointed to himself, and repeated his name; then making signs to me to do the same, I said, Hammond; and pointing to a kind of spade, the utensil with which I laboured, I showed him my name carved upon it, under which I had written with the same tool.

Deprived of friends, fortune, home, and country, a wretched slave in a foreign and barbarous land, here lingers out his miserable existence. Should death, or, by the blessing of Heaven, any other event, procure his release from captivity, and this be read by any future sufferers, let them commiserate the anguish he has endured, and trust, like him, in God: and may the prayer he now offers for his own release, be heard by that God for theirs!

He took the spade, but made signs that he could not understand the language; but repeated frequently, as if to endeavour to retain it, the name of Hammond. I pointed to the high wall which enclosed the garden, by way of asking him to favour my escape. He showed by signs that he comprehended my meaning and would endeavour to serve me. Many days, however, elapsed before I saw him again; and when he did come, instead of walking towards me as usual, he kept on the other side of the garden.

I now feared I was again betrayed; and was relapsing into my former despondency, when, being employed to work in a part of the garden near to the harem of the Moor, I heard a female voice in a song repeat my name. I started, and listening with attention, heard these words sung very distinctly. "Fear not, Hammond, to confide in the Spaniard; he pities you, and will obtain your freedom." Astonished and transported, I scarcely dare trust my senses, and believed myself in a dream. When the first emotions of amazement were over, I listened again, and again heard the same words sung, but no others. After they had been repeated thus for nearly an hour the voice ceased. I returned thanks to Heaven for the prospect now opened to my view; and performed my allotted portion of labour with cheerfulness and alacrity. This sweet influence of hope banished in a moment every idea of present suffering; and though all was yet doubt and uncertainty, I have known few days happier than the one which succeeded this. One only other day passed, in which my impatience to see the Spaniard again became extreme, before he entered the garden. I would have flown to meet him, but prudence forbad; and I was obliged to wait till he came towards me, appearing to direct me as usual. I endeavoured by signs to assure him of my gratitude, and to repeat my prayers for assistance, when dropping a letter upon the ground, and covering it with a piece of turf he removed with his foot, he left me with a countenance and air of affected severity. I was careful not to quit the spot, yet some hours passed before I could seize an opportunity of taking up the letter; at last, however, I found an opportunity, and no one being near me, opened it with trembling impatience. But what was my astonishment at sight of a well-known hand! The letter I read too often, and it is too deeply engraved on my heart for me to find any necessity to have recourse to it now: but before I repeat it, I must go back to a circumstance which befell me at school, and which I omitted to mention in its place.

Among my school associates was a Jew boy named Israeli, an orphan, whom the loss of all his friends and gratitude to his deceased father, had placed under the protection of a worthy clergyman who kept the school. As he was good-tempered and obliging and, above all, oppressed and unfortunate, since, on account of his religion he was hated and ridiculed by every other in the school, I felt a pity and even friendship for him which induced me to take his part when insulted, and my companions in consequence called me Smouchy the second. I was insensible to their ridicule, and performing a part dictated by duty and humanity, persisted in defending him when unjustly attacked. He was destined for a merchant, and different pursuits separating us, I never saw him after I left school. Imagine, therefore, my surprise when I found that this letter was from him and that to his friendship and grateful heart I should, in all probability, owe my freedom. The letter, which I should despise myself if I could forget, was this.

To the kind heart of the noble Hammond I have been, many and many are the times, indebted for comfort and protection. His situation is misery itself! And what were I, or what should I deserve, if, when I have discovered his distress, I could call my fortune my own till it had restored him to liberty? The hand of God, whom, however we differ in other tenets of belief, we both worship, has guided us to the same country, and enabled me, I hope, to repay a part of the obligations I owe to you. Here fixed as a merchant, my fortune is ample: I have offered as much of it as is necessary for your ransom. My offers have been at last accepted; and tomorrow morning at daybreak, if the wind serves, the generous Hammond will embark in the vessel destined to conduct him to his home and country. Too, too happy shall I be if he sometimes remembers with friendship and esteem his sincere and grateful,

AARON ISRAELI

Judge of my feelings when I had read this letter! Snatched at once from the lowest abyss of misery to happiness and freedom, and that by the generous exertions of one whom pity and common humanity alone had induced me to befriend, and for my trifling services to whom I never expected nor thought of a return. I would have given the world to have seen him and expressed my gratitude; but there was no one to whom I could apply, and I was obliged to leave to his own generous heart the task of speaking for me, and assuring him of all I felt.

I continued my toil as usual, and remarked no difference in the treatment I received, till the evening, when, instead of being locked into my little hut by the side of that occupied by the negroes, as had always been the case before, I was suffered to continue in the garden. Had the companions of my toil evinced the smallest traces of compassion for my sufferings, or even appeared sensible of their own, I could not have parted from them without compunction of heart, nor have left without pain, other sharers of a misery from which I was on the point of being delivered: but they had always seemed unconscious of their own misfortunes and regardless of mine, which at this minute was a consolation to me, and prevented even the shadow of a regret at leaving them behind me.

The night was still and calm. The moon now glimmering through a cloud, appeared yet more resplendent through the veil which covered her, and now sailing beyond it 'serene in cloudless majesty' cast her beams on the palace of the Moor, or darted them through the trees across the paths I traversed. No sound was heard – not even a breeze disturbed the leaves above me – no voice interrupted the universal calm of nature. Here, even at the hour of midnight, in the most remote village, some sound intervenes to break the gloomy silence, – the dog 'bays the moon,' the owl screams, the wind agitates the trees, or some stream murmurs in its course – but there, all is hushed as death. Struck by the gloomy stillness, had fear instead of hope had possession of my mind, sorrow and despondency instead of exultation and joy, my feelings had been overpowered, my faculties suspended, and nature must have sunk under the depression. But the veil of misery was removed – fair prospects opened once more on my enraptured sight, and the face of nature formed but a contrast to the animated delight that glowed in my breast. With an impatience more easily imagined than expressed I counted the hours till morning should arrive.

The morning at length came – and every added moment increased my impatience; at first, joined only with hope, even that impatience was delightful, now, mingled with fear, it was becoming agony, when, with delight and transport unutterable, I beheld the approach of some Moorish sailors. They opened the massy gate and conducted me to the sea shore, where the vessel lay at anchor. A brisk gale arose – we set sail; and with a heart overflowing with gratitude to Heaven and my deliverer, after an absence of six years, I found myself returning to my country, and, dearer yet, as I then fondly hoped, to my sister.

To my equal astonishment and delight, I was addressed by my name, and in my own language, by a female voice, which I instantly recognised as the same I had heard in the harem. I turned round, and beheld a lady young, beautiful, and interesting. Her fine black eyes sparkled with intelligence, and her countenance beamed with the most animated pleasure. On my expressing my surprise and joy at this unex-pected meeting –"

"I am sure," said Miss Cassandra, "before you go any farther, I am sure you fell in love with her."

Hammond smiled and continued. "On my expressing my pleasure and surprise, she informed me that to one and the same person we both owed our deliverance."

"It will be as I said," cried Miss Cassandra, "I am sure of it."

"Conceal the assurances of your penetration for a few minutes only," said Mrs. Herbert, "that we may be convinced whether or not they are just. Mr. Hammond, go on; I am all impatience."

"When we had both sufficient collection of spirits to speak with coolness of the several events that had befallen us," pursued Hammond, "she informed me, that she was the daughter of a Spaniard, who having formed a friendship with Mr. Ammerville, a young merchant then on his travels, had introduced him to her; that they soon became attached to each other, and her father, notwithstanding the difference of country and religion, approving the connection, they were shortly after married, and she returned with him to England, where she became the mother of two infants, now under the protection of their father. Anxious to see her parents and her native abode once more, she went on board a vessel intended to conduct her to Spain, leaving her children to the care of her husband, whose numerous and extensive mercantile concerns prevented his accompanying her. The ship in which she was a passenger was captured by a pirate and taken to Algiers, where she was given as a present to the Moor; but in continual dread of being conducted to his presence, and distracted at the separation from her husband and children, her health began to decline, and she was sinking fast into the grave, where only she dared hope for release from sorrow, when the Spanish renegado, who, by his application to the noble Israeli afterwards effected my deliverance, by accident discovered her situation. He had been a servant to her father, and anxious, therefore, to obtain her freedom, applied to Israeli, whose liberality he well knew, to offer a sum of money for her ransom. This was readily complied with; the Moor consented to the terms proposed, and everything was determined upon for her departure, when the Spaniard found means to inform her that a countryman of her husband's, whose name was Hammond, was a slave there; that he wished to procure his freedom, but that once deceived by another, he saw I suspected his sincerity; that this rendered him miserable, since it was now become his only consolation to expiate in some measure by services to his fellow creatures the crime he had, through the dread of death, committed against his God. He therefore entreated her to let me hear her speak from her apartments, which now, since her ransom had been agreed upon, and she was allowed more freedom, she could with ease, and to assure me of his sincerity. In the meantime, he would contrive to have me employed near her, and to prevent premature suspicion, would himself treat me with distance and coolness, if anyone was present, or likely to observe us. 'And this,' continued Mrs. Ammerville, 'was the cause of the voice you heard, and which must to you have appeared the effect of enchantment.'

After being delayed for some time on our passage by contrary winds, we were at last safely landed at Gibraltar, where we were to continue till some English vessel should arrive to take us to our country. Some months elapsed, during which our impatience was extreme. At length a Moorish vessel touched at Gibraltar, the master of which was charged with a letter for Mrs. Ammerville. She had no sooner opened it and read a few words, and she dropped the letter, burst into tears, and exclaimed, he has escaped – he is free – thank God! Thank God! Having never heard her say that she had left any friend in captivity, I enquired with astonishment, who had escaped – who was free? 'Israeli!' she said, 'the noble Israeli! Yes, Mr. Hammond, I can no longer conceal, no longer bury in silence, an act of generosity that will melt your very soul! Unable, by his largest offers for your ransom to obtain it, the Moor, at last, on his repeating his solicitations, replied, that he wanted slaves not money, and that if he would obtain your freedom, he must work himself in your place. This taunting offer, which it was never imagined would be accepted, Israeli eagerly embraced; and the Moor, finding a ferocious pleasure in humbling one whose fortune and general esteem he had acquired had made him long the object of his hatred and envy, consented, on this condition, to your freedom.'

At once astonished – shocked – and penetrated with gratitude and admiration, I became for some minutes insensible of everything, and Mrs. Ammerville's endeavours with difficulty recovered my senses and reason. When I had regained sufficient composure to hear what she had yet to relate, she assured me that he was now at liberty; that, in spite of his religion, which renders those who possess it more hateful to the Moors than even Christians, he was so generally beloved, that he effected his escape with a considerable part of his property, and would soon, as the Spaniard assured her he doubted not, arrive safe in England. But why, O why, said I, did you not tell me this? I would have flown to rescue him, and have endured a slavery ten thousand times more dreadful, rather than that another should suffer this for me! He was aware of that, replied Mrs. Ammerville. He knew your heart, and was convinced that you would act thus if ever his situation came to your knowledge; as he conducted me to the vessel, therefore, by supplications and entreaties which I knew not how to resist from my deliverer, he obtained from me a solemn promise not to reveal his situation to you. That situation, heaven be praised, now at an end, I am absolved from my promise."

"Noble! Noble Israeli!" said Mr. Crawford; "and Noble Hammond! For I was well aware that you would not be outdone in generosity! I was convinced you would have flown to rescue him at the expense of your liberty. The contest of the Damon and Pythias, being the consequence of a long and tried attachment, and as death, to one prepared for it, is less dreadful than life on such terms, was not so noble. Forgive my interruption; but my heart was full, and I could not suppress my admiration. And have you met since?"

"We have not," replied Hammond; "but I have every reason to believe from the information I have since received, that he is safe, and on his passage to England. The first English ship which arrived at Gibraltar conveyed Mrs. Ammerville and myself safe to England, and I had the satisfaction of conducting her to her husband and family. Immediately after which I set out to meet my sister.

The destruction of my hopes, and my subsequent anguish, I need not, nor can I paint. Thanks to the seraphic sweetness of the kindest of friends," continued he, looking at Agatha, "my mind regained a calm I could not have conceived possible: though there are yet moments when the remembrance of my loss is agony."

Hammond now ceased speaking, and Miss Milson observed that his sufferings had indeed been severe; "and doubtless," pursued she, "souls possessed of sensibility feel the poignancy of affliction more exquisitely than others: yet to cultivated minds, minds stored with information, there are numberless, consolatory reflections not known to the unlettered and ignorant. For instance, in your captivity, by recurring to the page of history, you might have reflected on Alfred when once a cowherd, on the imprisonment of Robert, brother to the Conqueror, on that of Richard the second in Pontefract, and of Edward the second in Caernarvon Castle; and remembering how many others had suffered, nay, that perhaps, at that moment, there were some in yet greater distress, have found your own mitigated."

"That is a mode of consolation which I have often found recommended," said Agatha, "yet to me it has always appeared incapable of answering the end proposed. Were I unhappy, the knowledge that others were more so, would, instead of lessening, add to my afflictions. I would rather reflect on those who were happy. I would say to myself – 'tis true I am wretched – but thank Heaven all are not like me: there are some, endued with the same feelings, who at this moment enjoy all their hearts can wish; whom the sun rises but to bless, and sets but to see them close their eyes in peace and contentment. Yes! Thank Heaven, all are not like me! – On reflection, do you not think with me, Miss Milson?" asked Agatha.

"My lovely friend is singular in her ideas," said Miss Milson; "yet there is much justice in the remark; and, for want of weighing the reasoning of the authors I have read, I am, perhaps, too apt to adopt their mode of argument."

"I had no patience with the Portuguese renegado," said Miss Cassandra; "he behaved so very ill-natured and deceitful. But Mrs. Ammerville should not have been married, and then the story would have been very natural, and just like what one reads in books; for when two people have been unhappy together they always fall in love and marry."

"A similarity of situations and distresses is without doubt a strong cementer of attachment both in friendship and love," said Hammond.

"And yet there is something selfish in that," said Mrs. Herbert; "for unless we pity distresses from which our own situation is exempt, with as much sincerity as those we may or do actually feel, we cannot be truly compassionate. The rich man tortured by the gout, should commiserate with the penniless wanderer, doomed to endure sufferings he is never likely to experience, as truly as he does his affluent neighbour labouring under the excruciating torment of his own malady: if he does not, his pity is selfishness not sensibility."

"It is certainly right, thus to search every sentiment to its source," said Mr. Crawford, "nor to take any opinion on trust, however plausible it may appear. We shall thus learn to retain those only which are founded in justice and propriety, and to discard all that are erroneous and specious. But we must at all times remember that it is as unjust universally to reject, as it would be to embrace opinions because they are among those commonly received."

"I am determined," said Miss Cassandra, "that for the future I will always enquire and know the meaning of everything. One thing very much surprises me, Mr. Hammond, and that is, that considering you worked so much in the sun you should be no browner than you are."

"Excepting during the months of July and August," said Hammond, "the heat at Algiers is by no means intense; and in almost all the sultry climes, Providence has so ordered it, that the trees afford a shade impervious to the sun."

"Yes," said Miss Cassandra, "Providence, I see, takes care of even our complexions. I have learnt a great deal this morning, and I will try to remember it, I am determined."

"We have all learnt a great deal," said Mr. Crawford; "and, I trust, there is not one of us who will not return to the house both wiser and better than when they quitted it. The act as a friendship, generosity, and heroism we have now heard, will be forever recorded in our hearts; while the glorious emulation a deed like this inspires, shall whisper to us, with the voice of Angels, 'Go, and do thou likewise.'"[18]

---

[18]Luke 10 v.37.

Chapter 9

After some further conversation, it being too late to pursue any other employment that morning, they returned to the house. Hammond seized an opportunity of entreating Agatha to grant him one half hour's conversation. Agatha at once wished and feared to consent. She now knew her own heart, and trembled at complying with its dictates, lest they should be contrary to prudence or propriety. That love was at all times, and in all shapes the most dreadful of evils, and therefore to be guarded against and shunned she had always been taught, but how it was proper to conduct herself when she loved and was beloved she had never been instructed, and with a mind that anxious on every occasion to act aright, she trembled lest she should ignorantly commit a fault or incur blame. On her hesitating to comply with his request, Hammond repeated his solicitations, assuring her that he wished only to clear his conduct from the charge of inconsistency, caprice, and ingratitude which he was conscious it merited in her eyes, and that, denied this, he should be miserable; he therefore conjured her to indulge him with some minutes only in the *Cassetta* the next morning. This, after what had passed, she positively refused; but, at last, won by the earnestness of his solicitations, she consented to walk with him towards Jemima's cottage some time in the afternoon, if it was possible to disengage herself from the company: or, if prevented that day, to endeavour to gain an opportunity some time in the next.

In the afternoon she attempted, but in vain, to perform her promise. She had scarcely reached the walk leading to the road, before she was joined by Miss Milson. Hammond, overtaking her, could with difficulty conceal his chagrin and disappointment at the sight of Miss Milson.

The remainder of the day was no more favourable to their wishes; and Agatha, anxious to give Hammond pleasure, and anxious to receive the promised explanation, was almost tempted to seize the only certain opportunity, by rising early in the morning, as he had at first proposed. But reflecting that if she did, it would in all probability be known and remarked, and that she should lay herself open to the jests of others, if not of Mrs. Herbert, she determined to avoid it if possible, and to make one other attempt at least before she had recourse to a method she could at any time adopt.

When at night she retired to her room, she sat down to ruminate on the events of the day. Hammond, whom the various distresses he had endured, had endeared to her more than ever, she was now convinced loved her with all the tenderness and sincerity possible, while her own heart, she was equally certain, returned his affection as it deserved. One only idea alarmed her and embittered the pure pleasure she would otherwise have felt. Her parents might not approve the choice her heart had made; sworn enemies to love, they might perhaps condemn her indulgence of it, and bid her throw from her bosom all that now charmed and delighted it. Yet Hammond's character was unexceptionable; his rank in life, though perhaps not equal to her own, placed him, she imagined, beyond the reach of a refusal on that account, since wealth and grandeur she knew Lady Belmont condemned, and had always declared incapable of bestowing happiness. What then should impede her wishes? Nothing! No! The aversion to love, which they had always inculcated, might be intended merely to guard her heart against its seductions till she met with an object on whom it could with justice and prudence be bestowed: that object they had never seen – for they knew not Hammond. The clouds which had on the first reflection obscured her promised felicity thus dispersed at once a prospect brighter than ever opened to her view. She determined, however, not to give full scope to her imagination; since, though it was highly improbable, it was alas possible her hopes might be checked; and after she had granted the promised interview to Hammond, which justice to him and to herself equally demanded, to shun, as well for his sake as her own, whatever might tend to the increase of an attachment as yet unsanctioned by parental approbation.

The next morning passed nearly as usual. In the afternoon she made another attempt to walk out alone, and was not interrupted. Hammond pursued her with eager and impatient steps, and just as she had opened the gate at the termination of the grounds, he overtook her.

"Dear! Dear Miss Belmont!" he exclaimed; "How shall I ever be sufficiently grateful for this condescension? Happy! Happy moments! Dearest of my life!"

"Be assured," said Agatha, colouring, "that your happiness has never been indifferent to –"; the time had been that she would not have feared to say to "me" – but she hesitated and was unable to proceed.

"I am, I am convinced of what you would say," said Hammond; "and nothing but the sweet hope of my happiness has been sometimes the object of your wishes could have emboldened me to confess every feeling of my heart: those feelings have often led me to act with inconsistency and apparent ingratitude. I have seemed cold and indifferent when most I have loved, and insensible of your sweetest efforts to restore my peace of mind at the very moment when that peace depended wholly on you.

From the first moment when, like my Guardian Angel, you recalled me to life and reason, when your soothing voice taught me resignation to the divine will, and enabled me to bless his name who gave and who therefore has a right to take away, from that moment I felt that all the future blessings of my life were centred in you. It seemed too as if Heaven mercifully intended thus to recompense me for all I had suffered, since the same hour which saw me robbed of one beloved object, bestowed another.

Some days had passed before I knew and recollected that Miss Belmont, Agatha Belmont was the daughter of Sir Charles and Lady Belmont, whose names together with their ample possessions I remembered formerly to have heard mentioned. As you simply call them by the names of father and mother when you spoke of them, the improbability that a daughter of theirs should be in the friendless and unprotected state in which I found you never suggested the idea that they were your parents. When at last I learnt it, the fatal intelligence struck like ice to my heart. My own easy, and till then I had thought, affluent fortune dwindled into nothing when compared with that of the heiress of Sir Charles Belmont; and I determined, as much as possible to conceal an attachment which every hour increased, that I might avoid the possibility of endangering a happiness infinitely dearer than my own.

Sensible that the world might condemn your continuance with me, I determined to hazard everything, even the loss of your friendship, rather than purchase my own pleasure at the expense of your future estimation in life. Repeatedly had I endeavoured to introduce the painful subject, and as repeatedly been prevented, when Miss Milson's proposal enabled me to urge your departure, though at that moment I felt to have lost in you every hope of happiness forever.

Dangerous as I knew the indulgence, how I could not resist complying with Sir John's entreaties to continue here for some time, not aware of the many sweet yet fatal circumstances which would throw me off my guard. Your assurances of friendship, your artless endeavours to speak comfort to my distracted heart, were but so many sources of misery, since they increased the value of a prize I dared not hope to obtain. At length, the tears you shed accompanied by the sweet and artless evidence of an affection surpassing, as, at that moment I first fondly hoped, even the generous friendship you had professed, forbad any longer concealment, and surmounted every determination I had formed. I avowed my love, and had even then laid open my whole heart to you, had not your exhausted spirits prevented my pursuing a subject they were then unable to sustain.

Every spot that has been visited by a beloved object, every scene that calls to mind a moment of delight passed with them, is sought again with avidity, and beheld with enthusiastic reverence. We can even quit those for whose sake we love that spot to retrace in idea the blessings it has bestowed: and I fled from even you to visit the scene I loved for your sake – to kiss the table whereon you had leaned – to gaze with rapture on the room where first I learned to hope you loved!

But now, will you – can you forgive what I am going to relate? Will you not accuse me of dishonour – of want of generosity? – I dare not say it, till you have first promised you will forgive me."

He paused, and Agatha, from the excess of her emotions, was silent. He repeated his request, and she at last replied, "Yes – I must forgive you; for you cannot act dishonourably – 'tis impossible."

"See then this paper, dropped by you in a spot thus rendered doubly dear. These lines were folded outwards, and I read them – trust me – believe me – my beloved Agatha! I read them before I knew they were yours or what they were:

In him 'twas sweet – how sweet to trace
The semblance of Maria's face;
And still, as friendship lent its balm,
By gentle arts his griefs to calm,
To hush his many cares to rest,
And blest, blest talk, to make him blest!

How! O how shall I tell you – how quaint my feelings when I read those sweet lines! – And will you – can you – do you forgive me?"

"O Mr. Hammond! Indeed – indeed when I wrote those lines I had no idea that my heart was sensible of any feelings beyond those of friendship."

"When you wrote those lines – dear, dear, confession! Then now Miss Belmont – my all – my Agatha! Now then you have –"

Agatha burst into tears. Hammond implored her forgiveness, while by the most tender endeavours he strove to recover her agitated spirits, and at length drew from her a confession of every sentiment of heart.

Recollecting that their absence might be remarked, Agatha proposed to return to the house; and Hammond, though he could have wished those minutes prolonged for years, acquiesced, sensible of the propriety of returning without delay, since the half hour had already been exceeded.

Agatha, her mind agitated though happy, leaned on his arm, while his other hand held and pressed tenderly the one which rested on him.

When they were near the house they observed a post chaise driving towards them. It approached, and stopping the moment it had passed them, the chaise door opened, and Sir Charles and Lady Belmont jumped out and ran to Agatha, whom with an astonishment apparently almost amounting to terror, they saw leaning on the arm of Hammond.

Agatha, in equal astonishment at meeting them, thus suddenly and unexpectedly, ran to her mother and fainted in her arms. Hammond terrified, flew he knew not whither for help – then returning to them almost instantaneously, he took Agatha, yet insensible from the arms of Lady Belmont, and supported her in his own – conjuring her in the most tender manner to look up – to speak to – but once to speak to him. Sir Charles turned to Hammond, and said, in a tone of equal pride and indignation putting at the same time his own arm under Agatha's head – "She will be better directly, Sir – do not give yourself any farther trouble – leave her to me: the assistance of strangers is unnecessary. Agatha! My child! Look up; it is your own father that supports you!" Then turning again to Hammond, "If you will procure us a little hartshorn, Sir, I shall be obliged you."

By this time however the whole family was assembled round them. Mrs. Herbert held her salts to a Agatha's nose, while Lady Belmont chafed her temples, and she began to revive. A chair was then brought, and they placed her in it. Lady Belmont supported her on one side, while Mrs. Herbert went to the other; which Sir Charles observing, he with very little ceremony, moved her on one side and took her place. Agatha now recovered apace, and Lady Belmont observed that it would be better to return home immediately.

"Better to return home immediately?" said Sir John Milson; "but upon my honour and credit it won't though. Why my Lady Belmont, do you think it shall be said in the country that Sir John Milson baronet and your equal in rank, would not give you a dish of tea and a bit of bread and butter after your journey? No, no, that won't do neither."

"We are obliged to you," said Sir Charles, "but we must return immediately."

"Upon my honour and credit, but I say you shan't though, Sir Charles. That would be no how, indeed. And I don't want to part with Miss neither; she's a nice lass, and we're all in love with her. Besides, the man has taken the horses off, and they must fill their bellies too, or what will the world say of Sir John Milson? Come, come, you must stay, Sir Charles – you must indeed."

Sir Charles and Lady Belmont finding remonstrances vain, and that they would only prolong the disgust Sir John's manner and address inspired, at length consented to stay to tea, on condition that he would permit them to go the moment it was over.

Agatha was by this time sufficiently recovered to walk into the house, Sir Charles supporting her on one side, and Lady Belmont on the other.

When they were all seated in the drawing room, Sir John turned to Lady Belmont, and said with much exultation of countenance, "now Miss is a little better, one can begin to talk to you a little my Lady – Would you believe it, we had liked to have stole a match upon you – Nay, come, however my Lady I will not go so far as to say that neither; but if you had stayed a little longer, I do not know what might have happened: upon my honour and credit I think it's very likely we should have been lucky enough to get your daughter off your hands before you came back."

"Sir," said Lady Belmont, with an air of equal contempt and indignation; then looking at her watch, "I am unwilling, Sir," she said, "to put you to any inconvenience; and as your tea is not ready, we will return without – for it grows late, and we have some affairs to settle at home tonight."

"It shall come di–rectly, my Lady," said Sir John; and after ringing the bell, he returned to his seat and pursued his subject. "Why, my Lady, he thinks you look rather glum about this marriage affair. But, however don't go to think that we'd have matched your daughter badly. No, no, that would have been no how; and I have too much respect (and a proper one it is too) for my own rank, to do anything to let down your Ladyship's. But my son William there, I have a sort of a guess has a sneaking kindness for her nowadays, and there's another young man – there he sits – Mr. Hammond – a gentlemen, and likely to be a baronet, that has cast a sheep's eye at her a long while – and has stuck so close to her these two days, that upon my honour and credit, he'll hardly vouchsafe to look at the victuals on his plate."

"Love and marriage, Sir," said Sir Charles, "are not proper subjects, for such a circle as this; and indeed the less they are spoken of, or indeed thought of, anywhere, the better – especially where a person is so young as my daughter, and therefore incapable of distinguishing the miseries or comforts attending either a married or a single state."

"A single state?" repeated Sir John. "Why sure, Sir Charles, you would not have your daughter an old maid! Would you?"

"I would have her adopt that mode of life," replied Sir Charles, "which, on mature deliberation, she, as well as her parents, shall judge most conducive to her happiness."

"Then you may be sure she'll think the married one – or I'll be hanged: Won't you Miss?"

Mr. Crawford observing Agatha's confusion, and anxious to divert the conversation to another channel, enquired if Sir Charles's journey had been unattended by any accident, and if his short passage by sea, had been a pleasant one. Sir Charles with more complacency of countenance than he had yet discovered was preparing to answer his questions, when Sir John exclaimed hastily, "Upon my credit but I never thought of that! I dare say you have been among some of them rich Mounseers to pick out a husband for your daughter." Sir Charles made no reply.

"Marriage," said Mr. Ormistace, "is by no means a thing of course. It is a state which confers exquisite happiness or exquisite misery; and no married person ever new a mediocrity of either. To a mind of sensibility, therefore, an attachment little short of adoration is necessary if they would not be the most wretched of human beings. Do you not think so?" continued he, turning to Mr. Crawford.

"Not entirely," replied Mr. Crawford. "To minds uncommonly refined and susceptible there may possibly be no mediocrity of happiness in a married life: but of such the world does not in general consist: it is chiefly composed of persons of moderate wisdom and moderate sensibility, to whom marriage is a state of common comfort, neither very happy nor very miserable. United most frequently from motives of prudence and liking, rather than love or romantic attachment, they journey through life together, satisfied rather than pleased with their lot. But I do not mean by saying this to pass a censure on marriage: far from it. By giving us one to share the pains and pleasures incident to human life, it diminishes the one and increases the other; and for happiness equally exquisite and durable we must look beyond an existence which hangs but by a thread, and all whose gayest colours, like the vivid hues that paint the air-blown bubble, may vanish in a moment, destroyed by the very breath which created them."

"You are perfectly right in your last remark, Sir," said Sir Charles; "those who expect happiness in this life pursue a phantom which constantly eludes their grasp: we have only therefore to wish for that situation likely to make us least miserable."

"No," said Mr. Ormistace; "be it my lot to know no medium of bliss! I would rather purchase one moment of delight by years of agony, than not to have known that moment's exquisite felicity. It is better to endure all the torments of love than not to have felt its delicious emotions."

"Love, as it teaches generosity, benevolence, and honour, is doubtless a source of happiness," said Mr. Crawford.

"I beg your pardon, Sir," said Sir Charles interrupting him sternly, "of misery you would say; for its pains sooner or later counterbalance all its pleasures."

"I am entirely of your opinion, Sir," said Mr. Craggs. Sir Charles, who found that the conversation was destined to take no other turn, rejoiced at hearing someone at last prepared to argue on his side; and bowing his head, as a mark of approbation, he desired Mr. Craggs to proceed.

"I said your sentiments were mine," pursued Mr. Craggs; "for love, by occasioning frequent sighs, as I have more than once remarked it does, is an injury to the constitution, and induces a lasting impairment of the vital principle. It is a vulgar supposition that every time we sigh a drop of blood falls from our heart: this is not just. But thus far is certain:

every sigh we heave presses upon a corner of the heart and indents it, as it were; and those who have died of what is commonly called a broken heart, have, on being opened, been found to have a hole in their heart, the consequence of sighs: sigh's therefore shorten the duration of our existence. Then an agitation at sight of the beloved object, which I have likewise noticed in lovers, both shakes and weakens our nerves. Now the nerves are a kind of invisible network covering the muscles and extending over the whole frame, beginning from the brain; and therefore whatever injures them, impairs the brain likewise; and by every wound of the brain we endanger the seat of the soul, and the habitation, as I may call it, of our reasoning and thinking faculties: which next to life, we ought to study to preserve. One other motive to avoid love you will find in Doctor Buchan's *Domestic medicine*,[19] a volume which, though of no deep erudition, is useful enough to the unlearned practitioner; and that is, his assertion that often nothing can cure love but the possession of the object desired. Now this being often through the perverseness of parents, guardians, and other malicious and evil-minded persons, difficult, nay sometimes impossible to be obtained, it is most prudent to avoid it altogether."

Sir Charles listened in mute astonishment. When Mr. Craggs had done speaking and had resumed his former pensive position, Sir John arose and advancing towards Sir Charles, exclaimed – "But, upon my credit, Mr. Craggs talks finely – does not he, Sir Charles? O, he knows more than fifty doctors and parsons put together. He is the Honourable Mr. Craggs too, Sir Charles – head to the noble title of my Lord –"

"Very possibly," said Sir Charles; then rising to ring the bell, Sir John stopped him. "Why you won't leave us yet, Sir Charles? Come, come – now do stay a few days with us, and we'll be friendly and sociable as we ought to be."

While this proposal was repeated by Sir John, and as repeatedly rejected by Sir Charles, Agatha, whose spirits were beginning to recover from the shock they had sustained, went to Mrs. Herbert and Miss Milson, and taking each of them by the hand and leading them to Lady Belmont, said, as they approached her, "I must introduce two of the kindest of my friends to my mother. When I was in great distress, Madam, Miss Milson was a mother to me, since in your absence she supplied your place, and brought me hither with the kind motive of recovering my spirits. To Mrs. Herbert too, I am indebted for a thousand acts of kindness and friendship, and when you know her you would delight like me to call her friend."

---

[19]W. Buchan, M. D., *Domestic Medicine or a treatise for the prevention and cure of diseases, by regimen and simple medicines*, Milner and Sowerby, Halifax, 1759.

"My sweet girl!" said Mrs. Herbert, "you interpret into acts of kindness all those little attentions which your own goodness and sweet disposition inspire; and it were impossible not to love you. I am sure I shall feel to lose my better half when you are gone: I cannot bear to think of it!"

"We shall often meet again, I trust!" said Agatha; "yet absent as well as present our friendship will remain unchanged."

"'tis a jewel I would not part with for worlds!" said Mrs. Herbert.

"Ours too, my dear Miss Milson," said Agatha, "I meant to include it in the wish."

"Yes, my lovely friend," said Miss Milson, the tears standing in her eyes.

"You see, Madam," said Agatha, "how fortunate your Agatha has been – what kind of friends she has found in your absence."

"I shall always think myself under obligations to them both," said Lady Belmont, curtseying condescendingly.

"There are others I must point out to your notice," said Agatha. "That middle-aged gentleman whose countenance bespeaks the sweet serenity of his mind, that dear and excellent man is Mr. Crawford – he is beloved and esteemed by all, and has been remarkably indulgent and kind to me. The lady who sits next and is now speaking to him, is Mrs. Valentine Milson, who if you knew you would love; her own assertions are centred in her children, two lovely boys, to whom she is the most instructive and indulgent of mothers." – Agatha now came to Hammond. She coloured and hesitated, and knowing her own inability to speak of him with composure, was tempted to have passed him over; but reflecting in a moment that this would appear particular, and anxious too to introduce him to her mother and to interest her in his favour, she assumed courage, and with as much calmness as possible proceeded. "That is Mr. Hammond, brother to the dear friend we have lost; and he is as good, as amiable as she was."

"He does not bear the smallest resemblance to her either in person or manner," said Lady Belmont, coldly.

"Your ladyship astonishes me," said Miss Milson, "the likeness strikes everyone."

"The next," said Agatha, who had somewhat recovered herself, and was anxious to pass on to another, "is Mr. Ormistace – the noble Mr. Ormistace, I call him; for his acts of charity and benevolence almost exceed belief. I have a long and sweet story to tell you of his goodness."

The carriage was now announced. Agatha, who amid the various emotions that filled and almost overpowered her mind, had never reflected that the moment of departure was so near, turned cold as death, and sitting down on the nearest chair, covered her face with her handkerchief, and burst into tears. Lady Belmont, who from Agatha's countenance on the entrance of the servant, was apprehensive of another fit, was careful not to interrupt the tears which she believed so salutary, and as everyone was assembling round Agatha, waved her hand, and expressed by signs that she wished them not to appear to notice her.

Agatha, greatly relieved, now rose, and making an effort she knew to be necessary, without allowing herself a moment for reflection, advanced to take leave of everyone. Going first to Lady Milson, she said, holding out her hand to her, "Lady Milson – farewell. Ten thousand, thousand thanks for all your kindnesses! – Miss Milson – my dear friend – do not forget me – nor you, my dear Mrs. Herbert. Heaven bless you, Mr. Crawford farewell – God bless you, Mr. Ormistace – Mrs. Milson – Mr. William Milson – farewell all – Mr. Hammond –" but here her voice faltered, and she had no power to speak, and she left in his the hand she had held out to him and everyone else and she took leave of them. Hammond held her hand and supported her as she walked, in spite of Sir Charles's endeavours to prevent him and to take his place; nor did he quit her till he had put her into the chaise. Sir Charles followed immediately after, and Agatha in vain attempted by leaning forward to take a last look of those she had left; Sir Charles, who sat on that side of her, leaned forward himself to take leave of Sir John, and the chaise drove off.

Chapter 10

With tears and depression Agatha had entered Milson Hall; she had then parted from one she esteemed, and whose society was even then dearer to her than every other: but her depression at entering was happiness compared to what she felt at leaving it. Hammond's presence had enlivened every scene, had rendered every conversation delightful; it was now become necessary to her happiness, and life seemed blank without it. Mrs. Herbert was become justly dear to her, and for Miss Milson she felt a grateful regard. What then were her feelings at quitting them thus suddenly! While Lady Belmont's countenance more strongly marked with sternness and severity than she had ever known it before, equally terrified and distressed her.

A silence of some minutes ensued, which was only interrupted by the sobs Agatha in vain endeavoured to suppress. At length Lady Belmont said, "The hurry of spirits you have sustained in the perplexing tumult of company has been too much for you, Agatha. A little quiet and repose will restore your wonted serenity."

"It will, I am convinced," said Sir Charles; "home, as it is the sphere of virtue, is that of comfort likewise."

Agatha, unable to dissemble, made no reply; she was well aware that they imputed her uneasiness to a wrong cause, and was surprised they should themselves mistake it.

They soon after turned the conversation to the events of their journey, and other ordinary subjects, in which Agatha joined by degrees as cheerfully as she could, fearful they might imagine the pleasure she ought to feel at their return was lost in the grief she experienced at parting from her other friends. Alive to every feeling of nature and virtue, she had always loved her parents with the tenderest affection, had made their wishes the law of her life, and had never intentionally displeased or offended them. To meet them again after their absence, was a source of the purest pleasure, which was only suspended by the mingled emotions that filled her breast, and her sudden separation from him in whom her hopes of happiness were centred, and from others deservedly dear to her. Her first grief, however, being subsided, and Lady Belmont's countenance softening by degrees, amid all the weight which yet sunk her heart, she was sensible of unfeigned pleasure at their return; and a ray of hope sometimes darted into her mind that her separation from Hammond was but temporary; that when they were sensible of his worth he would be no less dear to them than his sister had been; and that they could not destroy the happiness of their only child when they knew on whom it depended.

When they arrived at home, Lady Belmont told Agatha that finding herself rather unwell, she wished her to sleep in her apartment, and for that purpose had ordered another bed to be put into it.

"In your room, Madam?" said Agatha with astonishment.

"Yes, Agatha. Does it give you pain to hear that you will enjoy more of your mother's society than formerly?"

"Certainly not. I was only surprised –"

"Agatha! The time has been that that surprise would have been mixed with pleasure not chagrin! But others – butterfly friends – the acquaintance of a day, have estranged your affections from me!"

"Heaven forbid! I would not for the world you should think so. Indeed! Indeed! I do not deserve this," said Agatha bursting into tears.

"Come my dear girl," said Lady Belmont, much softened, "forgive me – I fear I spoke harshly – I did not mean to distress you thus; but I thought you did not express any pleasure at what I imagined would give you equal delight with myself." Then kissing her, she wiped her tears, and changed the subject.

During the remainder of the evening, Sir Charles and Lady Belmont evidently studied to amuse Agatha. They conversed on several subjects, apparently with no endeavour but to interest her. They spoke of music, books, of everything in short but the subject next to her heart – the friends she had quitted – and that, and everything that led to it they studiously avoided. Too grateful to appear indifferent to their efforts to please her, she joined in the conversation with all the cheerfulness she was able to assume; but her heart wandered in spite of herself to other scenes and other subjects, and fled from the present, as void and insipid. She sighed for night, that in the indulgence of silent reflection her mind might stray where only it could find repose, and counted the minutes till the hour of retirement came.

At length it arrived: but the blessings it had promised were denied. Lady Belmont continued, not without marks of kindness, her endeavours to amuse her; she enumerated every minute particular of her journey, and mentioned a thousand trivial and uninteresting occurrences. Agatha would have given worlds for some minutes of silent and solitary recollection. At length, her mind harassed, and her spirits worn out, she feigned sleep as her only resource. This procured her the silence she sought; but one idea crowded so fast upon another, that all was tumult and confusion, and it was some hours before she could obtain sufficient composure of mind to arrange her thoughts, and to reflect calmly on her situation. When she did, she saw herself on the brink of a precipice: she saw that she had unwarily engaged her heart without the sanction of those she was bound to obey; she saw that their aversion to love was as violent as ever – and prejudices of so long growth it seemed madness to expect to eradicate. Her father had said she should adopt that mode of life, which, on mature deliberation, she as well as they should judge most conducive to her happiness. The recollection of this assertion was her only comfort, the only anchor on which she rested; and like the shipwrecked mariner she clung to this one feeble prop, and blessed the fate that gave a single refuge from despondency. That Lady Belmont sought to efface every remembrance of the friends she had left, was but plain; that she feared to trust her out of her sight, or even to leave her in possession of her own thoughts, was equally certain – since the indisposition she had mentioned as a plea for putting her in her own apartment was palpably an excuse. That Hammond was not received as the brother of a friend was too, too evident: their distant manner, their averted looks, and silence since, with respect to him, were all too many fatal proofs of their prejudice against him. Yet wherefore this prejudice? It was unjust – it was cruel! Hammond was every way amiable – deserving their highest esteem; others not blinded by partiality thought as she did. What should she do? Strive to forget him? Forget Hammond! Impossible! His idea was interwoven with her very existence, and to forget him seemed a species of death. Till this separation she knew not half how dear he was to her. Should she then love him still in opposition to the wishes of her parents? Heaven forbid! No – she would hope that they would indeed suffer her to adopt that mode of life which she as well as they thought necessary to her happiness. This promise (for such it might be called) could not be retracted. In the meantime, she would study to oblige and please them, and by using every innocent art to interest them in behalf of Hammond, in time, perhaps at some future far distant period, she might obtain their sanction of her love. If that were impossible, it must be conquered; if her heart refused to bend, it should break! But what would become of Hammond? She dared not think of this!

The morning came, and saw her still in the same state of doubt and fear. Unable to sleep, she wished to rise: but wherefore rise when every employment had lost its relish and was become insipid? If she played or sung, Hammond was not there to listen; if she drew, he was not there to look over and commend – to give vigour to her genius and inspire her pencil; if she walked, he would not be present to enliven every scene by his conversation – to point out the beauties of nature, and bid her remark graces before unheeded. If she went to her library, there his lamented sister was retraced to her imagination: with every page her idea was blended, while her persuasive eloquence, giving new force to truth and adding lustre even to the precepts of virtue, now for ever mute, every wound of her heart would bleed afresh, and she should remember with agony the friend whom she had now, more than ever, cause to lament, and whose counsel she now more than ever stood in need.

Moving her curtain on one side, she was surprised to see Lady Belmont up and already dressed; since though Agatha had never once closed her eyes, Lady Belmont had arisen with so little noise, in the fear, as she now told her, of waking her, that she had not even heard her move. She enquired after Agatha's health with much tender solicitude, and was evidently shocked at observing the paleness of her countenance. Agatha now rose, and Lady Belmont renewed her attempts to amuse her. She stayed with her while she dressed, and attended her downstairs.

They found Sir Charles with several prints before him on a table, and on another some new publications; all of which, he informed Agatha, he had purchased for her on his journey. The examination of the prints passed an hour not unpleasantly; and when that was over, Lady Belmont taking up a work of humour which had recently appeared, desired Agatha to read it to her. She complied without hesitation, though her mind was little inclined for a performance of that kind. A large collection of music was afterwards produced, and Agatha desired to play. Music she dreaded: she knew that in the moments of depression, however soothing it may be, it adds to that depression in the end; and by softening our hearts, increases the sorrows it promises to mitigate. She rose, therefore, with a heavy heart, and walked slowly to the instrument.

"You will be delighted with some of those lessons," said Lady Belmont, "if you knew how charming they were, you would be more impatient to play them Agatha. But you have lost your alacrity, my dear."

"I have, indeed!" said Agatha, sighing.

"You must not give way to this, my love," said Lady Belmont. "Our spirits depend, in a great measure, on ourselves – if we fancy we are cheerful, we actually become so: without that imagination the gayest scenes are lonesome, and with it the most perfect seclusion is lively. Besides, you know you assured me that you felt pleasure of my return – let me see it then."

Agatha took the lessons and played one. She then turned over a volume of songs; but except some few which were entirely unmeaning, could find none but songs of humour or drinking. At last, and she was putting it down again, having seen no one likely to please her, she accidentally opened to one, the air and words of which, as she glanced her eye over it, seemed to be superior to the rest. She read the first verse, and pleased with its simplicity and the appearance of the air, and desirous to comply with her mother's wishes, she began to play and sing it. The following is a copy of the words.

THE CHILD OF PEACE

Poor Laura was the happiest maid,
That danced beneath yon chestnut shade
Still sportive, cheerful, and serene,
Her smiles enlivened every scene –
Her very look bad sorrow cease,
For Laura was the Child of Peace!

Childhood forsook its darling play,
By Laura's side to pass the day
While tottering age its crutch threw by
To steal new life from Laura's eye –
Her smiles bad every joy increase,
For Laura was the Child of Peace!

At length poor Laura's smiles are fled,
Pale languor takes their place instead.
No more her dance, no more her song,
Makes summer shine the winter long –
Her sighs still heave, her tears still flow,
And Laura is the Child of Woe!

Inhuman love has filled her breast,
And robbed her soul of peace and rest!
A lover faithless – friends unkind –
Who now shall heal her bleeding mind?
Ah none! Those tears shall ever flow,
For Laura is the Child of Woe!

No pitying bosom can remove
The festering wound of hopeless love.
At last she sickens, droops, and dies –
In the cold grave poor Laura lies –
And there once more her sorrows cease,
And Laura is the Child of Peace!

The air which was sweetly simple, and which joined with the subject at that minute too near to her heart, could not fail to affect her, was almost more than she could support: her voice faltered as she came to the last verse, and she could scarcely articulate the concluding words.

"The air of that is pretty," said Lady Belmont, not appearing to remark her emotion, "but the words are silly enough. I wonder how it came among the collection. The end, indeed, expressive of the fatal consequences of love is just; but then it gives a power to the passion which it can never have but over weak minds; for which reason you will observe that it is much more rarely a ruling passion in men than in women – their minds are stronger and their understandings more enlarged. It is not without reason that love has been drawn blind by poets and painters, and it is intended to afford us an excellent lesson; for who would commit themselves to a blind guide? The mere girl, indeed, may whimper and sigh, and dress up some ideal object of adoration, and to this sacrifice her time, her duty and her fame; but women of cultivated minds have nobler aims in view! If, for a moment, imagination has deluded their minds with the dreams of love, they awake at once to sense and reason, cast off the film from their mind's eye, and become again themselves. They look beyond this world and its spiritless enjoyments! Darting into futurity, they tear off the veil which covers it from their view! In Heaven only will they deign to place their Heaven, and thus, by anticipating its joys, they actually share them even on earth."

Day after day passed in this manner; Lady Belmont constantly inculcating the same ideas, and Agatha, aware of the impracticability of the attempt, not daring to endeavour to change her sentiments. Hammond's name she once mentioned, but he was heard with such marked aversion that she dared not repeat it. One minute she wondered he made no attempt to see her, the next recollected that he must be convinced of the fallacy of such an attempt from the cold and indignant reception he had met with from her parents at Milson Hall. Her love thus hopeless, her mind sunk into a dejection which she wanted power to overcome; and which Lady Belmont's efforts to divert, by obliging her through gratitude to assume a serenity to which she was a stranger, served only to increase.

She had continued in this situation some weeks; Lady Belmont never suffering her to quit her, never permitting her to pass a moment unemployed, and not even allowing her time for thought, except what she stole at night by pretending to sleep. Yet the blessing she feigned to share, too often forsook her pillow; and when it did deign to visit her, it was

Still interrupted by distracting dreams,
That o'er the sick imagination rise,
And in black colours paint the mimic scene.

Lady Belmont's endeavours to amuse Agatha became in time evidently forced. She would suddenly forget the subject on which she was speaking, and change to another without being herself sensible of the transition. She became thoughtful, absent, and melancholy; and at the very moment in which she was assuming cheerfulness, and perhaps affecting to laugh, a tear would start in her eye, – she would gaze wistfully on Agatha for some minutes – then turn from her with a look of terror. Her sleep was interrupted by starts and sighs. When she believed Agatha asleep, she would frequently rise in the night, and walk in disorder and agony across the room – her hands folded and raised to Heaven. Then she would fall on her knees, seem to say a short prayer, and return to bed, apparently more tranquil: and this she would repeat several times a night.

Agatha terrified and shocked, feared a derangement of her faculties, and wished to have opened her mind to her father; but he shunned her presence. She seldom saw him – never but when her mother was present, and then his own mind appeared little more at ease than hers. In this dreadful situation, she would have given worlds for some friendly bosom on which to have reposed, and confessed her misery and terror.

One of the servants, she had remarked, whenever she came into the room for any purpose, looked at her frequently, endeavoured to catch her eye, and seemed to make signs that she wished to speak to her. She endeavoured, but in vain, to seize an opportunity of meeting her. Lady Belmont never suffered her to be out of her sight. She would often take her hastily by the hand and desire her to walk with her into the garden, would say that she had something there to unfold – something to communicate to her dear child: and on Agatha's attending her as desired, would sometimes change the subject – say that she had forgot what she meant – sometimes that she would speak of it another time – in another place.

Agatha grew more and more alarmed. Some dreadful evil she believed she saw impending over her head; an evil which it seemed impossible for her to foresee as to avert: whatever it were, she prayed to Heaven to give her strength to support the trial whenever it should arrive; and armed with the consciousness of internal innocence, and cheered by a firm reliance on the protection of Him, who never is implored in vain, her mind became calmer and better able to sustain its present dreadful state of doubt, anxiety, and terror.

She now, in her turn, strove by every effort in her power to amuse her mother's mind, and chase the gloom that hung upon her brow. When her own heart was almost breaking, she would read, sing, converse, leave no attempt untried to divert her melancholy. But her endeavours, though received with kindness, were seldom successful; and Lady Belmont, from the latent grief which preyed on her mind, was seized with an illness which confined her to her bed. Agatha never quitted her night or day; her attention was unwearied, and in her anxiety for her recovery, even Hammond was almost forgotten. Agatha's tenderness seemed to endear her more than ever to her mother; she appeared to have no peace except when looking at her – nor could sleep unless she held her hand the while. After a fortnight of severe though not dangerous illness, she gradually recovered, and with her health, seemed, in some measure, to regain her spirits: she was less absent and less agitated than she had been before, though still melancholy and dejected at times.

When she was sufficiently recovered to walk in the garden, Agatha was pointing out to her notice several shrubs, and admiring their beauty.

"You love shrubs and flowers?" said Lady Belmont.

"Surely!" said Agatha; "it is one of the tastes you early taught me to cherish; and it is a perpetual source of amusement."

"You shall always have some," said Lady Belmont, "and every variety of species my fortune can procure. They will flourish far better in that soil than in this."

"In that soil, my dear mother? What did you mean?"

"Nothing! But that you shall have a new and far more beautiful garden – I believe my thoughts were wandering I knew not whither. Do not ask me the meaning of any trifling incoherences in my manner – Agatha – a little time – tomorrow – today perhaps. But of this be assured, I love you more than my own life! And would lay down that life to make you happy."

Agatha, though somewhat relieved by the kind assurance which concluded the sentence, was, nevertheless, greatly alarmed. Some fatal secret was to be revealed she was now convinced. But whatever its nature, she wished it told, since she could not conceive a horror beyond what she felt in this constant state of suspense and terror.

Chapter 11

At night Lady Belmont complained of feeling fatigued, and retired with
Agatha to her apartment an hour earlier than usual.

When they were upstairs, Lady Belmont shut the door, and taking
two chairs desired Agatha to sit on one of them; she herself sat down on
the other, and taking her hand, "I think you love me Agatha?" she said.

"Think I love you! And is not my mother assured of it?"

"I am – I am, Agatha – I am assured you love me with all the
affection, and more perhaps than ever daughter felt for a parent."

She paused; and Agatha was too much alarmed by the solemnity of
her manner to interrupt the gloomy silence. After some minutes she
continued.

"Agatha – my Agatha has a strong and noble mind – a mind
superior to the feeble pleasures of this fleeting life – a mind capable of
spurning every earthly bauble, to ensure her mother's happiness in this
world, and to preserve her from damnation in the next."

"Good God!" said Agatha, dropping on her knees. "What do you
mean? What would you say? For God Almighty's sake relieve me from
the agony I feel. Do not – do not break my heart, but tell me all!"

"Rise Agatha! 'Tis I that should kneel – 'tis I that am the suppliant:
a mother imploring at the hands of her child peace and salvation!
O Agatha! Agatha! Do you indeed love me? Swear then to obey me."

"This fatal mystery undisclosed, I dare not swear," said Agatha,
"yet all that I can do – all that my feeble nature can sustain – I will do
to give peace to my mother. But if you would not break my heart – if you
do not wish to sink me to the grave with terror and apprehension, hold
me not in this dreadful suspense."

"Hear me then Agatha; and may the Blessed Virgin give you strength
and courage to support the recital! With a guilt which years of contrition
could not expiate, I disobeyed my mother. I was destined, for what reason
I knew not, as an offering to my God; and had only quitted the convent
where I had been educated, and to which I was destined to return for the
remainder of my life, to spend a few months at my mother's habitation
previous to my leaving it forever, when I saw and loved your father. His
affection for me was equally strong; and I consented to fly with him from
my mother, my home, my country – and in the perishable pleasures of
worldly enjoyment, to abjure the enthusiastic transports of a life of pure
devotion, and the Heavenly Spouse for whom I had been destined. Believe

me Agatha when I say, that all the comforts annexed to wealth, society, and liberty, were inadequate to atone for the remorse that filled my guilty breast. I had disobeyed my heavenly and my earthly parent; and Heaven by denying me offspring seemed in vengeance to forbid any fruit of my guilty love.

Years had passed, and no forgiveness from my mother could be obtained. I travelled to see her, time after time, and was forbidden her presence. I wrote, and all my letters were returned. At last, on her deathbed she sent to me – I flew to meet her – to confess my crime and obtain pardon ere she expired. I travelled night and day, and arrived while she was yet possessed of sense and speech.

'Agatha,' she said, 'I yet live to forgive and bless you – yet live to tell my tale of horror. Born with dreadful and violent passions, which had been from my youth upwards suffered to assume the mastery of my reason, I lived a slave equally to love and hatred: ardent in my attachments, implacable in my resentments. Your father whom I adored won by the beauty and artifices of a widow who sought to seduce him, treated me with coldness, contempt, and aversion. With a soul unable to brook the slightest injury, one barbarous as this, stung me to the quick. To revenge alone I looked for retribution. I employed assassins to waylay and murder him. He was brought home, bleeding, and almost lifeless. At that moment all my love returned. My crime appeared in its blackest dye. I wept – I raved – and, in the bitterness of my heart, vowed to God that the child I then bore, should be devoted to him if his mercy spared my husband. He was spared. You was that child – and you fled from me, and this forbad the fulfilment of a vow from which I hoped for an expiation of my crime.'

'O Agatha,' she said, 'if your heart feels any shadow of pity for the agony of mind, O swear that if ever you are a mother your child shall be destined to the life from which you fled! Swear, swear it Agatha, and I shall yet die content. Years of contrition and remorse have in some measure, I trust, atoned for my crime: but this single request – this dying adjuration can my child deny me?'

I paused – I trembled – 'O forgive me,' I said, 'and think not that Heaven requires this at our hands: the sacrifice of a penitent and humble heart alone it seeks, and that you have offered.'

'Agatha!' she cried in horror, 'you deny me then. You will see your mother expire in all the torments of remorse and falsified vows – barbarous that thou art! No – if thou canst not bear this, expect not my dying benediction: I cannot, will not bestow it.'

How could I act – thus miserable – thus distracted? I had no child, was not pregnant, and Heaven seemed to have ordained that none should call me mother. By this vow I could obtain her blessing and forgiveness, and after she had passed a life of agony, remorse, and horror, I could yet send her grey hairs with peace to the grave. Her soul quivered on her lips. The cold damp of death were spread over her frame. She looked at me with ineffable tenderness; with supplication, the supplication of a sinner at the tribunal of his Eternal Judge. She made a feeble effort and seized my hand. 'Save me, my child! Swear to me!' was all she could utter.

'I do! I do!' I exclaimed, with the fervour of awakened devotion; 'and as I keep my vow may the Eternal prosper me in this, and bless or curse me in another world!'

'Bless you then!' she said; and casting a smile of death upon me, sunk in my arms, and expired."

Agatha trembled violently, raised her hands to Heaven in agony, but without speaking, and Lady Belmont proceeded.

"Agatha, the want of offspring which had before embittered every blessing, was then no more: I trembled lest I should bring into the world a child who wanted virtue, courage, and heroism to forsake it for my sake. But when the will of Heaven ordained your birth, I resolved to prepare you, even in infancy, for the life to which you was destined. I gave you every resource that solitude can desire: you have a little world within yourself. I painted society to you, different, it is true, from the colours in which I should have drawn it had you been designed to mingle with it; since then, I would have softened evils you was necessitated to sustain, nor have torn the mask from vices with which you was condemned to associate. But my colouring was just and true: such as the world is, such as I found it, and such as it will ever appear when the tinsel of novelty that decorates it is tarnished by the hand of time. Say then, my Agatha, my saviour, my preserver. Speak! Shall thy mother glory in her child, and fame tell to future[20] ages her duty and obedience; or shall she have to weep over her weakness and ingratitude, and blush to own herself a mother."

Lady Belmont stopped, took both Agatha's hands, and looked at her with eager and trembling solicitude. Agatha was unable to speak – she was unable to weep. She gazed wildly at her mother, and for some minutes seemed lost to the recollection of everything.

Lady Belmont, terrified at her appearance, screamed aloud; then kneeling down to her, "Agatha! My child! My love! My darling!" she exclaimed, "have you forgot me – forgot your mother? See, see I kneel to you – love you – O Agatha, beyond my life!"

Her recollection returned, and with it a sense of misery beyond all she had before known or imagined. "Rise, rise, I conjure you," she said,

---

[20]Original has "after".

folding her mother's hands between hers, "rise, nor break at once a heart that merits not the misery it endures.

For you, for my mother, the best and dearest of mothers, what dreadful sacrifice would I not make – yet this –"

"Bless! Bless my child!" said Lady Belmont, interrupting her hastily, "she consents, she consents –"

"Hear me – hear me speak," said Agatha, "hear a child to whom you have given life but to render it miserable, hear her plead the cause of virtue, of humanity, of religion even! Did God Almighty give me life – did he give me every tender affection of the human heart – pity for the afflicted, joy for the happy, and friendship for the good; did he plant in my bosom a delight mingled with veneration at the endearing names of wife – mother – friend – but to tear me from every sweet connection, but to snatch me from those witnessed blessings, and immure me in the cold cheerless cell of cloistered penance? Impossible! No, you yourself have said that Heaven seeks not this at our hands, that the sacrifice of a humble heart is all his mercy requires."

"Agatha, do I live to hear this? It is enough. You deny me. Yes Agatha – I am satisfied, and the dreadful forfeiture of my vow I will pay for your sake: to make you happy here, your mother will endure an eternity of misery! Millions and millions of ages multiplied to infinity shall see her among the heirs of perdition, consumed by the worm that never dies."

"Talk not thus, speak not so dreadfully," said Agatha, "if you would leave me sense and life to fulfil your dreadful mandate. Hear only what I would urge. You vowed – my mother vowed to devote me to Heaven – to Heaven cheerfully I devote myself, and have from my youth upwards."

"What is it I hear?" said Lady Belmont, in an ecstasy of joy, and folding her to her heart, "My child! My Agatha!"

"Yet hear me," cried Agatha. "To devote myself to God is to do his will on earth: he lives not in a temple built with hands; it is the heart of innocence he delights to inhabit. Him therefore will I serve."

"Mistake not," said Lady Belmont. "You would divide between the world you love, and Him your duty compels you to serve, that heart which should be wholly his. You cannot serve God and mammon; and while your lips were paying forced devotion, your heart would wander to the vain allurements of worldly and sensual delights. No! Deceive not yourself: this cannot be effected."

"Once more then hear me. That world I will renounce, though with it I forsake all hopes of happiness, and dreams of bliss as pure as they were delightful: yet I will forsake it for you; will retire to some lonely spot, where no society shall cheer or bless me, where no human foot has left its traces, and all is silent and solitary as the grave. There buried in retirement, will I devote my nights to prayer, my days to filial duty. But force me not to leave you. How would you endure to lose your Agatha? How, on the bed of sickness would you call for your lost child! No friendly eye to watch you as you slept, no one whose prayers and tenderness could soothe your pain, and call returning health once more to bless you:

What pillow like the bosom of a child?

O, force me not to leave you; nor by commands I had rather die than disobey, oblige me to take a vow at which my heart recoils, and nature sinks within me!"

"If you hesitate not to renounce the world, my Agatha, why fear it to take those vows which, by rendering that renunciation a duty, would, to a heart like yours, render it delightful? Come, my child, a little, little resolution, a small portion more of that heroic spirit which already animates your soul, will make your mother the happiest of beings on earth, and ensure her an eternity of bliss in Heaven. Think, O think you see her – imagine that in another world you behold her a sharer of immortal and exquisite felicity – think that to you she owes it. Think that after you have endured a life of privation here, whose short period compared to eternity is less than a thousandth part of a drop of water compared with the ocean, think that then you shall meet her in this pure and ever enduring state of felicity! O Agatha! Does not your noble heart glow at the picture?"

"I know not what I would say – what I would think," said Agatha, "all within is tumult and distraction. O, give me leisure to reflect – my mother is too generous – her soul would spurn the thought – to owe to a moment of agitation, and sensibility roused even to torture, a consent which should be the consequence of cool and determined reason. Thus far will I promise; I will think, I will reflect, and if convinced what you ask me is my duty, my heart shall break if it refuses to fulfil it."

"Enough – enough – my Agatha! My child! My angel; for such you are."

"One thing beside I ask," said Agatha. "Deny me not time or opportunity for reflection; allow me hours of retirement."

"Of retirement, Agatha?"

"Yes, nor fear them for me: they will enable me to conquer rather than to indulge every feeling my duty shall prompt me to surmount. I ask this for your sake as well as for my own; and without it, my mind, agitated by a thousand conflicting passions, must sink into hopeless melancholy, or lose in madness the remembrance of its sufferings."

"My Agatha shall never ask in vain; she shall not have a wish ungranted which I have power to gratify. Would you like your own apartment, my love?"

"Take it not unkind, nor believe I wish to quit you – yet it would be an indulgence."

"Tomorrow night then, tonight, if you wish it, your bed shall be prepared."

"Tomorrow, if you please; tonight my spirits are not sufficiently collected to reflect as I would wish."

"Would my sweet girl wish to go to bed now, or shall we sit up longer, and converse on ordinary subjects?"

"I am unable to talk, and dare not think."

"Then you shall go to bed, my love. Shall I sit and watch you, or go to my own?"

"Ten thousand thanks for your goodness! No, I will try to sleep."

"God send you that and every blessing, my Agatha! And make me in future deserving such a child, the only treasure her mother possesses! Good night, my love! May Angels guard thy pillow, and give thee that peace this world cannot give!"

Then kissing her with the utmost tenderness, she assisted in undressing and putting her to bed.

Dreadful is that situation where sleep is the only refuge from calamity; where the mind shrinks from reflection; where the future and the past are alike the harbingers of sorrow; where to look back retraces to our view scenes of happiness never to be renewed, and to look forward presents a spectacle of misery we shudder to contemplate. Agatha in vain endeavoured to avoid reflection, and to lose in sleep the remembrance of her sorrows: her mind wandered in spite of her. Unable to sleep she attempted to collect her thoughts and to reflect with all the calmness possible on her situation and the dreaded prospect before her. Yet though it was impossible to banish thought, she found it equally so to force her thoughts into any regular channel; all was terror, misery, and despair.

Chapter 12

When Lady Belmont rose in the morning she was terrified at the appearance of Agatha. She saw that her delicate frame had been unable to sustain the agitation of her mind; while the burning heat of her hand, her parched lips, and tremulous voice were but too plain indications of fever. "Merciful Heaven!" exclaimed Lady Belmont as she felt her pulse, "I have killed my child!"

"Why this alarm?" said Agatha faintly. "Why should my dear mother thus terrify herself? I am not quite well, it is true –"

"Not quite well! My love! My life! You are in a high fever! And 'tis I – barbarous that I am – O Agatha! Agatha! What will become of me?"

"I have not felt well for some days," said Agatha, (wishing by this sweet deception to ease her mother's mind, and to prevent her imputing her illness to herself) "this little complaint has hung upon me."

"And are you sure, quite sure you were ill before?" said Lady Belmont eagerly.

"Indeed I was," said Agatha.

"And you never complained. Why did you not tell me? I would have died ere I would have distressed you when so little able to endure it."

"My illness was very trifling, and is still," said Agatha. "I will rise, and shall be better."

"No, I will send for Dr. Harley immediately."

"Pray do not. Wait but a few hours. I am sure I shall be better."

"Will you not take some saline mixture?"

"Surely I will; that or anything you prescribe or wish me to take. But calm these apprehensions, my dear, my kind mother your terror magnifies an ailment which proceeds merely from a cold that I think I caught by the evening air a few days ago."

Agatha now attempted to rise, but her head turned round, and as she essayed to stand, she fell into her mother's arms. Lady Belmont then forced her to return to bed, and dispatched a servant for Dr. Harley. The servant had orders not to stop a minute, and he was to entreat the doctor to come without delay. The distance was short, and he arrived in less than an hour. When he had seen Agatha, he made Lady Belmont much easier by assuring her that he did not apprehend any danger from her daughter's illness; that her fever was doubtless high, but not so much so as to be alarming; and that, by keeping her perfectly quiet and her mind at ease, together with the necessary medicines, he had no doubt they should effect a cure.

"Once, Madam," he continued, "on a melancholy occasion I was called to this sweet young lady when you was absent; and found her nearly in the same state in which she is at present; her disorder was then occasioned entirely by uneasiness of mind, and her frame is of so delicate a texture that it will not bear the slightest shock. When nature gives to the world a blessing like this, it delights to show us that it is mortal, that, by convincing us by how frail a tenure we possess it, we may learn, from the fear of losing it, to prize it the more dearly."

Lady Belmont felt the force of this remark. O Agatha, she thought, what a treasure have I condemned myself to lose! How spotless a heart have I sworn to torture – a heart how unequal to the conflict! At the very moment in which I idolise my child, I plunge a dagger in her bosom! And indeed severe as were Agatha's sufferings, those of Lady Belmont exceeded them. In a moment of anguish and horror, she had made a vow which she then believed she should never be called upon to fulfil, and which was extorted by the agonies of a dying parent. That vow, whether justly or not, she conceived herself bound to perform. She was far from believing the world such as she presented it to Agatha; and though she had felt much repentance on account of her own deviation from duty, and a sincere and fervent desire of reconciliation, she had not felt all the remorse which, lest her daughter might be tempted to follow her example, she had thought it prudent to describe. The fatal secret of Agatha's destiny she had concealed from everyone but Sir Charles, whose sentiments on the subject agreed with her own, and Miss Hammond, to whom it had been a source of perpetual though unavailing regret and sorrow. With the world such as she described she did not imagine that Agatha could be desirous to associate; and with unremitting care she guarded her from every other impression. A pleasure neither known nor imagined cannot be regretted; and she conceived, therefore, that there would be a very small species of cruelty in depriving anyone of pleasures they have never known or believed to exist. A desire of going herself in search of a convent, the situation and regulations of which would be most conducive to Agatha's comfort, had induced her to go to France; not foreseeing that during her absence she should lose the only friend to whose protection she dared confide her child; that all the ideas she laboured to instil should be destroyed in a day; that the veil should be withdrawn, and society in all its charms appear to her view. A single look of Hammond's was enough to reveal all; and in their disappointment at the frustration of their long concerted plans, Sir Charles, and Lady Belmont, forgot for a time their affection for their child, and were only sensible of anger and vexation. From the hour in which they had been made acquainted with Agatha's change of abode, it had determined, lest she might indulge in the remembrance of the scenes they wished her to forget as soon as left, that she should sleep in her mother's apartment, and never pass a moment but under her eye; while it was agreed, that by unremitting assiduity they should endeavour to amuse her mind, and destroy every dangerous impression. Lady Belmont loved her daughter; and when she saw the struggles of her soul on the disclosure of the fatal secret, would have died to shield her from the impending evil; would have endured anything except the breach of that vow which she had always believed she ought rather to perish, nay, to behold her child expire, than violate.

Agatha's illness soon gave way to medicine; and in less than a week she had lost all remains of fever, though she still continued weak and languid. – Being now, however, well enough to require no farther attendance, she slept in her own room, and there

Had room for meditation e'en to madness!

She saw that she must either render her mother guilty of a crime which threatened her with the eternal vengeance of Heaven, or be herself a victim immolated at the shrine of superstition, and renounce friends – lover – everything! Yet could her mother suffer for a crime which she caused her to commit? No, that were impossible. On whom then would the guilt fall? On herself: on her, who, spurning a mother's tears, anguish, and entreaties, had dared to prefer her wishes to her duty. Dreadful – dreadful alternative! Whichever way she turned misery seemed to await her, and, like her shadow, pursued her whithersoever she fled. Her mother had said that no pleasures the world had bestowed could compensate for the contrition she had felt since her our own deviation from duty. If such had been her mother's remorse then, who knew not that a vow would be broken by her disobedience, how much greater and more bitter would be her own? Hammond's esteem she prized beyond even his love; and would not that be lessened by the knowledge of her disobedience? How should she say to her children, be it your study on all occasions to perform your duty, nor let pleasure or any views of self-gratification tempt you to swerve from it, if her own conduct had been in opposition to her precepts? How too could she bestow on Hammond a heart divided betwixt love and duty – sinking with sorrow, and bleeding with remorse? And could she endure to make wretched a parent whom nothing but an irrevocable vow would have forced to contradict a single wish of her heart; and who, in preparing her for the life to which it destined her, had devoted her whole time to the cultivation of those talents from which alone she could derive comfort in retirement? Had she loved her less, she would have been regardless of her peace, would have neglected her education, would have suffered her to mix with the world till a fondness for it had become habitual, and then have dragged her from it to misery and seclusion. But no! It had been her whole study to fit her daughter for her allotted station. She had therefore the strongest claim to her gratitude, and she could not oppose her will without remorse. And how far sweeter would be a life of sorrow with a consciousness of internal rectitude, than one possessed of every pleasure but that which alone can constitute actual happiness – a self-approving heart! And whose every joy was sullied by repentance!

Her mind ceased to waver, and she determined to devote herself a willing though heartbroken sacrifice to duty and obedience. Yet lest time and further reflection should change a resolution which she was determined nothing less than a contrary conviction of its injustice should effect, she resolved not to make known to her mother for some days the result of her melancholy deliberation.

The morning after these reflections, as she was dressing, someone knocked gently at the door, and the maid servant, whose signs she had remarked so long before, but with whom she could never seize an opportunity speaking, entered softly, shut the door after her with an appearance of much secrecy and caution, and then coming near to Agatha and speaking low, and curtseying at the same time – "If you be pleased Miss to hear me," she said, "I can mayhap be of more sarvice to you than you think for. I have tried and tried, and fretted and fretted, and contrived and contrived, and all to no end, till now that my Lady lets you have a little bit of time to yourself."

"I am much obliged to you, Hannah; but what is it you want with me?"

"O Miss! You shall hear it all, if so be you'll have patience. Excuse my freedom, Miss, but a prettier faced gentleman I never seed in my life. But you shall hear it all. As I was passing by the back door that goes to the harb garden one day with a pail of water in my hand, who should I see but the nicest young gentlemen I ever set eyes on, but he looked sad and sorrowful and moped most dismally; and so he put his hand into his pocket, and told me if I would contrive to give that letter to Miss Belmont, he should be internally obliged to me. And so, Miss, as I could not go to refuse a fellow creature in distress, and moreover one that was so pretty spoken and goodly-looking into the bargain, I took it, and to this blessed minute have never had any likelihoods of giving it to you. Then putting her hand into her pocket, she recollected it that she had forgot to bring the letter with her, and had left it locked up in her box of clothes, but promised to fetch it immediately."

"You surprise me greatly," said Agatha, who had no doubt that the letter was from Hammond. "What was the appearance of the gentlemen?"

"Tall, Miss, and as I said, very pretty faced."

"Of a complexion rather dark?"

"No, Miss, rather fair, as one may say; with the whitest hand I ever saw besides your'n and my Lady's. There is to be sure a gentleman that neither so fair nor good-looking, and yet not brown as one may say neither, that often walks about the park and grounds, and Robert Mathers was a little afeard he might be a poacher, as they say'n he oftenest comes towards night; but he was telling us other sarvants about him, and John said my master seed and spoke to him and seemed as if he knowed him one day, and so Robert said no more about him. Nay for that matter," continued Hannah, who plainly perceived from Agatha's countenance that the dark gentleman was the favourite, "I don't go for to say that one mayn't be as handsome as t'other, beauty's all fancy, you know Miss; you may happen like rough faces, now a pretty, snug, neatly looking face was always the face for my money. Howsomever, be it which it will, any sarvice I can do you I'll do it as freely as if it wants to sarve myself." So saying, she went out of the room as cautiously as she entered it, leaving Agatha in equal astonishment and agitation. That the person last described was Hammond she had no doubt; that he had seen her father, though she had not been suffered to see him, was now certain; and from his never repeating his visit the answer given him was too plain: how indeed could it be otherwise, destined as she was to abjure him and all the world? Who the other person could be did not strike her; but certain that he was not Hammond, she waited though with curiosity yet without impatience the return of Hannah.

Hannah was some time before she returned; when at last she came in, "O Miss!" she whispered, "we had it liked to have been all blown. I met my Lady upon the stairs when I went from you, and so she said, 'Pray where have you been Hannah?' 'Been! Your ladyship,' says I, 'I only went to fill Miss's water bottle, because Jenny had forgot to fill it overnight.' And so, Miss, if she should axe you a thing about it, you know your cue – that's all." She then gave Agatha the letter, and not daring to stay for fear of Lady Belmont's coming, went out of the room immediately. With equal surprise and pity Agatha read the following melancholy letter.

I have known love, and I have known sorrow in consequence, yet never, adored Miss Belmont, equal to what I have felt since I saw and have been divided from you. This heart imagined it loved another till your angelic form and mind chased the illusion, and convinced me I but dreamed of love before. Your parents deny themselves to everyone; and for what barbarous motive I know not, baffle every attempt to see you – formed as you are to make a Paradise on earth wherever you appear.

With not a ray of hope to cheer me, I yet dare to address you – despair gives me courage. Fortune is nothing to those who love! I have enough for both – enough to make my home a Heaven would you but consent to share it. O, then imagine what I dare not express! Yet you cannot – will not – hope I have none. Pray then for me. Pray that that *Heaven which sees my sufferings may end at once or mitigate them. Dare I write the name of*

William Milson.

Agatha had just time to put the letter into her pocket before Lady Belmont entered. She examined Agatha's countenance with an anxious and scrutinising eye, but forbore to ask any questions. After breakfast Agatha proposed walking and asking Lady Belmont to accompany her. When the mind is ill at ease it seems to find relief from exercise: perhaps the change of posture and of place with the variety of objects may promise a suspension of suffering; from whatever cause the relief proceeds the wretched have always had recourse to it. They walked for more than an hour; each sedulously avoiding the subject which occupied their minds.

Chapter 13

In the afternoon, Agatha went to her room to read again Mr. Milson's letter, and to write the answer to which she thought it entitled. Lady Belmont, remembering Agatha's request, made no attempt to follow her. She wrote the following reply.

Gratitude for the many instances of hospitality and friendship which I have received from every part of your family, together with that I feel for the generous sentiments expressed in the letter I but this morning received, induces me to do, what in other circumstances I should condemn – to make reply to a letter clandestinely sent. Much as regard so disinterested as yours deserves, were I even permitted to dispose of my own heart (which I am not) gratitude and esteem would be the only returns in my power to make.

Be assured that the peace and welfare of yourself, and every individual of your family, will ever be dear to me; and that I will not forget to number *in my prayers friends so deservedly entitled to every mark of gratitude and regard from*

Agatha Belmont.

When she had folded up and sealed this letter, she put it in her pocket, designing to give it to Hannah the first opportunity she had of speaking to her; and not wishing to be absent longer than was necessary, she went downstairs immediately afterwards. Not finding Lady Belmont in the drawing room, and imagining she might be walking, she went into the garden. She did not find her there, and her mind, intent on a melancholy prospect which forever occupied it, ensuring a state of misery little short of distraction, though firm in her resolves to perform what she believed her duty, she strayed to the gate which opened from the garden into the park, and from thence to the road adjoining. She had not gone far when she was awakened from her melancholy reverie by observing a gentleman on horseback galloping towards her. He jumped from his horse when he came up to her, and with equal surprise and pleasure she was addressed by Mr. Ormistace.

"Miss Belmont!" he exclaimed in transport, "how shall I express my delight at meeting you! Scarcely a day has passed in which I have not taken this road in hopes of seeing you; since a private meeting was all even I could expect, denied as you have been by your parents to everyone: and though my age and appearance precluded every idea that I came on any other footing than that of a friend, I have been denied like the rest. What are their intentions towards you God only knows; but of this I am certain, nothing can justify their locking up such a jewel, and that if they fail in their duty towards you, yours as a child is[21] cancelled towards them."

Agatha burst into tears. "O! Mr. Ormistace," she said, "the kind and generous concern you take in my fate I never can repay. But accuse not my parents; indeed they deserve it not. If an inviolable necessity forces them to relinquish for themselves and me the friends they would otherwise embrace with transport, their situation merits pity rather than blame. Of this be assured from me; they have made my happiness their study; to me have devoted all their hours, and are entitled to every act of gratitude and obedience in my power to pay."

"Good God! Is it to study your happiness to seclude you from the world? At an age when the soul is tuned to pleasure, when the heart beats high with hopes of social delight, when every eye adores you and every tongue is loud in your praises? O Miss Belmont! Is this to study your happiness? Good God! You might as well be a nun at once."

This dreadful word struck like death to the heart of Agatha. The blood forsook her cheeks; and all but fainting, she turned away her head to conceal her emotions. When a moment's reflection had somewhat recovered her, "Mr. Ormistace," she said, "business of necessity will shortly call my parents to France. If we should continue to reside there, shall I trouble you with the remembrances to those dear friends, whom, as it is possible we may be obliged to leave England suddenly, I may be unable to see before I quit them, perhaps forever. To Mrs. Herbert give every assurance of a friendship that shall end but with my life. Tell her I will write her – will love her – will pray for her happiness; that I will never lose nor part with her little smelling bottle; and ask her to accept this in exchange – and when she looks at it to think of me, and repeat my name. Assure Miss Milson of my gratitude for all the hours of pleasure I passed under that hospitable roof. Tell her I will never forget her; that I shall think of her often, and always with affection. Assure the good Mr. Crawford of my regard and veneration; and ask him to remember me in his prayers: the prayers of a good man are always heard. There is one other," continued she hesitating, "yet why should I fear to name him? Mr. Hammond! Tell him I regard, esteem, value him beyond every other friend; and that

> – *without a prayer for him*
> *my orisons shall never close.*[22]

---

[21]Original has "it cancelled ..."
[22]William Shenstone, *Jemmy Dawson*, lines 35 -36.

Tell him that if he prizes my happiness he will himself be happy –
that nothing on earth can give me such comfort as to know that he is so.
But perhaps you need not – perhaps I may – yet it may be impossible –
say then this for me –"

"But Miss Belmont! Sweetest dearest young woman! Why must all
this be? My heart is almost too full to reason with you; yet another
opportunity may never be obtained. Hear me speak then. You love these
friends; it is misery to that charming heart to part from any one of them:
and Hammond you love with a tenderness that would make him and
yourself the happiest beings on earth. Why? For what cruel purpose are
you to be divided? No duty exacts such a sacrifice. Your parents you say
love you – curse on their love if it is to make you wretched! We have no
right to give life to those to whom we purpose to deny happiness. Life of
itself is no blessing: no, when debarred the comforts it requires it is the
heaviest curse. But the moments are precious. I dare not waste them.
Trust to me that no duty binds you to forsake Hammond; a man that
loves you as his own soul! Consent to fly with me. Emma is at home, and
will receive you with transport. I will procure chaises instantly, and
she shall accompany you with Hammond to Scotland. If they refuse
to forgive you (which is not likely) half of my fortune shall be yours.
Hammond as well as William Milson offered to your father to settle the
whole of your fortune upon you – mine therefore shall be yours instead:
it shall be divided between you and Emma. She has a soul that will glory
in the division – if she had not, it should all be yours. Come! Not a
moment is to be lost. Suffer me to conduct you at once from tyranny and
injustice, to freedom, love, happiness, and Hammond."

"No, Mr. Ormistace; it is, it is indeed impossible. Beyond my life,
and every comfort of my life, I prize what I believe my duty."

"And does no duty bind you to Hammond, a man that adores you,
whose whole happiness is wrapped up in you? Can you delight to make
him miserable?"

"Delight in it? No! Heaven forbid! – No, Mr. Ormistace, I would die
to make him happy – do anything but renounce my duty; and to that an
immovable resolution has determined me to adhere. I dare not stay
longer. God bless you, and reward you for this goodness!" then taking
one of his hands, and folding it between both of hers, "fare – farewell,"
she said; and not daring to trust herself with him a moment longer,
darted from him with a strength and swiftness almost supernatural; and
ran through the park into the garden. When she had reached a seat she
threw herself into it and burst into an agony of tears.

"Where has my sweet girl been?" said Lady Belmont, who came up
to her at this moment; "I have been looking for you everywhere."

Agatha trembled violently and was unable to speak.

"Surely something has terrified you, my love?" said Lady Belmont. "Tell me – speak to me – what – whom have you seen?"

Agatha, who scorned deceit, and dared not confess the truth, was still silent; and Lady Belmont, perceiving her unwillingness to reply, urged her no farther, but made at the same time a secret determination not to trust her so long out of her sight again.

In the evening Agatha attempted to read and work, but her spirits were too much agitated to suffer her to pay attention to either.

She then endeavoured to paint, but her hand shook so violently she could not guide her pencil. Still, however, her resolution continued firm. Though more than ever sensible of the misery of her lot, though more than ever regretting Hammond, and for his sake, the world, she yet determined to pursue her dreadful purpose; assured that the sweet consciousness of performing our duty, repays us in the end for every sacrifice it enjoins; or at least if it does not repay us, so mitigates every sorrow that it enables us to endure it with resignation.

After a night of anguish, though of unshaken fortitude, she was awakened from a short sleep by Hannah, who with a great precaution entered on tiptoe, and opened her curtain.

"Well, Miss," she said, "have you got a letter wrote?"

"I have," replied Agatha, "and if you can find any means of sending it to the gentleman from whom the other came I shall be obliged to you."

"To be sure I can," said Hannah, "match me who can at contrivances. Though my Lady to be sure keeps a pretty sharp look out. But what of that, when the body has a mind of a thing! I defies anybody to stop a young lady or her sarvant either, in the persecution of a scheme. But what I wanted mostly for to say to you, Miss, was this: that I hopes you have given a pretty kindly answer to the gentleman; and if so be, he should not be the very man you had a mind of, why what of that? This world, as the parsons tell us, is a state of purgation and trial, and a body can't have everything they want; and so, if belike you can't get the very indiavittle husband you may be chanced to choose, why you should take up with another, and be thankful you can get any. Nay, for the matter of that, a man's a man, and I don't see no great difference among 'em for my part."

"I am obliged to you for your advice, Hannah," said Agatha, "but the letter I have written is such as on consideration I judged the most proper."

"Nay, to be sure you ought to know your own business best, Miss," returned Hannah "but mayhappen I could tell you something you little dream of, and that's what makes me so agog to get you married. You must know, Miss – but it's a shocking thing to say to you – but as sure as you're alive and now sit up in that bed, your Mamma means to make a nun of you."

"What reason have you to think so, Hannah?"

"Reason enough, and too much o' conscience. But I'll tell you all, Miss. You must know that Mrs. Wildys, my Lady's woman, happened to be in my Lady's closet laying up her muslins out of the wash, and my Lady had no more suspicions of her being there, than she has of my being talking to you now. Well now, though to be sure Mrs. Wildys would not go for to listen upon no account, yet ears are ears, and a body can't help knowing what's said in one's hearing. So she heard my Lady and Sir Charles both come in and talk of a sakerfice: and then they talked about nuns and abbeys and things I knows no more than the Pope at Rome. Howsomever, the long and the short of the matter is this: she made out that all their notion was to make you a nun."

"I am much indebted to you for your concern on my account, Hannah," said Agatha; "but I am certain that my father and mother will neither make me that nor anything else without my consent."

"Why, Miss, I think it is sartin sure you would never be rash enough to consent to that. Why, Lord bless you, your nuns what do you think they do? Why they live in a monstrous grate, and they're all shut up together, and ben't allowed to speak to their own fathers but through the bars. O, I'd rather be an old maid fifty, nay a hundred times over; and that is bad enough seeing they're the laughing stock of everyone. But matrimony is a holy constitution, and quite another matter. And so, Miss, if you'll be ruled by me, let ne'er an old crab of 'em all govern you, but make off with this young gentlemen sharply, and my life for it you never repent it."

"I shall never repent doing my duty," said Agatha "and no persuasions shall induce me to disobey my parents."

"Nay, Miss, if you come to that," said Hannah, "I don't know that you could do any manner of thing more inducive to your Mamma's anger, than having letters and writing answers to 'em unbeknown to her. When you have gone so far as that, I don't think you need make much bones of marrying the gentleman."

Agatha, who now felt that she had acted imprudently in receiving the letter and afterwards in answering it unknown to her mother, was shocked at the last insinuation, but recollecting herself, she said, "The letter you gave me, and which I have answered, is of a peculiar kind, and one which I could not without ingratitude refuse to reply to. My answer to it is such, that if my mother herself saw it she would approve it; and I shall neither receive nor write any more of the kind."

Hannah somewhat displeased that her advice was not taken, or, at least, received with the gratitude she expected, muttered two or three "Very well Misses," and putting the letter into her pocket went out of the room.

About noon, Agatha having retired to her library to indulge in a few moments of melancholy reflection, Hannah came and informed her that a young woman was then at the door who asked to speak with her.

"With me?" said Agatha.

"Yes, Miss, with you; and a very goodly looking young woman she is too; and this is a matter of the fourth time she has come to axe for you, but my Lady's so plaguey cunning that she always contrives to pack her off again. Howsomever this time I was resolved for to let you know it, come what would."

"I will go down immediately," said Agatha, "but I have no idea who it can be." She then ran downstairs, but before she had reached the hall the person was gone. "Mayhappen she's not out of sight," said Hannah. Agatha then went to the door, and looking along the avenue saw a young woman whose figure she thought she recollected, walking slowly from the house. Agatha pursued, and overtook her with little difficulty.

"Ah Madam!" said the person, whom she immediately recognised as Jemima Simmonds, now Mrs. Arnold, "How, how happy am I at last to meet you! Time after time that I have come here to see you, for never have I forgot, and I pray to Heaven I never may forget all your goodness to me; and how you pitied at all my sorrows; and now that I am as happy as the day is long, I could not bear but to come and tell you so, for I knew your kindness would take part in all my happiness as if it was your own."

"Happy indeed am I, my dear Jemima, to see you so," said Agatha, "and heaven preserve you that peace you so richly deserve! And how does Mr. Arnold?"

"O Madam! My dear Harry is well and happy as his Jemima: and not a day goes over our heads that we do not bless Mr. Ormistace, and you, and Mrs. Herbert."

Lady Belmont observing from the window someone in conversation with Agatha, joined her immediately; and Agatha presented Jemima to her, saying at the same time, "this, my dear Madam, is the sweet girl whose kindness to her aged parent I have so often described to you, and who comes now to give me the welcome assurance that she is rewarded as she deserves."

"Far, far indeed beyond my deserts," said Jemima, "almost beyond my desires; for never could I think of such a happy life as I lead. O Madam, surely there is no happiness on earth like that of true lovers. I often think that if it was not for knowing that this life cannot last forever, we should seem to be in heaven already."

"The first months of a married life are the happiest in it," said Lady Belmont, who by no means approved of this picture for her daughter. "Love owes its best charms to novelty; and when time has familiarised a

116

married pair to each other, the affection they at first felt is remembered as a dream."

"O Madam, forgive my boldness," said Jemima, "but this can never happen in true – real true lovers. The more they see and know one another, the more they love, for every day, Madam, gives them some new mark of kindness to remember; and by degrees, as a very great warmth of love, as I may say, wears off, it leaves behind it something more happy yet! If I had but had education, I think I could describe what I mean – a kind of softly – gentle goodwill towards each other, as I may say."

"I am glad to see you so happy, young woman," said Lady Belmont, "and I hope you will continue as much so as it is possible to be: but unless you can walk in, I will not detain you."

Jemima curtsied modestly, and was preparing on this hint to take her leave, but Agatha, taking her hand said in a tone of most tender affection, "Nay, my dear Jemima, I cannot part with you yet; I shall insist upon your coming in with us and taking some refreshment after your long walk." She then led her into the library, and Lady Belmont followed, evidently little pleased with her guest, and trembling at the impression her artless descriptions might make on Agatha's mind.

"And is your grandmother as well as usual?" asked Agatha, as they entered the library.

"Better, Madam," said Jemima. "Our happiness seems to have made her young again: and Harry tries to prove his love for me by watching and attending her. He was always a scholar, and when his work is done, will read to her by the hour together. O Madam, I can hardly ask such a favour, yet if you would but come and look in upon us and see how our little cottage is trimmed and adorned it would make us so proud. We have everything about us that the heart can wish. In an evening, before Harry returns from work, I trim up the little parlour, put everything in order, and spread a cloth upon the table; and our brown loaf and home-made cheese eats so sweet a lord might envy us. Then too I take delight in decking out the chimney with flowers, and when he praises my bow-pot I feel as proud and as happy – O Madam, them only that love and are married know what it is to be happy: God send that one day you may be so too, that wedded to some great gentleman that loves you and that you love, every day it may be like mine happier and dearer than the last; till full of years and honoured and loved by everybody, you shall, as the holy David has it, see your children's children!"

Agatha burst into tears: and Lady Belmont, unable to suppress the agony she felt, put her hand to her head and walked hastily out of the room. Jemima had touched every string of their hearts; Lady Belmont's vibrated at once with pity, maternal tenderness, and remorse. She saw – she felt the force of Jemima's artless delineations. She knew that a heart like Agatha's was framed for the blessings of the most tender attachment, which though differing in minute circumstances from Jemima's description, owing merely to the difference of station, would not be less sweet, less pure, nor simple; and she never felt before the full value of the sacrifice she required. Agatha, who saw herself deprived forever of a life of exquisite felicity, and condemned to one at which her heart recoiled, felt at the same moment the greatness of the sacrifice; yet firm and decided in whatever she believed her duty, her purpose remained unchanged: no temptations could allure, no fears deter her from it; and the greater the sacrifice the greater she was sensible would be the merit of enduring it in the cause of virtue.

After a minute's silence, "My dear Jemima," said Agatha, "will want no remembrance to remind her of her friend, yet if she will accept of this little locket – I am going far away; it is possible may never return to England."

"God forbid that you should not, Madam!" said Jemima, "many will be the poor that will suffer if you leave them."

"We know not what may happen," replied Agatha; "but of this be assured, I will never forget you, and every comfort you enjoy I shall think adds to my happiness. O Jemima, that I had been born in a station like yours! That that brown loaf and home-made cheese had been my lot! With such – just such a faithful, generous heart to share them with me! O Jemima, you are happier than a Queen. May heaven preserve to you, long, long preserve to you the blessings you possess! I cannot be quite wretched while those I love are happy."

Lady Belmont now returned, followed by the servant with refreshments, whom she ordered to wait. This prevented any farther conversation as she had designed; and Jemima soon after took her leave. Agatha attended her to the door. "God bless you, my sweet Jemima," she said, "do not forget me, and pray that if I am condemned to sorrow in this life, I may bear it with the constancy and resignation you did."

"O, I will pray that you may never have any to bear," said Jemima; then taking Agatha's hand, she kissed it, and wept over it. Agatha pressed her to her heart, and after looking at her in speechless anguish, not daring to trust herself longer with her, she ran upstairs.

"When our spirits are inclined to be depressed," said Lady Belmont, as she entered the room, "how mere a trifle is too much for them! The description of cottage happiness has, indeed, something in it peculiarly affecting: a white loaf and Parmesan cheese would not have excited a tear in either of us. But indeed Jemima's happiness is superior to all I ever knew; for it is the reward of filial piety: and with that consciousness of virtue which possesses her mind, and which, though she does not know it, is the sole source of all her blessings, she would have been equally happy in every other situation; separated from the man she loves as well as united to him. To believe ourselves blessed is eventually to be so; and who can believe themselves otherwise when they enjoy the approbation of Heaven and of their own conscience?"

Agatha, whose spirits were too much depressed to converse on any subject, but especially on one which had so recently affected her, made no attempt to reply to assertions, which if just were at that peculiar moment unfeeling at least. The contrast between the misery of her own and the blessings of Jemima's situation was too strong to be lessened by reasonings much more convincing than those Lady Belmont used. Yet while she was rendered more than ever sensible of her own distresses, her generous heart exalted in Jemima's happiness; and shrinking with horror from the darkness in which her own fate was involved, she turned to contemplate the cloudless sunshine of Jemima's future days; and blessed heaven for that felicity which could never be her own.

END OF VOLUME ONE.

Agatha 2

Chapter 1

Some days now passed in which nothing new occurred. Lady Belmont by degrees grew more impatient to know the event of Agatha's reflections. She watched every turn of her countenance with eager and inquisitive anxiety, yet did not dare ask, lest the question might imply a doubt of her acquiescence. In order, however, to give her an opportunity of introducing the subject, she never started any other, and with care avoided breaking silence, hoping that every one would terminate in the wished yet dreaded explanation.

Agatha was no stranger to what passed in her mother's mind; she saw her anxiety, and now convinced that however her heart might suffer, nothing could effect a change in her sentiments, and assured that the resolution she had formed, dreadful as she knew it to be, was founded on justice and duty, she thought herself no longer justified in keeping her mother in a state of doubt and suspense from which it was in her power at once to free her. After a night therefore in which she revolved in her mind every idea which had before occurred, and every reasoning which gave[23] rise to her determination, she arose, without having even thought of sleep, pale, faint, and trembling, yet firm and decided in her purpose; and determined to make known to her mother in the course of the morning her obedience to her will. "Yes," she said, looking at the sun as it broke through the clouds into her apartment, "before that sun shall have reached its zenith, it shall behold me the obedient victim of my duty, and the very wretch its beams illumine: lost to friends – to all – outcast of every earthly hope!"

The wandering beggar as he journeys from door to door, and takes the scanty morsel, churlish plenty with threats and cruel chidings, grants at last to his prayers, enjoys a Paradise compared to the lot awaiting me; for he is free to wander where he will: the sun shines not on that country of which he is not lord, which he may not traverse: he may drink of the brook, lie down upon its banks, and arise refreshed, free, and happy: no

---

[23]Original has "give".

121

vow compels him to renounce home – country – friends! While I, a slave within the narrow precincts of those walls, never – never to be released,[24] shall linger out a miserable existence – a perpetual prisoner! O freedom! Liberty! Happy, happy those who are permitted to enjoy thy blessings! What others can they ask? Then falling on her knees, "Father of mercies," she said, "support thy feeble child! Give her fortitude to sustain the trial which it is thy will she should endure, for O, thy blessing can only make her equal to the conflict!" From this short prayer she arose greatly relieved, and sensible of a courage she had before believed impossible. While yet this lasted, she determined to hasten to her mother, to pronounce the awful mandate, and seal at once her fate.

Inspired by this newly-acquired though momentary resolution, she rather flew than ran downstairs; but when she reached the door of the room where she imagined her mother was, her spirits and strength forsook her – she walked back a few steps, leaned against the wall, and had neither power nor courage to advance. After a minute's pause, she again approached the door; again shuddered and drew back. At last she heard someone walking in the room: and dreading to see her whom she came to seek, she attempted to go again upstairs; but her knees tottered, and she found she was not able to walk. The door opened, and Agatha terrified, screamed aloud.

"Why Lord have mercy upon me! Miss," said Hannah, who now came towards her, "you have scarred me out of my wits. I had no notion of anybody's being up so soon as this, then I was just a dusting at the parlour as I heared your foot upon the stairs."

"My mother is not down then?" said Agatha, recovering.

"No, Miss – down? Why bless you it ben't six o'clock; and I should not have been about my work so arly myself, only I miscounted the clock. You seems but poorliesh, Miss, shall I get you a cup of anything?"

"If you will fetch me a little water I shall be obliged to you," said Agatha.

Hannah then ran for the water, and as soon as she returned with it, "Ah Miss," she said, "you may say what you will, but it's all along of these nasty abominable nun notions that makes you so badly; I'm sure I'd do anything to keep you from any manner of thing of that sort – seeing a body ought to do as they would be done by, you know; and I should be glad to sarve you in your private despondence with that gentleman or anybody else, if so be you wishes it will."

Agatha thanked her, and assuring her that the uneasiness she had remarked, proceeded from a cause with which she was totally unacquainted, went upstairs again with her assistance, and she sat in

---

[24]Original has "repassed".

her own room to wait the hour of Lady Belmont's rising. She took up a book, endeavouring to banish the remembrance of her situation, and to think no more of the dreaded consent she meant to give, till she was present with her mother, and the moment actually arrived. But though she read the words of the author, they conveyed no ideas to her mind; and she read the same page over and over again without being able to understand it. Looking at her watch she found it was now past eight, the hour when Lady Belmont usually came down to breakfast; she therefore left her room, more composed than she dared to hope, but endeavouring still as much as possible to avoid reflection.

She found Sir Charles and Lady Belmont both in the breakfast-room; and sat down with them to breakfast with tolerable composure. In about half an hour afterwards, Sir Charles left them to take a morning ride, and Lady Belmont remained alone with Agatha. Agatha looked at her mother for some time, opened her lips but the words died upon her tongue. Lady Belmont remarked her manner, and looking at her with tenderness, "Surely," she said, "my sweet girl has something she wishes to say to me?"

"O, I had," said Agatha, trembling violently.

"Speak then, my beloved child. Am I the happiest, most blest of mothers that ever drew breath, and my Agatha the noblest of women?"

"Yes," said Agatha, rising, folding her hands, and raising her eyes to heaven, "I do – I do devote myself to Heaven and you! This world, and all that it contains, here, from this moment, I renounce – forsake forever!"

She heard something fall, and, turning round, beheld Lady Belmont lifeless on the floor. Shocked and terrified, she attempted to raise her, but finding her efforts ineffectual, she rang the bell violently. A servant came. She desired him to dispatch someone in search of her father, and to send Mrs. Wildys and whomever else he first found to her instantly. Mrs. Wildys, Hannah, and another female servant came immediately; and with their assistance Agatha raised her mother, and laid her on a sofa. She then threw open all the windows and chafed her temples; but every-thing proved ineffectual, she sent another servant for Dr. Harley.

Sir Charles now returned; and soon after he came, Lady Belmont began to revive. She attempted to speak, but most of her words were unintelligible, and the few they could comprehend were incoherent. By degrees, however, her speech returned; but only to shock Sir Charles and Agatha by convincing them that her senses were totally gone.

"Where is my Agatha?" she screamed, "give me my child – my innocent, sacrificed lamb! See – she bleeds upon the altar!" Then bursting into a compulsive laugh, "No she does not," she said, "see Sir Charles, see my love, she is mounting to Heaven! Look at the white robe she wears, see the flowers – O, sweet flowers! And so she is dead? Well!

Heaven be praised! But 'twas I that murdered her – it was indeed – I put the knife into her heart, her very heart – but that knife had a key to it, and nobody can unlock that gate. O, no – she's fast forever." Then laughing dreadfully again, – "but you know she does get out when she dies."

Agatha in vain endeavoured to comfort her; "My dear mother," she said, "I am here – I am not dead – I shall live long I hope to do all, and everything you wish."

"You my daughter!" she returned, "no, wretch! She is not like you – she is an angel of light."

Dr. Harley, who was now arrived, advised them not speak to her, as all attempts to restore her reason would be vain for the present. He ordered her to be kept perfectly still, and giving her a composing draught, advised that all but two attendants should leave her: no entreaties, however, could prevail upon the Agatha to go, she therefore by his advice, went to a distant part of the room, removed from her sight.

Lady Belmont continued to rave during the whole of the day, and great part of the night following; towards morning she sunk into a sleep, from which she did not awake for fourteen hours; and when, at last, she awoke, though she spoke faintly, she appeared perfectly reasonable. She asked for her child. "I am here, my dear Madam," said Agatha.

"How came I in bed, at this time, my love?"

"You have been but poorly, you know; and we thought it better for you."

"Ill have I been? I have no remembrance of it, nor any recollection how I came here – but bless you, my sweet child, for the kind cares I am sure you lavished on me, while I was insensible of your tenderness."

In a few days Lady Belmont was perfectly recovered, and in the presence of Agatha, informed Sir Charles that her request was granted, and her child the noblest of human beings. Sir Charles appeared much affected, and folding Agatha in his arms, called her their angel.

"I have one request," said Agatha, "which your illness prevented my making to you that fatal morning; yet do not – do not refuse it me."

"Can my beloved Agatha entertain a doubt of my consent to whatever she shall propose?" said Lady Belmont, "No, unheard I promise to grant it."

"It is then," said Agatha, hesitating, "to see Mr. Hammond."

"To see Mr. Hammond! Good heavens!"

"To see Mr. Hammond!" repeated Sir Charles at the same instant.

"Yes, and why should you fear it? Is not the consent I have given you irrevocable? Yes, nothing shall call it back."

"But his entreaties, his artful insinuations," said Lady Belmont, "if they do not change your resolution, may make you submit to it with greater reluctance."

"Mr. Hammond is incapable of artifice; and a resolution built on the firm foundation of deliberate reason, no blast, however severe, has power to shake."

"Shall you then inform him of what has passed, of the life to which necessity has destined you?"

"Perhaps not – I cannot tell; yet to see him once again before I quit him forever is a consolation no duty forbids."

"You shall then, my Agatha. My child shall never think that what I could grant was denied her. But you will not object to your father or me, or both, perhaps, being present at the interview?"

"Yes, I must entreat, as the last favour I shall ever ask, that I may see him alone. Wherefore these doubts? I do not deserve them."

"Say no more – forgive them my Agatha! It shall be as you desire. And when would you wish him to come?"

"The day is immaterial," said Agatha, sighing deeply, "if I may know it beforehand?"

"Surely. We will ask him to come tomorrow: Sir Charles shall write immediately."

Sir Charles then wrote the following note which he gave to Agatha for her approbation.

Sir Charles and Lady Belmont send compliments to Mr. Hammond. As they are going very soon to leave England to make a long residence in France, they, as well as their daughter, from respect to his late much valued sister, will be happy to see him any time tomorrow, to take their leave of him previous to their departure.

The note was sent accordingly but Hammond being out at the time it arrived, no answer was returned that day.

Agatha spent a night of unspeakable anguish. The prospect of seeing Hammond, one moment buoyed up her sinking spirits, the next, the recollection that it was for the last time, plunged her again into misery beyond all she had ever felt before. She endeavoured to recollect everything she wished to say to him, and to arrange it in order: but something new every moment occurred and she fancied that if she were to indulge in saying all she wished, their conversation would never have an end. She wished that the interview had been delayed for some days, at least; not only that she might have had more time for reflection, but that the blessing might then have been all that time in expectation, and thus have cut off so many days of sorrow; for O, when it was passed, what a blank would be the rest of her existence! Dreadful to think that one day more, and this last, and only blessing would be gone – gone forever! The morning arrived, but from this last reflection she sickened at its appearance, and wished the hours prolonged which were to be the only ones that had a ray of hope to cheer them.

While she was dressing, Hannah came in with a look of much pleasure, to inform her, that the brownish gentleman, for she was sure it was he by John's description when he took him the letter the day before, had sent a servant already to inform her master that he would wait upon him at four o'clock. "And so, Miss," she said, "as Sir Charles sent word he should be glad to see him, it looks as if matters went on a little better. I don't so much wish it now," pursued Hannah, "but I did wish most mortally that my Lady might have kicked the bucket that time she was about it, and then, you know, Miss, you might have managed Sir Charles instead of her."

"Of whom do you speak in that manner?" said Agatha. "Never let me hear a disrespectful word of either of my parents: they are very good to me, and never wish to deny me anything in their power to grant."

"Nay, Miss," returned Hannah, "I don't see there was anything disinspectful in what I said; and as to a wife's managing her husband as they call it, it's what every woman would do if so be she could; and for the matter of that, men are much better to be managed, let 'em have an inch and they take an ell, as the saying is, and when once a body lets 'em have their own way, they never thinks they have enough of it, but gets as many whims and vagaries as dancing bears."

Hannah, imagining she heard her Lady's foot, now went away in haste, to Agatha's great relief, whose spirits were ill-calculated at that moment to endure her vulgar conversation; and she had more than once repented, that by consenting to receive and return a letter through her means, she had given her a licence to talk to her with a familiarity she would not otherwise have thought of assuming.

When she went down, Sir Charles informed her that Mr. Hammond had sent a verbal message to say he would be with them at four o'clock. "You will, therefore," he continued, "think of whatever you wished to say to your friend, whom, as the brother of Maria, I am not surprised you should wish to see."

Agatha, turning pale, and trembling, replied that she had endeavoured to think of everything.

"How long," said Lady Belmont, "shall you wish your conversation to continue, for I do not wish to interrupt you?"

"Heaven knows!" replied Agatha. "For pity's sake, my dear mother, do not distress me thus," then pausing and recollecting herself, "perhaps an hour or rather more," she said.

"Enough, enough, my love," said Lady Belmont, "I will not mention it again." After a minute's deliberation she continued, "Perhaps my Agatha repents of her intention; if so, it may, and shall yet be avoided.

To a feeling heart there is something painful in taking leave of the most indifferent person."

"O," replied Agatha, "it will be my last, my only comfort; think not that I can repent it. My mother's solemn word was given."

"I know it, my dear," replied Lady Belmont, "and was far from needing to retract. What I said sprang from regard to you and your feelings: had you had a common mind I should not have feared it for you; but I note the merest trifle affects you, and I wish to spare you unnecessary pain."

Lady Belmont now changed the conversation, and spoke of indifferent subjects. Agatha endeavoured to attend to her, but her mind wandered – she was absent and thoughtful – she did not shed a tear, but at intervals, though she strove by every effort in her power to suppress it, sighed as if her heart would break.

The wished yet dreaded hour, at length arrived. Before the dessert was removed, a servant announced Mr. Hammond. Sir Charles ordered the servant to show him into the library, and to inform him they would attend him immediately.

"Now then, Agatha," said Lady Belmont, "are you ready? Shall I go in with you, or go and speak to him first?"

Agatha trembled violently, and had neither power to move nor speak.

Sir Charles poured out a glass of water, and gave it to her; then after walking hastily up and down the room several times, he said angrily, as he approached her, "It was very silly to expose yourself to this uneasiness." Agatha now wept; and raising her hands and eyes to Heaven, "Thank God!" she said, "for these tears – I shall be better now. I thought my heart would have broken." Lady Belmont pressed her to her bosom, and wept over her. "Now, my dear girl," she said, while tears almost choked her utterance, "shall we go? – Or shall Sir Charles go to him first?"

"If she is well enough," said Sir Charles, "I think she had better go. Come, my dear," continued he, taking her hand with some tenderness, "endeavour to recover your spirits: you have a heroic soul in spite of these womanish feelings."

"She has," said Lady Belmont, "she is every way an angel; and if ever one human creature idolised another I do her. I look up to her as to a being of superior order. Come, my sweet girl," she continued, kissing off her tears, "no more of this: such weakness might fit well on an ordinary character, but does not become my Agatha."

Agatha now rose, and without daring to trust herself to speak, leaned on her mother's arm, and 'with fainting step and slow,' went with her out of the room. When she had almost reached the door of the library, she stopped, shuddered, and was unable to proceed.

"Come, my love," said Lady Belmont, "resume your courage: remember who you are."

"O Madam!" said Agatha "pray, pray for me, and pity me."

"My Agatha," said Lady Belmont sobbing, "for you before myself, before my husband, I am bound to pray. I more than love or pity, I adore you! Be comforted then my sweet child."

Agatha now made an effort to resume her courage, and opened herself the door.

Hammond, who had been walking up and down the room, on hearing the door opened, turned round with a countenance of agony and terror, yet mingled with a look of momentary joy at the sight of Agatha. He flew to meet her, and taking her hand, pressed it to his lips. "My Agatha," he said, "and do I – do I see you!"

"Mr. Hammond!" said Agatha, her voice faint and faltering, "Heaven preserve you!"

Hammond, unable to bear the sound of that voice, on the accents of which he had delightedly[25] hung in happier days, now tremulous and every tone expressive of sorrow, sunk upon a sofa, then putting his hands before his face, hid the tears which flowed down his manly cheeks.

Agatha, in his sufferings once again forgetting her own, went towards him, and taking hold of his arm, "Mr. Hammond – my dear – my best friend –" she said, "recover yourself. Think where you are – whom you are come to see. Be comforted for pity's sake, for my sake."

Hammond let fall his hands, and gazing wistfully on her face, "O Agatha! Is it come to this? Do we meet to part forever?"

"No Hammond – not forever!"

"Say that again, thou Angel! And I will worship thee!"

"No, we shall meet again in a world where no duty forbids me to love thee; where we shall never part more, and enjoy an Eternity of bliss together!"

"O Agatha! What, never to meet till that sweet frame has sunk into dust, till those eyes are closed for ever, and that voice – O Agatha!"

"It is but a few short years, my Hammond! It is but enduring a little sorrow."

"A little sorrow!"

"No, I meant not so – it will indeed be dreadful; but then its continuance will be short. Every day draws us nearer to our end – every clock that strikes shall tell us we are one hour nearer to felicity."

Lady Belmont, unable to bear this, went out of the room, in an agony not to be described.

---

[25]Original has "delighted".

"But now, my dear friend, my kind Hammond," said Agatha, "let us assume a little composure, nor waste this precious hour in unavailing tears. I have much to say to you, had more, but my memory fails me."

"I will my love, my angel! I will be composed: speak, and on those sweet accents let me hang forever."

"A necessity as fatal as it is unavoidable obliges my parents to take me to France; there to live perhaps forever."

"But what is country, my Agatha! O, let them fly to the most desolate spot on earth, and I will follow thee, and live upon thy smiles."

"No, my Hammond, that must not be. They forbid me to think of you."

"And canst thou forget me, Agatha?"

"Never while life remains will Agatha forget thee; but I must remember thee but as a friend – as that, dearer than life, and all that it could give, you will ever be."

"O, Agatha! And shall another? – I cannot speak it –"

"Never Hammond. No other shall ever call me by a dearer name: of this rest assured. I never did, never will love anyone but you; nor will it be demanded; but a necessity, dreadful and inviolable compels me to denounce thee in every other but the dear light of a friend – as that, no duty can forbid me to think of you; and that is surely a blessing! Remember those happy days when you were only a friend to me – remember how dear was that title to you then."

"O days of bliss, never, never to return!" said Hammond, relapsing into his former agony.

"Once more, my Hammond," said Agatha, "let me conjure you not to lose these precious minutes. I have a favour to ask at your hands. Promise, promise to grant it."

"O bid me do anything but leave thee!"

"I would, indeed, that were never to be! But since it is the will of Heaven we must submit, my Hammond; and that Heaven which sees and enjoins will reward our obedience. What I implore of you, is, for my sake to be happy. Shut out myself from happiness I could yet enjoy it in you. Think, Hammond, and remember that every hour of comfort you experience will be reflected on me. When we are far apart, and the friends who adore you, the society you adorn, shall strive to enliven you, resist not their influence, shut not your heart to their endeavours: say rather, my Agatha claims it, and I will be happy. Something whispers me that you can never know a joy but my heart will share it with you, will vibrate with sympathetic pleasure. Think of this."

"Thou angel!" said Hammond. "But now hear me. You say, my Agatha says that I shall still call her friend; shall I not then, dare I not hope to see you? Were it but once a year, I would live upon those dear moments, and all the rest should seem as nothing."

"No Hammond, we must not, must not meet: dreadful to think!" Then turning from him in speechless agony, she seemed for some moments lost to recollection.

"Once again hear me, my angel," said Hammond. "Is it not, O, is it not barbarous in your parents to condemn us to this misery! Why, O, why should it be given to one human being to rule another with a rod of iron! No just reason can bid them to tear our hearts asunder. My fortune, my birth, though below theirs, are not contemptible; and I have so studied to live that I know not an enemy. What then should divide us! Can any duty compel us to submit to the decrees of caprice and tyranny?"

"I will not deceive you. Nothing but a vow made to her own parent at the point of death, could have induced my mother to deny me that happiness she would glory to bestow. But that vow which forbad her child to marry, invoked at the same time, the most dreadful curses on herself in case of its violation."

"Merciful God! And shall my Agatha be its victim? And what – for mercy's sake, unfold all – what could induce a mother to exact such a vow?"

"A crime of which she had herself been guilty, and for which she conceived this an atonement. More I dare not reveal, and I conjure you not to ask it.

"And can a vow like this be binding, extorted perhaps in a moment of delirium, and made, when the mind, distracted by grief, is not mistress of itself – its reason?"

"Heaven only knows how far a vow thus made is binding! But the curses my unhappy mother imprecated on herself, I dare not draw down upon her head: no Hammond, though one dearer than life be forfeited by my obedience!"

"But O, then my Agatha, though all other hopes be denied us, we may yet meet, yet live as friends, forbid to call each other by a tenderer name – this still shall bless us; from friendship sprang our love, and to that sweet – that sacred source it shall return."

"It shall, my Hammond: but to meet is – O, it is impossible!"

"Impossible! Gracious Heaven! What vow forbids?"

"O Hammond, seek to know no further – I dare not – cannot say – but we must not meet."

"Distraction! Misery! O Agatha! That I had never lived to see this day – that the death which menaced my early years had not been withheld! That in the grave, where only I can hope for peace, I were now laid forever!"

"My Hammond, speak not thus. Let us, O let us arm ourselves with fortitude. God Almighty sees our distress, his ears are open to our prayers, and he will not permit us to suffer beyond that we are able to bear. The meanest[26] wretch that crawls upon the earth, knows not a misery beyond what I have endured for some dreadful weeks – yet while torn by a thousand conflicting sufferings, I have found consolation in religion. For you I will never cease to pray – no, Hammond, the last word these lips shall utter shall be your name!"

Sir Charles now came in, and, addressing Hammond with cold politeness, began to speak of ordinary subjects; but Hammond was unable to reply to him beyond a mere assent to whatever he said. After some minutes thus passed, Sir Charles turned to Agatha, and said, "your mother wants you Agatha." She turned pale as death, and as she offered to rise, sunk again into her chair. Hammond took her hand, but could not speak.

"I am sorry it so happens, Sir," said Sir Charles, "but unexpected business will engage me for the rest of the evening; had not that been the case, I should have been happy to have had the pleasure of your company longer. Agatha, my dear, I do not know if you heard me?"

Agatha now rose, and turning to Hammond, sunk into his arms. "God bless you," she at last said, "God ever bless you – preserve you – comfort you!" Hammond kissed her in speechless anguish. Faint and trembling, she again offered to go, but Hammond again took her hand, and again she turned back and looked at him with unutterable anguish. Blessings, blessings light on thee! He now strove to say, but his voice failed, and his words were scarcely audible.

Sir Charles now took the hand Hammond held, and leading Agatha out of the room conveyed her almost lifeless to her mother, leaving Hammond in an agony little short of distraction.

---

[26]Original has "veriest".

Chapter 2

Lady Belmont, who after the moving scene she had witnessed, had retired to her room, regardless of Sir Charles's efforts to console her, now rose from the chair into which she had thrown herself, and as Agatha approached, held open her arms to receive her; Agatha sunk into them, and sobbed upon her bosom. When the first tumult of grief had subsided, Lady Belmont strove by every expression pity and maternal tenderness could suggest, to soothe the distresses she would have died to alleviate. "O, my Agatha!" she at last exclaimed, "would to Heaven this tongue had forgotten its office, ere it was bid to pronounce that fatal decree! How barbarous to condemn my innocent child to sufferings which all my tenderness can never mitigate! I now feel I ought to have died rather than to have uttered those cruel words."

"Do not thus accuse yourself, my dearest mother," said Agatha, endeavouring to recover herself and to speak peace to the wounded bosom of her self-condemning parent. "Those only who have been in that dreadful situation, who have heard a parent's dying request, can know how hard it were to resist it. Who could have acted otherwise? And O, be not distressed for me – the worst is over now."

"O Agatha! How should I have glorified in granting every wish of your heart; how delighted to unite you to one you seem born to love! But from this moment I will no more seek to influence or control you. In your reason, your better judgment I confide: if you should yet think my vow can be dispensed with, I am ready, I am willing to submit to your decision, whatever be the consequence."

"O tempt me not," replied Agatha, "to abandon the duty I have bound myself to fulfil. Now," continued she, firmly, "that determination which every suggestion of reason, every hour of deliberate reflection, served only to confirm, sufferings, greater if possible than these, shall never subdue."

"Noblest of all human beings!" said Lady Belmont, "how, every moment, do you rise in my estimation! Come to my arms, angelic girl! And if the constant and unwearied endeavours of my whole life can lessen the pains and increase the comforts of yours, doubt not that you shall receive them. I will have no thought, no wish but your happiness, and art and nature shall be ransacked to give you but a moment's pleasure."

Nearly two hours were passed in this manner; Lady Belmont one minute endeavouring to comfort Agatha and soothe her sorrows, the next expressing the veneration her conduct inspired. At last, faint and dejected, they left the room, and were proceeding to the library, where they usually drank tea; but Agatha stopped at the door, and by a look which expressed more than words, told her mother that she had not courage to enter. Lady Belmont but too well comprehended its meaning, and turning to the dining room, said, "On recollection it will be cooler here, and we will order tea in this room." – Sir Charles had left word that he was gone out on business, and they did not see him till very late in the evening; when he returned, his spirits appeared little less depressed than those of Lady Belmont and Agatha, and unable to support a conversation, they retired soon after to rest.

Agatha had passed several nights without sleep; but nature, long harassed, was at length exhausted, and, though more unhappy than she had ever yet been, she sunk into a sweet and refreshing slumber, from which she did not wake till late in the morning. She blessed heaven for this temporary cessation of suffering; and though she awoke with a confused sensation of regret and uneasiness, she felt, by degrees, more calm and resigned than she had yet done.

After some days, her grief settled into a kind of patient melancholy. When Lady Belmont, forgetting her own distress, strove to console and enliven her, she received her tender attentions with the most endearing gratitude; and would even sometimes force herself to smile – but it was the smile of dejection, and faint and cheerless as the momentary glimmerings of the just-expiring taper.

Lady Belmont, by degrees, ventured to introduce the subject of their departure from England, and spoke of the country they were in future to inhabit. Agatha listened to her without emotion or apparent uneasiness: she was resigned to her fate, and looked forward to its completion with melancholy composure. A long continuance of sorrow blunts, for a time, at least, the edge of our sensibility.

"We have searched," Lady Belmont one day said to Agatha, "almost every province in France, to discover a situation the romantic beauties of which might diminish the pain of a continued residence in it, and in quest of a society as free as possible from every monastic austerity. The lady under whose care you will be placed is of noble birth, and refined manners: the world contains few more deserving the friendship and confidence of my Agatha. You will not be wholly separated from us: we have purchased an estate less than a mile distant from my Agatha's residence; and not a day shall pass in which we will not enjoy some hours of her society." Agatha enquired the name of the place and the province. "It is," replied Lady Belmont, "about two miles from Issoire in the province of Auvergne; a country and climate infinitely surpassing what your ideas can form, from having lived only here. Nature produces spontaneously the most delicious grapes, and other fruits in equal perfection; and did the industry of the inhabitants keep pace with the fertility of their soil, there is not a comfort or luxury which they might not enjoy. But nature seems to have ordained, that in every country the industry of the people shall be in exact proportion to the necessity they are under to exert it; and when the earth gives her treasures without culture, man is too indolent to court an increase of her favours.

The time for their departure was at length fixed; and now it was, that Agatha's sensibility returned, and with it brought a sad renewal of all her former anguish. She gazed with avidity on every spot of ground, on the very walls around her, soon to be quitted forever – and quitted for what? A perpetual prison!

Lady Belmont would not suffer her to take part in the preparations for their departure, but gave herself every direction to the servants: Mrs. Wildys and three other maids, with two men servants being all who were to accompany them; the rest of their household was to be hired in France. Hannah was not in the number of those who were to go with them; she told her Lady that she could not think of leaving her naked country for nobody; and she could not help hinting as she was no longer afraid of giving offence, and was desirous of showing her own sagacity and discernment, that she was afraid they might choose to make a nun of her.

The dreaded day now arrived. It was on the 25th September 1788. Agatha, to whom that agony of her mind acted like the false and temporary strength occasioned by fever, left not a room, a walk, a spot of ground untraversed. She took a little earth from the garden, kissed it, and put it into a little box. This, she said, shall be my darling treasure, a consolation when all others are denied me. Perhaps on this very dust Maria's feet have trod. Perhaps in those happy days when I leaned on her arm, and learned the lessons of virtue from her lips, while my heart expanded with hope and youthful pleasure, perhaps on this dear earth she stood. Perhaps – poor, poor Hammond – perhaps, with bleeding-heart he wandered over it! Come then to my bosom dear remnant of my native soil and country: speak for its yet dear inhabitants, and be my companion and comforter in their stead. She then went to her own little library, and kissed the walls – the table. Here it was, she said, in infant years my little toys were laid. Here it was my mother would sit and take me on her knee, and reward at night the dear labours of the morning. Here too Maria's voice yet seems to vibrate in my ear: O, sounds of pleasure, of delight, never, never to be heard again. Here she would sit – here, in this very spot – here did we read – here work together. O, had she lived to see this day, her heart would have broken. Blessed be the mercy of Heaven that took her hence and spared her gentle breast the conflict!

She now visited the library below. Here, here it was, she said, my Hammond sat: my Hammond; no, never to be mine! On this sofa he sat.

And how he looked at me! How kind! As if he only thought of me, only wept for my sorrows! And so he did. O, he has a heart that would not leave a sorrow in the world if he could rule! Heaven bless – bless him for it! And here, O dreadful spot, I saw him for the last, last time! O, that look! Never shall I forget it – I feel it now! Then screaming she ran into Lady Belmont's arms, who came in search of her, almost deprived of sense and life.

In this state she was rather carried than led to the carriage which waited for them at the door, and after she was put in it fainted away. The moment she began to revive, not daring to stay for fear of a relapse on beholding once more objects so dear to her, they ordered the chaise to drive on, and before she was perfectly sensible, or able to look around her, they were many miles from their abode.

She had no sooner recovered her recollection than, unconscious how far they had gone, she leaned out of the window, in hopes of catching one other view of some object she had been accustomed to see. There was one clump of trees, which, being in an elevated situation, was visible for more than two miles around. She looked for them, but was unable to discover them, and the road in which they now were, being new to her, she was soon but too certain how far she was removed from a spot which was infinitely dearer to her than till this day she had every imagined, and where all her hopes and affections seemed now centred.

The face of nature was little in unison with her feelings. Everything smiled around. The sun shining with unusual splendour, gilded the yellow leaves with which autumn had intermixed the foliage of every tree. They passed a cheerful group, who, resting from their labour, were refreshing themselves in the shade with their frugal repast. Ruddy health glowed on their cheeks, contentment sat on their brows, and the coarse and hearty laugh was heard as they passed them. Happy, happy peasants, thought Agatha, and free as happy! My heart is not yet so hardened by its own sorrows as to take no share in your joys: long may they be preserved to you! O did ye know the distresses of those stations which at some moments ye may be blind enough to envy, how would ye exalt in your own!

The variety of objects insensibly dissipated from Agatha's mind, in some degree, the remembrance of her situation. She now began to look around her, and, peace being banished her own breast, to seek it in the countenances of others, or lose in the contemplation of the beauties of nature the sad recollection of the griefs she had known, and those which yet awaited her.

Their journey presented nothing remarkable; and they arrived at Dover in three days without any circumstance having occurred worth noting.

The moment of Agatha's quitting Dover, of leaving her country forever, was another of those marked with peculiar misery. There is something in the name of our own, our native country, endearing to every heart, and conveying a thousand fond remembrances to the mind: or why is banishment so dreadful when the other lands are open to receive us, others, perhaps, which present to the eye numberless superior beauties, and afford the comforts and luxuries of life in greater abundance? But no other blessing can atone for a separation from that soil on which our infant feet have trod, that air where first we drew our breath.

Their passage from Dover was, like their journey to it, unmarked by any peculiar event; and they arrived safely at Calais, where the novelty of the scene again banished, in some measure, the remembrance of Agatha's sorrows. They remained one day at Calais, and from thence proceeded southward by easy stages, passing some hours in every place through which they passed which presented anything curious to the traveller; and arrived at Issoire during the second week in October.

The estate Sir Charles had purchased had every advantage of situation to recommend it; and Agatha turning to Lady Belmont, said as they were admiring the various beauties around them, "O, had this been my destined abode, how – how happy were I yet? Yes, though divided from my country and friends, still to be under one roof with my parents, bound by no dreadful vow."

"Would to Heaven it were so, my sweet girl," said Lady Belmont, "yet in idea only is that vow dreadful; and trust me the beauties of this scene fall infinitely short of those of the charming spot which is destined to be your residence: art and nature have combined to render it delightful."

Agatha sighed deeply; and Lady Belmont pressed her to her bosom with unutterable tenderness.

Several days passed, and Lady Belmont made no proposal of visiting the convent. Agatha trembled whenever she spoke, lest the dreadful subject should be mentioned; and blessed even these joyless days, and sighed as every hour of them passed, since these were yet days of freedom, though marked with sorrow and fear.

Lady Belmont, accompanied by Agatha, walked every day to different parts of the country; frequently to the distance of several miles. In one of these rambles Lady Belmont complained of feeling fatigued, and proposed to Agatha to return by a nearer road; they accordingly turned from the path, and proceeded straight through a small wood. Just as they had reached the end of it, Lady Belmont sat down, and confessed she was unable to proceed farther. Agatha alarmed and uneasy enquired if she knew of any habitation near them. "I do not," replied Lady Belmont, "unless the large gate I observe through those trees should lead to one." Agatha looked, and discovering a very high wall to which there was a large iron gate, said she imagined that they were near the garden of some nobleman. "It may be the Marquis de Blevarde's," said Lady Belmont; "he has an estate near Issoire; and since hospitality is nowhere more practiced than among the French nobles, I will venture to try if one of the keys belonging to our own gate, which I recollect having with me, will open this."

She now attempted it, and the key unlocked it without the least difficulty. They had no sooner opened the gate, than another of the same size and materials presented itself. Lady Belmont again searched her pocket, and found a key somewhat smaller which unlocked that with equal ease.

"Good God!" said Agatha, shuddering as they opened the second gate, "if it should be –"

"Should be what, my love?" said Lady Belmont.

"O, I cannot speak it. Pity me – hold me – let them not tear me from you!"

"Why this alarm, my love? If this should belong to the Marquis, what injury can you possibly suppose?"

"O, but if it does not; if it is that dreadful place – yet you have seen it, and must know."

Lady Belmont turned from Agatha to conceal her emotion; and now, taking the precaution of locking the gates again, she took her hand and led her along the winding walk through a beautiful grove the trees of which grew in some parts thick and were impervious to the sun, and in others, planted thinner, admitted its setting beams through their foliage, or sprinkling, as it were, with light the path before them. Among the trees a small clear stream meandered over pebbles, which here and there was brought to wind across the path, and one rustic arch led them over it. As they proceeded further, the trees became gradually thicker, till, by transition as momentary as it was delightful, they opened on a beautiful semi-circular lawn. Seats formed of green turf, and canopied with flowers and fruits, were ranged within the crescent. Turning round, they saw, opposite to the seats, a long vista terminated by a superb temple. Attracted by its beauty they proceeded along the vista, and now discovered that the temple stood on an island, surrounded by a small lake; a boat with sails painted in lively colours floated on the water, and added to the gaiety of the scene. Observing a rising ground on one side of them, Lady Belmont proposed to ascend it, as they might have a view of the house from thence, and by that means discover which road they ought to pursue to lead them to it. They accordingly ascended it, and Agatha remarked with surprise that Lady Belmont had entirely forgotten the weariness of which she had complained. From the top of the eminence they looked around them, and saw, on one side Mount Dor, its lofty summit appearing buried in the clouds, and on another the town and lake of Issoire, as the evening sun gilded the summits of the houses. "O," said Agatha, "all ideas I could have formed of romantic scenery fall short of this, and did not something strike like death itself to my heart, I could never be weary of contemplating it."

Lady Belmont made no reply, but pressing her to her bosom, called her her beloved daughter. They now descended the way they came, and having yet seen no appearance of a habitation, Lady Belmont proposed to return back through the vista to the grove, and thence to the gates by which they entered; but the moment they had reached the grove, and were entering the impenetrable gloom of that part which opened onto the lawn, they heard the sound of a bell at a little distance. Agatha started and turned pale.

"Why this alarm, my love?" said Lady Belmont.

"It is – it is too true, and that bell rings to Vespers." Then holding Lady Belmont, she looked around her in wildness and terror.

"My dear girl," said Lady Belmont, "you equally shock and terrify me; be more composed or what will become of me?"

"O, tell me the truth, and I will strive to bear it! But deceive me not thus, nor keep me in a suspense more dreadful, if possible, than the reality. Is this indeed the convent?"

"Hear me, my darling Agatha. Be composed, I conjure you, and hear me. I wished to spare my sweet girl the pain of a formal introduction to a place, which, seen with other ideas, could not fail to charm; I wish to leave you to admire the loveliest scene in nature before I told you to whom it belonged: your fears anticipated the discovery, and eluded my intentions."

"Just Heaven," said Agatha, falling on her knees, "thy will be done. O, look down upon me, and support me in these awful moments!"

Then rising and looking around her, "this then," she said, "is the boundary of my existence: tenant of this scene till death. Yes, these trees, which now, for the first time, I have beheld, day after day, year after year, in unvaried succession I shall contemplate; lost to that world I shall have sworn to renounce."

"My beloved Agatha," said Lady Belmont, "would to Heaven it were my lot to forsake it for you – with what transport –"

"Heaven forbid!" replied Agatha, "No, I would not purchase a moment's pleasure or exemption from pain at the expense of anyone, how then at that of my mother; so kind a parent, so dear a friend! At this moment, my spirits and strength seem renewed; now, while they last, lead me forward to –"

"To the house, my love?"

"If you please," said Agatha, trembling violently, yet studying for composure.

"This way then, my Agatha; it is on the other side of the grove."

Agatha leaned on Lady Belmont, unable to walk without support. Now, for a moment she stopped, wanting courage to proceed; and now again walked with hasty steps, the sooner to terminate the trial. Passing by the iron gate, they proceeded a small distance farther to the other side of it, where the grove terminated in a lawn, in which the convent, and, adjoining it, the chapel stood. The building, which was spacious and lofty, was of Gothic structure. The stone in many parts was overgrown with moss and in all the hand of time had left its traces. The female choir were performing Vespers as they approached; and as the harmony of their voices joined to the pealing notes of the organ struck their ear the moment they were passed the grove, it seemed as if Heaven itself were opening on them. Agatha stopped; and in the mingled transport and devotion it inspired, forgot, for a moment, both her terror and distress, and raised her eyes and hands to Heaven in speechless ecstasy.

"Shall we proceed my love," said Lady Belmont, "or shall we remain longer to enjoy these seraphic sounds?"

"We will go on if you please," said Agatha faintly.

They now approached the building: a Gothic door, under a portico overgrown with ivy, was the entrance. Lady Belmont recollected that they could not enter till the service was concluded. This delay proved fatal to Agatha. The courage she had assumed, and which was renewed by the rapturous harmony she had heard, forsook her by degrees, till at last as she heard footsteps within, and someone unbar the door, she fainted.

When she revived, she found herself in Lady Belmont's arms, in a small room, furnished like an English parlour, and a lady, in a long white veil, tall, elegant, and of a figure at once majestic and interesting, using different applications to recover her, and in the most tender manner studying to console Lady Belmont. As Agatha revived, she addressed her in a tone of equal affection and respect, and with the soothing tenderness of a mother, enquired if she was better: then turning to a beautiful young woman in the habit of a nun, "Sister Agnes," she said, "if, now this sweet lady is rather better and able to swallow them, were we to give her some drops of our distilled herbs, I think it would revive her." The beautiful nun brought them instantly, and Agatha felt almost immediate relief from the medicine.

Lady Belmont now said, "I must introduce my Agatha to this excellent Lady as to a second mother; it is, my Agatha, Madame the Marchioness de St. Clermont, who as abbess of this sisterhood has retired voluntarily to devote herself to Heaven."

"Happy, indeed, shall I think myself," said Madame de St. Clermont, "if this Lady should ever regard me as a mother; it shall be my constant study to deserve her friendship."

"Suffer me to introduce to you," continued Madame St. Clermont, "our beloved Sister Agnes. She was a daughter of the late Count de Vermueil, and is a valuable member of our little community."

Agatha, whom the countenance of the lovely Sister Agnes had interested the moment she saw her, held out her hand to her on this introduction, and amidst the depression which yet sunk her heart, felt secretly grateful that among the few with whom she was hereafter to associate, there were two whose appearance spoke so warmly in their favour.

But Agatha with a heart exquisitely tender, was blessed with that sweet disposition of mind which seeks rather to draw good from the evil, than evil from good. If in the thorny paths of adversity one comfort raised its kindly head, she saw and cherished it, nor disregarded its sweets on account of the baleful weeds by which she was surrounded; and if every rose had its thorn, and every joy its allay of sorrow, or in the fragrance of the flower she endeavoured to forget its prickles, in gratitude for the blessing, to lose sight of its attendant uneasiness.

Lady Belmont mentioned the temple, the beauty of which had struck them greatly.

"That temple," said Madame St. Clermont, "is a source of much innocent pleasure to us; and, in order to render its influence the greater, it is never visited but on particular occasions; on festivals instituted in honour of the virtuous actions of the father, mother, brother, or sister of one of our society, or on account of any benevolent or charitable deed which in our confined sphere we have been so fortunate as to perform. A few days before that destined for visiting the temple, such of the community as choose it, write a few lines of poetry on moral or religious, and sometimes on sprightly subjects, which are given to me to deposit in a vase in the temple, according to a custom which an English traveller who visited our convent informed me was practised in a villa near Bath in England. On the day appointed we all proceed to the temple where there are fruits and sweetmeats set ready, and after refreshment the vase is opened and the verses read, and a trifling prize, such as a work box or any other becoming our situation, is bestowed on the successful candidate."

Lady Belmont now spoke of the semi-circular lawn, and dwelt on the beauties of the seats around it.

"That lawn," replied the Lady Abbess, "is our theatre; and opposite to those seats some of the sisters perform such little theatrical pieces as I find unexceptionable. The seats you admire are themselves the reward of industry. The flower garden you probably did not see, since that is separated from the rest. Everyone has a small part of it allotted to her care, and on a stated day the flowers are produced, and the sister who can display the most beautiful collection receives one of those seats as a reward; the one who has possessed hers the longest resigning it to her: and in those they work, read, play on the guitar, or drink tea occasionally."

"Thus even in solitude," said Lady Belmont, "you enjoy some of the vaunted pleasures of the world; and for a few which are denied you, you are amply repaid by an exemption from the cares and uneasiness attendant on them. Honours, riches, and beauty, the most valued of worldly advantages, besides their precarious duration, subject us to envy, and sharpen the arrows of detraction."

"We come not hither," said Madame St. Clermont, "in quest of earthly but of Heavenly joys. To do the will of God is our supreme delight. But as his mercy forbids not some sweetness of this existence, some cessation of that worship which would expire or grow languid if it knew no intermission, we study to pursue those recreations which we deem the most innocent; nor do we seek even these purely for their own sakes, but chiefly to enable us to return with redoubled ardour and satisfaction to that devotion which is not more our duty than delight."

Agatha grew insensibly more tranquil; she found the conversation of Madame St. Clermont every moment more interesting, as every moment displayed some new proof of the goodness of her heart, and of her warm yet unaffected piety. After they had continued in conversation for nearly two hours, a sister informed Lady Belmont that her carriage waited.

"Sir Charles," said Lady Belmont turning to Agatha, "knew whither I purposed to come, and sent it to my request." Agatha, pale and trembling, uncertain whether it was intended that she should remain at the convent, or return for the present, looked at Lady Belmont with a countenance of supplication and fear.

"Why that look, my love?" said Lady Belmont. "Surely you did not imagine that as I brought you hither by surprise I meant to leave you in the same manner. No, you shall fix your own time, make every preparation you wish, and not depart from my house for months, unless you desire it."

"Nor could I consent," said Madame St. Claremont, "to receive Miss Belmont thus; and now nor ever must she join our society unless she feels the same pleasure on entering it that we should have in receiving her. The life I have myself chosen I am far from recommending to others, unless they feel the same predilection for it which I have done. When next I enjoy some hours of your society we will speak of the penances enjoined, as we have now done of the indulgences allowed us: for I never consent to receive anyone till they have a previous knowledge of every rigid rule necessarily attendant on our state."

Chapter 3

In order to familiarise Agatha to the scene and society of the convent, Lady Belmont attended her thither almost every day, and spent some hours in conversation with Madame St. Clermont, who described to Agatha, as she had promised, the austerities they obliged themselves to practice; their cells, where no indulgence or luxury could be allowed them, their fasts, and the service of Matins, which compelled them to rise at midnight to attend the service in the choir, and which nothing but severe illness could dispense with. Agatha heard her with little emotion: the distress of quitting her friends, her lover, her parents, her home, her country, absorbed every other idea, and would have rendered her callous to penances far more severe than any of those Madame St. Clermont described. Alas, she thought, what are these hardships to a heart that bleeds with keener anguish? Could a bed of down afford me ease? Alas, no – I wake to misery, and dream but of horrors in all the luxury of my chamber – can my cold cell add to the terrors of my sleeping or my waking thoughts? And when I rise at midnight to offer prayers to him who only can give me peace, shall I not return to my bed tranquil and revived? – Yes, a mind at peace perhaps might shudder to contemplate the austerities here practised: to me they are as nothing.

Agatha was introduced to all the nuns in turns; but except the lovely Sister Agnes, whom she had first seen, and Sister Frances, a young nun, whose vivacity amused her when she had spirits to bear it, there was no one whose society appeared to merit a distinction from the rest.

Lady Belmont always accompanied Agatha to the convent, nor ever left her while there. One day, however, Madame St. Clermont seized an opportunity of speaking to Agatha alone, as a message from Sir Charles called Lady Belmont out of the parlour. "I have watched for this opportunity, my sweet lady," said Madame St. Clermont, "ever since the first moment I saw you, when your distress and terror convinced me you did not make a voluntary choice of the life for which you are intended. Confess the truth: do you not feel repugnance to the veil, or a desire to continue in the world? Do you not leave behind you someone whose image when your soul should mount to Heaven, will call it back to earth? – Speak, my charming friend; fear not to answer me, and if it be as I suspect, every persuasion in my power should be attempted to turn your parents from their purpose."

"Alas," said Agatha, "I know not if I ought to disclose the reasons which compel me to embrace a life which I have always contemplated with dread. Duty and necessity have obliged my parents to choose for me, and me to consent to what otherwise neither they nor I should have desired. The reasons, I dare not, without my mother's permission, reveal; but I will endeavour to obtain it, and the gratitude this kindness inspires shall never be forgotten."

"Speak not of that, my sweet friend," returned Madame St. Clermont; "the service I offer you is no more than I think myself bound to perform; and there are many whom I have been so fortunate as to restore to the world they wished not to renounce. But to one question you did not reply. Are you sure there is no one dearer than the rest?"

"Ah," said Agatha, "there is indeed! But time and my unremitting endeavours, when my vow shall have made it a duty, will I trust, enable me – not to forget him, for that can never be, but to remember him only as Heaven itself shall authorise. I will consider myself dead to him and all the world, yet will pray for his happiness here and hereafter. There will be no crime in that: think you there will? For more I could not do!"

"Come to my heart, sweet lady!" said Madame St. Clermont. "No, in thus regarding him there can be no crime. Yet have a care that this idea obtrudes not itself on your devotions, except at the moment in which you pray for him with others who claim your prayers. Remember you will be the spouse of God, and not even a parent must wean your affections from him."

Lady Belmont now returned, and Agatha attended her home. She informed her, in part, of the questions Madame St. Clermont had put to her, and asked her permission to inform her of the vow by which she was bound. Lady Belmont consented, and suffered her to go unattended by herself to the convent. She informed Madam Saint Clermont of the fatal vow, and its occasion, with every particular concerning herself, and the unfortunate attachment which made the world thus dear to her. Madame St. Clermont heard her with tears; and when she had concluded the recital, "hard indeed," she said, "has been your fate: innocent victim of the guilt of your mother's mother. Yet how could she imagine that to dedicate her child or her child's child to Heaven, could expiate her own offence! She ought to have retired herself to a monastery, thereby the most rigid penance have sought to atone for a crime whose punishment she wished rather to cast on others. I say punishment; for where the heart prompts not its adoption, the life of a nun is that of punishment; where it does, it is a life of reward and blessings. Cruel as it is, I dare not advise the breach of that vow. Your own conscience, my dearest lady, is your guide, and that you will obey. Had Lady Belmont chanced to have adopted a different method, had she educated you among us, you would insensibly have loved the life you now dread, we should have been endeared to you from infancy, and you would have been spared the pangs your unfortunate introduction to society has given you. But she was guided by maternal affection, and in this state of darkness and imperfection, it is not permitted us to see into futurity; our longest and apparently best-concerted plans, are defeated by a thousand inevitable and unexpected events. Yet, if all the tender cares of friendship, all the affection of a heart that shares your distress and bleeds for it at every pore, can heal your sorrows, believe it, sweet lady, they shall be healed." Agatha with tears expressed her gratitude; and Madame St. Clermont's affectionate attentions endeared her to her every day more and more, till she never met her but with sensations of pleasure, nor left her without regret.

When rather more than a month had passed, Agatha, sensible that the fatal day, however delayed, must arrive at last, after a painful and severe struggle, introduced the fatal subject, and proposed to Lady Belmont the commencement of her year of probation. She heard her with tears of regret and tenderness; and with anguish yet greater than her own, looked forward to the day fixed for her departure. Agatha watched her mother's countenance, she saw her distress, and strove to alleviate it by feigning a serenity foreign to her heart. She would retire to weep, and return to smile. She expatiated with sweet deception on the influence the various beauties of the garden had already over her mind and spirits. She would then speak (and here her praise was unaffected) of the charms of Madame St. Clermont's conversation and that of sweet Sister Agnes. In the first emotions of grief, she would say, I did not conceive that I could have felt so tranquil; but till a trouble arrives, we know not how easily it may be endured, nor what blessings may be reserved to mingle with it, and lessen our affliction.

The fatal day too soon arrived; and Agatha, whose sufferings no effort could now conquer or conceal, gazed wistfully on every object around her, soon to be seen no more.

"My sacrificed innocent," said Lady Belmont, whose feelings almost overpowered her reason, "Yes – I have murdered thee – for I have stabbed thy peace, and what is life without it!" then kneeling to Agatha, she said, "Do not – O, do not curse me! Yet if thou dost, I can, and will forgive thee!"

"My dearest mother," said Agatha, "rise for pity's sake, and talk not thus. To suppose me capable of such guilt is to torture me beyond every other suffering. Grieve not thus for me, I conjure you. I will not deceive you. I am not happy, it is true; but I am more tranquil and more composed than I could have imagined it possible to have been; and time, reason, and religion, will give me that peace you wish me. Be comforted if you would have me so, and if you would not add to my troubles one greater than all."

Soothed by her tenderness, Lady Belmont became more composed, and, accompanied by Sir Charles, attended her to the convent at the appointed hour, with melancholy resignation.

The separation from Sir Charles was not marked with less anguish than that from Lady Belmont; and all the kind efforts of Madame St. Clermont were exerted to each by turns, while her benevolent heart bled for their distress.

After the usual prayers at the commencement of her novitiate, Agatha was received as one of the society. She attended the several services, and performed her part in the appointed devotions. At night, after the service of Complin, which is that performed after sunset, Madame St. Clermont, taking her hand with an expression of the most tender affection, led her to her little cell, "this my beloved friend," she said as they entered it, "contains all the indulgence we think right to permit ourselves in our apartments; and there are many who would deem even this too great a luxury. But though I judge it right to place our supreme happiness in devotion, I do not therefore believe that Heaven enjoins that extreme austerity which many think it their duty to practise. But till your spirits have recovered the first shock they will sustain in a change so great as that from your own splendid chamber to this narrow retreat, I will not quit you."

"Fear not for me," said Agatha, "this is nothing. O, Madame St. Clermont, a heart at ease is all; and blessed with that even this little cell would seem a palace."

"God grant it you, my sweet lady," said Madame St. Clermont. Then seeing Agatha more tranquil than she had dared to hope, she left her to her repose, after embracing her with the utmost tenderness.

The cell was a small square apartment. The walls of stone had no covering. On a table of the same materials placed underneath a high Gothic window, stood a lamp already burning, and by the side of it a small taper ready to be lighted to conduct her to Matins. The curtains of the bed were of white stuff. On one side of it stood a solitary chair, and on the other a small chest, intended to contain changes of linen, their only wardrobe.

Agatha, not daring to think, after endeavouring to compose her spirits by prayer, hastened to bed, where, harassed and exhausted, she dropped asleep. She was awakened by a loud bell. At the first moment unconscious where she was, or why it tolled, she started and screamed. At this minute Madame St. Clermont entered, "I was indeed fearful," she said, "that the bell calling us to Matins might alarm you, and came to warn you of it."

"It was kind indeed," said Agatha, "but you are, and will be a mother to me!"

Madame St. Clermont remained with Agatha while she rose; then, taking her hand, she conducted her along the gallery to a passage which communicated with the chapel. It was midnight; and except the heavy toll of the bell at intervals, no sound interrupted the stillness of the night. Everyone entered the church in silence, her taper in her hand; and as they walked slowly along the aisle a hollow echo repeated the sound of their feet. As all were not yet assembled, Madame St. Clermont led Agatha to the place allotted her, and kneeled herself near her in silent devotion. Agatha now endeavoured to collect her thoughts, and to implore in these solemn moments, the blessing and protection of Heaven. "And bless, O bless," she said, "him for whom it is no crime to implore their mercies! Shield and preserve him in the silent, awful hour! Guard him from every danger! Sweet may be his slumbers, and may angels hover around his pillow, and bless his sleeping or his waking thoughts." Then not daring to dwell longer on this fatal theme, she offered up her prayers for every other friend. The service now began; and, with a heart glowing with devotion, she joined the choir, and seemed at that moment, to soar beyond this world and its circumscribed possessions: Heaven itself opened to her view!

The service ended, Agatha returned to her cell; but not to sleep. Her agitated spirits forbad even a momentary slumber; and when the bell called her to Prime, (the devotion performed at sun-rising) she had not closed her eyes. She arose, and did not again return to bed; but when the morning service was over, walked with Sister Agnes during more than an hour. She returned refreshed and revived, and strove by different employments to divert her mind, and chase the depression which hung upon it. Lady Belmont now arrived. "And how is my sweet girl?" she said, as she entered. "My spirits," replied Agatha, with assumed cheerfulness, "are almost all you would wish them. And see, my dearest mother, how much my industry has already performed," showing her a drawing she had began. "I see," said Lady Belmont, "that you are an angel!" Agatha turned her head to conceal the tears, which, amid her feigned serenity, forced their way, in spite of every effort she made to suppress them.

Lady Belmont remained with Agatha the greatest part of the morning, and, as she had promised, passed some hours with her during every day; Sir Charles frequently accompanying her.

The serenity Agatha had assumed, now, in some measure, became real. Her spirits grew more composed, and her attempts to render them so were unceasing. She never suffered herself to pass a minute unemployed, nor to indulge the fatal idea of Hammond; except during those moments when she prayed for his happiness. If his beloved image obtruded itself, she would whisper, "Heaven bless him!" then force her thoughts to another subject, cool as was the transition, and sweet as would have been the indulgence.

These efforts, painful and appearing scarcely possible at first, became, by slow degrees, less difficult; and before the year of her novitiate was expired, she remembered him with that serenity of soul with which a sainted spirit looks down on those they have left behind; still, perhaps, desirous of their happiness, and wishing for the moment that shall unite them in the realms of bliss, but that desire and those wishes, though firm and constant, yet mild and gentle, and incapable of interrupting the peace of superior beings.

Agatha had written to Mrs. Herbert immediately on her arrival at Issoire; assuring her of her inviolable friendship, and informing her of the life to which she was destined, but conjuring her keep the place of her retreat a secret from everyone, and, above all, from Mr. Hammond, or her uncle, whose benevolence might lead him to pursue her, and to endeavour to snatch her from the fate to which necessity compelled her, and which his generous efforts, without a possibility of changing, would only render more painful. To Mr. Hammond she entreated her to give every assurance of an unalterable friendship, to soothe his sorrows, and to endeavour to pour the balm of consolation to his bosom. "To the mind of a man of sensibility, my dear Mrs. Herbert," she wrote, "there is something in the tenderness and pity of a female heart more soothing, I have always imagined, than there can be in every exertion of the most assured friendship from one of his own sex. A man to a man may blush to own those sorrows and those weaknesses which to our more tender and more susceptible minds he will not fear to reveal. Be you then this friend to my Hammond." She then requested her to break to him, by degrees, her destined situation, which, by totally destroying his hopes, might enable him to conquer his attachment, and restore to him that peace for which she daily prayed.

She received an answer from Mrs. Herbert, expressive of the most tender affection for her, and the severest sorrow at the information her letter contained; conjuring her to reflect before it was too late, nor to plunge herself into fatal and irremediable misery; to listen to the voice of friendship, of nature, of religion even, nor to shut up from the world one whom Heaven had formed to adorn and delight it, to give an example of virtue, and to impart blessings to thousands of her fellow beings. She informed her that Hammond had been dangerously ill soon after her departure, that her uncle's attendance upon him had been unceasing, and that his health was then nearly re-established, but that his friends, believing it likely to be equally serviceable to his health and spirits, had prevailed upon him to consent to travel, and that, in the space of a few weeks, he was to set out with Mr. Ormistace for the Continent; that they proposed visiting Italy and others of the southern parts of Europe during the winter, and in the summer were to go to Petersburg, Stockholm &c.; that during their absence she should spend the greatest part of her time with Mr. Crawford and his family, and some probably at Sir John Milson's, as she had no occasion now to fear adding fuel to Mr. William Milson's flame by her society, since it was entirely extinguished by his new though hopeless passion for her friend. She promised to break Agatha's situation to Hammond in the most tender manner possible, and assured her that if it were within the limits of possibility she would yet one day enjoy the pleasure of her society by visiting Auvergne; but that she trusted she would yet reflect, nor inflict perpetual misery on herself and all to whom she was dear.

In reply to this, Agatha assured Mrs. Herbert that her conduct was the consequence of long and mature reflection; and that, severe as had been the struggle, she had, at last, she trusted, forced her wishes to be subservient to her duty. She assured her of the gratitude her kindness inspired, and blessed Mr. Ormistace for his friendship to Hammond. She promised to write often, and entreated Mrs. Herbert to do the same, and to inform her of Hammond's health, peace, and safety; but to dwell no further on a theme, which, dear as it yet was, she must eternally renounce: yet, though dead to him and everyone on earth, it would be no crime to hear and know that he was well and happy. She then anticipated the period when she should enjoy the blessing Mrs. Herbert promised of her society in Auvergne; a blessing infinitely sweeter than she had dared to hope was reserved for her in this existence.

Chapter 4

The winter and the summer glided away. Agatha, resigned to her fate, and steady to her purpose, strode daily to acquire that presence of mind which should enable her to sustain the dreaded trial with becoming fortitude.

At length the fatal period came. She beheld its arrival with melancholy yet unshaken resolution. Every preparation was made for the awful ceremony. Lady Belmont had procured the habits necessary for the occasion according to Madame St. Clermont's directions. In persons of birth and fortune it is usual to wear a dress remarkably splendid before they adopt that which bespeaks their renunciation of every worldly ornament.

On the morning of the appointed day, (which was, as is commonly the case on such occasions, one of those marked by the Romish Church as a festival) Madame St. Clermont attended Agatha in her cell. "I come, my beloved friend," she said, "to request your attendance, if, yet firm in your purpose, you determine to embrace the life for which you are prepared."

"Yes," said Agatha, raising her clasped hands to Heaven. "He who knows all hearts sees that mine is sincere."

"Come then, my beloved friend," said Madame St. Clermont, "the bishop waits to put the necessary questions." Then bringing the dress which had been provided for the purpose, she assisted Agatha in putting it on. It was a loose robe of silver muslin, fringed with silver intermixed with pearls; necklaces of the same covered her bosom, and one row of large diamonds confined her hair.

Supported by Madame St. Clermont, she now attended the Bishop, a venerable prelate, whose countenance bespoke him the practicer as well as teacher of every moral and religious duty. With gentleness and benignity he asked her the accustomed questions concerning her situation, her intention of receiving the veil, and determination to adhere to the vows she was soon to make. He explained their nature and the dreadful consequences of their violation, and repeated the question, if she chose the life she was preparing to enter.

She replied to all his questions with firmness and courage; but when Lady Belmont came; when she beheld the parent under whose roof she was never more to sleep, whom with every other that was dear to her she was preparing to renounce forever, her fortitude forsook her, and she was obliged to retire some minutes to subdue her feelings, and to endeavour by prayer and supplication to Heaven to revive her fainting spirits.

When Agatha returned, Lady Belmont dared not trust herself to speak to her, but catching her hand, and pressing it to her lips, gazed on her in silent anguish. Agatha feared equally to speak to her, but by her countenance whenever Lady Belmont observed her, endeavoured to say, "Grieve not for me, my beloved mother, for I am not unhappy."

The bell now summoned them to Mass, and warned them that the solemn hour was arrived. Agatha, supported on one side by Lady Belmont and on the other by Sir Charles, and followed by two of the oldest of the nuns, was led to the bishop in the chapel, who began with the usual Mass for the day. Agatha trembled – but armed with the fortitude she had long studied to obtain, betrayed no other mark of weakness or terror; and, joined in every response with animated piety. The priest her confessor now chanted an anthem, importing, that the bridegroom was coming and their lamps should be prepared; and as he sung, Agatha was led by the nuns to light her lamp at a fire kindled for that purpose. The priest then presented her to the bishop, and, kneeling before him, she repeated the vows by which she renounced the world, and lived henceforth to God alone. The Bishop now rehearsed the duties of her state, and the crosier[27] in his hand, gave her a solemn benediction; after which she retired to put on her religious habit, attended by the two nuns. Her beautiful hair was now cut off, and stripped of every ornament and clad in the plain vestments of a nun, she was led once more to the chapel to complete the ceremony. The choir chanted as she entered, and being again led to the Bishop, he put on the ring, signifying her mystical union with Christ, the virgin crown, and veil. She was then conducted to the centre of the aisle, where, falling prostrate on the earth, she was covered by a black pall, and the whole choir surrounded her, singing on their knees the following requiem to her soul, mystically departed from[28] its earthly abode.

> Dead to the world, and all the world contains,
> Thy body to its grave we now consign;
> Life's fleeting joys thy soaring soul disdains,
> For Heaven and Immortality are thine!
>
> See from this dust her fainted spirit flee!
> Father of Heaven! She lives! She lives to Thee!
> Mark where Ambition, Pride, and Sensual Bliss,
> Stabbed in this grave, expiring curses breathe!
> While, on her child, Religion prints her kiss,
> And Fame for her prepares a deathless wreath!

---

[27]Original spelling "crozier".
[28]Original has "departed its earthly abode".

Lo! From the dust her fainted spirit flies!
It mounts! It mounts! A Sister of the Skies!

Myriads of Angels hail her spotless soul,
And 'grave on adamant the Virgin Vow:
Born on their wings behold her reach the Goal!
Vile lump of earth! Where are thy pleasures now?

She flies – she spurns them for that blest abode,
Where, dead to Sin, she only lives to God!

When the words "Thy body to its grave" were sung, a dreadful scream was heard, and Agatha recognised her mother's voice, who, unable to bear the solemn scene before her, screamed and fainted, and was carried lifeless out of the church. With agony not to be described, Agatha waited the termination of the solemnity; while, regardless of her own situation, she thought only of her mother, felt only for her. The anthem ended, little remained to be performed. With an exhortation to the Lady Abbess to whom Agatha (now Sister Constance) was presented by the Bishop, the service closed.

Agatha now flew to Lady Belmont, whom the exertions of Sir Charles and of the servants of the convent had nearly recovered. At sight of Agatha in the habit of a nun she again screamed, and was with difficulty kept from fainting.

"My mother! My dearest mother!" said Agatha, kneeling to her, "bless, bless your child. Do you not see me – know me?"

"My child!" she exclaimed; then, looking at her dress, and turning from her in agony, "dreadful, dreadful change!" she said.

"What changed, my beloved mother? Am I not still the same – still your Agatha, your own Agatha? – What is this trifling alteration of dress! Can the most splendid habit confer a moment's peace upon an aching or repentant heart? No! How many wretches who have bartered their integrity for gold, have felt the fallacy of such a hope? This plain garb will be dear to me, will make me happy, since every time I look upon it, it will remind me that I have done my duty to God and to my mother."

"Excellent creature!" said Sir Charles, his voice faltering, and the feelings of his heart almost too great for utterance.

"I know not when I have felt so happy," continued Agatha. "When anything we have feared has actually come to pass, our minds seem relieved, as from a burden. Our apprehensions render almost everything more terrible than we find it in reality. Do they not, Madam?" pursued she, appealing to Madame St. Clermont, as if to entreat her to assist her in speaking comfort to her afflicted parents.

"Certainly, my dear sister," said Madame St. Clermont, weeping as she spoke.

"Then too," said Agatha, "have I not to thank you for giving me another parent in my dear Madame St. Clermont? Fortunate, fortunate Agatha! To be blessed with two mothers – two such mothers!"

"Do you hear her?" said Lady Belmont, turning to Sir Charles, "do you hear the sweet suffering angel?"

"Call me your child, your Agatha; call me not a sufferer. What are the sufferings of those who enjoy the sweet consciousness of a self-approving heart? Bless then your daughter, your resigned, and, could she see you once more tranquil and happy, she would be your happy Agatha."

"God bless thee, my soul's darling!" said Lady Belmont, "and make us humble instruments in his hands to reward your unexampled excellence!"

"Yes," said Sir Charles, "it shall be the sole study, as it will be the only comfort of our lives to administer to your wants and wishes."

During the whole time Sir Charles and Lady Belmont continued at the convent, Agatha used every exertion to lessen their grief by appearing to feel none herself. Madame St. Clermont saw her efforts, and trembled for their consequence; and with much reason, for when at night she attended her to her cell, she found her too ill, and her spirits too violently agitated, to make it safe to leave her.

"O, Madame St. Clermont!" said Agatha, as she entered her cell, "have I indeed committed a crime when I thought to perform a duty? Heaven knows, but I have a sensation of horror I never felt before, a consciousness of I know not what of terror and repentance."

"No, my sweet friend," said Madame St. Clermont, "you have acted nobly, and Heaven which sees your virtue will reward it ultimately, though you suffer now. The sensation you describe springs not from guilt or from a consciousness of crime; it is the pain attendant on the recollection that you have done a deed, which, though virtuous, is irrevocable. Time, as it habituates you to the idea, will soften the pain, and, with a soul heroic as yours, fear not but you will yet be happy."

Thus kindly did Madame St. Clermont attempt to soothe Agatha. When she was in bed she sat by her in silence, in hope she might drop asleep; but if for a moment she closed her eyes, she started and awoke in horror. Madame St. Clermont observing that her watchfulness greatly increased the symptoms of fever, gave her a strong opiate, which had the desired effect; she sunk into a slumber as sweet as it was salutary. And when, at last she awoke, she appeared resigned and calm, though so feeble and languid as to be unable to walk without support.

Sir Charles and Lady Belmont, whose sufferings had not been less than those of Agatha, were little better. When they sent early in the morning to enquire after Agatha's health, Madame St. Clermont wrote to assure them that they had no cause for apprehension; but she advised them not to attempt to see her that day, as she was convinced the efforts she would make to seem well and happy in their presence would again overpower her delicate frame. Assured of Madame St. Clermont's tenderness to Agatha, and scarcely able themselves to bear the interview, they consented to delay seeing her till the day following.

When they came the day after, they found her infinitely better than they had reason to expect. The forced vivacity she had assumed was fled; but in its place they saw a calmness and composure which promised to restore in time the peace they so ardently desired her to possess; and to procure which they would have endured every possible calamity with transport.

Agatha became by degrees more tranquil than she had felt before her vows. She renewed her own endeavours to engage and interest her mind by every innocent pursuit; while the society of Madame St. Clermont and Sister Agnes was a perpetual source of comfort and delight. Sir Charles and Lady Belmont received from London a monthly supply of new publications, music, and prints; and, in their seasons, they were supplied with the roots and seeds of the choicest flowers: anxious in every trifle to give her pleasure, they even procured some roots from Haarlem at a considerable expense. Agatha received their endeavours to amuse her with a gratitude which even pained her; and her generous heart always reproached her as wanting in the acknowledgement with which she strove to repay their attentions. "Be happy, my Agatha," they would say, "and we are more than repaid; be happy, and we shall not think we live in vain." But Agatha looked beyond her own gratification, and felt the better half of her pleasure from the ability thus afforded her of amusing and pleasing others. Idolised by every sister in the convent, she delighted to return their kindness by imparting pleasure to each; and her books, her flowers, her prints, and her music were not less the property of every other than of herself.

But a source of delight more noble and more congenial to her heart she now discovered – which repaid her for all she had suffered, made existence a real blessing, and rendered her not only tranquil but happy. In the sublime consolations of Charity she sought and found relief from every lurking sorrow. Daily supplied by Lady Belmont with sums for the purpose, the sick, the aged, and unfortunate came to her grate, told their tale of woe, and departed relieved and happy. The orphan found in her its lost parents, and she made the widow's heart to sing for joy. On young women, who, with the approbation of their parents, bestowed their hearts on those who deserved them, and whose virtues in other respects entitled them to her favour, she bestowed small portions at their marriages as a stimulus to virtue, and a reward for filial piety. Nor did her charity stop here. Independent of pecuniary assistance, many were those who had reason to bless her as their preserver. She instituted a little school in the convent for the instruction of a number of poor girls, and by the virtues she inculcated made them examples of virtue and piety to others. She had early studied among other pursuits, the general principles of medicine, and had received instructions both from her mother and Miss Hammond, by whom she had often been led to the sickbed of her poor neighbours. That study now became, from the power it afforded her of bestowing benefit and easing sufferings, a source of the purest delight and highest satisfaction. Numbers of poor from even distant parts of the province flocked to the convent, on the days appointed, to receive her medicines and advice. Her piety and charity rendered her the theme of every tongue, and the subject of many a prayer; and she was generally known by the name of the Angel of Auvergne.

Chapter 5

Two years thus passed, and Agatha became at length, peaceful, serene, and happy. Sister Agnes, whom every day more and more endeared to her as the purity and tenderness of her heart became daily more evident, was walking with her one evening, and expressing the friendship which attached them to each other, "one only proof," she continued, "remains to be given of it, and that has always been withheld: we have never confided to each other the story of our lives, nor of those sufferings in the world which have induced us to take refuge from its tyranny in this peaceful retreat."

"The circumstances which have befallen me," said Agatha, "are some of them such as I should not think myself justified in revealing, even to you; and there are others I fear to retrace, which to repeat might open afresh wounds long since healed, and renew feelings which it has cost me months of misery to subdue. The same motives may not render concealment a duty in you; yet reflect seriously, and if on recollection you are sensible that you may revive sorrows now passed, joined to a fatal remembrance of the world you have quitted, let me advise you to withhold from me and everyone the dangerous recital, however sweet may be the temporary indulgence it might afford you. I want no fresh proof of the friendship which has been so long a source of delight to my heart, and the sincerity of which I have never for a moment suspected."

"For worlds, my dearest friend," said Sister Agnes, "would I not solicit a relation which would distress you; and forgive me, that, ignorant of the consequences, I ventured to ask it. But from my recital I have nothing to apprehend. Each event; long since over, passes every day in review before me. The blessings I once knew I remember but as a dream, which was too sweet to be lasting; and from the contemplation of the fleeting and delusive enjoyments of this life I learn to look forward with increased transport to that for which I am preparing myself, where every bliss shall be as lasting as it is exquisite."

"Yet once more," said Agatha, "let me warn you not to deceive yourself. Snatching from memory a shadow only of departed bliss, you may perhaps find a sad reality of misery."

"Far from it, my kind friend," said Sister Agnes. "Here, serene and peaceful, if not happy, I look back on the world as on the cruel surge which wrecked my hapless vessel, and bless this haven where I rest secure from future storms. Not less sweet is it to the traveller to recount the dangers he has escaped, while his family eye him with wonder and delight, than it will be to me to repeat my trials past, and the sorrows I have been enabled by religion to sustain.

Losing my other sisters and a brother very early in life, I was left an only child to parents, whose memory I am bound to revere, and who, had it pleased Heaven to spare them to me, might have saved me from the evils I have since known. My father, the Count de Vermueil, on the death of his own son, adopted in his place Lewis Henry Dorville, then only six years of age. Destined for each other, if no repugnance on our part prevented it, we were brought up together; and now affection was all their most sanguine wishes could desire. Dorville had no thought, no wish but his Emily, while, even in my childhood, I delighted to believe I lived only for him. The only contest we ever knew was who should sacrifice most to the wishes of the other; but in this Dorville was generally the victor, and forced me to accept in his stead the offered pleasure, or to suffer him to perform for me the unwelcome task. Every little treasure we possessed belonged equally to each, and every trouble as well as every pleasure was shared between us. If I wept, his tears flowed in concert; if I smiled, he was gaiety itself. As the amusements of youth supplanted those of childhood, these still were only dear to each in proportion as they were so to the other.

When we were of years to govern with prudence and propriety, the household committed to our charge, my father purchased an elegant habitation for us, and the day that was to unite us inseparably was fixed. But a malignant and contagious distemper broke out in the neighbour-hood. My father and mother both fell victims to it; Dorville and I, though attacked by it, were enabled by youth to struggle with the malady, and lived to pay the last tribute of grief and affection to their remains. Duty, propriety, and filial tenderness, equally prompted us to delay the promised blessing of our union, and we determined that not less than a year should be passed in paying that respect to the memory of our parents to which it was so justly entitled. Equal sufferers, it was the sole endeavour of each to mitigate the afflictions of the other, and we blessed Heaven that, on the trying occasion, we possessed one friend in whose tenderness we could seek and find relief.

After somewhat more than a month had passed, and the first violent emotions of grief had began to give way to mild regret, a person came to settle in a house near to ours, who, whenever she met us, attempted, by every possible attention to us both, to show the part she took in our distress, and the interest our tender attachment inspired. Delighted, as she would say, to witness a love which raised its possessors above the common herd of mortals, she longed to be admitted to our society and friendship; and we knew not how to resist entreaties which flattered at once our feelings and the dearest vanity of our hearts; for if there was anything in which we took a pride it was our love. Till then, all the world to each other, we had neither sought nor admitted any other society.

Madame Frevillarde, which was her name, was far from young, but she was sprightly, animated, and interesting. Tall and large, she was rather handsome than pretty; but struck by the quick sparkle of fine eyes you could hardly contemplate her other features: and well – too well did she know to employ them!

By degrees, her attentions to me diminished, and those to Dorville increased. Whatever I happened to advance in conversation, she had the art, though in the most polite and respectful manner imaginable, to prove was erroneous in its idea or principle; and unaccustomed to the subtleties of logic, I knew not how to controvert arguments, which I often discovered to be specious. Dorville's remarks, on the other hand, she as highly applauded, and, by reasoning equally artful, proved the justice of every position of his. Dorville thus learned, by degrees, to condemn my poor abilities, and, charmed by the flattery of Madame Frevillarde, to admire his own, and hers who discovered them. Men are, I believe, notwithstanding the general opinion to the contrary, more the dupes of flattery than women. He requires, perhaps, a more judicious and guarded application; but, where it is judiciously applied, it rarely fails of effect.

Madame Frevillarde had a delightful voice, and sung with equal taste and judgment. Dorville was passionately fond of music, and nature had not gifted me with a voice – though to please him I had learned several airs on the harp, with which I accompanied his violin, and which, in former times, he thought delightful. But my poor harp was neglected and despised. If I attempted to play, the instrument was out of tune, the strings jarred, the air I began was insipid, and *if we wanted music, Madame Frevillarde would perhaps oblige us with a song.* Desirous to exert my little efforts to please, I more than once offered to accompany her voice; but she discovered that it did not accord with the harp, and to the violin only she had been accustomed to sing.

Dorville was fond of poetry, and in some moments of tenderness had often written a few lines which he presented to me as tributes to his love. I received them with delight and preserved them as sacred treasures; and though I possessed not the talent myself, was charmed with it in him: Madame Frevillarde unfortunately did. She took up, one day, a book of receipts, which, at my poor mother's request, I had collected and copied in order to assist me in housekeeping. In the first page of this, Dorville had written with a pencil.

Take near a hundred harmless wiles,
And full ten thousand charming smiles,
The downcast eye, and crimson'd cheek
Which own a love no words can speak;
With many a vow, (our joy and pride!)
To know no other love beside.
These form the dear, the true receipt,
Which makes our tenderness complete,
Makes every hour replete with bliss,
And every moment sweet as this.

Madame Frevillarde took up the book as it lay in the window, and read the lines to herself. Dorville coloured as she read them; perhaps imagining the simple effusions of his heart in a moment of ingenuous tenderness too incorrect for her inspection, and perhaps ashamed of that love which had been once not more his delight than pride. She smiled, and holding out her hand, said, 'lend me your pencil Dorville.' He gave it her in some confusion, yet apparently encouraged by the look of approbation she gave him when she had done reading. She wrote these lines under his.

Not one among those charming lines
The real force of love defines,
'tis mingled still with chaste respect,
Love's genuine cause and sure effect.
Though heir to every miser's pelf,
T'will own no treasure but itself.
True to the object of its choice,
It hears no music but her voice.
Though twenty learned sires might preach,
't'would own she only knew to teach.
Nourished by doubts, with tremors fill'd,
By cold security 'tis killed.
Who would its genuine transports gain,
Must it with each pleasure know a pain.

'Delightful!' said Dorville, as he read the lines over her shoulder. 'You shall read them presently, Emily,' said Madame Frevillarde turning to me, 'and shall tell me if they bear any resemblance to your own reply to the sweet verses before us.'

'I made none,' said I coldly.

'What! Not to a line? Surely they were entitled to an answer at least!'

'Emily has no talent for poetry,' said Dorville, with a contempt I had never seen him express before.

Unable to bear treatment so different from what I had been accustomed to receive from him, I could not refrain from tears, though my pride made me struggle hard to check them.

'Really,' said Madame Frevillarde, 'I think the poor dear girl is jealous of our talents, Dorville.' Then turning to me, and taking my hand with affected condescension, 'I would not have had you hurt, my dear, at a superiority which springs merely from accident; Dorville and I possess the talent of poetry from nature, and it is not therefore a merit in either of us.'

'I desire no talents,' said I, withdrawing my hand, with an anger I did not endeavour to hide, 'I desire no talents, which may be perverted to the worst of purposes; to plant the thorns of discontent in the bosoms of the innocent, or to tear asunder two hearts connected by duty, habit, and inclination.'

Madame Frevillarde, whose tears were always ready to flow when it was proper or necessary to call in their assistance, burst into tears. 'This from you, Emily!' she said, 'I neither deserved nor expected it. Dorville, speak for me, 'twas in defending you that I incurred the anger of our mutual friend. Surely,' pursued she, 'there can be no crime if nature has given us a similarity of sentiments and tastes: where this is the case, the mind naturally seeks the society of its counterpart.'

Dorville had beheld my real tears, which he saw me at the same time endeavouring to suppress, with coolness and indifference; those of Madame Frevillarde, forced and indulged, appeared to wound him to the soul. 'Cruel girl!' said he to me, indignantly; then, turning to Madame Frevillarde, he took her hand with an expression of tenderness and pity, conjuring her to be comforted.

She did not appear insensible to his efforts to console her, and taking my hand, 'Come, my friend,' she said, 'I was perhaps too easily wounded; but all hearts are not alike – and mine cannot bear the shadow of unkindness. Dorville, here is my other hand; and now we are all friends, and happy as before.'

'My dear Madame Frevillarde!' said Dorville, kissing the hand she gave him.

'Why always Madame Frevillarde?' she replied, 'I call you Dorville, the Mademoiselle de Vermueil, Emily, with the familiarity of an old friend: let me then be Clara. Observe me – I desire it of you both as a mark of friendship.'

Dorville promised to obey her. Incensed at her artifice, which would have been palpable to all eyes not blinded by vanity and self-love, I made no reply. I could not have spoken with temper; and I feared to irritate

Dorville, and increase his indifference to me and partiality to her; too well assured, from the specimen I had already had, whose part he would take in a quarrel.

Madame Frevillarde had had two husbands, and was therefore, perhaps, an adept in the art of pleasing and managing mankind; and an artless girl, with no guide but nature and sincere affection was little able to cope with the artifices of a woman who had made their foibles her study, and knew how to turn them to her advantage; and who was arrived at that age of which it has been observed, that if a woman is less lovely, she knows better how to love.

I wished to speak to Dorville alone, but he never gave me an opportunity. If I brought my work to sit with him, he pretended business; or if he remained in the room, took up his violin, and when I spoke, either did not, or affected not to hear me. Certain, however, inexperienced as I was, that a wandering heart is not to be recalled by anger or ill humour, I studied to be as attentive to his wishes as formerly, and if he signified his desire of any trifle, made it my business to procure it instantly. But in vain. My attentions passed unheeded; and every day gave added proofs of his attachment to Madame Frevillarde, and indifference, if not dislike, to me. Yet even then, though stung by jealousy, and mortified by coldness, I loved him, and preferred his happiness to my own. My parents had bequeathed their property equally between us, not doubting that it was the same thing to which they left it, and wishing by this to say, as with their last words, that they considered us both as their children. Had Madame Frevillarde possessed the qualities of mind and heart which would have ensured Dorville's happiness in a union with her, I would not have hesitated a moment; I would not have sought to recall a heart which might have known superior happiness in the possession of another: his fortune should have been his immediately, and I, the only bar to his wishes, have been removed forever from his sight. But I was but too certain that he never could be permanently happy with a woman of her character; the veil must at last drop-off, he must see his infatuation and lament its consequences. I determined, therefore, to wait with patience; and, in the meantime, to leave no means untried, in my power to devise, to please him, and regain his lost affection.

But how shall I tell you the sad sequel of my love? O, Sister Constance, if ever you have known what it is to love, to feel your happiness depend upon another, in whom every hope and wish is centred, you may imagine what I felt when I waited in vain for Dorville one fatal morning. I had dressed the breakfast table with flowers, had gathered our grapes with my own hand, and sat down expecting his arrival. Hour after hour passed, and no Dorville appeared. I enquired of the servants, but he had not been seen. I sent one of them to his room, and he was fled, O, Constance, fled forever, and with Madame Frevillarde, as I soon, too soon discovered.

I received no message from either of them for more than a week, nor could learn what route they had taken. At length I received a few peremptory lines from Madame Dorville, as she then, alas, was, demanding her husband's fortune. From Dorville himself I received none – he was withheld from writing either by shame or remorse. It would have been in my power to dispute his fortune, and probably with success, since my poor father's will ran, 'To Lewis Henry Dorville, my adopted son, and intended husband of my daughter, Emily de Vermueil, I devise one half of my property to be paid him on the day of their marriage.' But this was so far from my wishes or intentions, that, had all the fortune been left at my disposal, he should have had half of it to share with my happy rival. Certain, however, that her integrity was not to be depended upon, and wishing, for his sake even, to whom it might hereafter be serviceable, not to lay myself open to her artifices, since she might probably claim the whole of my property, under pretence that his share had not been received, I sent the amount of half my possessions of every kind, which I had first had legally estimated, by a person on whom I could depend, to receive a written release from Dorville as to any further demands upon me. I then sold the house I inhabited, since every spot around me awakened some dear and fatal remembrance, as well as that which had been purchased for us by my parents, and took a small one several leagues distant from my former abode. There I resided two years, a prey to dejection and sorrow; with no other consolation than the consciousness that I deserved not my fate, and that, my dearest sister, is of all others the greatest. No! Let my happy rival, I would say, exult in the blessings she has unjustly acquired. I would not exchange this lonely abode, this isolated life for hers – for her feelings where every joy is poisoned by remorse, and the purest sources of felicity polluted by treachery and guilt. But may Heaven bless Dorville, and preserve him from remorse! O, may he forget that there exists one, whose life he has robbed of all that rendered it desirable, one whose hopes he has blasted, as the pestilential vapour destroys at once the source of vegetation, and leaves the face of nature a desert – one, who deserved his love, deserved a better fate!

Still anxious for Dorville's happiness, I employed a person to enquire, and give me secret information from time to time of his situation and domestic comforts; and learned, to my sincere regret, that he was far from happy; that his circumstances were believed to be deranged, partly owing to debts contracted by Madame Dorville before her marriage with him, and partly to her extravagance afterwards. As I lived at a small expense myself, I could afford to spare sums from time to time, which

I contrived to send under feigned names, and on different pretences; since I could not bear that, for his sake, for the sake of what I knew he would suffer, he should know from whence they came.

At length I heard that Madame Dorville and he were at variance, and had separated, it was believed, forever; and some time after, learned, from too certain information, that he laboured under a dangerous malady, and was thought to be hastening to his grave; that Madame Dorville, immersed in the gaieties of Paris, appeared indifferent to the relations sent her of his illness, and left him to perish, friendless and unattended.

This was too much. My love, outraged as it had been, returned with more tenderness than ever: my heart bled for his sufferings; and I determined, be the consequence what it would, to fly to, and comfort him in his last moments.

I took post immediately, attended by the gentleman, a man of years and respectability, who had procured me the melancholy intelligence, and one female servant, and arrived, after travelling without intermission during four days and nights, at the chateau of Aylmer in Normandy where he was resided.

Our chaise stopped at the gate. The driver went to the house, and knocked repeatedly at the door – but no one came. During this interval we contemplated the melancholy scene around us. The garden, which had gone to ruins, bore yet some vestiges of former magnificence. The gates were superbly carved; and images which had once been beautiful, were placed on pedestals on each side of them. But the pedestals themselves were broken and tottering. The high wall, which surrounded the garden, was broken down in many places, and fragments of it lay scattered among the few herbs which grew wild beneath it. Those which had formerly been the walks were overgrown with grass; and everything around had the appearance of an uninhabited and neglected spot.

At last, an elderly woman, pale, feeble, and dejected, opened slowly the door. We inquired if M. Dorville did not reside there. 'He lives here now,' said the woman, 'but for how long Heaven knows; for he is almost at his last gasp.'

'And Madame Dorville?'

'O, she never comes nigh him; and thank God she does not, that he may at least die in peace.'

'Great God! And what advice has he?'

'He had a doctor; but the doctor could do nothing for him – the disorder, he said, lay upon his mind. And well it might; for they say he left the best of young creatures to marry the wickedest lady that perhaps ever breathed.'

'And who nurses – who attends him?'

'I do; and one girl, and his own man. And we sit up with him in our turns, and would do anything for him, for he has been the best of masters. God help him! As for Madame Dorville, she has got all his money in her own hands, and he would have starved long ago, for he has not spirits or courage to seek after her and get his own, if somebody or other had not sent him money from time to time; and it has seemed to drop from the clouds, as one may say, for he never knew why it came, nor where it came from.'

I could not bear this, my dearest sister, and sunk into my maid's arms, who supported, and wept over me. When I was somewhat relieved by my tears, I enquired if we might not be permitted to see M. Dorville. I said I was an old friend, and had always a great value for him, and wished to comfort him in his illness. She said she would ask him; but it had been so long since he had seen anyone but themselves and the priest who came to pray by him, that she did not know how he would bear it. She now conducted us into a saloon, where she left us while she went to him.

When she was gone, we consulted on the best method of breaking my arrival to him; fearing that, in his weak state, the shock would be too great for him, if he saw me without being prepared for the interview. M. Loverd, which was the name of the gentleman who accompanied me, proposed that he should go to him first, and tell him, that he had seen a friend who had enquired much concerning him: that he should break to him, by degrees, that that friend was Mademoiselle de Vermueil; and, at length, when he was become familiar with my idea, should confess that I had accompanied him to see and attend him, if by my attendance I could be any consolation to him. As we could devise no better method, this was, at last, agreed upon.

The woman returned, telling us, that M. Dorville rather wished than otherwise to see us; but advised us not to go up together, lest the sight of three strangers should be too much for him. This was what we had intended; and M. Loverd went with the woman, leaving me and my servant in the saloon.

The inside of the house, though less ruinous than its appearance without, bore, like that, the marks of decayed magnificence. The tarnished gold fringe on the chairs and curtains, the soiled, and in some places, torn hangings, spoke their owner like themselves fast falling to decay.

After waiting nearly an hour in a state of terror and suspense, M. Loverd returned, and assured me, that Dorville, though dreadfully agitated at first, was now calm and prepared to see me: that, shocked at the mention of my name, it had been long before he could render his spirits sufficiently calm to enable him to bear the disclosure of my being actually there. M. Loverd then, in the most tender manner, conjured me to support my own spirits, nor to add by my agitation to the sufferings of Dorville. He bid me expect to see one whom remorse and sickness had worn to the shadow of what he once had been; whose feeble voice could scarcely be heard at a small distance; while his words were interrupted at intervals by groans which would pierce my very soul.

I endeavoured to assume the fortitude so requisite as well for his sake as my own; and leaning on my maid's arm, was conducted by M. Loverd up a stone staircase, and from thence, through a long and gloomy gallery, to Dorville's apartment at the end of it.

Unable to lie down in his bed, he was supported in it by pillows; and the image of death itself was imprinted on his languid and emaciated countenance. Those eyes which, when I had last seen them, sparkled with the fire of youth and vivacity, now, sunk in their sockets, were dim and lifeless. Those lips, which had been wont to give utterance to a thousand animated and interesting subjects, now, white and parched, seemed to have lost all power of motion.

He turned his head as we entered, and with a faint and agonising smile beheld my approach. O, that smile, never will it forsake my memory – methinks I see it now – 'Emily!' he said; and held out his poor trembling hand.

I flew to him, and kneeled by his bedside. 'My Dorville! My friend! And do I again see you? And I pressed his pale hand to my lips.'

'O Emily! How – how have you been avenged, dear, injured saint!'

'My Dorville, speak not thus: we meet, and all is forgotten.'

'O Emily! Soon, soon indeed it will be, and I shall be no more. Fast sinking to the grave you see your execrable Dorville; victim of guilt and barbarity. If yet thou canst forgive me, speak it and those accents shall attend me to the grave, and cheer my dying moments.'

'Dorville, you have not offended me. Betrayed by artifice against which your youth and inexperience could not guard, call not yourself guilty. Yet if it will be a consolation to you in these hours of illness, hear that your Emily, your own Emily forgives you from her soul, and she looks for forgiveness of her own errors at the throne of Heaven.'

'Bless! Bless you then! Do not withdraw your hand, my Emily, these are the last moments of comfort I may ever know. Dear hand, how many times delighted have I pressed it, and sighed for the hour when it should make thee mine! Dear face, how often have I gazed upon it with fondness! – 'tis still the same: mine, Emily, you hardly could have known; yet (for I know that heart) it will be dear to thee even in ruins; and when buried in the grave, you will love the dust which covers it. Dear girl! How kind this is! O, canst thou bear these poor parched lips to take one last – one parting kiss?'

I leaned towards him – and – holding out his feeble arms to receive me, he sunk upon my bosom and expired.

O, let your imagination paint my feelings, for words cannot.

With difficulty was I torn from the breathless corpse. I kneeled by him – kissed his cold cheeks – and, at last, deprived of sense and life, was carried from the melancholy apartment. My maid conducted me home as soon as I was well enough to be moved, and M. Loverd remained behind to pay the last sad debt to his remains.

I settled a pension on each of the servants who had attended Dorville, and having disposed of my house and furniture, and visited and wept over his grave, retired hither from a world which had no longer a single blessing in store for me.

What became of Madame Dorville, or how she bore the death her own barbarity had occasioned, I have never heard. But I do not forget to pray for her – to pray that she may repent her crimes and obtain forgiveness; and that in her last moments she may find that consolation she neglected to give him."

Chapter 6

Sister Agnes had no sooner finished her melancholy recital, and received from Agatha, whose feeling heart took but too great a part in her sufferings, every consolation which compassion and the sympathising voice of friendship can bestow, than accidentally looking behind her, she saw a young man at some distance from them. "Merciful Heaven!" exclaimed Sister Agnes, "look there!" Agatha turned her head, and saw a youth of low stature, dressed in black, who, on their observing him, fled to hide himself among the trees.

"Were I not convinced of the reality," said Agatha, "and had we not both seen him, I should have believed it a dream; since by what means anyone could enter here, or for what purpose, is equally astonishing. But we seem to have little to apprehend, since he shuns us as much as we could him. It will be proper, however, to make Madame St. Clermont immediately acquainted with the circumstance."

They went to the house immediately, and informed the Lady Abbess of the person they had seen. Madame St. Clermont, equally astonished and alarmed, requested everyone to attend her, and advise that they should proceed, without delay, to every part of the garden; and first, to that in which the young man had been discovered.

Agatha, besides that the figure did not correspond with his, was well assured that Hammond would never attempt to violate her sanctuary; and she had heard from Mrs. Herbert, that he was then in England. Mr. Ormistace, Mrs. Herbert had informed her, was then on the Continent, but where she knew not; and from his romantic generosity, she would not have thought it wonderful, if, with a view to free her from a situation which she knew he regarded with abhorrence, he should have had the temerity enough to have attempted such a plan: but the low stature of the person again tranquillised her mind, and assured her that it could be no one that had the remotest connection with her. As they proceeded along the grove, she was, notwithstanding, alarmed by observing the letters A. B. carved on a tree; but was again relieved by seeing, at a small distance farther, the initials of Mademoiselle de Vermueil engraven on another by the same hand.

After traversing every part of the garden, and leaving not a spot unsearched, and after examining that the gates were fast, they returned to the house more astonished than before; since, if anyone had been there, they must have escaped by miracle. The Lady Abbess observed,

166

that it was absolutely impossible for anyone to climb over the wall; and that the locks of the gates were so constructed that no keys but her own could open them; which, except at the earnest request of Lady Belmont, when she wished to introduce her daughter by surprise to the beauties of the garden, had never been out of her possession.

"It is, however a charming circumstance," said Sister Frances, "for it is so long since we have seen anything but women, that the novelty will be delightful. For my own part, if I can but discover a tree that bears any resemblance to the figure of a man, I am ready to worship it."

"Fie, Sister Frances," said Madame St. Clermont, "this is certainly not a subject for jesting. Should it be rumoured abroad how much injury should we sustain?"

"Then let us keep it secret," said Sister Frances; "which may very easily be done. I'll engage to be secret for one; and this little gentleman will make a charming variety in our society."

"It seems to me," said Madame St. Clermont, with more anger than was usual to her character, "that you have totally forgotten your vows, Sister Frances. Ask Heaven to forgive you conversation so unbecoming the habit you wear."

"I have not indeed," said Sister Frances, "a very strong predilection for my dress, and I must confess that the one I formerly wore was infinitely more becoming, and consequently more agreeable to me. But I would venture to lay any wager, that the gentleman, whoever he is, would never have come to the convent if I had not been in it."

"Sister Frances," returned Madame St. Claremont, "must I again entreat your silence? You must have much levity in your disposition, not to feel the consequences of such an affair."

"We will keep them secret too, if you please," replied Sister Frances, in a half whisper, not daring to speak aloud. Assuming courage again, however, in a few minutes she continued. "But it strikes me that this adventure, instead of injuring our fame, may, in the end, redound to our eternal honour, for it will give us an opportunity, like the nuns of some place, (I forget where), of destroying our beauty to render ourselves objects of disgust to the invader. I for one, will promise to set the example; for I assure you faithfully, that, if ever he comes again, I shall think it right to be disguised to the best of my power."

Madame St. Clermont, though offended that what appeared to her and to everyone else in so serious a light, should be made a subject of ridicule by Sister Frances, could not forbear smiling. After examining carefully every lock and door in the convent, the general terror began to subside, and they attended Vespers as usual.

Several days now passed, and nothing more being seen or heard of the object of their alarm, it was generally believed in the convent, that it was a mere creature of the imaginations of Sister Agnes and Sister Constance; and had either of them seen him without the other, they would themselves have thought the same; but they believed it possible they could both be deceived.

As Agatha was walking with Sister Frances one morning some time afterwards, Sister Frances told her that believing her very discreet and prudent, she thought her deserving the confidence of one equally discreet; and she therefore entreated her to keep a very important secret which she was on the point of disclosing to her.

"I cannot, indeed, promise to keep the secret," replied Agatha, "unless I know its nature. You may perhaps have mischief in view to which I should not choose to be accessory."

"O, it is gone and past, and your divulging it can be of no service. But somebody I must reveal it to, or I shall die with the pain of concealment; and I had rather trust your prudence than to that of anyone else. You must know then, that I can inform you who the gentleman was that terrified you all."

"Good Heavens!"

"Nay you need not appeal to the Heavens – they had nothing to do with it – he did not drop from the clouds. It was I."

"You?"

"Yes, no creature beside, upon my honour; but I was wearied with the eternal sameness of our life, and wished to frighten you all for a little variety. And nothing could divert me more than the Lady Abbess – poor soul! I believe she thought he was come to run away with her. Now I am sure if there had been such a person, he would have taken you, or me, or half a hundred in preference to her. She is handsome enough, I confess, but then so formal and stately, that if I was a man I should as soon think of falling in love with the picture of my great grandmother."

"And did you feel no compunction when you saw the uneasiness we all suffered?"

"Compunction! Why my dear creature, it was by far the happiest day I have spent since I entered the convent. I enjoyed the pretty confusion visible in every face, and wanted nothing to complete my happiness but to have been in reality what I pretended to be, for the sake of perfecting your terror. But as you and Agnes were my particular friends, my scheme was particularly levelled at you."

"We were greatly obliged to you."

"Yes, and for this reason, I carved your names upon the trees, and chose to appear to you."

"But how could you possibly contrive –"

"O, I had one of the servants in my plot. She procured me the dress; and I went the shortest way back, and had taken it off, and was properly attired, before you returned to give the alarm."

"Certainly nature never intended you for a nun."

"Most certainly not; and nothing but my father's perverse will could have made me one. But he fancied that I was not so handsome as my sisters, and therefore not so likely to marry to advantage; and the fortune, it seems, was not sufficient for us all. But I assured him, with great force of argument, that if I had not such regular features as they had, there was a certain vivacity in my air and conversation, which was infinitely more fascinating. I assured him, that if I was not *touchante* I was *piquante*, which in a Frenchwoman is highly characteristic, and never fails of its effect. Not that my person could be found fault with neither – for, except my mouth being rather wide, and my nose somewhat exceeding the common size, my features themselves were far from ugly; and then, I had, as you may perceive, a charming pair of black eyes, which I told him would do more execution in half-an-hour than the languishing blue ones of my sisters would in a twelvemonth. And I do assure you, that my complection, when set off with a little rouge, was then excellent for a Frenchwoman; but I have neglected it since I came here, and it is horribly tanned: but no wonder – when one's confessor is so old and ugly, it is not worthwhile to preserve one's beauty. But all my arguments failed. The old gentleman was inexorable – and take the veil I must. Finding all my reasonings fruitless, I attempted to work upon his feelings, which, I confess, would have been ungenerous in any other case, but was surely excusable in this; and with my pathetic eloquence I intermingled a little flattery – the last resource in a desperate case. 'Consider, my dear kind Sir,' I said, affecting to weep, 'how terrible it will be for a young person like myself to be shut out from the society she most likes – that of the sex she values for your sake. Consider too, that she, who would glory to give to the world a son resembling, in every respect, his beloved grandfather, – with that mild countenance, those virtues which adorn you, would be placed where, (dreadful to think!), such a hope would be impossible!' But this moving and very flattering address had as little effect as what I had before urged; and it has always been my unfortunate fate, that where I expected to move tears, I have excited laughter. And so here I am, without any hope of transmitting to posterity the image of my respectable papa."

"But it surprises me," said Agatha, "that, with the repugnance you had to the veil, your sisters could endure that to promote their interest you should be sacrificed. If they had less gaiety than you they were better calculated for a monastic life."

"O, with regard to that, my sisters were very fond of me, and loved me better than anybody except themselves; but we were none of us born with that heroic virtue, nor did we inherit it from the dear old gentleman, (not withstanding my flattering eulogiums), which is willing or desirous to sacrifice its own happiness to that of others. They did not wish me to be a nun, nor I them; but since the evil must fall upon one of us, each was desirous that one should not be herself."

"Cruel policy!" said Agatha, "which to aggrandise one part of the family sacrifices another!"

"But in truth," pursued Sister Frances, I never knew what it was to be unhappy; and there is a kind of light-heartedness in my disposition which makes me sport even with misfortunes, chained to the oar, I think I should find some subject for laughter, or, if I found none, should create it. A solemn face always diverts me; and when I am believed to be saying an Ave Maria very devoutly, I am very likely caricaturing the Lady Abbess upon my nail."

"There is something in Madam Saint Claremont," said Agatha, "which mingled with the affection her goodness inspires, excites such veneration that I am surprised ever you can make her a subject of ridicule."

"O, I neither love nor esteem her the less because I laugh at her. I have every reason to love her; for she left no stone unturned to induce my father to give up this horrid plan – and she would not have consented to admit me, if she had not found that he was determined I should go to another convent if she was unwilling to receive me, and she knew that it would be in her power to make my life happier here than elsewhere. Here, then, since it must be so, I came; and poor Mademoiselle Henrietta Rouvine was converted into Sister Frances, and became, for the rest of her life, what neither nature, nor her own inclination intended her for – a nun. If it had not been for these excellent spirits, I must have died of the vapours; for needlework is my aversion; books, except those which are very diverting, I detest; and music is worse than either. I had a master to teach me the harpsichord; but never being able to pay regard to more than one thing at a time, while I attended to the treble, I forgot the bass – and while I attended to the bass, I forgot the treble: and there ended that accomplishment. I had then a drawing master; and I believe I might have excelled in drawing, but for an unfortunate, and, as some thought, misplaced instance of filial affection. I was painting the Flight into Egypt, and in the face of the ass caricatured my father. Politeness was so strong that everyone discovered it. My father himself observed it, and was highly offended, notwithstanding I assured him I really took his likeness from pure affection; and meant to destroy the rest of the picture, and have that head set in a bracelet. The offence however was so great, that I was not permitted to have a master any longer, which put an end to my only talent."

Thus did the lively Sister Frances go on; sporting with her own misfortunes, and happy from that very hilarity which seemed to make her unfit for the station it enabled her to support.

The happy period at length arrived, when Agatha was to enjoy a blessing to which she had long looked forward with delight. A letter from Mrs. Herbert informed her, that she would take advantage of accompanying a family then preparing to visit the South of France; and would persuade some of the party to attend her to Issoire.

Agatha counted the weeks and the days which were between the time of her receiving the welcome intelligence, and that in which she flattered herself her hopes would be realised. "Happy! Happy Agatha!" she would now say to herself with that sweet disposition of mind which dwells on the blessings within our reach instead of repining at the want of those beyond it. "Happy Agatha, to have found a friend whose attachment time and absence have only served to strengthen, who flies to me with equal affection and delight! How sweet it will be to press her to my bosom after this long, long separation; to behold her a pleased spectator of the scenes, where, all my trials past, and my mind taught to be resigned to its fate and cheerful under it, I pass my peaceful, happy life! No cares to interrupt the sweet calm of every hour – religion, as my beloved Madame St. Clermont once observed, not more my duty than delight. How sweet will it be to introduce her to that dear friend; to bid two hearts, formed alike in the mould of virtue, give to each other the esteem they merit; to the dear, unfortunate Agnes to introduce one formed to compassionate distress, and to love its victims! Yes! Heaven only knows what situation will conduce to our happiness. Perhaps, in the world I so reluctantly forsook, I might have found trials I wanted virtues to sustain, or calamities which might have bowed me to the earth, and made me languish for the grave as the only asylum from misery. Here, secure from trial, and sheltered from the storms that wreck the peace of thousands, I await, equally without dread or impatience, the dissolution, for which it is the business of my life to prepare."

As Agatha was straying alone one evening among the various beauties of the garden, and was contemplating with calm delight those objects which she had first viewed with terror and agitation, Madame St. Clermont joined her, and entering into conversation with her usual sweetness, enquired how soon she expected her friend Mrs. Herbert. Agatha replied that, calculating the time her journey must occupy, if she set out at the time proposed, there was reason to hope she might arrive in less than a week.

"What would you say, my beloved Sister, if I were to assure you that I was apprised of the time of her arrival, and could give you certain information when you should see her?"

"Happy, happy tidings!" said Agatha, her eyes sparkling, and her whole countenance animated with pleasure, "and how? When? My dear Madame St. Clermont do not keep me in suspense."

"Let me then see you more tranquil, and I will tell you everything. What would you think if she were now at Issoire?"

"At Issoire? O, happiness not to be expressed! In a few dear hours I shall see her –"

"Yes – in less than even that time; in a few minutes. She is now in the parlour. She wished to meet you by surprise, and to give you the pleasure of seeing her unexpectedly; but I, who know you better, my sweet Sister, knew how little able you are, even now, to support such an agitation of spirits as the unexpected sight of a friend so dear would occasion, and without difficulty have prevailed upon her to suffer me to give you notice of her arrival."

"Kind, dear Madame St. Clermont, how shall I ever return the thousand, thousand marks of tenderness and friendship I have received from you! Of what materials must this heart be composed, if I did not feel and acknowledge myself happy – if I could repine at the privation of the few pleasures I am forbidden to desire, when so many, many others have fallen to my lot?"

As Agatha approached the house, her impatience to see Mrs. Herbert made her attempt to quicken her pace; but her tottering limbs refused their office, and she was obliged to stop, and lean on Madame St. Clermont, while she endeavoured to quiet her agitated spirits.

"However our rules forbid it, my dear sister," said Madame St. Clermont, "it is my request that you would join Mrs. Herbert in the parlour. It is in my power occasionally to dispense with forms, and it were cruel indeed to exact their observance on such an occasion as the present; especially, as Mrs. Herbert is alone, and there will be no gentleman present."[29]

As Agatha entered the parlour, Mrs. Herbert met her with every expression of the most tender affection; yet her sensations, which were those of mingled pleasure and pain, of joy at meeting one she tenderly loved and of sorrow at meeting her thus lost to the world, rendered her words scarcely audible. Agatha wept, and pressed her to her heart with all the friendship and tenderness that heart dictated.

When the first emotions of pleasure were over, Madame St. Clermont seeing Agatha's spirits so tranquil as to stand in no need of her friendly exertions, left the room; imagining that her presence might be some restraint since, though she had been long a friend to Agatha, she was yet a stranger to Mrs. Herbert.

With much hesitation, yet with a countenance expressing the most tender solicitude, Mrs. Herbert now said to Agatha, "I almost feared to

---

[29]**Author's note.** It is well known that in all convents there is a threshold over which the nuns ought not to pass when visited by strangers.

pain my beloved friend by the inquiry, yet it would be the sweetest satisfaction to me to know; to be assured from her own lips, that she is indeed happy: or if, alas, otherwise, I should yet find a consolation in the hope that the soothing voice of friendship might lessen her pain. May I then ask – or will you think me impertinently inquisitive?"

"With gratitude greater than I can express," replied Agatha, "do I witness your generous anxiety for my happiness. Yes, my dearest Mrs. Herbert, you have no cause for apprehension; believe me when I assure you, with a sincerity I should be hurt if you could mistrust, that I am happy. Many and severe were the struggles my mind underwent – struggles which had well nigh overpowered a constitution not naturally strong. But a sincere and fervent desire to pursue what I believed to be my duty, supported me under every suffering, healed every wound, and at last converted what I had deemed misery into a state of happiness as great as I can or ought to desire in a world where I am but a creature of a day: and this excellent lesson has taught me, which I seek by every means in my power to teach others – *that to a mind sincerely disposed to perform them, the severest duties become, by degrees, supportable, and even sweet.* The cup of pleasure, to those who drink deeply of its delicious draughts, leaves a bitter on the palate which they vainly seek to lose; while, at the pure fountain of virtue and duty, the more copious the draught, the more delicious the beverage: the bitter dregs of disappointment mingle not with its uncontaminated waters – which flow forever sweet, forever pure. Yet I am not shut out from pleasure here – from pleasure of the purest kind. I had painted myself a little Heaven of happiness in this sweet idea of being one day called by the endearing name of mother; or seeing around me a little group of smiling faces – infants who owed to me much more than life – happiness and virtue! I figured to myself their filial tenderness. I saw myself in the days of age in decrepitude the object of their cares: I saw the anxiety with which they would hasten to support my tottering steps, and sweeten existence on the verge of its decay. O, Mrs. Herbert, these, and a thousand other delightful pictures had of my fond imagination drawn; but, forced to relinquish them, others appeared on the canvas, the colours of which, though less glowing at first, are more durable, and become more and more beautiful as they are mellowed by the hand of time. Death might have robbed me of those children, or, more terrible yet, of their father! I might have followed them to the grave, where my peace should have been entombed with their dust; – or I might see them, in spite of the principles I had laboured to inculcate, abandon their duty, and thus bring my grey hairs with sorrow to the grave. Even here I am blessed with children, who, if it pleased Heaven to rob me of them, will cost me no tears but those of humanity and mild regret. The poor, the sick, and the unhappy are my children; and on them do I bestow that tenderness, those duties which had else been lavished on my own; and, if less dear to me individually, collectively they are not. Then in the society of Madame St. Clermont and of Sister Agnes, whom I have repeatedly mentioned to you, and whom I shall delight to introduce to your regard, I find a pleasure as sweet as it is pure."

Mrs. Herbert listened with tears of affection and admiration, and when Agatha ceased speaking, expressed the delight she felt at seeing her happy. She said, that Madame St. Clermont's appearance and manner, with the affection she discovered for Agatha, had given her a pleasure as unexpected as it was welcome, since, notwithstanding the high encomiums she had bestowed upon her in her letters, she could not help imagining a Lady Abbess such as fancy commonly pictures her, ceremonious and austere, with the words lock and key written on her countenance. "But pray, my dear," pursued Mrs. Herbert with her natural vivacity, "is your priest as handsome and interesting as your Lady Abbess? If that be the case, I shall think the situation of his flock less safe than pleasant."

Agatha smiled, and assured her that his age and venerable appearance were she to see him, would at once destroy every idea of the kind. "But he is," continued Agatha, "an epitome of everything that is valuable and excellent; and we look up to him as to a father and guide. In his countenance and his benignant smile, he often reminds me of Mr. Crawford; but perhaps there is a resemblance in the truly good of every country and religion; the same benevolent sentiments fill their minds, and thus become imprinted on the face."

Agatha now enquired with an agitation she had hoped never again to feel, concerning Hammond. "Speak, Mrs. Herbert," she said, "and remove the only weight which now ever lodges at my heart, is he well? Is he happy?"

"His health," replied Mrs. Herbert, "is perfectly re-established. I will not deceive you by saying he is happy, for there is a dejection on his countenance at times which shows that all is not right within; but his spirits are, on the whole, infinitely better than they were. He does not shun society, but makes a part in it, sometimes with apparent cheerfulness, but always with polite complacency. When I broke to him the fatal tidings of your situation –"

"Hush," interrupted Agatha, "I must not hear you – I could not bear the dreadful detail of his sufferings. I bless Heaven that he is so tranquil and it is my fervent and daily prayer that he may one day be not only peaceful but happy. Assure him, Mrs. Herbert, if you think it will be any comfort to him, that I wish and pray for his happiness; yet, if you think the mention of my name may revive any dangerous remembrance, withhold it entirely. And now we will close this subject – close it forever," said she sighing deeply. Then making an effort to suppress feelings the sight of Mrs. Herbert and her conversation had for a moment renewed, she assumed immediately her natural serenity, and spoke of other subjects with cheerfulness and composure.

Madame St. Clermont soon after joined them; and Agatha, calling both of them her friends, entreated them for her sake to be such to each other. She then introduced Sister Agnes and the lively Sister Frances to Mrs. Herbert, who, having been at the convent nearly two hours was preparing to depart, when a message arrived from Lady Belmont requesting Mrs. Herbert's company and that of the gentleman who was with her, at her house during her stay at Issoire. Agatha's pleasure at this politeness to her friend is not to be described; and she felt more than ever grateful for being blessed with parents who foresaw and prevented every wish of her heart.

Mrs. Herbert informed Agatha, that the gentleman who accompanied her was Mr. Harold Crawford, a youth of about nineteen, and the eldest son of Mr. Crawford, who with her had joined the family of Mr. Melorane on their journey to the South of France for the health of the latter. Mrs. Herbert then asked Madame St. Clermont if Mr. Crawford might be permitted to attend her on her next visit to the convent; to which Madame St. Clermont cheerfully consented, but entreated Mrs. Herbert to excuse her if the rules she had dispensed with on her account were observed in the presence of another; since she might be severely censured if the nuns committed to her charge joined the guests in the parlour, which formed no part of the convent.

Mrs. Herbert now took leave of Agatha, promising to return the next morning.

As the next day happened to be one of those appointed for the sick and poor to visit her grate, and receive medicines, advice, and clothing, Agatha without assigning her reasons, entreated Mrs. Herbert to come to her immediately after the service of Sexte, (that performed at noon) knowing that her poor pensioners would all be dismissed before that time.

Mrs. Herbert, who imagined there must be some reason for delaying till past twelve, a visit which she was assured Agatha desired as impatiently as herself, enquired, and very soon discovered the reason. Determined, therefore, to see her by surprise the second time, though the Lady Abbess's prudence had forbidden it the first, she asked and obtained Lady Belmont's permission to go to the convent, attended by Mr. Crawford, at ten o'clock instead of one.

Chapter 7

When they arrived, they found Agatha dispensing benefits to more than twenty persons of different ages and descriptions; while her countenance, illuminated by benevolence, bespoke her what she had been so often and so justly called – the Angel of Auvergne!

"The best blessings of Heaven light on you, Madam!" an aged venerable woman was saying to Agatha, as they entered, "you have saved the life of my son, the only support of his family. O, could my poor husband look down from Heaven, how would he bless you for saving us all! Jeanot can work now, Madam, and is as healthy as ever; and to you he owes it."

"I rejoice to hear of his recovery," said Agatha; "yet to God not to me the praise is due: the medicines I have been so fortunate as to give you owed their efficacy to his blessings who delights to protect the good and industrious."

Some children now advanced to lisp their gratitude, and received, with the clothes she had provided for them, lessons of piety and virtue.

Agatha, intently engaged in her works of charity, did not see Mrs. Herbert and Mr. Crawford as they entered. When she discovered them she coloured and felt confused; but recollecting herself – recollecting that she had indeed no cause for shame while performing acts of virtue, she pursued her benevolent task till all were served, and departed, loading her with blessings and grateful acknowledgment, which she in vain endeavoured to silence, by fixing the gratitude where she believed it due – on Him whose steward and almoner she considered herself.

Mr. Harold Crawford possessed all the goodness of heart, and sweetness of disposition of his father, with all that openness, candour, and generosity, which are the loveliest characteristics of youth. On his very handsome face, and regular but manly features, mildness and serenity were most plainly written, but blended with that noble ingenuousness which bespoke him incapable of performing a mean or illiberal action. Though polite to all, his politeness to his parents and sisters had been always most conspicuous; and if ever he was deficient in attention, it was not to them. Sensibility was not generally esteemed the leading feature in his character; yet he rather concealed than was wanting in it – and perhaps this was the only part of his conduct which borrowed the disguise of art: but ashamed to discover that feeling which he had taught himself to suppose was derogatory to the dignity of man, he never owned himself affected by distress, and his impatience to relieve it, constantly betrayed that he was so.

Deeply interested and affected by the scene before him, he could scarcely conceal his tears. He shook his head in order as it were to force them back again; and, as he blew his nose, affected to cough at the same time. Fancying the Lady Abbess had remarked his tears, and might impute them to their real cause, as soon as the poor visitants were departed, he complained of having caught a cold. Madame St. Clermont remarked that it was a disorder very common in the English.

"And particularly so to Mr. Crawford," said Mrs. Herbert; "he is sure to take cold immediately on beholding an object of distress; or witnessing an act of generosity."

"Indeed Mrs. Herbert," said he colouring, "you are very much mistaken."

"You are conscious that I am not," returned Mrs. Herbert, "and you had better avoid an argument in which you know I always come off victorious. I have told you a thousand times, and I will repeat it to your utter confusion in this company, that you are not destitute of feeling. But observe, that, when I say this, I neither mean to praise nor condemn you. I never imagined sensibility a virtue in itself. It is a gift of nature, which, though it may render even you more interesting than you would be without it, as it is not of our own creating, cannot have the name, or deserve the reward of moral virtue. It often, indeed, prompts noble and generous actions; but a person who, without being impelled to those actions by his own feelings, should perform them because he believed duty, humanity and religion required it, would be quite as meritorious as one who performed them to gratify the propensities of his nature which would hardly permit him to act otherwise. But I will not torment you longer with this subject."

Mrs. Herbert then informed Madame St. Clermont and Agatha, that when Mr. Melorane was perfectly recovered, his family were to travel northwards through France, and were to visit Paris in their way, where Mr. Ormistace was to meet them, to enjoy with them the sublime spectacle of a King giving liberty to his subjects – a King, whose humanity, and desire to make them happy entitled him to the adoration of his people. "I have but one fear," continued Mrs. Herbert looking at Mr. Crawford, "and that is – that some people will have very bad colds on the occasion."

"God grant," said Madame St. Claremont, "that my countrymen make a good use of the liberty their Monarch has so generously given them."

"I hope there is no doubt of it," said Mrs. Herbert.

"I hope not," rejoined Madame St. Claremont. "If I can judge of the dispositions of the nation in general, by those of the Nobles, they certainly will not. They are liberal minded, benevolent, and humane, and make the most temperate use of the power given them over their vassals and dependents. Of the disposition of the lower class it is impossible to judge; but in a state of subjection that they are mild and gentle-spirited, humble to their superiors, and courteous to their equals, with whom they lead a life, happy, gay, and thoughtless to a proverb."

"Your remark is certainly just," said Mrs. Herbert. "It is impossible to judge of the real disposition of one who has never been endued with power to exert it; and those who when ruled have been mild and docile, frequently become when they are rulers intractable and tyrannical. But if the French should acquire a spirit of tyranny with their freedom, if they should not only kick down but trample upon the ladder by which they rise, they will have reason, perhaps, as well in this world as the next, to wish they had been vassals still."

"It is certain," said Madame St. Clermont, "that the power given to the Nobles of our country over the peasantry, however temperately they have used it of late years, is such as no one, for the honour of human nature, ought to have it in his power to exert over another; and I have often looked with envy towards your country, where the same laws protect the person and property of the peasant as the lord, and where every subject enjoys as perfect liberty, as in a world where absolute perfection is unattainable, it is possible to do, consistent with his happiness and safety. You may smile inwardly, perhaps, at my speaking of freedom, and think it resembles the well-known story of a prisoner confined for debt in England, who exclaimed, when the nation was in dread of a French invasion, 'My dear friends what will become of our liberty?' But I certainly cannot wish, though I impose restraints upon myself voluntarily, that others, which are unjust, should be imposed upon my countryman involuntarily.

To return to what I was saying in praise of our Nobles: during the dreadful storm which laid waste several leagues of our most fertile provinces last year, every exertion that humanity could devise was employed by them to repair the losses their tenantry had sustained. Besides affording them immediate and ample support, they remitted them a year's rent, and purchased seed to sow the land the year ensuing. The King sent more than a million of livres to the sufferers, and remitted them a year's taxes."

"The generous hearts of Englishmen would hardly have prompted them to do more," said Mr. Crawford; "and they would not, I am sure, have done less."

After some farther conversation on this and other subjects, Mrs. Herbert again took leave of Agatha till the afternoon, when she promised to return and pass some hours with her.

Mrs. Herbert and Mr. Crawford remained six weeks at Lady Belmont's, who took a pleasure in paying every possible attention to her guests, when, Mr. Melorane's health being perfectly re-established, they set out to meet his family on their way to Paris. Lady Belmont requested Mrs. Herbert to pay her a yearly visit, and she promised to profit by her kindness whenever it was in her power. This hope softened the pangs of separation; yet still they were severe – and all Agatha's own fortitude, and Madame St. Clermont's kind attentions, with those of Lady Belmont were necessary to enable her to bear the separation from her friend. Time, however, together with the hope of meeting again before very long, restored her former serenity.

The next year passed the same as the two which preceded it – Agatha, in the duties of Religion, Charity and Friendship, still enjoying "that peace which the world cannot give."[30] The sweet talent of poetry which had early formed one of her amusements was not neglected; and her verses sometimes claimed and obtained the prize among those which were consigned to the vase, but more often were the amusement of her solitary hours. The following is selected from among others which she wrote about this period to pass away some minutes not claimed by more important business.

To Tranquillity

Dear smiling source of ev'ry lasting joy!
Still o'er my bosom hold thy gentle sway.
Still give the peace that knows no rude alloy,
Still ev'ry hour in thy white robes array.

Far from the wearying world thy spirit flies,
To where the Vestal breathes her silent prayer,
There thy mild accents court her to the skies,
And bid her seek thy richest blessings there.

Thy modest beauties fly from vulgar sight,
To scenes where Contemplation loves to rove.
While the mild moon emits her azure light,
O'er the still lake or gently-waving grove.

Dear smiling spirit! Still these haunts pervade,
Soothe every breast with thy benignant power,
Nor, like these flowers which only bloom to fade,
Live but the blessing of a fleeting hour.

---

[30]John, 14, v. 27.

Mrs. Herbert wrote to Agatha regularly, but not being able to find among her acquaintance anyone who had thoughts of going to France, and her uncle, who would with pleasure have accompanied her, having business which called him elsewhere, she was obliged, however reluctantly, to relinquish the hope of visiting Issoire the year after she left it; from the next she hoped for better fortune. But the next year that spirit of tumult, which had long been fermenting, exceeded all bounds, and rendered travelling in France equally unpleasant and dangerous. To the pain of the deprivation of her friend's society was added the fear which Agatha, in common with almost everyone else, felt on the alarming situation of public affairs. Property, and the life of anyone who had the misfortune to possess it, was no longer held sacred. Rapine, massacre, and bloodshed were common throughout the kingdom. The King, who had made his subjects free, was himself a prisoner. His friends and adherents were murdered and instead of the liberty of opinion so long and so ardently desired, instead of the spirit of toleration which the lenient measures of the present reign had sanctioned and promoted, everyone dreaded to avow his sentiments if they were in opposition to those of the ruling faction, or, were he hardy enough to avow them, found death the consequence of his temerity. The monks and nuns in the convents near Paris, received at first permission, and afterwards commands to quit their sanctuaries. Some few who, contrary to their wishes or inclinations had taken the cowl or the veil, and who yet languished for the world they had quitted, received the summons with pleasure; but by far the greater number, however reluctantly they might at first have quitted society, having now no provision out of their convent, and most of their friends or connections being either dead, dispersed or fled, left their asylum with regret and dread.

A rumour at length was spread at Issoire, that the convent there, which, on account of the riches of many of those possessed in it, had long been beheld with envy by those whose ideas of liberty consisted in appropriating to themselves the property of others, would not long be suffered to remain inviolate. Sister Frances on the first mention of this, acknowledged that the idea gave her infinite pleasure. "O my dearest Constance!" she exclaimed, "I shall, I shall after all, perpetuate my dear father's image and his virtues. And how shall I glory in convincing him that I can marry better than either of my sisters! Yes – the sprightly Mademoiselle Henrietta will eclipse them both, and break the hearts of half the men she sees."

"For Heaven's sake," said Agatha, "do not talk thus. Though convinced that your volatile spirits only occasion it, and that your principles are really good, such conversation must appear to me and to everyone equally ill-timed and improper. Remember your vows."

"Yes, that I have long done to my sorrow. But I am serious upon my honour. I will try at least, what conquests I can make, if I should be set at liberty. My hair is grown long enough for dressing – I only repent that I have not been rather more careful of my complexion. But who could have foreseen what has happened?"

"And can you then indeed," said Agatha, "contemplate without dread the breach of vows so solemn?"

"Most certainly I can. For my poor father indeed, I shall feel a few apprehensions; for I recollect picking up a charming book in his library – it was in English, but worth all the French ones I ever met with – I forget the title – but four of the lines I remember were,

He that imposes an oath, makes it,
Not he who for convenience takes it.
Then how can anyone be said,
To break an oath he never made.[31]

Now, this being the case, the breach of vows will be my father's, and I shall have no consequences to apprehend – and for imposing them upon me he is entitled to some punishment."

But however lightly Sister Frances treated the subject it became very soon a serious cause of alarm to Agatha and to everyone else in the convent. The terror of Sister Frances became at length even more evident than that of the rest; for light and inconsiderate minds are often most deeply impressed by fear when they are brought to feel it.

Though determined not to quit the convent till compelled to it, almost everyone endeavoured to provide for her safety and support, in case necessity should force her to return to the world. Those who had relations or friends wrote to request their protection; others, whom death or accident had robbed of this resource, strove to devise some means of maintenance, and hoped to earn a subsistence by their needle or pencil; while some, whom age and ill-health had enfeebled, and whose minds, long accustomed to struggle with hardships, had lost in this peaceful retreat their natural activity, shrunk from the impending evil with dread and horror: to them their country was worse than a desert; since it left them not only nothing to hope, but everything to fear. Religion, and all who possessed it, were branded with infamy; and the habit of sanctity was become the signal for insult – perhaps destruction.

It was determined that whenever the fatal period should arrive, Agatha should return to her parents, and with them proceed immediately to England. Sister Agnes, whom, on account of her friendship for

---

[31]Samuel Butler, *Hudibras*, part 2, Canto 2.

Agatha, Lady Belmont considered as a second child, was to accompany them, and was entreated to regard their house as her home in future. To Madame St. Clermont Lady Belmont made an offer of her house and protection; but she had relations in Spain who had strongly urged her return to them, and therefore declined accepting the offer, though with the most grateful acknowledgments.

After having determined what steps to pursue, everyone continued her duties of devotion as before, and awaited with fearful expectation the event too certainly foreseen. Some months, however, passed, and no new report having reached them, and the country around being in a state of tolerable tranquillity their fears began, in some measure, to subside; and Agatha was beginning once more to indulge in the hope that she should be suffered to remain in a retreat which duty and habit had equally endeared to her, when a new and far more dreadful cause of apprehension and terror made her regardless of every other. The lives of her parents were threatened. Their immense property, known by the sums they bestowed in charity, was intended to be seized; and from one of those false accusations which have been so often ingeniously fabricated in France, their lives were said to be forfeit. The intelligence reached them by means of a faithful servant who had heard it whispered among the peasantry in the neighbouring village. Their only chance of safety was flight; but as they learned that the *Officers* of *Justice* were not expected till the week following, they believed they might allow themselves time to secure some of their most valuable articles before their departure. The fatal intelligence reached them early in the evening, and they determined to set out during the following night, intending to employ that night and the next day in the most secret though expeditious preparations. Agatha, dearer to them both and the lives which for her sake they were anxious to preserve, they could not endure to leave behind them in a country and situation, where, if she was for the present screened from danger, her safety was precarious, and every day it might expose her to insults and misery they shuddered to contemplate. After consulting with Madame St. Clermont, it was therefore agreed, that Agatha, with Sister Agnes, should come to them immediately after Matins, under the guidance and protection of the venerable counsellor; and that, under cover of the night, on horseback, and in the disguise of peasants, they should travel as fast as possible towards the southern coast, and from thence to embark for England by the first opportunity. They wished to have taken Agatha with them immediately, but believing that it might excite a suspicion of their intentions, they judged it most prudent that she should remain at the convent till the moment of their flight.

Their plan being arranged, and everything determined upon, they left the convent soon after Vespers. Agatha, a prey to extreme terror, could scarcely endure to part from them, though so soon to be restored to them forever. She clung to Lady Belmont, wept on her bosom, and when the necessity of their quitting her to hasten the preparations for their departure was urged, she seemed to awake as from a dream, and with wildness in her countenance, conjured them to go – to lose not a moment; while her imagination, anticipating the horrors which awaited them in case of delay, almost deprived her of reason. With anguish not less than her own, they tore themselves from her; and imploring Heaven to bless her, and preserve their lives for her sake, left her almost lifeless in the arms of Madame St. Clermont.

When her parents had left her, Madame St. Clermont endeavoured by every means in her power to calm Agatha's fears, and to restore her to reason. She urged the necessity of her assuming fortitude on the dreadful occasion; since if, by giving way to the agitation of her mind, she should suffer in her health, her illness might impede their journey, and occasion the misery she dreaded. She assured her that she had little cause for apprehension, since, as their flight was not suspected, there was little danger of its being prevented; and she conjured her in the most tender manner, if not for her own sake, for that of her parents, to endeavour to moderate her fears.

Soothed by her tenderness, and convinced by her reasonings, Agatha became more composed, and proceeded to prepare with Sister Agnes the disguises necessary for them both. Some of the clothes which had been intended for her poor pensioners, when they had undergone a trifling alteration could be worn by them both; and employed in this task, Agatha had not been in bed when the bell called her to Matins.

"Ah!" she said, "tomorrow night at this hour, I shall fly to my parents! Tomorrow night. Gracious Heaven! Shield and preserve them! Once more then – and once more only shall I hear this solemn sound – once more only shall it call me at this hour to do homage to my Creator. Tomorrow night I quit this cell – quit it forever!"

She now lit her taper, and with trembling steps traversed the gallery that led to the chapel. The bell yet tolled, and few of the nuns were assembled. Agatha proceeded to the place where she usually performed her devotions, and kneeling down, was engaged in silent prayer, when a noise in the outer body of the church startled and alarmed her. The chapel in which the nuns assembled was separated from the church itself by two grated folding doors of iron. The noise, which had been heard by the other nuns who were present as well as Agatha, had alarmed them all; but having ceased, they were preparing to begin the service, when they heard it again, and louder than before, and could distinguish that it was made by someone striking one of the windows, the glass of which they heard fall, and immediately after a man's voice pronounced, which the vaulted roof conveyed to them in a deep and hollow tone, the name of Agatha. Madame St. Clermont now approached Agatha, whose terror had almost deprived her of life, and proposed that they should unlock the iron doors and go towards the window whence the voice proceeded, since it was probable, she thought, that it might be a messenger from Lady Belmont, who might have something of moment to communicate to her daughter, which would not admit delay. She therefore gave the keys to one of the nuns, and supporting Agatha, and followed by the other nuns, proceeded towards the window. The noise had ceased, but they observed something white on the ground under the window, a pane of which lay shattered on the pavement. On approaching nearer, they discovered it to be a paper. Madame St. Clermont took it up, and found it was tied to a small box, with the word Agatha written upon it with a pencil. She gave it to Agatha, whose hand trembled too violently to open the paper without her assistance. It contained these words:

> My Agatha – God preserve thee! We are beset. Every avenue filled with armed men – we try to escape, Heaven knows whither! But a private passage – we cannot fly to thee, the murderers are between us. If we live you shall hear from us. God preserve thee!

Of the box, which contained some jewels, one of the nuns took charge, while the others supported and endeavoured to recover Agatha, who had fainted before she finished reading the billet. They carried her to the parlour and used every means to restore her, but without effect for a considerable time; and when at last she recovered her senses and speech, it was only to feel and express an agony, which not all the soothing tenderness of Madame St. Clermont or of the weeping Sister Agnes could alleviate for a moment. She passed a night of horror and misery not to be described.

Early in the morning the holy father arrived, and brought the blessed assurance that Sir Charles and Lady Belmont had eluded the vigilance of those who came to secure them, and had fled, no one knew whither. Agatha returned thanks to Heaven; and for some time, in the joy of hearing they had escaped, forgot the dangers which yet threatened them.

More than a week now passed, and Agatha having received repeated assurances that they were not taken, began to hope they were past danger, and perhaps out of the kingdom, when one evening a poor girl came to the convent and asked to speak with her, at the same time saying, that she brought a letter which she was to deliver into no hands but hers. Agatha, attended by Madame St. Clermont, went to her in the parlour, and the girl gave her a sealed letter, written in English but without any superscription. The hand writing was Lady Belmont's, but it had no signature. The contents were as follows:

My beloved child
We are safe at present, and wait for you. The bearer of this will conduct
you and sister A – to us. Change your habits, and travel as little as
possible by day. You will be told what it is not safe to write.

Agatha, in extreme agitation, enquired who had brought the
letter. The girl replied, that it was a man who had fallen sick, and now
lay at her father's cottage, where he had been three days: that his illness
appeared to be occasioned by the fatigue of travelling, and they did not
now think he would recover: that he was of the same opinion himself,
and had promised her all the money he should have about him when he
died, and had given her some more already, in case she would take a
letter to the convent, and give it into the hands of one of the nuns named
Sister Constance, and would promise him faithfully never to speak of it
to anyone. Agatha enquired where she lived, and learnt that it was at a
village about two leagues distant. She enquired with equal anxiety and
concern, if the person had had no medicine or attendance. The girl said,
that till that day he had had nothing but such things as her mother could
give him; for that though they believed he had a good deal of money
about him, he had seemed very sparing of it; but that now, thinking
himself in danger, he had consented to have a doctor, and he had ordered
him something. Agatha with tears conjured the girl to pay him every
possible attention, and promised her that if he recovered, she should be
very amply rewarded.

As soon as the girl was gone, Agatha sent for the confessor, and
entreated him to go to the poor man immediately, to take with him some
wine and cordials, and to see that he was treated with the utmost care
and tenderness. She showed him the letter she had received from Lady
Belmont, and desired him, if it were possible, to seize an opportunity of
speaking to the messenger alone, and to gain all the information he could
respecting her parents. She desired he would extort from him a solemn
promise to regard no expense during his illness, assuring him that
she had jewels the value of which was more than sufficient to defray
all the charges of their journey. She would have given worlds to have
accompanied the father herself; but aware that her presence, however she
might be disguised, would excite suspicion, dared not indulge her wishes.

The priest did not return that night nor the next day, and Agatha's
terror every moment increased. At length he arrived, but with a
countenance too plainly indicative of the melancholy news he brought.
The faithful messenger was speechless when he arrived, and though he
lingered in that state four and twenty hours, before he left him, had
breathed his last.

This dreadful intelligence was a dagger to the heart of Agatha.
Besides the grief which equally from humanity and gratitude, she felt on

account of the death of one whose fidelity to her parents, and solicitude to serve them, had probably brought him to the grave, she had now lost the hope of being restored to them; while the reflection that they were perhaps delaying their own journey, and exposing themselves to danger while they waited for her, and were enduring at that moment all the anguish of suspense and apprehension on her account, was another and severer source of sorrow. She would have fled to them now, but the fatal precaution of not mentioning in the letter the place where they were, had rendered this impossible.

In a state of terror and misery little short of distraction, she passed a dreadful fortnight, during which she was unable to gain any intelligence concerning her parents. One moment her imagination painted them seized and imprisoned, the next beheld them enduring all the miseries of a mock trial and false accusation, and perishing at last under the axe of the executioner. Her only comfort was derived from the hope that if they had been taken, the fatal tidings would by some means have reached her.

Chapter 8

As she was wandering alone in the grove one evening, indulging the melancholy which oppressed her heart, her memory reverted to the blessings she had enjoyed a few months past, when she was sure every day of beholding the parents by whom she was idolised, of enjoying the sweet delight of their approving smiles; when, without a care or fear to embitter the tranquillity of every hour, she knew no anxiety but for the poor objects of her bounty, or how to repay her debt of gratitude to the most indulgent of mothers. Now, sad reverse! She saw herself threatened by evils with which she knew not how to contend – deprived of her parents when most she might want their succour; and, more terrible yet, every moment trembling for their safety!

From this melancholy reverie she was awakened by the sound of several voices on the other side of the wall; and in the same instant Madame St. Clermont approached her, exclaiming, as she folded her arms in an agony of terror, that they were undone – that at that moment there were people breaking down the wall, and preparing to destroy the convent. She had scarcely spoken, when the iron gates were forced open, and the mob entered. Madame St. Clermont, with a firmness and dignity, which inspired at once awe and amazement, instead of flying from, now advanced towards them.

"My friends and countrymen," she said, "what have we done, how behaved towards you, to deserve this treatment? To this convent we retired to worship God; to devote to works of charity those fortunes which might else have been squandered in luxury. Who is there among you that has been sick or unfortunate, who, coming to our grate, has not obtained relief? To your wants and necessities it has been equally our pride and pleasure to administer. Enough to supply the common exigencies of nature is all we desire; to you – to the world we give our superfluous wealth. You are free. I rejoice in your freedom. I have thanked Heaven for it. But deprive us not of liberty because you have obtained your own. We are not free if you compel us to quit the convent to which we have chosen to retire. And shall the champions of Liberty be tyrants? Shall they use their freedom as a cloak for maliciousness? And because secured in their own possession deprive us of ours? Because no insolent invader dare trample on their rights, or withhold from them the fruit of their labour, shall not we be suffered to eat our morsel in peace? No – I will not believe it possible. You cannot act like wolves and tigers prowling for their prey. You are my country-man, men heretofore generous, liberal, and humane, who would have scorned to insult the defenceless, or to trample upon the worm, because it can neither resist nor return the injury."

The mob, awed and astonished, suspended their work of destruc-tion, and without making a reply, retired in apparent confusion.

"Heaven be praised," said Agatha, when they were out of sight, "Heaven be praised, that has given to your lips the eloquence of angels!"

"Alas, my sweet sister," said Madame St. Clermont, "we have little cause for exultation; yet I bless Heaven for this temporary release – temporary as I fear it will be. But let us employ this interval to provide for our safety. They will return, I doubt not; everything of value, therefore, that we can carry secretly we must hasten to secure, and quitting the convent, fly as Heaven shall direct our steps. I, alas, can ill protect you – myself long since obnoxious on account of my nobility, and perhaps rendered more so by this appeal to them, though it has suspended their fury for the moment."

Agatha and Madame St. Clermont now hastened to the convent, where, having secured the doors, the Lady Abbess assembled the nuns, and took a tender and affecting leave of each in her turn; and admon-ishing everyone to remember her vows, and to suffer neither the terrors nor temptations of the world to induce their violation. She advised them to go to their friends, in pursuance of their former intentions, and told them, that she should travel on foot and alone, having learned from too certain information that her life was threatened, and she would not therefore involve another in her danger; since, to be found with her would be a sufficient ground for accusation.

Agatha, sister Agnes, and several others conjured her to suffer them to share her fate – and Agatha implored her not to rob her of her second mother; but Madame St. Clermont, firm in her determination, resisted their entreaties with tears of grateful affection.

Agatha, accompanied by Sister Agnes, determined to proceed towards the southern coast, in hopes that, as there was a possibility of it at least, they might find or overtake her parents.

A loud noise, accompanied by songs and shouting at intervals was now again heard; and from the windows of the convent they saw the mob busied in destroying the trees, and every other ornament of the garden. With ferocious pleasure, the flowers and shrubs were trampled under foot, or torn up by the roots; the beautiful seats were hewn in pieces; even the lawn did not escape their fury – the turf was dug up, and not a blade of grass suffered to remain; and in little more than an hour, scarcely a vestige of cultivation was discernible.

During this time, flight was impossible. Some of the mob surrounded the convent, while the rest were employed in laying waste the grounds around it.

It was now almost dark; and some of them were heard to propose to retire for the present, declaring they would return the next day to complete their work. With reiterated shouts of applause, they now therefore abandoned their prey.

When the ravagers were out of sight, Madame St. Clermont once more bad every one farewell, and proceeded to unlock and unbar the doors.

Agatha went to her cell, to bid a longer and last adieu to a scene which, dreary and comfortless as it had once appeared, was now become dear to her, and was never entered but with mingled awe and affection. The stone table, the lamp, the bare walls, as the feeble remains of light were just sufficient to permit her to discern them, she viewed as so many friends from whom she was about to part forever. She now remembered with astonishment the pain she had once felt on contemplating each; and comparing her present comfortless situation – destitute of a home – divided from her parents, about to wander exposed perhaps to all the miseries of want – with only one companion, whose presence, great as was the comfort it would afford her, could be no protection from insult or danger – comparing this melancholy situation with that when first she entered her cell, it seemed a crime to have repined at a fate which now appeared to have been so replete with blessings.

Commending herself to Heaven, and putting the jewels in her bosom for the greater security, she now left her cell, and went in search of Sister Agnes. She went to Sister Agnes' cell, but she was not there; she called, and no one answered. She was met by a nun flying in terror towards the chapel. "Where is Sister Agnes?" said Agatha, detaining her. "I know not," replied the nun. "Let me go, for God's sake! – save yourself – they are coming again." In inconceivable terror, Agatha now ran to every part of the convent, calling aloud to Sister Agnes. But no one answered. Everyone appeared to have fled, and she seemed alone in the convent. She returned again to the cells – entered each of them – but saw no one.

She could now distinguish shouts at a distance at intervals; and passing through the gallery, descended to the chapel. She here again called to Sister Agnes; but was answered only by the echoes of the vaulted roofs repeating the sound. The iron gates were open. She passed through them into the body of the church. It was now so dark that she could scarcely distinguish any of the objects around her. She went to the great door, which stood open, and heard the shouts repeated, and seeming to be nearer. Breathless with terror, she leaned against a pillar at the door. Someone now glided by her. She caught hold of them; but with that inconceivable swiftness they escaped from her hold. Agatha would have spoken; but speech was now denied her – and faint and sick to death, she sunk upon the pavement.

The shouts, heard yet more distinctly, again roused her; and with an effort of strength, which terror gave her for the moment, she rose, and ran from the convent she knew not whither, endeavouring only to fly from the noise.

Chapter 9

Agatha ran till she heard the shouts no longer, when, breathless and exhausted, she again fell down. She, who, till now, had never been divided from friends whose delight it was to cherish and protect her, who "would not suffer even the winds of heaven to visit her face too roughly,"[32] now, without one friend or human being near her, convulsed by fear, and almost bereft of life, lay on the damp grass, with scarcely a ray of light from heaven to cheer her. She, who never saw a sorrow that she did not seek to mitigate, who, in her infant years, fancied her little heart would break on beholding an object of distress, had now no kind hand to raise or support her, heard no friendly voice to call her back to life and reason.

She lay in this state some hours. At length awaking to a sense of her situation, she endeavoured to rise, but twice sunk down again in the attempt. At last supporting herself by a tree, near which she chanced to have fallen, she arose, and walked slowly on.

Some drops of rain now fell. Apprehensive of more, and something dark before her having the appearance of a wood, she feebly walked towards it, and soon found herself in a forest, the thick trees of which promised her shelter from the storm that seemed to be approaching. But here she had new cause for terror. She distinctly heard the howling of wolves at a small distance from her. Yet even in this dreadful situation, in a dark and tempestuous night, alone in a forest, hope and conscious innocence supported her. She had never intentionally offended heaven in the most trivial instance; and when her spirits became sufficiently collected to reflect, she felt assured of its protection: or, should she perish, death would be but a release from future sufferings; and from a world of care and trouble, she should awake in one of pure and endless bliss.

Consoled by this idea, her spirits became more calm; and after revolving in her mind the sad prospect before her, she at length determined to remain in her present situation, terrifying as it was, till daylight appearing, should enable her to pursue some track to a village or town, where she might perhaps find shelter under some hospitable roof, till she could procure a guide to conduct her on her melancholy route. She now felt for her jewels, alarmed, lest in her fall she might, by some means, have dropped them from her bosom, and found they were safe.

---

[32]Paraphrase of Socrates' description to Aristotle of the creator giving us eyelashes to protect us from the wind. (From *The Memorabilia*).

The day, at length, broke; and the sun, as it burst through the clouds of the horizon, gave to the face of nature an appearance, which, contrasted with the horrors of the preceding night, seemed to Agatha gay and delightful. The birds awakened, sang on the branches over her head; innumerable moving insects were discernible among the leaves; a squirrel hopped on a tree adjacent; a hare ran across the path before her; all bespoke her surrounded by the peaceful inhabitants of the forest, from whom she had nothing to fear, and whose presence enlivened the scene, and seemed a consoling substitute for the society of man. A thousand delightful scents regaled her. The wild thyme and laurel-rose peeping through the underwood rendered the path she was preparing to traverse as fragrant as it was beautiful.

Turning into a little winding alley, on which the prints of human footsteps were now and then discernible, she walked, as she conjectured, more than three miles along the track before she discovered any termination of the forest. As she went along, she picked a few wild berries, and was stopping to gather some more, when a beautiful little bird perched on a branch near her, and pecking some of the berries, seemed jealous though fearless of the invader of his little treasures. The idea struck Agatha as the bird seemed to watch her motions. "Forgive me," she said, a tear starting in her eye as she spoke, "forgive me that I rob thee of thy food: I alas, have no other – or I would not take a berry from thee."

The path at last led her to a little lane at the end of the forest, nearly covered with grass. Continuing along this for some time, a wider and apparently more frequented road crossed it. Agatha was uncertain whether to turn to the right or left; since no appearance of any habitation was to be seen on either side – when, after hesitating some time she fancied she heard the voices of children on her left, and took that road. At some distance she saw two little boys picking up leaves under a tree, and inquiring the way to the nearest village or town, was directed by them to continue in the same road, and she would arrive at the village they came from, which was not more than half a league distant.

Animated by hope, weary and faint as she was from walking, and from want of sleep and refreshment, she soon arrived at the village. The first house in it was a cottage, the door of which stood open; and a tall, thin, masculine woman came out of the house as she approached it. Her countenance had nothing in it which bespoke kindness and hospitality, but Agatha, feeling faint with fatigue, and being sensible that every step she took she grew worse, stopped at the door of her cottage, and asked permission to go into the house and rest herself for some minutes.

"Not that you know of," replied the woman, "I take no lodgers I assure you."

"I did not ask to lodge with you," said Agatha, "but I have walked many miles, and am faint and weary. I wished but to sit down for a few minutes."

"I shall harbour no such people, I can assure you," replied the woman, "I never let nuns come into my house – it might be the worse for me if I did."

"Alas," said Agatha, "I hope you may never want a home to shelter you."

"I hope not," returned the woman, "but I know better than to beg for one if I did."

Agatha now attempted to go; but faint and weary, her tottering limbs refused to support her and, scarcely able to stand, she leaned against the wall. Feeling herself sick through want, and absolutely incapable of proceeding without something to sustain her, cruel as was the treatment she had already experienced, she ventured to ask for a morsel of bread.

"I tell you," replied the barbarous wretch, "I never give anything to beggars. Why we have nuns coming here continually, and all of them with these dismal stories, and if we were ever to serve them there would be no end of it."

"God help them!" said Agatha.

"Aye, aye, God must help them now, they have nothing else for it. The convention knows better than to maintain a pack of fat, lazy monks and nuns in idleness. No, no, they must all troop, and learn to work or starve: and so 'tis fit they should."

"Give me but a drop of water," said Agatha, growing fainter and fainter.

"Water!" said the woman, "no, no – you nuns and friars like a draft of something better than water – that's your characters of old time."

Then laughing at her own wit, she turned round, and walked away; when a little girl about six years old, seeing Agatha's distress, ran into the house, and bringing a little mug of water, held it to her with tears in her eyes. Agatha offered to take it from her, but her trembling hand was incapable of holding it. The little girl then, drawing a block of wood nearer to her, stood upon it, and putting one hand behind Agatha with endeavour to support her, and holding with the other the cup to her quivering lips, "Here Lady," she said. Agatha swallowed the water, and turning to the sweet child, who was essaying to support her in her little arms, her tears fell upon her neck. The little girl stroked them off, and looking up in Agatha's face with an expression of the most tender concern, repeated several times, in a voice of pity, "Dear Lady! Poor Lady!"

Agatha, revived by the water, and the tears which the little innocent's kindness had brought to flow, was now able to walk, and was preparing to go, when the woman returned, and seeing the child attending on Agatha, called to her, in a tone of anger, "Mary, I charge you, let her alone. You know I bid you never to go to them." The child, however, watching till she was again out of sight, renewed her gentle endeavours to comfort Agatha, who, putting her hand in her pocket, found a small enamelled box. "Here Mary," she said, "keep this; and whenever you look at it, pray to God to make you always thus kind to the poor and unhappy." Then kissing her little hand as she put the box into it, she walked with feeble steps from the cottage, and felt, for the first time in her life, what it is to be a beggar!

Agatha asked admittance at several other houses, but was always denied; by some, indeed, without insult, and by others even with an expression of pity and concern – yet still she was denied. *Eh quoi! – recevoir chez moi une Fanatique – une Religeuse! C'est impossible!* "What receive into my house a fanatic – a nun! Impossible!" was the general reply to her solicitations. In the haste and affright in which she quitted the convent, she had forgotten to take with her two Louis which were all that remained of the last sum which her mother had brought her to dispense in charity: money, therefore, she had none; and the fear of exciting suspicions of her birth, or perhaps being plundered of them, she dared not offer any of the jewels in return for the kindness she solicited.

She had now reached the last house in the village, and weary with fruitless solicitations, could not bear again to plead in vain; but unable to walk farther, sat down on a green bank by the side of the road. Here, at least, she said, may I rest my wearied limbs. The poor, forlorn, and hungry wanderer here may sit, under the canopy of Heaven; here rest till want and sorrow send her to a kinder home – till she 'rest from all her labours.' But shall no friendly hand close my dying eyes? No one watch over my poor remains, and consign them with tears and prayers to their native dust? Alas, no. But that is nothing, I shall wake in Heaven; and in the presence of my God look down as on a dream on all my sorrows past.

Lifting up her head, as it rested on her hand, she observed a man at the door of the house opposite, in whose rough features there seemed an expression of pity, and of something which bespoke the workings of humanity as he looked at her. Her applications had hitherto been to those of her own sex; and having found cruelty where most she looked for compassion, she thought she might perhaps experience kinder treatment where there was less reason to expect it. She therefore feebly rose, and directing her tottering steps to the cottage "I almost fear," she said, "so often have I pleaded in vain, to ask if you will suffer an unfortunate traveller to rest in your house for some hours, and will bestow the farther benefit of a little refreshment – no matter what."

The man, whose stern features seemed but to have relaxed into a momentary kindness to induce her to implore his assistance, assuming instantly an appearance of severity, and said in a loud and imperious tone, looking around him as he spoke, "No wretch – I have neither food nor lodging for the religious of either sex." Speaking now in a lower voice, he said, "Go into that garden and take what fruit you find. Look near a root of Eryngo." Then, again raising his voice, "Yes, the refuse of my garden is all I can allow you – but dare not enter it till I permit you."

The man now left her and returning in a few minutes, beckoned to her to go into the garden. Agatha, struck by the singularity of his manner, in which compassion and cruelty appeared by turns predominant, hesitated whether to accept his hardly-granted favours, and take the "refuse of his garden." Alone and unprotected, fear too withheld her. The little kindness he betrayed might be assumed. It might be known or suspected, that she was the daughter of Sir Charles Belmont; since she was known to many by the alms dispensed at her grate. He might wish to trepan and imprison her. A thousand dreadful ideas crowded into her imagination, made the miseries of want seem light in comparison. Yet recollecting that, if indeed he wished to betray her, such an artifice was unnecessary, since, were he to seize her in the road no one would offer to protect or screen her from his power, believing too, that an appearance of distrust might increase her danger, if any there were, with a trembling hand she opened the little wicket, and entered the garden. She saw no one, nor any fruit in it, but going towards an eryngo as she had been directed, close to its blue stalk she found a loaf of bread, and near it some olives and dried grapes. As she took up the loaf it broke asunder and six francs fell out of it. Raising her hands and eyes to Heaven, she was returning thanks for this unexpected relief, when a little boy ran to her, saying in a whisper, "Take what you have found, nun, hide it, and go directly;" and without waiting for reply, was out of sight in a moment. Agatha, who now discovered that fear for his own safety had alone occasioned the harsh treatment she received from her generous benefactor, felt a sensation of self-accusation on remembering that she had suspected his sincerity, and obeying the directions given her, hid the loaf and the francs, and hastened out of the garden; the man bidding her be gone, as she passed the door, in a tone of anger.

"Unhappy country," said Agatha as she walked slowly along, "unhappy country, where cruelty under a thousand hideous shapes, dares show herself, and glory in her deformity; while charity, if she would escape danger, must skulk under the same hateful forms. Wretched people, who, if ye would, dare not be virtuous!"

When she was out of sight of the village, she sat down on the grass, and spread her humble repast before her. She had eaten nothing since eleven o'clock the day before, and so refreshing and delicious seemed the homely meal, that, had but the friends she loved and lamented been present to share it with her, she would have thought it delightful. But when her own sufferings were less intense, her apprehensions and anxiety for her parents increased. She shuddered to reflect, that perhaps they were enduring evils far more terrible than her own – evils, from the bare idea of which she shrunk with horror. Could she have been assured of their safety, she would have borne her own distresses, severe as they were, with cheerful resignation, grateful for the preservation of lives which she had ever held dearer than her own.

Having finished her solitary breakfast, and slaked her thirst at a brook near her, she rested some hours, and then proceeded along the road, in hopes of arriving at another village, where perhaps all would not be thus unkindly fearful of giving protection to the wretched. Surely, she said, some hospitable door will open to receive me. Some mother, who perhaps trembles for the fate of her own daughter, will pity and receive me for her sake; or, at least, direct my wandering steps, and enable me to return to my native country, where the weary traveller seldom pleads in vain; where no dread of impending danger withholds from the unfortunate the shelter and protection of the cottage; where virtue needs but to be seen to be beloved: where real freedom reigns; not that factitious liberty which tyrannises here, and like the viper, wounds the bosom that has nurtured, and warmed it into life.

Agatha pursued her lonely journey for some miles without meeting anyone, or arriving at a habitation of any kind. At length, dejected and weary, she had sat down under the shade of a spreading tree to rest herself, and recover strength to proceed, when she observed two men at a distance, who, on espying her appeared to speak to each other, and quickening their pace, advanced towards her. Their dress and appearance bespoke them above the lower rank; yet there was something in their manner which alarmed her, and made her desirous to avoid them. But no means of escape were practicable. No friendly dwelling was near in which she could seek shelter; and were she to attempt it, she could not run so fast as they could pursue. Believing, therefore, that there would be less danger in appearing to disregard them, than in betraying her fears, she rose, and seeming not to have observed them, walked slowly, and tremblingly on.

"You had chosen a very romantic situation, fair nun," said one of them as he overtook her, "a shepherd and his flock would have made it perfect Arcadia to you. You have reason to thank your countryman for throwing down the walls that enclosed you. What a shame it was," continued he, turning to his companion, "to shut up such a lovely young creature from us! My dear," taking her hand, "how long has your cage door been open?"

"For pity's sake, Sir," said Agatha, greatly alarmed, yet fearing to incense him by betraying any resentment, "for pity's sake do not detain me – I have friends waiting for me."

"O, they would wait with pleasure if they knew how agreeably you were detained. Besides, I have certainly more gallantry than to suffer you to proceed alone – Fainrive, take the lady's other hand. You see, Madam, I am not like your father confessors, who wish to engross all the treasures themselves." Then snatching a kiss, he bade his companion take one likewise.

"Blessed Virgin, protect me!" said Agatha screaming, and forcing her hands from their rude grasp.

"Nay, nay," said one of them, again catching hold of her, "that blessed Virgin Lady herself was no nun, if I remember right; and she would be very glad to see you so well disposed of. Upon my honour, if all nuns were as pretty, they would be in a state of requisition presently, and the next generation of Parisians would be all the bantlings of *les Mesdames Religieuses*."

"O Sir!" said Agatha, again forcing her hands from them, and folding them together, in an agony of terror and supplication, "if you have any wife, sister or daughter or your own, think, O, think of them! Think if they were thus friendless and unprotected, how you would bless those whose benevolent hearts pitied their distress, and forbore to insult and torture them. For God Almighty's sake suffer me to pursue my journey, and the latest hour I live I will bless your goodness."

"Why my dearest Madam, you have certainly been an actress, and sick of the theatre, in a fit of jealous or religious frenzy, have played the fool, and ran into a nunnery. Come, be sincere with us. Is it not so? But, however, since you want a *protector*, I am very much at your service. When your dress is a little modernised, you will make a charming figure as the conductress of my *petit soupers*." Then, with the assistance of his companion, he was dragging her along, while Agatha, almost deprived of reason, in a voice of distraction and despair, called on her father – her mother – then, with wildness in her voice and gestures, again besought their pity, when a blow from an unseen hand, felled her insulter to the ground. The other instantly fled, leaving his companion wounded, and apparently lifeless on the ground.

Overpowered by terror, Agatha fainted in the arms of her deliverer.

"My Agatha – Miss Belmont! Best beloved of my soul! Look up," said a voice, whose tender accents called her back to life.

Agatha looked up. She was in the arms of Hammond.

"Mr. Hammond! My preserver – my deliverer!"

"Miss Belmont, my angel! And do I see thee again? And dost thou live?"

"Yes, to bless the hand that saved me. Yet is it possible? Mr. Hammond!"

"More than a year concealed in these environs – but another time I will tell you all. We must now fly, and with all the speed possible. The villain who escaped will alarm the neighbours, and they will return with him to seize me."

"O, let us not lose a moment," said Agatha.

The wounded man, who, sick with pain and loss of blood, yet lay on the grass, now conjured them not to leave him to perish.

"Little as is the compassion you deserve," said Hammond, "who felt none for another, I hazard my own safety and that of one infinitely dearer, to preserve your life."

While he spoke thus, he bound his handkerchief over the wound to stop the bleeding; then, taking the hand of Agatha, fled with her from the fatal spot. Fear for the safety of Hammond, and joy of meeting thus a friend and protector when most she wanted one, gave wings to her feet, and she rather flew than ran with him, till they arrived in a valley, where a thick coppice screened them from view.

Chapter 10

In order to elude pursuit, they had quitted the road, and taken the most unfrequented path. Believing themselves, however, not yet safe, when Agatha had rested some minutes, they again fled towards a hill, on the declivity of which was a hollow, where Hammond, charmed with its romantic beauties, had passed many solitary hours; and where, as the path to it was difficult, and, to those unaccustomed to its windings, extremely dangerous, a river dashing with impetuosity against the stones at the bottom of its almost perpendicular side, they might, he was assured, remain secure, till the welcome cover of night should enable them to pursue their journey to the coast. Perfectly acquainted with every part of the country, he purposed to travel during the nights, and in the days to rest in some of the unfrequented spots, of which he had acquired a knowledge.

When they had reached their place of refuge, Agatha enquired of Hammond by what strange, yet blest chance he had found and rescued her from insult.

"When from Mrs. Herbert I learned the fatal intelligence," said Hammond, "which planted everlasting daggers in my breast, when I learned from her, that a cruel and fatal necessity forced you to abandon the world, which, when you had forsaken it, had not a blessing to give me, I believed that my reason would have sunk under the burden of my sorrows. I haunted as a ghost every spot that had been endeared by your presence. O, my Agatha! Lost in the luxury of woe, I was indeed dead to the world. My friends spoke to me – I heard them not; they sought to comfort me – and I shrunk from their endeavours to divert your image from my soul, as the pious Christian shrinks from the specious arguments with which the vainglorious philosopher seeks to undermine the tenets of his belief, and tempt him from his God. To forget you, though but for a moment, seemed a crime. There was a shrub in my garden, which had fallen neglected, to the earth. Alas, poor thing, you said – it has lost its mistress – and how it droops! You raised it and propped it, while your tears fell upon the leaves. Those leaves – O, my Agatha –"

"Mr. Hammond, forbear, I conjure you!" said Agatha, greatly affected. "I must not hear this. May Heaven preserve and bless you! But we must forget, forever forget those moments when it was no crime to hope to call each other by a dearer name than friend. Do not therefore, I again conjure you, renew this subject – quit it, for both our sakes, my dearest friend, and revert only to the period when you came to this distracted country."

"Merciful Heaven!" said Hammond, "and is it become a crime but to remember that I once was blest? Can my Agatha – my Agatha, did I say? No; I have been forgotten by her, while years and years have been witness of my attachment."

"Hammond, not less fervent, not less sincere has been – is still my attachment to you. Heaven is my witness that my own happiness would shrink to nothing in my estimation when compared with yours, were both in my power. But I have vowed to devote myself to God; and should 'your image steal betwixt my God and me?' No – my best friend – my preserver – I were indeed unworthy of your friendship had that been possible. Would the Eloisa of Pope deserve the esteem of Hammond? No, with sentiments noble as are yours, ideas of rectitude pure and spotless as I know you to possess, you would not desire to live as other than as friend in a heart that could not without a crime be yours. Here then let us close this fatal subject. And now, will my deliverer and friend pursue his narrative?"

"Noble, noble Miss Belmont! Every way my superior! Yes, I will endeavour to be all you desire. Yet suffer me once more to return to the commencement of my relation; I will conceal as much as possible what I then endured. From the state of despair and misery I have represented, I was, at length, in some measure, recovered by the perusal of a fragment which I accidentally found among my sister's papers. It was written by her hand, and was probably her own composition, since the sentiments contained in it, were those by which her conduct was regulated, and which equally adorned it and ennobled her character. Struck by the justice of the lesson it inculcated, I no longer believed it a virtue to indulge my grief; and though the admonitions of an angel could not have obliterated your idea, I strove to dwell upon it with less anguish, to fulfil the duties I owed to society, and for your sake even, (remembering your earnest entreaties during the agonising hour which preceded our separation) to be no longer insensible to the benevolent attentions of my friends."

"Do you recollect any part of the fragment?" said Agatha.

"It was too deeply impressed on my mind ever to be effaced," replied Hammond. "It began –

Child of sorrow, why in this pilgrimage through a world of woe, dost thou seek to heighten thine affliction? Why by unavailing regret, make rugged every path before thee? Why spurn the admonitions of thy friends?

Is it a crime to be comforted? Art thou guilty, if, forgetting thine own sorrows, thou administerest to the wants and necessities of the poor? Or when thy voice diffuses cheerfulness through the little society around thee?

Darest thou undermine thy constitution by sadness? Darest thou say
'Love is my God! And on his Altar I will sacrifice this fabric, will sap
its foundations, and glorying in my crime, expect eternal honour for my
constancy?'
Live. Live for shame. Live to subdue a passion designed to be
subservient to thee, not thou the slave of its capricious will.
Or, if thou wilt still love, call the deeds of virtue, of heroism, the heart
of thy beloved: make them 'the gods of thy idolatry' – then, though
divided from her on earth, thou shalt deserve to be united to her, where
happiness is happiness, and "change shall be no more!"

"It seemed my Agatha, as if my sister had spoken to me from Heaven, had seen my distresses, and charged me to be comforted. From the moment in which I first read this solemn adjuration, instead of indulging, I endeavoured to combat my feelings; and, in compliance with the solicitations of Mr. Ormistace, consented to travel; leaving my generous deliverer Israeli, whom I had the exquisite happiness of meeting a few weeks previous to my departure, the inhabitant of my house during my absence. Change of scene and society, with the unwearied endeavours of my friend, rendered me, by degrees, less wretched. I enquired, and learned that my Agatha, resigned to her dreadful lot, was calm, and, as her friends hoped, happy. For worlds would I not have endangered that peace for which I hourly prayed, whatever were my own distresses – I therefore forbore, when I attended Mrs. Herbert to Issoire, to see you, nor would even suffer you to be informed that I was there."

"At Issoire with Mrs. Herbert?" said Agatha. "Good heavens!"

"Yes, my Agatha, I was indeed there; though fearing my presence might alarm your parents, it was not known even to them. I took lodgings in a village near Issoire. Every returning day beheld my solitary footsteps traverse the path that led to the convent; and hours and hours have I sat and gazed upon the wall which enclosed all that my soul held dear. Once I heard your voice accompanying a guitar – no words can paint my feelings at that moment – I hung upon the plaintive notes; and when the sound ceased, every enjoyment seemed to have died away with it: I would have given worlds for its continuance. Time after time I listened at the same spot; but never heard it again. Yet I breathed the same air, or beheld in part the same objects, saw faces on which you had looked not an hour before, and (though you knew it not) a few paces only divided us – to quit Issoire therefore seemed tearing myself from you; and all Mrs. Herbert's reasonings, all the gentle soothings of her friendship, were necessary to enable me to support the conflict.

When from certain information I learned last year that the religious throughout France would surely be compelled to quit their monasteries, and that those, once beheld with veneration by their countryman, were despised and insulted; when I learned too, that the Nobles, driven from their estates, were not less marked for destruction, my apprehensions for your safety, my Agatha, and, for your sake, for that of your parents, rendered it impossible for me to remain passively in England, and not to endeavour, at least, to shield you from oppression; yet conscious that my friends would combat the determination which they would believe pregnant with danger to myself, I concealed from everyone, and even from my bosom friend the generous Israeli, my intention of going to France: from him, indeed, I was obliged to conceal it, since his generous regard for me would not have suffered me to incur any danger alone. Aware that I was preparing to visit a country where the life of no one is secure, I provided myself with a hanger and a brace of pistols, and informing my friends by letter from Dover, that a design, which I would at some future period communicate to them, induced me to travel for some months, possibly years, proceeded, under an assumed character to Issoire. I passed for an American, travelling in pursuit of a youth confided to my care, who, in a fit of anger had left his friends and country, and had gone, it was believed, to France.

At Issoire, feigning to be charmed with the beauties of the country, and the newly acquired freedom of its inhabitants, and pretending to despair of finding the youth of whom I came in search, I have since lived, though not without being regarded with an eye of suspicion by the peasants around me. But O, my Agatha! To what scenes so complicated misery and horror have I been witness, scenes which imagination even shudders to contemplate! The ferocity of the Moors is humanity, is gentleness compared to the spirit of *murderous liberty* that reigns here.

A nobleman whom age and infirmity had confined to his bed, and who during fifty years had been the idol of his tenantry, among whom it was his delight and pride to distribute his wealth, was dragged from his bed; that bed and all his furniture burned in his sight, and himself afterwards murdered by those hands which but a few years before had been lifted up to Heaven to invoke blessing on his head. His feeble voice blessed his murderers, and asked forgiveness of their crimes. My Agatha, wilt thou believe me when I say, that I saw a child not ten years old wearing this unfortunate nobleman's sword – that sword which had been dyed in the blood of the enemies of his country – the badge of his honour – which, while youth and vigour nerved his arm, no one could have wrested from him – and while uttering horrid imprecations, unsheathing it to plunge it in the bosom of another infant whom he called an Aristocrat. I rescued the child, though at the hazard of my own life; but was afterwards regarded with so much hatred and suspicion that I could not much longer have remained in the neighbourhood of Issoire. 'Aristocrat' was whispered as I passed along; and a dagger once grazed my side from a hand out of a window of a cottage, which I had unguardedly passed too near. The cruel generally are cowards; and, on account of the weapons which I found it necessary to declare that I carried, no one dared attack me openly; but I had reason to believe that some species of vengeance was meditating against me, when the destruction of the convent rendered my continuance at Issoire no longer necessary."

"No longer necessary! – O, Mr. Hammond, and for me!" said Agatha, bursting into tears.

"My Agatha – why this? What was my own life when that of one infinitely dearer was at stake? And every danger is a thousand – thousand times overpaid by the blessing of having protected thee. Heaven surely inspired the idea, and guided my steps. The intention of seizing Sir Charles and Lady Belmont was kept so secret, that I heard not of it till the news of their escape caused a general tumult. Uncertain whether my Agatha was a companion in their flight, I remained some time in an uncertainty which I dared not endeavour to remove by enquiries. At length a traveller falling sick at a neighbouring cottage, was visited by the confessor of the convent, who brought him every relief his situation required; though, notwithstanding the assistance he received, he died the next morning. I heard not of this till some days afterwards, when the woman at whose house I lodged repeated the circumstance, adding her supposition that the Angel of Auvergne had heard of his illness and sent him the relief. 'For,' continued she, 'the wretches that have escaped the punishment their crimes deserved, have not taken the nun their daughter with them. No, no – they left her to pacify the rage of the people by charities and gifts; but that will do nothing, I can tell them. Angel or not, she is a vile Aristocrat; and where is the mighty goodness of giving away a property she had no right to possess?'

Thus, my Agatha, I learned that you were yet in the convent, and learned at the same instant, that the hearts of the wretches around me, scared by rapacious cruelty, were incapable of a single sentiment of virtue or humanity; for in the very sentence in which she acknowledged your goodness, nay, called you by the name your excellencies inspired, she made a boast of her ingratitude.

Passing my days chiefly in this solitary spot, (Ah, little did I know that my Agatha should one day bless it with her presence!) I conversed a little with the people around me: nor, indeed, was it safe; since the Inquisition itself, during the zenith of its power, was a merciful institution compared to the system of liberty prevalent here. A word of pity dropped accidentally for the fate of the murdered noble – a tear – a look of compassion even, are sufficient to involve another in his pretended guilt. Then the inquisitors could not be present, nor their spies for them, in every house, as is the case here, where every man's hand is against every man, and dark distrust, and brooding fear have closed the lips of the once flippant and garrulous Frenchman. To accuse another of pretended crimes is often the only way to screen yourself from suspicion; while, not infrequently, the same part is played by someone else on you, who, in his turn, falls a sacrifice to the temporary safety of another."

"Thus ever," said Agatha, "are the guilty punished by crimes resembling their own; and thus has the inventor of almost every instrument of murder felt himself its edge."

"The intention of destroying the convent was, I believe, sudden and unpremeditated," proceeded Hammond, "since, though I have conversed little with anyone, I must have heard it whispered, had it not been a hasty plan. Indeed it is probable that they would not suffer the inhabitants of the convent to have previous warning, lest they should secure some of those valuables which were the chief temptations to demolish it.

I had passed the day in this spot, and returning late in the evening, found no one in the house in which I lodged. Universal stillness prevailed, and everyone seemed to have forsaken their habitation. Unable to guess at the cause, I quitted the house, and walked to some distance, when the shouts I heard towards the convent first led me to suspect the truth. I hastened thither immediately. The mob was demolishing the walls, and scattering fragments of the stones around; cursing superstition, yet vowing vengeance on its innocent victims could they find them. Happily everyone had escaped, and their fury was vented only on the walls and furniture. In the cell of one of the nuns, they found a miniature of a young man, which gave occasion to several jests as low as they were illiberal. The picture was given to one of the leaders of the mob to be preserved as a monument of *Religious Purity*.

I wandered alone all night in every path around the convent in hopes of finding my Agatha. But Judge of my agony, when I was this morning addressed by a venerable old man, who declared to me and everyone he saw, that the Angel of Auvergne was dead: that not knowing whither to go, she had, it was true, taken shelter in his house, but that she had died with terror during the night, and his son had thrown her body into the lake.

There was something in the tale, and in the manner of the old man's telling it unasked, which at the moment that it struck like death to my heart, imparted a ray of hope that it was, for what reason I knew not, a fiction. With equal anxiety and terror I interrogated him further, but could learn nothing more from his replies. The more, however, I reflected upon it, the more reason I believed there was to hope that his story was false, and probably the fabrication of a grateful mind, which knew not how otherwise to return the benefit you might have conferred on his children, than by thus preventing any search that might have been intended after you, either on account of your parents, or of the riches you might be supposed to have received from them. Still, therefore, animated by hope, I determined to leave no part of the country unsearched; and chance, or rather Providence, directed my steps to the spot where I heard your screams – I saw the barbarous efforts of your insulters to carry you away, and flying to them with a rage and agitation not to be described, wounded one of them with my hanger, and rescued my Agatha."

When Hammond had finished his recital, and Agatha had expressed, as well as her feelings would suffer her, the gratitude which penetrated her heart on account of the dangers he had incurred and the risks he had ran for her sake, she related to him every circumstance which had befallen herself; while the miseries and terror she had endured affected him too deeply to suffer him to interrupt the mournful narration. When she had ended it, he could only press her hand to his lips, and bathing it with tears, return silent thanks to Heaven for having at last given her to his protection.

Hammond now took out the remains of his yesterday's repast – some dried fruits, wine, and biscuits, and Agatha adding to it what remained of her solitary breakfast, they prepared to partake of a meal, which the presence of each other, in a place of tolerable security, rendered sweet to them. They then consulted on the plan of their future journey, and Agatha, could she have been assured of the safety of her parents, comparing her present situation, under the protection, and enjoying the society of Hammond, with the desolate and friendless one in which he had found her, would have been happy; but her apprehensions for them, which Hammond in vain endeavoured to dissipate, damped every blessing, and embittered every moment.

When the dews of evening began to fall, and the day shut in, Hammond, fearing that Agatha's health might suffer from the damps rising from the water, and the little shelter afforded them from the night air, proposed, as she had suffered too much from fatigue and terror to be capable of walking far that night, to endeavour to obtain shelter in a cottage, the inhabitants of which he believed to be more humane than the generality; where they might perhaps not only procure shelter during that night and the next day, but might purchase provisions to last them during the great part of their journey.

Chapter 11

The moon now darting its beams through a clump of trees before them, as just appearing in the horizon, it began to illuminate the scene, promised to afford sufficient light to guide their steps; they therefore quitted the hill whose friendly-rugged path had secured them from the danger of pursuit, and proceeded towards the cottage which was about three miles distant. Agatha weary and faint, but for the support of Hammond would have sunk under her fatigue; but his friendship and tenderness, by soothing her spirits, seemed to give her new strength.

They were not, as Hammond believed, more than half a mile from the cottage, when the storm which had only threatened the night before, began suddenly with a violence which seemed to shake the earth to its centre. The moon disappeared in a moment. Bursts of thunder, each louder and more tremendous than the last, succeeded each other with dreadful rapidity. The rain fell in torrents; and the dazzling glare of the lightning alone afforded them a momentary view of the objects around them – while the violence of the wind, threatening to lift them from their feet, and scattering the branches of the trees around them, added to the other horrors of the storm. Thus dreadfully situated, with no shelter in view except the trees, under which they dared not take refuge, a vivid flash of lightning discovered to Hammond the ruins of a monastery at a small distance. He remembered to have seen it as he once passed it, when the magnificence of its ruins had caught his eye; and on enquiry he had learned that it had fallen to decay some centuries ago, and that the stones, as time or accident displaced them, were used by the peasants around to repair their houses, or for other purposes. Enough of the building yet remained, however to afford them shelter. Directing their steps towards it therefore, as the repeated flashes of momentary light discovered its situation, they arrived before long at the venerable structure. Going towards that part of it which Hammond remembered to have appeared least decayed, they entered what seemed to have been the aisle of a church. But here every clap of thunder threatened destruction. The tottering roof shook with the peal, and the wind, during the intervening moments, was hardly less terrifying. Unable, however, to find a safer shelter, they determined there to wait till the storm was over.

After some hours, the thunder having ceased, the wind, now whistling through the ruinous fabric, and now, seeming to collect additional strength, shaking the walls near which they stood, was the only cause of alarm. During some moments, in some of its gusts, it conveyed the sound like that of deep and hollow groans.

"The force of fancy, in such a night and such a place as this, is wonderful," said Agatha. "In every murmur of the wind my imagination conveys to my ear groans like those which superstition sometimes gives to the restless spirits of the murdered; and, though hitherto a stranger to such fears, I shudder at the sound."

"Be not alarmed," said Hammond, "yet something more than fancy, or the murmurs of the wind, occasions those groans – for groans I am assured they are. Perhaps some miserable being is at this moment perishing beneath these ruins. Perhaps someone murdered and expiring here. But conjectures are fruitless – I will listen whence the sound proceeds, and go towards it."

"O, do not," said Agatha. "You know not what dangers. The murderers as well as murdered may be here." Then, lowering her voice, she conjured him to quit the building, regardless of the storm, the fury of which was already abated.

Hammond endeavoured to calm her fears and having represented to her that it was possible some miserable wretch expiring with want, disease, or grief, might have taken refuge in some part of the building, the horrors of whose dying moments their pity and attendance might lessen; that perhaps the loose stones had fallen on some unfortunate traveller, who, like themselves, had sought shelter there; Agatha's humanity in a moment conquered every apprehension for their own safety, and following Hammond, she went along the aisle towards the place from whence they had heard the noise: but it had ceased. The wind was still, and nothing was heard but the echo of their footsteps. They, however, were still proceeding slowly along; though with difficulty, the loose stones under their feet rendering it scarcely possible to walk without a light when Agatha's foot slipped, and as she fell, endeavouring to save herself, she caught hold of something. It was a hand, which, with the cold damp of death upon it, feebly grasped hers as she touched it. Agatha screamed. "Alas, whoever you are," said a female voice, faint and gasping for breath as she spoke, "whoever you are that like me have taken shelter here, fear nothing – wretch as I have been, I cannot now injure you if I would."

The storm was now at an end, and the moon appearing, gleamed through the chinks and wide clefts of the stone, and discovered to them a female lying on the pavement, on whose pale and haggard face, convulsed as it was by the agonies of death, the remains of former beauty were yet discernible. "I am fearful," she said, again languidly speaking, "that I have greatly terrified you – yet by the mercy of that God whom my crimes have offended, I conjure you to give me, if it be possible, one drop of liquid to moisten my parched and burning lips. An inward fire consumes me."

"If we can give you the smallest relief, we shall indeed be thankful," said Agatha. "I am here, Madam – can you raise your head and rest it on my arm." Then sitting on the ground, Agatha put her arm under the head of the unfortunate lady; while Hammond, finding a few drops yet remaining of the wine he had with him, guided the bottle to her quivering lips.

"The blessing of one that is ready to perish be upon you!" said the lady, who, somewhat revived, now spoke with less difficulty.

"Generous strangers, whoever ye are, should ye ever behold her whom I have injured, will, O, will ye tell her how I am punished. Say, that with my latest breath I bless her, and ask of her forgiveness. Tell her, that she who robbed her of all she prized, perished thus miserably, indebted to the bounty of strangers for comfort and support in her last moments. Bid her not curse my memory – but when I am no more, pity and forgive the wretch who has fallen the victim of her own crimes. Should ye ever see or hear of Emily de Vermueil –"

"Emily de Vermueil!" repeated Agatha. "Good God!"

"Alas!" said the lady, "perhaps she is known to you – O, ask her to forgive me, that her pardon may be an earnest of the mercy of that God of whom I dare not ask it. Will you then give her this ring – last remnant of the fortune I robbed her of. Yes – I will avow all my crimes – O, that this confession might make atonement for them when I shall appear in the presence of that Judge in whose Eternal records they are written. I saw and loved (if that passion deserves the name of love, which seeks only its own gratification) Henry Dorville, the lover, the then happy lover of the spotless Emily de Vermueil. His person, his fortune were alike temptations to my guilty heart. By the basest arts I won his affections, and tore him from his undesigning and tender Emily. A few, very short months destroyed the illusion. From the love my artifices had created, he awoke as from a dream; awoke to remorse and anguish. Proud and vindictive, I disdained to court the favour of a heart alienated by returning love to another. I returned his coldness with contempt and aversion; and forsaking him, fled with the property, which I knew he had neither spirits nor courage to endeavour to wrest from my hands, to Paris, to lose in the pleasures of dissipation the remembrance of him and of my own guilt. There, even before his death, I formed a connection with a man, in my guilty attachment to whom every remaining spark of virtue was smothered in my breast forever. Regardless of the world and heedless of its censures, I gloried in my shame, and boasted of having fixed a heart which had hitherto been divided among many. But that love which has not virtue for its basis, is shaken by every blast, and has poison mingled with every pleasure. Another object at length attached him, and seduced him from me. In vain every art was essayed, in vain I strove by those allurements which had first pleased to win him back to my affections: what was intended to charm created but disgust, and my happy rival, triumphing in her power, joined her own insidious pity to his scorn. Stung by jealous rage, I denounced him to the people as a tyrant – an enemy to liberty! – My voice was heard. He was torn from the arms of my rival, and I met his mangled body dragged along the streets. Filled with horror and remorse, life was now a burden to me; and I dared to precipitate myself into the presence of the Eternal with all my crimes upon my head. I swallowed poison. But Heaven was merciful, and gave me time for repentance – yet can repentance wash out crimes of a hue black as have been mine? My stomach nauseated by the deadly draught, and enough only remained by lingering tortures to consume me. Determined to implore forgiveness of Mademoiselle de Vermueil, and having been informed that she resided in this province, I have travelled hither, on foot and alone. But my strength failing me, I have lingered two days and two nights among these ruins, in all the torments of pain and misery – outcast of everyone, with the aggravated horrors of knowing I deserved my punishment. And O, that this were all that in this life might end my sufferings! But in that which is to come, O, on the brink of what torments do I stand?" Then grasping Agatha's hand with a convulsive start, she trembled violently, and shuddering with horror, screamed as she held it.

"Alas," said Agatha, "What shall I say to speak comfort to you? Yet O, remember that the mercy of God is boundless, is infinite as his power – the repentant and contrite heart he will not, we are assured, despise. If my prayers, the prayers of one whose heart bleeds for your sufferings, can be of no avail, I do and will pray for you from my soul."

"Kind Lady!" said Madame Dorville, "if your prayers are not heard for me, they must, they will bring down blessings on yourself. And O, whatever distresses you are born to suffer, may you be free from crime, and you cannot, you cannot indeed be wretched! I have fallen a victim of violent and ungoverned passions – passions which from my youth I have sought to gratify, when it was my duty to have conquered them." At this moment a compulsive pang seized Madame Dorville. The strength which only seemed to have been lent her till she had confessed her crimes, forsook her suddenly. She attempted again to speak; but her words were inaudible. Her soul quivered on her lips; and supported by Hammond and Agatha, she uttered a deep groan and expired.

With sensations of pity, grief, and horror, they laid her lifeless corpse on the earth, and kneeling by its side, commended her spirit to God.

Then, no longer able to support the dreadful spectacle, they hurried from that part of the building, and returning to the aisle which they had first entered, sat down to compose their agitated spirits, and await the return of day, when they purposed to go to the cottage Hammond had mentioned, and remain there privately, if suffered to do so, till the ensuing night. The dreadful scene just passed had made a deep and melancholy impression on the minds of them both; and finding it impossible to banish its horrors from their remembrance, they experienced a relief from dwelling on the subject. "Never, O never!" said Agatha, speaking of the agonies the unhappy Madame Dorville had endured, "never may the sting of self-reproach wound my bosom! Secure from that, whatever wreck my hopes may sustain, whatever distresses I may be destined to encounter, all will not be misery; a ray of light shall break through the gloom, and cheer the scene. In religion I can seek and obtain consolation; in the soothings of pity and friendship feel my anguish mitigated, if not cured; but O, Hammond! No friendly hand can draw forth the arrows of affliction when they are barbed with guilt!"

"Your pathetic wish, my Agatha," said Hammond, "reminds me of some lines my sister gave me when a boy at school. The sentiments are nearly the same as those you have uttered, though differently expressed. These were the lines, which, from being learned in childhood, and given to me by one so deservedly dear, I can never forget.

> O! grant me Heaven! howe'er thy will,
> My cup with bitterness shall fill,
> Howe'er thy wisdom shall deny
> Each other good for which I sigh,
> O! grant – from ills the best defence –
> A shield of Conscious Innocence!
>
> Then, though each storm that others dread,
> Should burst on my devoted head;
> Though every friend on earth were lost,
> And every flattering prospect crost;
> My peace shall know one sure defence –
> The shield of Conscious Innocence!
>
> In every scene supreme its power,
> How shall it bless my parting hour!
> Content, when thou shalt will, to die,
> My Guardian Angel hovering nigh,
> Shall ease the pangs that call me hence,
> By whispering "Conscious Innocence!"

Day at length breaking, they quitted the monastery, the appearance of which as the light discovered to them the loose and mouldering stones which hung over their heads, made them shudder to reflect on the imminent danger of their situation during the night – shaken as the building had been by the fury of the storm.

Taking the path towards the cottage, they were met by a soldier, apparently bowed down by the weight of age and grief. Looking at Hammond earnestly, "Surely," he said, "your appearance bespeaks you the American who wounded the insolent and inhuman Morèe? If you are he, fly I charge you, for vengeance pursues you. Every house is searched throughout the Province. Wonder not that I wish you to escape. I had a daughter – sole comfort of my age. She was seduced and torn from my feeble arms by the villain you stabbed. Fly then. There is a thick forest near. Seek the dens of wild beasts rather than the haunts of men – for man is savage here!"

The old man then sitting down on the grass, wiped a tear that had fallen on his furrowed cheek, and again urged them to hasten to the forest. Not daring, therefore, to pursue their former intentions, they fled as they were directed; Agatha looking behind her at every step, and fancying every breath of wind conveyed the sound of footsteps in pursuit of them.

Breathless and fatigued, they at length reached the forest in which Agatha had taken shelter the night before. Here, believing themselves secure, they sat down to rest, when a noise at a distance alarmed them. They listened, and could distinguish the sound of horses' feet; and immediately after, looking around, discerned several horsemen not far from them. "Merciful Heaven preserve us!" said Agatha, "whither shall we fly?"

"We will seek a thicker part of the forest," said Hammond. Then flying, torn by briars, among the underwood, they lost, for a time, the sound of their pursuers, and were again indulging the hopes of safety, when the horsemen again approached, and by the exclamations of fury which they uttered left them no room to doubt that they were actually in search of them.

Flying for shelter yet farther from the beaten track, Hammond's foot slipped, and he fell among some briars, which he immediately discovered were placed over the mouth of a cavern, into which they could with ease descend. Not a moment was to be lost. Their pursuers were in sight; and, guided and supported by Hammond, Agatha descended with him a steep slope which led into the cavern. Having displaced the briars in their descent, lest this should lead to a discovery at their place of refuge, they again, though with some difficulty spread them over the aperture, standing on a step which seemed to be made in one side of the cave for that purpose. They now again heard the voices of the horsemen, and trembling lest they should by an accident similar to Hammond's discover the cavern, they proceeded to explore a narrow passage, which they observed on one side of them, in hopes it might lead to some more distant and secure retreat. The passage was serpentine, low, and narrow, and so totally devoid of light, that with difficulty they groped their way along it; and nothing but a terror far greater than any this gloomy retreat could occasion, would have given them courage to explore it: but smaller, and possibly ideal causes of fear shrink to nothing when known and real ones are apprehended.

After traversing the winding path for some time, they were struck by observing it become lighter, and by the glimmering of a lamp reflected on the stone. This subterraneous scene was therefore inhabited; and whether to proceed farther, or to continue where they now were till their pursuers might have left the forest, they were in doubt. At length, curiosity, added to the probability that it was the refuge of the unfortunate rather than the wicked, in a country where the innocent are persecuted, and the barbarous and guilty roam at large, they ventured to proceed; and turning to the right from whence they observed the light, saw a large circular cavern, resembling that which they had first entered, at the farther end of which sat a venerable figure in the habit of a priest, reading by the light of a lamp placed on a stone table before him. The floor was of earth; and as they walked slowly and silently along, they had time to contemplate his figure before he observed them. Every furrow in his face bore the print of benevolence. One hand supported his head, while the other, laid on his book, was now raised and then dropped again gradually, as the devotion excited by his missal inspired him. Raising his eyes, at length, and observing Hammond and Agatha, he started, and rose from his seat, while a blush rather of surprise than confusion for a moment overspread his face.

"Forgive us," said Hammond, "that we intrude on your retirement. Chance discovered to us the entrance to this cave; and pursued by implacable enemies, we gladly profited by the shelter it promised to afford us."

"You are welcome, sincerely welcome," said the venerable priest, advancing towards them; "and I bless Heaven that my peaceful abode has given you shelter and protection." Then, observing the terror yet imprinted on Agatha's countenance, with an aspect of mild concern, and an air of that genuine politeness which benevolence prompts and inspires, he took her trembling hand with respectful tenderness, and led her to the seat he had quitted; when taking an earthen cup from a corner of the cave, and filling it with wine, he entreated her to partake of the trifling refreshment which he was enabled to offer his guests; "for such,"

he added, "I shall be proud to consider you." He now brought two large blue stones and, there being no other chair but that in which he had placed Agatha, offered one of them to Hammond, and took himself the other. "You are no doubt surprised," he continued, "to find an inhabitant of a subterraneous spot like this, and it will perhaps recall to your minds the scenes of poetry and romance; but we live in a country, where, what would have been deemed extravagant in the pages of fiction, is now every day practised in real life. Many are the families, that, dreading the consequences of their former declarations of attachment to their King, have retired to the woods; and there, subsisting on such fruits and herbs as they casually discover, lead a life of wildness and dismay – alarmed at the approach of a human being, and dreading a murderer in everyone they meet. Others there probably are, who like me have interred themselves alive; and who, excluded from the light of day, bless a retreat, which, in more prosperous times, they would have beheld with terror. Intended from my infancy for the sacred garb I wear, and glorying in a religion, the pure tenets of which I have laboured to teach others, I was marked for destruction. Whithersoever I fled I was persecuted, myself and my profession ridiculed, and, because I scorned to deny what I firmly believed, I was branded with the name of hypocrite. Yet the time has been that the very persons who gave me the odious appellation, looked up to me as a father, and delightedly confessed, that they owed to my instructions the virtues, and, in consequence, the happiness of their lives. Convinced that Religion had lost many votaries by the harsh and forbidding form under which she has been too often represented, I endeavoured to paint her as she is – mild, soothing, and consolatory; to the innocent clad in perpetual smiles – soothing affliction and heightening happiness. True piety, I frequently said, forbids no one guiltless pleasure, enjoins an abstinence from no enjoyments but such as would endanger our real happiness even in this life: while by my example I endeavoured to enforce the practice of the innocent cheerfulness my lessons were designed to inculcate. I was a party in every innocent festivity. I looked on as the youths and maidens danced, and invited them to pursue the harmless pastime. I listened to the long stories of the aged, and pleased them by my patient attention. I gave little rewards to the children who excelled in any infantine feat; and 'father Albert is coming' made every little nerve be strained, and every effort of skill be exerted to obtain applause. I mention not this from vanity or ostentation, but to show from what a height of happiness I am fallen. Those very children, instigated by their relations, have since hooted as I passed them; and instead of 'dear Father Albert' as I was once called, I have been loaded with every term of abuse and execration which the most infernal heart can dictate, yet my conduct has been unchanged. I have not, that I am conscious, neglected a duty, or committed a crime: 'to do justice, love mercy, and walk humbly with my God'[33] has been, as far as in me lay, my constant practice. At length I believed it my duty to fly from a torrent which I was unable to stem. My life was threatened – and though few may be the years that are given me to sojourn on earth, and though with the calm resignation of a Christian I trust I am capable of meeting my end, yet not to provide for my safety when my death would neither reclaim the wicked, nor strengthen the cause of piety, I held to be criminal, and adverse to the principles of the faith I possessed. This retreat, from my intimacy with the Prior of a Monastery situated on the extremity of this forest, was well-known to me, and persecuted on every side, I fled to it as a last and only resource. Communicating, by a passage similar to that through which you passed, with the refectory of the convent, and from thence with another cavern which was the cellar of the monks during their residence here, I have wine enough to last probably during the few years of my solitary existence – enough too, to share with my welcome guests," pursued he, bowing, and smiling complacently, "and, attired as a peasant, I sometimes go to one, sometimes to another village or town to purchase provisions, which a little stock of wealth that

---

[33]Micah, 6, v. 8.

I providentially discovered, when digging for roots in the garden of the forsaken monastery, enabled me to do; but more frequently I explore the forest in search of wild fruits and herbs.

Thus, though innocent of crime, I endure in part the terrors of the guilty, and skulk under disguises, which they only ought to be forced to assume. But the ways of Heaven are just. Let them brandish their instruments of destruction over the head of trembling Virtue! In the breast of each there lurks an adder whose sting is worse than death – worse than any torments their power and malice can inflict. O, may it not sting in vain! Warned by its torments of those which are to come, may they repent and be forgiven! Yes! May Heaven of its mercy pity and pardon a deluded and infatuated people – a people who know not what they do!"

The venerable appearance of their kind host had greatly interested the travellers in his behalf, and this short description of his situation and sentiments confirmed the favourable impression. With equal ingenuousness they gave him a brief relation of the different events which had befallen themselves, and in particular of the circumstance which had driven them to take shelter in his cave.

The good priest, much affected by the recital, conjured them not to quit their present retreat till the search after Hammond might be supposed to be at an end, and they could pursue their journey with a probability of safety, requesting them in the meantime, partake of the simple fare he was enabled to set before them. They gratefully accepted his offer, and, thus happily screened from danger, enjoying the society of each other, and of one, whose conversation, enlivened by the cheerful serenity of conscious virtue, and tinctured by universal benevolence, rendered him every minute more and more an object of their esteem and veneration, they were comparatively happy. Yet when Agatha's grateful heart would have exulted in the blessings thus providentially bestowed, her anxiety for her parents, and fears for their safety again embittered every comfort; and neither the tender arguments of Hammond nor the friendly hopes suggested by Father Albert, could calm her apprehensions.

When Father Albert's timepiece warned him that it was time to retire to rest, he spread a coverlet on the ground, and making as convenient a bed as he could, insisted on Agatha's taking that, and retired himself with Hammond to different parts of the cavern.

Chapter 12

Agatha was now alone. The lamp burning on the stone table before her faintly lighted the spacious vaulted apartment. No sound was heard; and in the silence that reigned around her, she felt a depression of spirits to which she had hitherto been a stranger. Time had rendered her little solitary cell in the convent not only familiar but dear to her. But there, the wind at intervals shook her casement. The bell to call her to Matins, though once heard with terror, had been since heard and expected with delight, since it bad her to join that devotion she lived but to pay. But here – in this subterraneous apartment, no sound broke the dead stillness of the night, or dissipated the images of terror which fancy in a thousand fantastic shapes presented to her imagination; while her mind, harassed as it had been of late, was but too well suited to receive the gloomy impressions. At length, by an effort of reason and piety, she chased the fearful shadows of her imagination and commending herself to Heaven, lay down on her humble bed, and sunk into a sweet and refreshing sleep from which she did not awake till morning.

At an early hour she was joined by Father Albert and Hammond, and the little group, after uniting in prayers and praises to the dispenser of every comfort, sat down to their temperate breakfast, and passed this day as they had done the last, in conversation equally instructive and delightful; and a friendship which in the world might have been months, perhaps years, in forming, from a similarity of situations was already so closely cemented that the good priest was regarded as a father by his guests, while he considered them as children, whose safety he would rejoice to provide for, though at the hazard of his own.

On the day following, Father Albert's small stock of provisions being nearly exhausted, he assumed his accustomed disguise, and going to a neighbouring village, returned to them, after an absence of some hours, with a fresh supply.

Hammond had concealed nothing from the good priest, and had confessed the attachment which had taken place in his own and Agatha's heart before they knew that any duty would compel them to renounce each other. Accident revived the subject on the father's return.

"Does it not seem," said Hammond, appealing to him with an air of timid supplication, "does it not appear as if Heaven had interposed on my behalf, and, throwing down the barriers which divided us, smiled on our love, and designed a union to which it has thus removed obstacles which once appeared insurmountable? Has it not, by a chain of events next to miraculous, given my Agatha to my care, and placed us both under the protection of – a Priest?"

Father Albert was silent. Agatha, greatly agitated, was incapable of speaking, and Hammond, not daring to look at her, again tremblingly repeated his question.

"Alas!" replied Father Albert, "how shall I advise, when my inclination and reason will perhaps point different ways; and when the happiness of those, already dear to me as if they were actually my children, is at stake? You, my daughter, was, by your mother's vow, devoted to God. You have fulfilled her vow; have in the sense in which her word was given, devoted yourself to Heaven. Fate has restored you to the world. Perhaps it would be now no crime to devote yourself to Heaven in another, and, as I have always held, the truest sense of the word – by a life which would render you useful to society, and reward the faithful affection of one who deserves to be happy. Yet with doubt and hesitation do I offer suggestions by which I wish you not to be swayed. To your own hearts I appeal – if they forbid it not –"

"Enough – enough," said Hammond, starting from his seat in transport, "you do not disapprove, and Heaven itself sanctions my wishes! My Agatha, speak! Yet do not speak – that silence, my flattering heart assures me, bids me be happy – the happiest of human beings!"

"Indulge not the idea," replied Agatha; "for never can I have an earthly husband."

"Cruel, cruel Agatha!" said Hammond, awaking from his short dream of bliss, "you never loved me. You might make me happy – without the shadow of a crime might make me happy! Yet, exulting in your power, you triumph in my misery. No, you never loved me."

"Indeed, indeed," said Agatha, bursting into tears, "I have not deserved this. Can it be Hammond – my friend – my deliverer who speaks thus? Without the shadow of a crime say you? O, if without the shadow of a crime I could make you happy, can you believe that I would hesitate a moment? Be calm, consult your own reason, and you will know and acknowledge that I would not. Dearer than the life for the preservation of which you hazarded your own – generously, nobly hazarded it – do I prize your happiness; I would submit to any worldly misery to procure it, if it were so to be procured. But not even you shall tempt me to violate my duty; and, by a subterfuge as mean as it would be criminal, to draw down on both our heads the wrath of Heaven. A mad populace have unbarred the gates of my sanctuary, have forced me to abandon it; but could that action dispense with my performance of vows the awful solemnity of which will be forever engraven on my soul? Believe not that you would be happy were I to consent to your present wishes! The heart-rending idea that I had violated a vow, had committed a crime, to make you happy, would haunt your mind perpetually, and embitter every promised blessing: dreadful is it to lay to our own charge the guilt of those we love. And, after all, is there a blessing in a life, whose longest duration is a few fleeting years, which deserves to be purchased by the chance even of offending Him whose punishments and rewards are *Eternal?*"

Agatha stopped; and Hammond, struck by the solemnity of her manner, and the superiority of her virtue, was silent and abashed.

"Excellent young woman!" at last exclaimed Father Albert, "how little do I appear in my own eyes! I, whose weakness could plead in extenuation of a crime, because I believed it would promote your happiness! Who, by a 'mean subterfuge,' if not advise, at least permit you to forfeit a vow! But by specious arguments we too often deceive ourselves into an approbation of our wishes. An unbiased investigation of their inherent rectitude ought to precede all our actions; and, divesting ourselves of every partial prejudice, duty and reason should be our only directors."

"O Father Albert!" said Hammond, "plead too for me! I have accused my Agatha, angel as she is! I have accused her of cruelty – have said –"

"My Hammond," interrupted Agatha, holding out her hand, and advancing towards him, "say no more – all is forgiven – forgive me too, if anything that I have said has hurt my best friend – friend! My Hammond – let me repeat this sweet word, and be grateful to Heaven that forbids us not the dear privilege of friendship! And now, for the second *last* time," continued she, forcing a smile though the tears which yet glistened in her eyes, "we will close this painful subject."

She then gave her other hand to Father Albert, who, as he respectfully received it, gazed on her with a mixture of surprise and veneration, as on a being of a superior order.

But the serenity of the little party was not immediately recovered. Hammond, sanctioned by the reluctantly-given consent of the kind priest, who, accustomed to dispense felicity, knew not how to forbid it, had given the reins to hopes, which, once indulged, could not, without a severe struggle, be again relinquished. While Agatha, at the same time that she suffered severely from the pain she was compelled to inflict on her preserver, was but too sensible at that fatal moment, of the continuance of a love which she had believed forever subdued, and trembled at her own emotions. But in a heart long and firmly devoted to the cause of virtue, the empire of the feelings which oppose it, is weak and transitory. Agatha's reason and piety in a moment resumed their sway, and triumphed over her wishes; and she replied to Hammond with a firmness which at once dissipated the flattering illusion.

Almost a fortnight had elapsed, and Father Albert, apprehensive for the safety of his friends, and happy in their society, was yet unwilling to consent to their departure, and had prevailed upon them to remain his guests for some days longer, when, on his going one morning to purchase provisions, they were alarmed by his not returning at the accustomed time. They went repeatedly to the mouth of the cavern, and looked around for him; but to no purpose. Evening arrived – yet still he came not. And now, more than ever alarmed, they determined to go in search of him, though they knew not whither: they were ignorant what road he had taken, or to what village or town he purposed to go; and to enquire of any one they might chance to meet would equally endanger his safety and their own. But, in a state of anxiety and suspense, every plan, however vague, seems preferable to remaining passive. Believing it possible, that, fatigued by the heat of the day, a sudden illness might have seized him, they resolved to seek him in every part of the forest. With this view they left the cavern, but had no sooner quitted it, than they were convinced, by observing its situation, surrounded by brakes, and distant from every beaten path, that if they once ventured to stray any distance from it, all endeavours to find it again would be fruitless; especially as the night would overtake them before they traversed any considerable part of the forest; by which means, if Father Albert should return, he would be in equal terror on their account, and they might, in all probability never see him more; they were therefore compelled to remain in this painful suspense – listening every moment at the mouth of the cave, and in every rustling of the leaves endeavouring to discover the sound of his footsteps.

Hour after hour thus passed till twelve o'clock arrived. Still, however, they cherished the hope, that in the morning he might return to them; possibly, detained by accident, he had been benighted, and losing himself among some of the wildest parts of the forest, had been unable, during the darkness of the night, to discover his retreat. In the anxiety and agitation which they had endured during the greater part of the day, they had not even thought of taking any refreshment; but now, all expectation of seeing him that night at an end, they endeavoured to make themselves as easy as possible, and to await with patience the return of day, whose welcome light would they flattered themselves restore to them their venerable friend. They now therefore took their lamp, and proceeded towards the cellar of the monks, in order to fetch some wine and the few provisions that remained – but scarcely had they ascended the winding steps which led to the refectory, when they were alarmed by the sound of voices issuing from the cellar into which they were going. Apprehending with too great an appearance of reason, that Father Albert had been taken, and his retreat discovered, they turned back immediately, and, fearing the light of their lamp might betray them, should the persons, whoever they were, proceed to explore any of the other subterraneous passages, they blew it out, and groping their way as silently and quickly as possible to the part of the cavern they inhabited, with all the calmness and collection of mind they could assume, began to deliberate on the steps they should take to ensure their safety. To quit the cavern at the other aperture might be hazardous – persons might be stationed near it; or, at least, while some explored the cellar, others might remain above to receive tidings of the discoveries they made; and, to continue where they were, as there was an uninterrupted communication of their cave with the refectory, seemed equally dangerous. At length, in hopes the other aperture, from being covered with briars, might have escaped discovery, they determined to stand on the slope near it, ready to escape into the forest should they hear anyone in the passage, or to retreat into the cave, and to endeavour to effect their escape through the other passage, should anyone attempt to remove the brakes.

When they had arrived at the place they had fixed upon, prepared to advance or retreat as they find it necessary, they could distinguish several voices above ground not far from them; and the conversation, which they could not often distinctly hear, was interrupted by frequent bursts of laughter.

At length, the party above ground seemed to be joined by that which had been below, and they heard with inexpressible satisfaction that the search was intended to be abandoned for the present. But this momentary exultation at their own escape was soon converted into distress for the fate of the unfortunate Father Albert, which the last words they distinguished left them little reason to doubt was by that time determined. "We have kennelled the old fox," were the words they heard, "and are certainly welcome to the legacy of his wine, when he has no longer any occasion for it." This witticism having received its due share of applause, the sons of LIBERTY, elated by the wine they had copiously drank, and by the good fortune of having seized and murdered a PRIEST, departed in high good humour, while the forest resounded with their vociferous mirth.

When they were gone, and the barbarous tumult was succeeded by the solemn stillness of midnight, Hammond and Agatha again consulted on steps they should take to provide for their safety. From one of the expressions they had heard, they had every reason to believe that, as soon as it was light, the cavern would again be visited and its passages explored. To remain there, therefore, was out of the question, and whether or not the pursuit after Hammond was at an end was uncertain; whether too they could fly, or to whom have recourse for protection, they were equally at a loss. But the forest now visited, and all its haunts probably searched in expectation of finding other subterraneous dwell-ings, seemed of all others the most dangerous situation. At length they determined to go to the benevolent cottagers, to whom Hammond had before intended to apply, to ask for temporary assistance and protection. But dark as was the night, it was next to impossible to find the road, or perhaps to discover a path which would lead them out of the forest: and, already in want of food, how should they subsist, if, unable to find a path, they should be necessitated to conceal themselves in some part of the forest during the next day. As, therefore, in all probability, the whole stock of wine was not yet carried away, Hammond prevailed upon Agatha to return with him through the cave, every part of its passages being familiar to them, to take a small supply with them.

Agatha, trembling violently, and leaning on Hammond, prepared, once more, to traverse the gloomy passages; and walking with fearful haste, they soon reached the steps leading to the refectory. Before they proceeded farther, they listened for some minutes in silent apprehension, lest someone should have been left behind to keep watch for his companions – an idea which struck them both at the same instant, but which had not occurred to either when they ventured to return. At length, however, they ascended the steps; and arrived at the last, they listened again – but everything was still. They heard no one breathe – and struggling with their fears, they had half crossed the refectory, when they stumbled against something on the ground before them; and a hoarse voice inarticulately muttered an oath on being touched; but, endeavouring to rise, sunk down again, overpowered, as it appeared, by intoxication. Though this was probably someone, who, having drank more largely than his companions, was unable to follow them, and in that state had fallen asleep, and not, as they had apprehended, anyone stationed there as Sentinel, they dared not proceed; but hastening back the way they came, quitted the cavern, and entered the forest – wandering only as they were directed by chance, and without a ray of light to guide their devious steps.

When they had walked some time, ignorant to what part of the forest they had strayed, sat down, spent and weary, on the trunk of a fallen tree, and there awaited the return of day.

The morning light giving them a view of their situation, they found themselves on the skirts of the forest, within sight of a castle which Hammond remembered to have seen on his first arrival in Auvergne, and which, during his residence in the Province, had shared the fate of many others, and fallen a sacrifice to popular fury. Its walls were yet standing, but everything of value in or near it had been either carried away or destroyed. In its ruins Hammond however proposed that they should take shelter till the evening, when they would once more attempt to gain the friendly cottage. Before they left the forest, they gathered some wild berries, and with this slender supply of food, proceeded without delay to the castle.

"That castle," said Hammond, pointing to it as they went along, "was, a twelvemonth since, the residence of the Marquis de Villarme, a nobleman in the flower of his age who inherited it from a long line of ancestors not less illustrious for their virtues than their rank. His wife, one of the loveliest and most accomplished women of the age, terrified at the menaces of the mob who wanted to seize her husband on his return from hunting, was deprived of her reason, and in that miserable state received insults which humanity shudders but to think of.

The marquis returning, beheld her, her hair dishevelled and her clothes torn, bewailing in a frantic manner her murdered husband. 'Wretches! Devils!' he exclaimed, as he beheld the mob surrounding her, 'what – who are you! – My Life! My love! My Julia!' flying to her arms. 'I am not murdered – I am here to protect, to shield, to die for thee!' 'Here?' replied his Julia, 'No – no, they stabbed you here – and here – and here' pointing to her heart. 'Come, come,' said one of the mob, 'no more of this fond fooling. You are wanted, Sir, and must leave my Lady your wife for good and all.' 'Alive you shall not tear me from her,' he replied; 'death, death only shall divide us.' One of the wretches then endeavouring to force him from her, wounded his arm, and the unhappy lady, seeing the blood flow, wept over the wound, and from the relief of tears, recovered her senses for a few minutes – but recovered them only to wake to a sense of misery of the most exquisite. Her husband was torn from her arms, and murdered in her sight. She flew to his mangled corpse, and with an eloquence that might have melted a savage. 'Is it come to this?' she cried; 'have they taken him from me? Is he indeed gone – gone forever? Those lips that were wont to utter every kindness closed forever!' Then kissing them 'No – they are not yet cold – see – they move – yet quiver with the vows they made to save thy Julia. But all in vain – they would not suffer thee! Who would have thought it? We were once so happy. Madam,' turning to a woman who stood by her, eyeing her frantic grief with cold curiosity, 'you know not half how kind he was – how I loved him! But I hope Ladies and Gentlemen you are all happy – I was once – and our little boy – but then he had a father, and so, and so – but God bless you all – and I will bless you too, bid him but live!' then once more attempting to kiss his lifeless lips, she gave a deep groan, and expired without another struggle. The infant was, in the meantime, conveyed away by an old and faithful nurse, and perhaps yet lives to lament his murdered parents. The house was ransacked, and those are the remains. This dreadful tale was recited in my hearing, with dry eyes, my Agatha, by some of those who were present at the horrid spectacle."

Agatha, deeply affected by the melancholy relation, had scarcely strength or courage to approach the scene where these horrors had been acted. Hammond, not less moved, wept with her; and with silence and dejection they approached the desolate mansion, through what had once been a large paved court, but the chequered stones, of which had been many of them taken away, and others broken in pieces to glut the senseless rage of the destroyers. Through a portico, the strong and stately pillars of which had bid defiance to the blows they had received, they entered what had once been a saloon. A small part of the furniture yet remained. In one corner lay, covered with dust and cobwebs, part of a broken frame with embroidered satin fastened to it; in another, the shattered body of a harpsichord; and beneath it, a music book, which had entirely escaped the fury of the ravagers. Agatha opened it. On the blank spaces of several of the leaves some jagged lines were drawn in pencil, apparently by an infant's hand. "Ah," said Agatha, as she contemplated the wayward strokes, "with what delight perhaps thy wretched mother gazed on her infant as its little fingers traced those lines, and kissed the hand that formed them! Unhappy child! An orphan and an alien! That hand shall never more feel the tender pressure of a mother's lips! No – she is taken from thee ere thou art enabled to brave the storms of life. But may He who is a father to the fatherless protect and bless thee! Thou hast no mother, and a stranger shall offer up her prayers for thee. Alas, while I bewail thy fate, I myself have lost – dreadful thought – yet not forever. No – merciful Heaven forbid!"

The remembrance of her own sufferings, of her parents lost, perhaps forever, now obliterated every other idea; and, in an agony not to be described, she let fall the book, and dropping on her knees, implored Heaven to spare their lives.

Hammond, by every argument he could suggest, endeavoured to calm her sorrow and dissipate her fears. He represented to her, that Sir Charles and Lady Belmont, when they had quitted the province of Auvergne, as she had reason to believe they had by the time which had elapsed before their unfortunate messenger was dispatched to her, were in little danger of being recognised during their journey; and that while, by unavailing terrors, she was injuring the health of one on whom their happiness depended, they perhaps were already in England, and enduring no troubles but those which sprang from uneasiness on her account.

When Agatha was sufficiently recovered for Hammond to leave her, he went to the well of the castle, and in a broken teacup brought her the only refreshment he was enabled to give her, and indeed all they could obtain during the day, as, till the twilight commenced, they dared not pursue their journey.

The day passed in melancholy reflections, which every object around them conspired to increase. The memorials of the once happy inhabitants of the ruined dwelling – the view of the court where their lives were miserably terminated, and the dreadful scene had passed, struck a damp to their spirits, which they in vain strove to dispel; while a cruel death of the venerable and benevolent Father Albert – their own uncertain fate – the distresses they had already encountered, and those for which they might yet be reserved, completed the gloomy picture.

Evening at length approached, but before they left the castle, their curiosity led them to take a melancholy survey of those parts of the building they had not yet examined. At the farther end of the saloon was a door, which with some difficulty, they opened, and which led them through a vestibule to another apartment, smaller, but which had been apparently more elegantly finished than the saloon they first entered. The silver damask which had covered the walls was not entirely gone – a few scattered shreds yet remained here and there. The furniture, except one broken inlaid table, had been all taken away – but on the wall on one side of the room, there yet hung a picture, which appeared to have been taken for the Marquis and Marchioness. A lady, beautiful and interesting, dressed in a robe of pale blue satin, was sitting upon a sofa, contemplating with maternal fondness an infant that lay on her lap, and, smiling in her face, grasped her finger with its little hand. The Marquis entering behind was gazing on the scene before him with a look of ineffable tenderness. His appearance was marked with dignity, yet dignity softened by sensibility. "Unfortunate pair!" said Agatha, as she surveyed the picture before her, "you deserved a better fate – but there is a world of retribution – and again and again shall the prayers of the strangers who sought an asylum in your deserted mansion, ascend for the preservation of the infant ye have left." The canvas shook as she spoke. "Bless! Bless you for the prayer!" said a voice which seemed to speak from behind it – and at that moment a door by the side of it opened, and a decrepit old man entered leaning on a crutch. Agatha was speechless with astonishment, and the old man repeated his benediction. "I was Intendant," proceeded he, "to the father of that very nobleman. Many and many are the times that I have taken him on my knee and blessed the fate that gave a son, and such a son, to my kind master. From his childhood he had no thought but to bless the poor, and make his servants and all around him happy. Then he was so tender-hearted, he would not have hurt a worm! When he came to his estate, and married that sweet lady, his poor father, though dead and gone, was never forgotten – he would cry over his grave, and say to me, but Lawrence, we will do everything he wished, though he is taken from us and sees not. His deceased father's favourite dog was one of his dearest friends, and my dear lady's eyes were swollen with weeping when he died. Then their child was the sweetest infant! And it is gone, God knows whither. I had hoped to die in their service – with my last breath to have given them a blessing, and have left them behind me prosperous and happy! But – they were murdered – barbarously murdered! Cursed by the mouths they fed, slaughtered by the hands they filled with plenty; and that little bit of ground is all that's left of them! There, (pointing to a part of the garden) there they lie. I was gone to overlook another of my Lord's estates when the horrible deed was done. O, had I been present, old and feeble as I am, they should not have killed him: no, this arm, strengthened by a grateful heart, should have regained its youthful vigour – the villains should have felt it, or have taken first a life I should have gloried to lose for him. Now, old and past labour, despoiled of the small property I had saved in the family of my benefactor, I subsist on the charity of a distant relation, and every evening visit and cry over the grave of my master, and look at and talk to his picture. They may kill me for it if they will; but my life is no blessing to me, and therefore, perhaps, they spare it."

This moving though artless testimony of the virtues of those whose sufferings had already but too deeply affected her, in the present weak state of her spirits was more than Agatha could sustain. Hammond saw her agitation, and, fearing its consequences, with a voice that faltered with his own feelings, bade farewell to the faithful domestic, and forcing a few Louis into his hand, caught Agatha's arm, and hurried with her from the fatal scene.

END OF VOLUME TWO.

Agatha 3

Chapter 1

It was now evening, and the picturesque beauties of the scenery around were rendered more romantic by the 'sober twilight,' darkening the shades of green, and, by half concealing the distant view, giving scope to the imagination to delineate beauties created by itself, a little world of its own, superior to reality. To a mind ill at ease, there is something in the mild gloom of evening, which, like the sympathising voice of a congenial friend, by gently soothing dispels our sorrows, or, if they yet remain, softens them into a melancholy rather sweet than painful; while the broad glare of day, like the ill-judged efforts of the gay and thoughtless to dissipate distresses they are incapable of feeling, but increases the dejection it would seem to remove. Agatha felt its soothing influence – her mind grew more serene, and pointing out to Hammond the various beauties around them, lost by degrees in the pleasing contemplation the remembrance of her troubles; but weak and exhausted through want of food, long before they reached the destined village she was too feeble to proceed. A cottage, to whose inhabitants Hammond was a stranger, was in sight, and as Agatha was unable to walk farther that night, necessity compelled him to seek refuge there. After resting a few minutes therefore he supported her tottering steps till they reached the cottage. They stopped for some minutes at the window, the ivy which half covered it concealing them from view, in order to take a view of the inhabitants before they ventured to apply to them for protection.

At a distant corner of the room, by a candle which seemed that moment to have lighted, sat a beautiful girl about nineteen making lace. Over a small fire on the opposite side, an old woman, apparently her mother, was busied in preparing supper for her family. A middle-aged man sat near her, engaged in conversation with a youth about twelve years old, who appeared to be his son. "I would have killed the villains!" exclaimed the youth, in reply to some anecdote his father seemed to have been relating. "Peace! For Heaven's sake, Jeanot Pierre," said the beautiful girl, lifting up her face from her work, "you know not who may hear you. My dear father, why will you, when you know his temper, repeat stories to him which may ruin us all?"

"I do not indeed, wish him to speak with so much vehemence," replied the father, "but he must learn the difference between virtue and vice: he must hate the persecutors, pity the persecuted, and, if necessary, sacrifice his own life in their defence."

"Alas!" replied the girl, "what can Jeanot Pierre do, or you my father, or both together? Remember my mother and me, and do not abandon us to avenge the cause of strangers."

Agatha and Hammond listened no longer. What they had heard, with the interesting appearance of every one they saw, left them no cause for hesitation.

The door was ajar, and Hammond pushed it gently open, accosted the little family with that air of respect which the appearance of virtue, in whatever station found, never fails to excite; and in reply to his request for leave to pass that night at least under their roof, received a welcome as cheerful as it was sincere. The youth with studious attention immediately brought chairs for the guests, while his sister put down her work, and spreading a coarse but clean cloth on the table, assisted her mother in the preparations for supper.

"We knew not an hour ago, my Margaret," said the master of the house addressing himself to his wife as they sat down to table, "we knew not that we should have the happiness of these guests to share our humble meal with us; and never, O, never," added he with warmth, "shall the hope of reward, or fear of punishment, induce me to close my doors on the stranger, and to deny myself this first of blessings."

"Heaven forbid," said Agatha, "that your hospitality should endanger your safety!"

"Fear nothing," replied St. Valorie, "they know I have courage to defend myself, and dare not attack me; besides, I have another and better security – I have no property to make it worth their while. Wonder not, when I assure you, that I was among the first and warmest champions for liberty, till liberty became ferocity. I saw with pleasure my countrymen shake off the yoke under which they had groaned for ages. I exulted in the prospect of Gabelle,[34] every other heavy and unjust import being at an end, the extortions of Farmers General abolished, and the wings of Kingly power prudently clipped: but there I would have stopped – and did stop myself; nor will I abet by my countenance, trifling as is my power or influence, deeds at which human nature recoils, and at the bare thought of which my very soul sinks within me. To the desire of liberty I was stimulated by the misfortunes of my family; and perhaps we are never so zealous in a public cause as when we are goaded on by

---

[34]Author's footnote. "Duty on salt".

private injuries. I longed to see the day, when mild and equitable laws should take the[35] place of the severe code which condemns the innocent descendants of the criminal to perpetual obloquy, and, bereaves them of a property they have not deserved to forfeit. My father's father committed a crime, which, though not of the blackest dye, brought him to the scaffold. His estates were in consequence forfeited, his name rendered infamous, and his family degraded to the rank of Plebeians. My father, who was old enough to be sensible to the fall of his fortunes, never recovered it; it cast a gloom over his mind, which time, instead of dispelling, served but to increase, and which destroyed every comfort yet within his reach. In education only was he enabled to raise his children to the rank from which he had fallen – and this was his pride. Everything he had himself acquired, he transmitted to me: but I have not believed it prudent to act the same by my children. I have taught them to distinguish between virtue and vice, but, at the same time, I have given to their minds only that moderate degree of refinement, at which, without teaching them to soar beyond their station, makes them cheerful and happy in it, and gives them a few innocent resources in their leisure hours. Marianne reads tolerably well, and is sufficiently accomplished to be regarded with respect, though not enough so to excite envy among her associates: Jeanot Pierre the same. But what do I say? Society is now at an end; all its bonds are broken – and the neighbour and the friend are become the spy and informer."

Hammond on enquiry learned from St. Valorie, that Morèe, the man whom he had wounded, was recovered, and that all pursuit after himself was at an end. The greatest risk in pursuing their journey, was now, therefore, over; but St. Valorie advised Agatha to change her dress before she travelled further, and Marianne promised to assist in equipping her as a female peasant, under which disguise she might pass unnoticed, and no one would fear to receive her as a guest. It was immediately determined that Agatha and Hammond should remain at St. Valorie's cottage as long as was necessary for this preparation, which probably would not detain them many days. A bed was prepared for Hammond, and Agatha shared that of Marianne, whose artless manners, and natural serenity of temper, rendered her conversation always pleasing.

"It has often surprised me," said Marianne to Agatha as they sat at work the next morning, busied in preparing Agatha's new garb, "it has often surprised me, that anyone can consent to become a nun; to give up dancing – and then to lose all hopes of having a lover – I could bear anything but that."

---

[35]The definite article is missing in the original.

"You then have a lover?" replied Agatha.

"Not now, but I had once."

"And you are separated!"

"O, yes, and have been for a twelvemonth."

"And do you still grieve at the loss?"

"O, no – far from it; I did indeed at first, as well I might. La Tour was a young man that any woman must have loved; he danced admirably, played on the violin, sung nearly fifty songs, and was besides very good-tempered and industrious; and for two whole years we were constant to each other. I spotted him a handkerchief in my hair, and he gave me a work-basket of his own making, for he was very ingenious."

"And what divided you?"

"He saw someone else he liked better."

"That was hard indeed."

"It was rather so, but I could not help it, nor he neither. And so he left me and went to live near her, and what has become of him since I have never heard."

"But it did not deeply distress you?"

"Yes, indeed, it did – I was very unhappy for two days; but it was the season of the vintage and we were to have a dance at the Marquis's. La Tour would not be there to dance with me, and I had a great mind not to go, but I argued myself into reason, and so got the better of my love. Surely, said I, the sun will shine as bright, the country look as gay, the fiddles play as merrily as if La Tour was there, why then should I give way to a distress which only proceeds from my own foolish imagination, and give up pleasures which are still such if I can fancy them so? Besides, if from uneasiness I should fall sick, it will grieve my mother and make her ill too, and I can get another lover, perhaps, but if I should lose these, shall never have other parents. So I began in earnest to conquer my love, and, as I was born with a happy temper, I soon got the better of it. O, there is nothing like a light heart, it makes sunshine all the year through! And now I am as happy as ever."

"O," said Agatha to herself, "what a lesson does this artless girl give to those who, with minds more cultivated, and reason of course stronger, feebly yield to their feelings instead of endeavouring like her to conquer them. Few, indeed, are born with this happy serenity of temper; and those of my own country have not the light hearts of the French, many of whom can cry one moment and sing the next; but all may endeavour to conquer, and where the will is sincere, and the object proposed is generally obtainable: even the consciousness of an endeavour to think and act aright is in itself a reward for many a struggle."

In three days Agatha's new dress was nearly completed, and as, when she was thus disguised, and the pursuit after Hammond at an end, they could continue their journey without danger, it was determined that they should set out early the next morning, and travel leisurely every day, and at night sleep at different towns through which they passed, in some of which it was probable they might be fortunate enough to find a conveyance of some kind to take them part of the way. Agatha in vain endeavoured to prevail upon St. Valorie to accept some of her jewels as a testimony of her gratitude; his generous heart was amply repaid in the reflection of having served those who stood in need of his assistance.

Chapter 2

Hammond, in the evening previous to their departure, accompanied Jeanot Pierre to a neighbouring town in order to purchase some provisions to take with them. Margaret and Marianne went at the same time to visit a sick neighbour, and Agatha remained in the house alone. But the rest had not been gone many minutes, when St. Valorie, who had been cultivating his little garden, entered hastily, and with a countenance of terror conjured Agatha instantly to conceal herself in a partition in the wainscot which he opened, and which, as the last inhabitants of the cottage had been smugglers of salt, had been used by them as a place of concealment either for themselves or their contraband goods, as occasion required. There was no time for explanation, not a moment to be lost – for scarcely had Agatha entered the partition and St. Valorie closed it upon her, before she heard the voices of several men in the house, demanding of St. Valorie the Lady Abbess that lodged with him. St. Valorie assured them they had been misinformed, for that no Lady Abbess had ever lodged in his house.

"Our information, St. Valorie," answered one of them, "is not to be suspected; we know she is concealed here, and bid you at your peril detain her."

"I repeat it," said St. Valorie, "you are mistaken. But if it were as you imagine, if any unfortunate religious of either sex had taken shelter in my house, neither persuasions nor threats should induce me to violate the laws of hospitality."

"St. Valorie," replied one, "your patriotism is suspected. You have been seen more than once conversing with some of those holy hypocrites; and if you would save your own character and screen your family from danger, I advise you, as a friend, if anyone is here, to give them up to justice quietly."

"To justice!" repeated St. Valorie, with emphatic scorn.

"No sneers, if you please, Sir," said one, "or it may be the worse for you."

"If," rejoined St. Valorie, "my house had given shelter to a thief – a criminal – you might with reason bid me deliver them to the justice they deserved, and would with equal reason deem me an accomplice in their crimes were I to refuse to obey you; but when you demand of me an innocent person, a person whose situation in life was not perhaps their choice, and which, even if it were, comprehends in itself no fault,

232

nothing but a strict observance of a religion once held in veneration by yourselves, can you imagine I will be dastardly enough to give up such a one to injustice? But I repeat it, – no Lady Abbess lodges with me, or has taken refuge within these walls."

"St. Valorie we are not to be trifled with, or talked out of our reason by your specious arguments. We know from certain information that a female religious, a nun, if not an Abbess, is now in your house, and that, moreover, she is possessed of a large property, the savings of her convent, and by your leave, while I keep guard over you, my companions shall search your house."

"They are welcome so to do," said St. Valorie.

Every part of the house was now searched and every room examined, but the partition remained undiscovered. Still, however, unsatisfied, they persisted in their belief, and declaring they were assured that she was there concealed though their attempt to find her had been fruitless, they threatened St. Valorie with the prison prepared for her in case he persisted in his refusal.

"Did I not," said St. Valorie, "urge you to assert your rights as men? Did I not exult in the liberty you had obtained? And did I do this but to subject myself to imprisonment?"

"Take that," said one of them striking him, "and repeat your insolence and its reward shall be repeated."

"Coward!" said St. Valorie, "you dared not insult me, were there not numbers around you to protect you from my just resentment."

"Come, come," said another, "we will not quarrel, St. Valorie; we may all be friends, give but this nun to our vengeance."

"Yes," rejoined another, "choose St. Valorie – a prison and death are your portion or hers."

"My choice is made then," replied St. Valorie, with firmness.

"It is? Then I presume we shall see the lady"

"Behold her now!" said Agatha, opening the partition and coming forward.

Agatha's beauty, the elegance of her air rendered awfully majestic by the dignity of heroic virtue, the fortitude with which she spoke, added to the mellifluous sweetness of her voice, seemed to strike them at once with reverence and astonishment.

"Innocent as I am," said Agatha, "if it must be so, I am content to die, and I shall meet my fate with transport, if by my death I can preserve to his family a man whose virtues render it happy, and who has no crime even in your eyes but that of having sheltered an unhappy fugitive, who for two days before he consented in consequence of her entreaties to receive her under his roof, had tasted no food but the berries the forest afforded her; one deprived of parents, friends, home, everything! O, were

ye thus destitute, think how ye would bless the hand that was held out to succour ye, the door that opened to receive ye! 'I was hungry, and he fed me, a stranger and he took me in.'[36] Let him not suffer for that act of mercy here, for which, in the face of the whole assembled world he shall meet approbation and eternal reward hereafter. For me, I am content to suffer – yet how have I injured ye? Whom have I offended? How have I erred? Is it a crime to be destitute and friendless?"

"Madam," said one of them, assuming courage to reply, "it is a crime to take that money from the industrious, which they have earned, to enrich lazy ecclesiastics; to hoard up treasures to spend in private voluptuousness and – for we all know the lives the religious of either sex lead in private, however sanctified their outward appearance."

"I am not, as you have imagined, an Abbess," said Agatha, "but I was once, though a nun, possessed of fortune – poor as I now am. But I received not that fortune from the earnings of the industrious; it was my own, the gift of my parents – and I exulted in my riches because they enabled me to relieve the necessitous: this was the voluptuous purpose to which they were applied. Never did the beggar plead in vain at my grate:

---

[36]Matthew, 25, v. 35.

but I have been since a beggar, and have implored in vain for a scanty pittance of that bread I once bestowed on others."

"This may be very fine," replied one of them, "but it is not at all to the purpose. St. Valorie has taught you to preach, I find. Had you not led an idle life you had not been a beggar, as you call it; you had had an honest employment to support you; and the daughter of a Farmer General or haughty noble has no right to expect mercy at the hands of those whose due share of wealth they have for ages withheld, and, while they rioted in plenty, left us to starve. Besides, it is known, in spite of your protestations, that you have property still if you choose to produce it. But however, yourself and St. Valorie, who assists you to conceal it, shall proceed with us where, if you do not consent to give it up, you may be made to repent the refusal."

"Why? O, why," said Agatha, "involve the innocent St. Valorie in my implicated guilt? Take me, take my life, but spare him."

"No, Madam, till the fortune, till the riches of your convent are produced, St. Valorie suffers with you."

"Will you, O, will you," said Agatha, "if I produce the little wrecks of my property, will you spare him?"

"Not for worlds!" said St. Valorie.

"Peace! I conjure you," said Agatha, "will you, do you promise me to spare him?"

"I do. He shall be released, and never persecuted more."

"Enough," said Agatha, putting her hand in her bosom and taking out her jewels, "bear witness Heaven these are all I have in the world! And now I am indeed a beggar."

"God of Heaven!" exclaimed St. Valorie, raising his eyes and hands to Heaven, "God of Heaven preserve and reward her!"

The man took the jewels, and eyeing them with eager pleasure, "you recollect, Madam," said he, "that when you gave up these little wrecks of your property, as you elegantly phrased it, you made no conditions for yourself though you did for your confederate?"

"I did not," replied Agatha, "but my imprisonment or death will avail you nothing. That I am in your power I know – I am a weak and defenceless woman. But O, how poor the triumph where resistance is impossible!"

"At that rate, Madam, we might spare every viper of ye all, for you have no weapons to defend yourselves. However, it is in vain to reason, we had orders to seize you, and you must go with us."

"Not while I have an arm," said St. Valorie offering to rescue her as they prepared to seize her – but his hands were instantly bound by two of them, while the others surrounded Agatha.

"On my knees then," said St. Valorie, "let me implore you to spare her! Take, O, take my life, and spare hers!"

"No! Generous, noble St. Valorie!" said Agatha, "live, live, I charge you. I have no family, no child, no friends to lament me? Guiltless of crime I shall sink quietly into my grave, and bidding adieu to a world where I have had my portion of sorrow, go where sorrow shall be no more. O, envy me not this rest from all my troubles."

"Nay," said one of the men, unmoved by this noble struggle, "these compliments are very unnecessary; you are both welcome to go."

"No! No," said Agatha, "Take me. I only am obnoxious to you – take me then, and (terrified lest Hammond should return and be involved in her destruction) delay not my fate. Lead the way – I am prepared to follow you."

St. Valorie as he beheld them preparing to depart with Agatha, renewed his entreaties to spare her, and finding them in vain, in the bitterness of despair he exclaimed that she should not suffer alone.

"Nor shall she," replied one. "I promised her that you should be released and you shall, from all your troubles, and forever." Then seizing hold of him, bound as he now was and unable to defend himself, he dragged him along the floor, and was taking him with Agatha to prison, when Hammond and Jeanot Pierre returned, and almost at the same instant Margaret and Marianne.

Imagination can better paint than language describe the feelings of each at that moment. Hammond flew to Agatha, and, drawing his hanger, attempted to wound one of the men who held her, when another, perceiving his intention, caught his arm and with the assistance of two others, bound him as they had already done St. Valorie.

"Inhuman wretches!" said Hammond, "dread the vengeance of Heaven, dastards as ye are, ye withhold mine. My Agatha! My angel! Do I live to see thee suffer, yet be unable to rescue thee?" Then forcing against the cords that bound him, he released one hand, and seizing a stick which one of them held, felled him to the ground. He was, however, overpowered by numbers and his arms again tied down.

"Generous stranger!" said Agatha, "you doubtless mistake me for some friend; but do not, I charge you, involve yourself in farther trouble on my account. Forgive this unhappy unknown, I conjure you," she continued, turning to them, her hands supplicatingly clasped, "forgive him. He mistakes me for someone else, and thence the rage he has manifested; or perhaps his mind is deranged – spare him, therefore, in pity spare him; and let me not involve so many others in a fate I will gladly meet if suffered to meet it alone. Release this stranger, release St. Valorie, and I would cheerfully receive the punishment you tell me I deserve, and bless you for this mercy with my dying breath!"

"God of Heaven!" said Hammond, frantic with grief, "do I live to hear, to bear this?"

Agatha, endeavouring to drown his voice, supplicated them to take her without delay, and to release the others.

In the meanwhile, a scene not less affecting passed at the other part of the room. Margaret wept over her husband, threw her arms around his neck, and declared that death should not divide them – that she would perish with him; while the gentle Marianne kneeled by turns to her father and his persecutors, imploring him not to irritate and offend them, and them[37] to spare and forgive him. Jeanot Pierre, attempting to rescue his father, received a blow on his head which stunned him, and compelled him to desist.

At length the inhuman causers of this scene of complicated misery, wearied with, though unmoved by, the tears and supplications of the wretched family, tore St. Valorie from the arms of his wife, and prepared to take him, Agatha, and Hammond to the prison destined for their reception.

"No!" explained Margaret as they forced her husband from her, "think not that I will outlive thee – one grave shall hold us. O, we have done nothing to deserve this!"

"That we have not, my life," replied St. Valorie, "is my comfort. But O, live my Margaret! Live to protect and bless your children! You must now be father and mother both. We have known many happy days together, and for those I bless God! He has given, and He has a right to take away, – Jeanot Pierre, my boy – the darling of my heart, if we should never meet again – remember thy father – remember his precepts – remember that he suffered in the cause of virtue, and therefore exulted for his sufferings: let nothing tempt you to disgrace his name: act uprightly, and God will bless you here or hereafter. – Marianne, dry those tears for thy mother's sake – comfort her, she will have need of it. Be obedient and kind to her, and think that thy father's spirit hovers near you, and bless every virtuous action you perform. And now I am ready. Margaret, my love, fare thee well – if we meet no more – farewell forever. And now the worst is over."

The unhappy victims were now led out of the house, and the sad procession commenced. Agatha, guarded by two, walked first. Hammond and St. Valorie followed, guarded and surrounded by the rest.

The fortitude Agatha had exerted and which had been inspired only by the hope of saving St. Valorie and Hammond, now that her efforts had been ineffectual, and she beheld them sharers in her fate, forsook her entirely. She looked wildly around her, and seeing Hammond bound and guarded following her, anguish and despair on his countenance, she gave a shriek and fainted in the arms of the men who held her. Hammond,

---

[37]Original has "then".

whose eyes had been fixed on her, saw her sink into their arms, and strove again to break the bonds that held him, and to force his way to her; but he was forcibly detained while the wretches that witnessed his misery, triumphed in it, and ridiculed the *virtuous nun*, as they called her, and her *unknown paramour*. One of them, however, had the humanity to return to the cottage for some water for Agatha, while the rest stopped till she was able to proceed. Recovering to a sense of exquisite misery, she again looked around her, and beholding the situation of Hammond, was with difficulty kept from fainting a second time.

They now proceeded through a part of the forest, and after walking nearly five miles, reached the town where the prison was situated. It was late in the evening, and the inhabitants as they passed through the streets, surveyed the procession in gloomy silence, not daring to manifest either curiosity or pity.

The prison was at the farthest part of the town. Its high walls, small grated windows, with the dead silence that seemed to reign among its miserable inhabitants, would have struck terror to the breast of the most fearless. Its heavy doors were slowly unbarred at their approach, and immediately on their entrance, the prisoners were separated, in spite of the entreaties of St. Valorie, the tears of Agatha, and the frantic rage and wild despair of Hammond.

Agatha was conveyed by her guards to a solitary cell, which she had no sooner entered, and heard the rusty key grate as it turned in the lock on the other side, than she again fainted. Not even an enemy was now near to administer a drop of water. She lay insensible for some time, and when she recovered her recollection, beheld herself in a small room or rather dungeon where the faint remains of light, which appeared through a small barred window above her reach, were just enough to give her a view of its horrors; of the stone walls half green on which the drops of damp hung; and of the floor, where, fastened to an iron ring, lay a chain and collar. In one corner lay a bundle of something white. A kind of curiosity mingled with fear led her to approach and touch it. She screamed, and shrunk from it with horror. It was the corpse of an infant. "To what horrors am I not reserved," she said. "Yet whence this terror? From that lifeless infant what have I to dread? Alas, a few, few days, perhaps hours, and I shall be as cold myself – an object of terror to the next weak wretch that enters this dungeon! Poor child! It is at peace forever – that peace shall soon be mine: then shall I rejoin my parents, or wait with patient hope the minute that shall bring them to me, while I bless the prison that has given me everlasting liberty."

Endeavouring to conquer the remains of fear, she again went to touch the corpse, but twice shrank back with invincible horror – but at the third attempt she stroked its little hand. "Alas," she said, "how cold and valueless the casket when the treasure it contained is fled. A few days past, this breathed, and moved – pleasure, perhaps, sparkled in its little eyes, and amid the horrors of a dungeon, unconscious of its fate, it smiled on the mother that sustained it. And are these, the bewailings of the next stranger that is doomed to share thy fate, thy only obsequies? And shall they be mine? Shall some other inheritant of misery touch my clay, and lament my fate? Yet what avails it? Though no holy rites are performed, no grave opened to receive me, my soul shall burst its earthly bonds, and in the presence of its Redeemer, remember its past sorrows but as a tale that is told. Shall Hammond too?" But though she had calmly contemplated her own death, from the idea of his she shrunk with horror, and for some minutes lost her reason in the misery the dread of his sufferings excited.

When the small remains of light had been gone for some hours, and the objects of terror around her were indiscernible, the stillness of midnight was suddenly broken by screams from a distant part of the prison. The tumult every moment increased, and approaching nearer to her, the cry of fire was distinguishable from every quarter. She now heard the roaring of the flames, and as she distinguished the sound of feet not far from her, and heard several persons at intervals pass her cell, she screamed, and conjured them in mercy to open the door. But in vain – everyone was busied in providing for their own safety, and deaf to her prayers. The voices were now fewer. Several seemed to have escaped; and the dreadful sound of the flames, the cracking of some parts of the building, and the fall of stones from others, appeared to render her fate inevitable. Her dungeon was now filled with smoke that nearly suffocated her, and the flames began to burst through the crevices of the stone. She flew to the door, and pressing violently against it with the strength of despair and terror, burst the rotten panels that contained the hinges, and escaped from the cell.

Flying from the flames which had now communicated to almost every part of the prison, she arrived at an opening, and passing through it, escaped into the street. In the general consternation and tumult she was suffered to pass unmolested, and flying she knew not whither, stopped at last, breathless and exhausted at the corner of a street and leaned against a house.

A young man, supporting someone who appeared to be lame and to walk with difficulty, now passed her at some distance. "Who are you, and who are you taking away there?" said a female to the young man as she met him. "It is a good patriot who has been at the fire to watch that none of the prisoners escaped, and who has been wounded in his virtuous endeavours," replied a voice which she instantly knew to be Hammond's. "Brave fellow!" answered the woman, "I came out of my bed for the same purpose."

When the woman was out of hearing, Agatha who seemed as one risen from the grave when she heard the voice of Hammond, followed and overtook him, and making herself immediately known to him, conjured him to moderate the joy he was preparing to give way to, and in case they should be stopped by any future enquiries, to retain his presence of mind, and to answer in such a manner as to screen them from suspicion. St. Valorie, whom it was that Hammond supported, and who had actually received a wound, felt little less delight on beholding Agatha safe and once more restored them; but he prudently concealed his joy, and walking through the streets with apparent indifference, they excited no further suspicion and were asked no further questions.

Once out of town, their danger, for the present at least, was over. Agatha now related the miracle by which she had escaped, and Hammond and St. Valorie informed her, that though threatened to be confined separate, they were, after some consultation, put into one cell; and being near to that part of the prison where the fire began, their room was among the few which the person who kept guard had the humanity to open; but the wind rising, and the flame spreading rapidly, his regard for his own safety prevented his going on with the charitable work; and many, doubtless, were left to perish. Hammond said, that remaining among the flames in the hope of discovering the place of Agatha's confinement, St. Valorie had received a wound on his leg from the fall of a piece of timber, which forced him to quit the dreadful scene; that, sick with pain, and unable to walk without support, he was, when Agatha saw him, conveying him through the streets, determined as soon as he should have left him in a place of safety, to return without a moment's delay to resume the search for her, and to rescue her or perish in the attempt.

With all the expedition possible they now returned by the road they came, and animated by hope, weary as Agatha already was, and severely as St. Valorie suffered from the pain of his wound, they arrived in little more than an hour at the cottage of St. Valorie.

The wretched family were sitting over the embers of a fire, endeavouring to administer that comfort to each other which themselves stood in need of, while their attempts to soothe each other's sorrow served but to increase their own. Every face, as the faint red light gleamed upon it, bespoke despair and the deep sighs which interrupted when words scarcely articulate through grief, were heard several paces from the house. But the scene of distress was in a moment converted into one of joy as exquisite, the tears of anguish exchanged for those of a transport almost painful from its excess. "My husband!" "My father! My dear father!" "My Margaret! My love – and my dear children!" "And do we meet again! And are we happy! And what blest chance?" "I have scarcely a moment to unfold the scene of our miraculous preservation, my life," replied St. Valorie: "now, while the consternation and tumult yet prevail, we must escape, before search can be made after us."

Every little treasure that was portable was now hastily collected. – Agatha changed her habit, and as St. Valorie believed they should travel with less hazard of suspicion if they went in separate parties, St. Valorie and his family took leave of Agatha and Hammond with sensations of the sincerest regret, which would have been yet more painful but for the hope, however faint, of meeting again, St. Valorie having promised at the earnest solicitation of Hammond to fly for refuge to England, if it were possible to escape from France; and in case any fatal event should impede or prevent his own and Agatha's return, Hammond gave him, before they parted, a few lines which would ensure him a friend and protector in the generous Israeli.

As Agatha was incapable of walking far, Hammond, convinced that the report of the destruction of the prison could not yet have reached the inhabitants of any of the houses by which they passed, ventured to knock at the door of one to implore shelter for two travellers who had lost their way. A young man came to the window, and seeing nothing in their appearance to excite suspicion or fear, consented to receive them for the remainder of the night, exacting a promise, however, that they should depart early in the morning, as he knew not their patriotism, and might, he observed, get into trouble on their account. He now struck a light, and coming downstairs, let them in, and immediately conducted Agatha to his mother's chamber in which there was a bed unoccupied. Informing his mother of her guests, she replied, not in the most conciliating tone, that he was a fool, and would one day repent bringing strange people into the house – they might be Religious or Nobles for ought he knew. But, however, as they would come, they might stay that night, but must go as soon as it was light in the morning. Agatha, weary as she was, scrupled to remain where she had received so unwelcome a reception; but the young man with so much friendly earnestness entreated her to stay, desiring her in a whisper not to regard his mother who was always cross when she was waked out of her sleep, that she at last consented; and laying down her clothes, in spite of her strange and unpleasant situation, enjoyed some hours of rest, after an evening, the fatigue, agitation, and misery of which, exceeded all she had hitherto endured. In the meanwhile, the youth, with the greatest kindness, insisted on Hammond's taking his bed while he sat up during the rest of the night.

Chapter 3

Early in the morning Agatha was awakened by the young man, who entreated her to rise, lamenting the necessity of disturbing her so soon. On coming downstairs, she found a cloth spread and breakfast prepared for them by their attentive host, whom no solicitations could induce to receive the smallest recompense. At their departure, he gave them directions to a person in a neighbouring town of whom they might hire a conveyance to take them on their journey. Hammond now determined to pass for an Englishman, who, his wife having died in France whither she had come for the benefit of her health, was returning to England accompanied by the faithful English servant who had attended her mistress in her illness. This feint, which Agatha's present dress rendered plausible, prevented suspicion. They found means to hire carriages, mules or horses during the greatest part of their journey; and without meeting with any obstacle of importance, except a delay of some days on account of a fever, with which Agatha was seized in consequence of the fatigue she had undergone, they passed through the Province of Guienne, and arrived safe at Bordeaux.

A vessel bound for Bristol was in the harbour, waiting but a favourable wind to set sail. They immediately secured a passage on board her; and embarking overnight, a propitious gale arose early in the morning. With joy and exultation of heart they beheld the land lessen and the shores move from them; and in a few hours lost sight of a country where misery in almost every shape had presented itself to Agatha; a country she had entered with terror, but where the reality of her misfortunes had exceeded all the dark pictures her imagination had drawn. "O," she said, "let me, kind Heaven, but behold my lost parents! May the dear shores of England but have given refuge to them, and my happiness shall be indeed complete! But a blessing only less than that of meeting them was reserved for the vessel: the amiable St. Valorie and his family came on deck – and the joy to each on being restored to their friends, though prudence obliged them to moderate it, beamed in their countenance. Agatha, however, feigning to recognise them as persons who had been kind to her late mistress, embraced each in their turn; and animated by the hope of returning to those yet dearer to her, she seemed, in this moment, repaid for every past affliction, while her gratitude to Hammond to whom she owed her preservation, was visible in every turn of her speaking countenance.

When they had an opportunity of conversation on the subject, St. Valorie informed his friends, that with the assistance of the tale he invented, added to the meanness of their appearance which did not bespeak them fit objects of plunder, he travelled with his little family safely through Guienne; while the conviction of those who had taken him to prison that he had no property to lose, was possibly the reason why, when Agatha had escaped, they thought it useless to dispatch anyone in pursuit of them. Agatha expressed much surprise that her residence with him should have been so well known, since she was not conscious that she had been seen by any but those of his own family; and she was equally at a loss to imagine for what reason she should have been supposed to have been an Abbess possessed of wealth. This was easily accounted for, St. Valorie replied; as no habitation was secure from spies, there might be listeners at the instant in which she generously urged his acceptance of some of her jewels.

They arrived without accident or delay of any kind at Bristol, when the appearance of everyone they met formed a striking contrast to that of the inhabitants of the distracted country they had quitted: plodding business might be traced in the faces of some, the spirit of hardy enterprise in those of others: sedate cheerfulness was discernible in many, levity or vivacity in few; but in none that ferocious spirit which glorifies in trampling on every law human and divine stamped on the countenances of one half of those they had left, nor that fear which shrinks from the scrutiny of every beholder, dreading in everyone an enemy, too legibly written in those of the other. All here seemed to move in their own sphere; no virtuous exertion cramped by those laws which are the protection of their lives and property, the bulwarks of their liberty – and which are a scourge and terror to guilt alone.

"Happy, happy country, if you knew your own happiness," exclaimed St. Valorie, when he had heard Hammond's description of the laws and government of England; "had this been the government, these the laws of France, never had I desired or endeavoured to promote the fall of that fabric which had well nigh buried me under its ruins, as it has done thousands of others. Possibly as you observe, Mr. Hammond, even this government, excellent as it is, may not be perfect; there may exist faults which you say it is the opinion of many might be rectified: but it is not the season to begin to repair your own house when its foundations have been recently shaken by the shock given to the surrounding earth when that of your neighbour fell: especially, when the repairs attempted by him were necessary, and his house was barely habitable without; and when the imperfections of yours, if not imaginary, are, at least, so trifling, that you may reside in it with comfort and convenience in its present state. Men themselves are not perfect. In every character there is some blemish, which, though friendship may forgive or pass over, and self-love never discover, exists in proof that man is man and not an angel. Why then should we expect that the laws framed by man, the government planned by him should be without speck; enough if its merits outweigh, infinitely outweigh its defects? You have, I think, a proverb. *There was a man was well, wanted to be better, took physic, and died.* Quackery is one of the foibles of the English; nor is it less dangerous in politics than in medicine."

From Bristol Hammond, Agatha, St. Valorie and his family proceeded immediately to Hammond's house, where they were met by Israeli, whose transports on again beholding his friend after the apprehensions he had long been under on his account, could only be equalled by those of Hammond on once more meeting his preserver, and presenting Agatha to him.

A messenger was immediately dispatched to make every possible inquiry whether Sir Charles and Lady Belmont had been seen or heard of in England. During the absence of the messenger, Agatha's agitation of spirits, her alternate hopes and fears were almost too excessive to be endured. Hammond endeavoured by every effort in his power to calm her spirits and to arm her against the worst should it arrive, and should the intelligence received of them be fatal; the gentle Marianne wept with her, and St. Valorie raised his eyes to Heaven in silent devotion.

After an absence of several hours the messenger returned, but returned without bringing any intelligence but what Hammond was before acquainted with: the house formerly inhabited by Sir Charles and Lady Belmont and the estate around it had been sold by their orders soon after their departure, and the money transmitted to them in France: the agent employed to transact the affair was since dead, nor could he learn that from that period anything had been known or heard of them.

Hammond, by gentle degrees, broke the report to Agatha, endeavouring at the same time to encourage the hope that though they were not yet in England they might be safe; their return might be only delayed; and though a flattering idea she had indulged was disappointed for the present, it might yet be realised. In the meantime, for his sake, for her own, for theirs even, he conjured her not to give way to despondency; but, remembering her own next to miraculous preservation, to look forward with confidence to theirs.

Agatha's distress gave way by degrees to the hope Hammond strove to encourage: and though her dejection was but too visible, it was less extreme than he had apprehended. But where the least room for hope remains, the heart, when the first sensations of disappointment are over, again clings to it with eagerness, though, but an hour before, convinced by fatal experience of its fallacy.

Happy as Agatha was in Hammond's society, she judged it improper to make his house her place of residence, as well on account of the idea of impropriety the world might affix to it, as on his own, since his attachment to her in every light but that of friend she anxiously wished to destroy, and her continuance with him in a spot where their attachment began, but too evidently preserved and increased it. Yet whither to go she knew not – she had alas, no other home, no fortune to procure her one. Her jewels, her last dependence were gone. She would not have blushed to earn a subsistence by her own industry, but this, she was convinced, Hammond would never consent to while he had a fortune to support her. Her generous heart, indeed, conscious of the pleasure of bestowing felt no pain in receiving; and she was above that narrow pride which detests the sense of obligation even to those who are dearest to us. From Hammond, infinitely as she was indebted to him already, she could without pain receive pecuniary assistance; yet to leave him now, and thus to make that assistance immediately necessary, seemed indelicate. At last, as the least objectionable plan, she came to a determination, to reside with St. Valorie, whom Hammond purposed to place in a farm on his estate, as soon as he should be settled, and till that time to entreat Jemima to permit her to board in her family, exacting a promise from Hammond to consider her as his debtor for the sum she should want till the arrival of her parents, an event the probability of which she could not bear to doubt. She had written to Mrs. Herbert immediately on her landing, but she was out at the time the letter came; and now, anxious to see and consult with her she would have sent to her or written again, but on enquiry found she was not returned.

Several days had now passed, and everyone but more and more convinced Agatha that her continuance with Hammond would be fatal to his peace. She therefore seized an opportunity one morning of introducing the subject, and confessed her intention of leaving him; alleging, principally, the light in which the world might regard her residence with him. "To act merely for the world, Hammond," continued Agatha, "to act merely with a view to gain its approbation, is certainly condemnable; we ought to have higher and better incentives to propriety of conduct than the praise or opinion of the generality. But on the other hand, to condemn its censures is sometimes one step towards deserving them. There are persons, who, satisfied with the conviction of the purity of their own actions, dare and incur the censures of the world. Accident or inclination afterwards draw them from the path they are designed to tread – the world has censured – it can do no more – they have no character to lose, and thus are freed from one of the terrors of guilt. Besides, our example may give licence to others whose motives are less pure, and who learn from us to despise that world, whose opinion had otherwise, it is probable, kept them in awe."

Hammond heard Agatha's determination with pain though without surprise, and acquiesced with silent yet evident dejection.

"Think not, my best friend," said Agatha, observing with extreme pain the melancholy depicted on his countenance, "O, think not that there is a wish of this heart superior to that of promoting your happiness; and it is that, ultimately that, which is one, if not a principal inducement to me to propose a plan, for which, by separating us sometimes, may render other subjects the employment of your thoughts, and divest the heart of my friend of every lurking remains of that attachment which has disturbed its tranquillity."

"My Agatha," replied Hammond, "I know not how to oppose your wishes, even when they tend, as now, to make me miserable. But hope nothing from absence. A love which reason confirms and increases, which depends not upon personal attractions, and would continue were my Agatha divested of every charm which, till I knew the superior beauties of her mind, claimed my admiration – a love like this it is in vain to seek by absence to cure; it must exist while that reason maintains her seat. In this spot that love began. Here first I indulged hopes, never, alas to be realised, yet never to be forgotten – I had almost said, relinquished. On this very table I leaned, when my Agatha with a smile of plaintive tenderness at this moment present to my imagination, took out her pocketbook, and pointing to one of the leaves, bid me remark it. The melancholy day that brought me here, witness of a spectacle how dreadful, you had covered with black except one small space. When I asked an explanation, 'That space, Mr. Hammond,' you replied, 'is left to signify your coming – one *white event* in a day how dark beside!' My Agatha, judge of my feelings at that moment. Think you that I longed to press the dear emblem of that *white event* to my lips – my heart! Not daring to indulge my feelings, I rose to leave you, while with angel sweetness you followed, conjuring me not be pained by your revival of a dreadful remembrance, declaring you meant but to express your own friendship for me. O, my Agatha – yet you are here, and I am wretched!"

Agatha was for some minutes too much affected to reply. At length, "Hammond," she said, with assuming firmness, "are we not culpable when, because it is the will of Heaven to deny some of the wishes of our hearts, we believe we owe no gratitude for the blessings which are given us? In that agonising moment that separated us in the prison, would you not have given worlds to be assured you should be one day as happy as you are at this hour? Yet now that happiness is despised. All the comforts of your situation are disregarded, because it is not all you wish it. Recollect yourself, my dearest friend; recollect the precepts of your excellent sister, and *in thy pilgrimage through a world of woe, seek not to heighten thine affliction.*"

Agatha now changed the subject, and Israeli with St. Valorie and his family entering the room, she endeavoured with forced vivacity to introduce a general conversation in hopes of breaking the chain of melancholy ideas in Hammond's mind, when a post chaise stopped at the door, and in a moment Mrs. Herbert flew into Agatha's arms.

When the first emotions of pleasure had subsided, Mrs. Herbert, impatient to learn by what fortunate event Agatha had escaped, entreated her to inform her of everything that had befallen her. Agatha, acknowledging with tears of gratitude that she was indebted to Hammond for her preservation, related as succinctly as possible whatever had passed since the period when her distresses and precarious situation forced her to discontinue a correspondence that had been one of her greatest pleasures. When she came to that part of her narrative which described her obligation to St. Valorie, she presented him and his amiable family to Mrs. Herbert, who, looking first on them, and then on Agatha, Hammond, and Israeli, contemplated with tears of admiration so many votaries of virtue – so many in whom self-preservation had been despised in their endeavours to rescue others.

When Agatha informed Mrs. Herbert that she had thoughts of residing with Mrs. Arnold, if it were convenient, till St. Valorie was fixed in the farm in which Hammond was preparing to place him, Mrs. Herbert insisted on her accompanying her home. Mr. Ormistace, she said, was out, but she could be answerable for his pleasure on finding Agatha an inmate of his house at his return. "Indeed," continued Mrs. Herbert, "such an event will be the surest means of making my peace with him; for on my disbelieving the tale of a ballad singer whom he took into the house, and who has since his departure eloped with the greatest part of the furniture of her apartment, he left me in anger, threatening never to speak to me again. You will therefore be doubly welcome just at this time as a mediatrix between us. Yet with this single foible my uncle has a heart that does honour to human nature. Indeed his very faults are the offspring of benevolence; and I were undeserving the thousand acts of kindness I have received from him did I not take a pride in acknowledging it."

Agatha had half consented to Mrs. Herbert's request, when looking at Hammond and observing the distress impressed on his countenance, and reading a look which seemed to say it was at once cruel and ungrateful to leave him thus hastily, she retracted her consent, entreating Mrs. Herbert to excuse her for a few days only; and naming a day in the next week, promised faithfully that she would then come to her. Hammond, grateful for this respite, though but of a few days, now as plainly expressed by his countenance the joy he felt; while Mrs. Herbert, looking at them both with arch penetration, expressed by a smile no less intelligible that she perfectly comprehended the reason of the delay.

Taking Agatha aside at her departure, "my sweet friend," said Mrs. Herbert, "is not a nun in her heart now."

"Indeed," replied Agatha, colouring at the insinuation, "indeed I am."

"In deed you are, my dear, but not in thought, in wish – O, my sweet Agatha, when nature and love designed you and Hammond for each other, what a thousand pities was it, that the blind old lady Fortune in one of her moody humours should contrive to separate you. But, however, she has made all the separation in her power by bringing you together again; and I hope it will be so contrived that I shall yet see you as happy as you deserve to be."

"In the sense you allude to, never," replied Agatha. "But if I live to see Hammond subdue his fatal attachment, and feel himself happy, I shall be so. If I have the least knowledge of my own heart, I only wish my vows revocable for his sake – with regard to myself, I am yet, believe me I am, a nun in my heart."

Mrs. Herbert, with a look which seemed to say she must not in politeness contradict what however she could not be made to credit, now took leave of Agatha for the present, promising to send her carriage for her on the day appointed.

Chapter 4

The interval between Mrs. Herbert's visit and the day fixed for the departure of Agatha was passed in the most earnest endeavours on the part of Agatha, seconded by the arguments of St. Valorie, to reconcile Hammond to her absence, and on his, in reiterated promises to bear his fate with patience, every one of which was no sooner made than broken.

At length the dreaded day came, and the chaise with Mrs. Herbert in it arrived. With a pain she could neither conquer nor conceal Agatha prepared to take leave of Hammond – she would have expressed her gratitude to him, but her voice failed her. At last, turning to St. Valorie and Israeli, "Heaven bless you both!" she said. "Strive to amuse our dear and common friend in the absence of one of the happy group." Then giving her hand to Hammond, "I shall see you again – perhaps, in a few days, my dearest friend."

"Surely," said Mrs. Herbert. "Whenever Mr. Hammond will favour us with his company, I shall consider it a pleasure; and my uncle's partiality to him is too well known to render a particular invitation necessary."

With all the courage she could assume, Agatha now bad Hammond farewell, and attended Mrs. Herbert. Hammond led her to the carriage, and beheld it take her from the house which her presence had endeared to him with severe though silent sorrow.

The distance was not great, and they arrived in little more than an hour at the house of Mr. Ormistace. When the chaise stopped, some of the servants gathered around it at a distance, and others flocked to the windows to see the prodigy – a nun! "She is a pretty creature," one of the men whispered to another; "What a blessed thing it is she has got out of the nunnery! She may well bless the revolution, though the poor souls that now lie dead for it would tell you another story."

"Thank fate," whispered a female servant, "I am not one of the papishes; but if I was they should never have made a nun of me, I can tell 'em. I only see how dismal she looks, she has not overgot it yet, poor creature!"

Agatha had not been arrived more than an hour when Mr. Ormistace returned. In the earnestness with which she flew to Mrs. Herbert he did not even see Agatha. "My dearest Emma," he exclaimed, kissing her affectionately, "I have been wrong, very wrong. Can you forgive me? But indeed, my dear Emma, you are sometimes too hard as I was on this occasion too easy of belief."

"My dear Sir," replied Mrs. Herbert, "I always regard your heart with veneration, even at the instant in which I suffer from its preference of others who do not deserve your kindness. But we neither of us love recrimination. All this is past and forgotten. And now, as Mrs. Malaprop says, all our retrospections shall be to the future. But see," continued Mrs. Herbert, "one for whose presence I expect as many thanks as she has merits, for[38] you will have hours of pleasure in her company."

"Miss Belmont!" exclaimed Mr. Ormistace in transport, "this unexpected pleasure is great indeed! Let me welcome to a house which I should be but too proud if she would call a home, one I shall delight to consider as sister to my Emma, and share with her in every comfort I have to bestow. But you see what an impetuous fellow you have to deal with, and thus learn of Emma generously to forgive my faults. And yet she cannot condemn me for them half so much at the time, as I do myself afterwards."

Mr. Ormistace with unbounded kindness endeavoured to render every hour more agreeable to Agatha than the last, and seemed to have no study but to make her forget her troubles, and feel herself at home. Ringing the bell for one of the female servants, he bid her attend particularly on Miss Belmont, and consider her as her mistress during her residence with him and Mrs. Herbert, which he hoped would be very long.

Agatha now enquired of Mrs. Herbert concerning the family of Sir John Milson, in which she had been informed that several changes had taken place, and learned from her the following particulars. Sir John Milson had been dead several months, and his eldest son, now Sir Valentine Milson, was master of Milson Hall. The widow with her eldest daughter had taken a small house in the neighbourhood which was to be fitted up according to the taste of both; but they were at present at Scarborough for the benefit of Miss Milson's health. Mr. William Milson, after pining some years after Agatha, the object of his second tender attachment and the subject of his muse, convinced, at last, that his passion was utterly hopeless, had seriously resolved to conquer it: but being incapable of living without an attachment, had a third time surrendered his heart, to a daughter of Mr. Crawford, an amiable and interesting young woman, to whom, with her father's full consent, he had lately been married. Mrs. Milson, to whom his attachment had been rather that of friendship and esteem than love, possessed just enough sensibility to make her susceptible to every virtuous impression and alive to every feeling of humanity, without having enough to create imaginary troubles, or to increase by romantic extravagance the real evils of life.

---

[38]Original has "or".

As their attachment was that of reason, reason served but to increase it, and they were to appearance perfectly happy in each other. Miss Cassandra, Sir John Milson's youngest daughter, had been married almost three years to Mr. Besford, a worthy young merchant, who lived chiefly in London, but had taken a country house near Milson Hall for the summer, where his wife and children yet were. Mrs. Besford, was the same good-natured, and merely good-natured character she had ever been, without any alteration in her appearance except being grown immoderately fat.

Late in the evening a note arrived from Mrs. Besford, requesting to see Agatha as soon as possible, and she had something of importance to say to her. She added that she would have come to her herself immediately on being informed of her arrival at Mrs. Herbert's, but was forbidden, owing to an indisposition she had lately had, to quit the house.

Agatha, whose beating heart instantly presaged some tidings respecting her parents, was anxious to obey the summons immediately, till assured by Mrs. Herbert, that, in all probability, what Mrs. Besford wished to say was not of the importance she represented it, and was perhaps nothing more than congratulations on her arrival in England, or very likely some frivolous questions she might wish to ask her relative to convents.

In the morning, however, the chaise was ordered, and Mrs. Herbert attended Agatha to Mrs. Besford's. They found her amusing herself with her two children, one of whom was tearing out the leaves of a folio for his diversion. She arose on Agatha's entrance, and shaking her hand with hearty good-nature, "My dear, dear Miss Belmont," she said, "you can't imagine how glad I am to see you come safe back again. I was so sorry when I heard you was to be a nun, and was taken off to France all in that hurry, that I could have cried. And I wanted so sadly to hear how you got away that I could not rest till I had seen you."

Agatha thanked her for her friendly solicitude, and described the manner in which she was compelled to quit the convent.

"But my dear creature," said Miss Besford, "surely you did not want much bidding to make you leave the place? My goodness! They need but have opened the doors, and if I had been you I should not have wanted asking to go. I am sure I have always been very sorry for you, and when my poor father used to ask me in his joking way how I should like to be a nun, I always said that I had almost as lief be one myself as that you should, for I never liked anybody half so well as I did you. Well, and now do tell me all about it. There are two kinds of people I have always wanted to talk to, and those are, nuns and negroes. I always wanted to hear if nuns are really so comfortable sometimes as some people say they are, and whether negroes are really so cruelly treated as Mr. Sharp and Mr. Wilberforce say they are. I am sure if I thought so, I would never eat sugar again; indeed I did leave off it once, but somehow or other I forgot my resolution and drank it again. Well, and how did you pass your time? How soon did you dine? What did you generally talk about? And is it indeed true that you used to get up in the night to say your prayers?"

When Agatha had satisfied her curiosity as well as she was able in these several particulars, "O, dear goodness gracious!" exclaimed Mrs. Besford, "well, I would not be a nun – not for the world – I had rather have a child every week. But how glad my sister will be to see you! It will put her in mind of all the Kings and Queens that ever reigned in England. Not that I mean to laugh at Sophy for her learning – I am sure I wish I was half as clever myself. But somehow or other I never could be. I used to determine I would read, and so I began a book of history she gave me, and read almost as far as King William the Conqueror; but then as I never could tell whereabouts I was without I put a paper in my place, I used always to read the same over again, and so never got any forwarder. And when I did mark my place, I had always forgot what went before, and so was obliged to begin from the beginning every time I went to it. And now I am married and have children, and have something else to do."

After a little more conversation equally trifling, Agatha and Mrs. Herbert took leave of Mrs. Besford, and went to call on Jemima.

Old Mrs. Simmonds had been dead some years, and Jemima was mother of three children, who already promised by their sweet dispositions and attentive obedience to her wishes to pay back with interest her own excellent behaviour to her aged parent. Jemima, or, as she was now always called, Mrs. Arnold, met them at the door of her little dwelling with a face that expressed the sweet contentment of a mind at peace with itself, yet tinctured with that degree of care, which, without seeming to have invaded her comforts, bespoke her the mother of a family; betraying the fond solicitude of maternal tenderness and showing her, though happy, not supinely so. Harry was then busied in his farm, and Jemima had been laying the cloth, and preparing dinner against his return. She met her former generous benefactress with tears of pleasure, and respectfully led her and Mrs. Herbert into her little parlour, the furniture of which indicated that happy situation in life which is far above indigence, but in which luxury has created no artificial wants. The floor white as snow was covered by a small square mat near the fireplace, the stove in which had received its utmost degree of polish from the hand of its industrious mistress, and was now filled with the white pods of emblematic honesty, mixed with Michaelmas daisies. A curtain of light-flowered linen was festooned over the window, in which stood a pot of myrtle and another of mignonettes. On the chimneypiece were two busts in plaster of Paris of Shakespeare and Milton, which at once served as ornaments for the room, and playthings for the children; and a coat of arms that had been given to Harry by his godfather, was framed and hung up over them. The door of a cupboard in one corner of the room was open, and displayed their small stock of glass and china arranged in complete order.

Mrs. Arnold now set her bright oak table before them, and bringing a plain cake, and a bottle of cowslip wine, entreated them to accept of the poor entertainment she could give them. "And yet," continued Jemima, "to them who, like me, have known no better fare, this is excellent good. Our wine, which is seldom brought out but on great occasions, when it does come always makes us cheery and gay. We drink a health to each other and our little ones, and are as happy! And when we look upon our children, and see in their faces the goodness that is in their hearts, and think that when we are old and past labour they will love to work and maintain us; and when we think how we shall still love one another when time shall take from us all that beauty that is but a shadow, and shall even then find comfort in nursing and attending each other; and that we shall still feel young and gay when we see our children so around us. O, when we think of this, we look up to Heaven, and believe and say there is no lot like ours. Surely there is nothing like true love! It lightens every burden, makes greater every happiness, and makes old age seem as nothing. Then my little Betty and Jemima are already helps to me. Dear mother, little Mimy often says if she sees me fatigued, do not work so hard – I wish I was old enough to do everything for you. And Harry is a sweet sprightly lad, the image of his father."

Mrs. Arnold now went out, and returning in a few minutes with her children, presented them to Agatha, who, too deeply affected with this scene of domestic happiness, went to the window to conceal the tears that would not be suppressed. Mrs. Herbert went to her, and beckoning to Mrs. Arnold to take the children away, "My sweet – sweet friend!" she said, pressing her to her heart, "if I had had the least idea you would have felt thus, I would have gone a hundred miles elsewhere rather than have brought you hither."

"Be not distressed for me," replied Agatha, "it was a temporary emotion, and will soon be over. But O, Mrs. Herbert, when I reflected that a life of happiness equal if not superior to this might have been mine! Yet how selfish the thought! May you – may all I love be happy, and I shall, I will be so."

Mrs. Arnold now returning, filled another glass of wine for Agatha, and with the most tender solicitude entreated her to take it, while the tears stood in her eyes on beholding those of Agatha, though unconscious of what had given rise to her uneasiness. Agatha now making an effort to subdue her feelings, entreated once more to see the children, and giving a kiss to each, took leave of Jemima in the most affectionate manner, and with Mrs. Herbert quitted a scene that had left impressions on her mind which it required all her courage and self command to efface.

Chapter 5

When Agatha returned, she was informed that a young man, who said his name was Smith, had called to speak to her on particular business, but finding her out, had promised to call again in the evening. Agatha, whose heart always foreboded some tidings of her parents, and who could assign no other probable reason for a stranger desiring to speak to her, waited with impatience the time of his arrival.

At about six o'clock Mr. Smith came; and immediately on his entrance Mr. Ormistace and Mrs. Herbert withdrew.

"You have heard, I hope, Sir," said Agatha tremblingly, "and yet I almost fear to enquire – you have heard some intelligence of my parents?"

"Indeed, I have not, Madam," replied Mr. Smith, "which is the cause of my now troubling you. You are, I understand, the daughter and only child of Sir Charles Belmont?"

"I am, Sir."

"Sir Charles Belmont, Madam, was an excellent character, and I, for one, have great reason to bear testimony to his merit. When I was a very young man, just beginning business for myself, Sir Charles very generously lent me two thousand five hundred pounds, requiring only the moderate interest of three per cent. You probably may have heard him mention the circumstance, Ma'am?"

"Never in my life, Sir."

"Possibly not, Madam. You was young, I think, at the time he left England, and might not be made acquainted with all his pecuniary affairs. Now, Madam, as I have lately married a wife with a handsome fortune, and have no further occasion for the money, I should be glad to be clear of the world, as I may term it, and should wish, therefore, to pay back into the hands of the owner, or, in default of that, (he not being in England, nor to be heard of at present,) into those of his daughter, the sum I have specified; requiring only a proper discharge from her on the receipt of it."

Agatha assured him that she was entirely ignorant of pecuniary transactions, and entreated his permission to consult Mr. Ormistace on the subject, at the same time acknowledging her obligations to Mr. Smith.

"The obligations, Madam, are nothing on your side," replied Mr. Smith, "though great on mine; and as I am discharging my other debts, I shall think myself happy in being freed from this."

"But is it not possible, Sir," said Agatha, "that my father, intending merely to serve you, neither expected nor desired the sum to be returned? His never mentioning the affair seems indeed to render this supposition probable."

"By no means, Madam," answered Mr. Smith, "I paid him the interest duly, and he had my bond for the money."

"Then till that bond is destroyed you cannot securely pay it, I should apprehend," returned Agatha.

"Your discharge (Mr. Ormistace witnessing the payment) will be sufficient satisfaction to me, Madam," replied Mr. Smith.

Agatha now left him to consult Mr. Ormistace, who advised her to receive the money, since Mr. Smith was desirous of paying it, promising to take charge of it, and to place it for her in the funds. Agatha, therefore, according to his directions, received the sum, and wrote the discharge in the words dictated to her. And thus, by an event entirely unforeseen, she was no longer in a state of dependence; she had a fortune which, though small compared to what she formerly possessed, was considerable enough to enable her to possess a habitation of her own; and she immediately determined to hire and furnish a small house near Mrs. Herbert for her residence till the still-hoped-for period of her parents arrival.

As soon as Mr. Smith was gone, Agatha wrote to Hammond to inform him of the circumstance. After relating everything that had passed on the subject, she concluded her letter, "To my friend – my preserver – I shall not therefore be necessitated to apply for the assistance I could without pain have received from his generous hand; even though assured I should never have been able to repay him. And yet I do rejoice in my little independence, since I shall not now be compelled to rob the indigent, nor to take from my friend a portion of that fortune, the beneficent employment of which procures in the prayers and blessings of how many?"

Early in the following morning Hammond was announced; and the pleasure he felt on again seeing Agatha after even this short separation, added to the friendly welcome he always received from Mr. Ormistace, induced him frequently to repeat his visits, however dangerous the indulgence. Agatha saw with extreme pain the dejection with which he always took leave of her, were the expected absence ever so short; yet she indulged the hope, that by never giving him an opportunity of conversing with her alone, or touching on the fatal subject his unfortunate attachment would by degrees be lessened, and at length entirely destroyed, leaving only that friendship behind which might be cherished without pain or danger to either of them.

As Mrs. Herbert was not, any more than Mr. Ormistace, desirous of an extensive acquaintance, except the family of the Crawfords and some other friends equally estimable, they had few visitors. On a day appointed, however, Sir Valentine and Lady Milson with Mr. and Mrs. Craggs who were on a visit to them, and several other persons in the neighbourhood were to dine with them. Agatha would have been excused attending them, believing it right to mix as little as possible with the world; but in compliance with the earnest solicitations of Mrs. Herbert, who believed the caprices of Mr. Craggs might be a source of amusement to her friend, she consented to make one of the party.

Mr. Craggs had lately learned, either from his own cogitations or from the whim of some obsolete author, that the sun, as it is the centre of our system, is likewise the centre of all perfection – our Heaven in short, whither we all tend, and shall ultimately be assembled. "Do not the Persians," he would observe, "who no doubt draw their tradition from some sacred source, make it the object of their worship? Everything we see," he would further affirm, "whether in the animal or vegetable world, appears first in an imperfect state, and advances by degrees to maturity and perfection. It is, therefore, self-evident that mankind are born in that planet most distant from the sun in our system originally, from whence, after their migration to another, or, as it is vulgarly called, death, they proceed into the next; and so on, life after life, growing progressively more perfect in each, till they reach their sun or Heaven. Now," he would say, "it is our duty to continue as long as possible in each of the planets in which we are placed, for which reason I have taken all possible care to preserve my health in this. But that is not enough. I must begin to make some preparation for the next. Venus, into which I shall shortly go, will appear very hot on my first entrance, and no doubt during my infancy I shall be liable to feverish complaints; to prevent which, I hold it right to accustom myself to endure all the heat I can support in this. For though the soul is not material, it has a material covering as we may term it, and is sensible of pain from exterior and material circumstances. Does not a wound on the brain affect the soul or mind, call it which you will, and do not corporeal pains cause it to quit the body it inhabited, occasioning what is ordinarily called death? We ought, therefore, to make its habitation as comfortable to it as possible that it may not be induced to leave it. I wish therefore gradually to accustom it to the heats of the next planet." Mr. Craggs would frequently assert, that he had some recollection of his residence in Mars, a fainter yet of what had passed in Jupiter; of Saturn he confessed he remembered very little, and of the Georgium Sidus[39] nothing at all. He alleged in favour of his system, the phrase used by the North American Indians,

---

[39]Georgium Sidus was the name Herschel gave to the planet he discovered in 1781 which we now call Uranus.

who say, that a person has *changed his climate*, when they would signify that he is dead: and thence he adduced the truth of his position: since unenlightened nations by traditionary evidence have frequently the best and least perverted ideas of past events.

In compliance with his new system, Mr. Craggs was habited very warm, in order to induce an artificial heat. He wore, on his entrance a complete dress of flannel lined with fur, though the weather was mild and warm. His hands were covered by a large muff, and his little emaciated face was just discernible through the aperture of his green baize cap. At dinner he desired the servants to make liquor somewhat more than blood heat, about 99 degrees as nearly as they could guess.

"I am thinking," said Sir Valentine Milson, "how excessively foolish you are Mr. Craggs."

"Sir," said Mr. Craggs, raising his head, and discovering his face turned paler by anger, and rendered more ghastly by the hue given to it by the green baize cap which more than half covered it.

"Why I mean," continued Sir Valentine, "that when you go to that monstrous hot place, it's fifty to one but the water's cold. For I heard my Dame teaching the children the other day, that there was the burning mountain and a hot spring in Iceland. Now, you know, if that's the case, very likely there's cold springs in the place you talk of going to."

"There is some semblance of reason in what you observe," replied Mr. Craggs, relaxing from his severity, and eyeing Sir Valentine with more complacency than usual, "there probably may be cold springs even in Mercury; but then they will be as rare, in all probability, as hot ones are in our planet; and I may not reside near one. I thank you, however, for the hint."

"You are heartily welcome," returned Sir Valentine, "and I think if ever there was a good man you are one."

Mr. Craggs bowed.

"Because," continued Sir Valentine, "you do what very few other people do, think nothing of this world to prepare for the next; though, to be sure, there's few but you that would like the thoughts of going into a very hot one. You understand me?"

"No, sir," replied Mr. Craggs, disappointed at the conclusion of the speech. Then returning to his meditations, he seemed to forget that anyone was present.

When the company were gone, Agatha lamented to Mrs. Herbert the perversion of faculties which made Mr. Craggs a slave to imaginary apprehensions, and destroyed every comfort of his life.

"Call it rather a derangement of intellect," replied Mrs. Herbert. "But be that as it may, an excessive attention to preserve a life valuable to no one but himself, was the primary cause of it. We should be very careful to what propensities we give way in youth, since they generally grow upon us as we advance in life; and there are few foibles for which self-love cannot find an excuse, as there is seldom a hypothesis, however absurd, for which we may not distort a few arguments to satisfy ourselves."

Several months now passed, and no intelligence was yet received of Sir Charles and Lady Belmont. The house Agatha had hired was almost ready for her reception, and she had engaged two female servants who were to be all her household. Yet, though more than ever alarmed on account of her parents, Agatha felt much more easy concerning Hammond whose tranquillity seemed in a great measure restored. The dejection, formerly so visible, was now lessened. He listened to Mrs. Herbert's sprightly conversation with apparent pleasure; and though his essential regard for Agatha was not in the least abated, though he yet looked up to her as to a being of superior order, and hung with delight on every word she uttered, the starts of passion, the gloom of dejection which had embittered the hours he passed with her, were now no more. He left her with pain, yet without anguish; and met her with pleasure, though without transport. In short, their attachment was that of love refined into a friendship of the sweetest kind; a friendship similar to that which, in married life, succeeds to and surpasses the first transports of love.

Mr. and Mrs. William Milson were the most intimate of their friends, and the most frequent guests at the house of Mr. Ormistace. On one of those days when they and Hammond only were expected, and less welcome visitants excluded, the conversation after dinner turned on a first love.

"I am certainly," said Mrs. Milson, "one of the least jealous persons in England, for my most intimate friend, my sister excepted, was my husband's first love, and another of my best friends was his second."

"True," said Mrs. Herbert, "but poets, you know, seldom marry their Delias. There must be a subject for the muse, who or what is immaterial. Shenstone's, I have been told, though I will not vouch for the truth of it, was either his cook or his washerwoman."

"But what is strange," said Mrs. Milson, "though I have married a poet, he has never addressed a single distich to me – yet, stranger still, I am perfectly satisfied without. I flatter myself he regards me with that esteem on which I build all my hopes of happiness. I allow him to think fifty women handsomer, but I hope he will never find one of the rectitude of whose intentions or conduct he will have a higher opinion. I feel a pleasure in tracing the youthful emotions of that heart towards others, whose serious and lasting regards are fixed on me. Besides my very name shut me out of the poetical world. What a figure would Sarah have made in a poem! You must absolutely new christen me, Mr. Milson."

"Not for the world!" replied Mr. Milson with energy, "I would not exchange even a letter of your name."

"Thank you a thousand times," said Mrs. Milson. "One compliment like this spoken in prose and from the heart is worth all the verse in the world. But will you be displeased if I produce the little poem that pleased me so much when I found it by accident, addressed, I believe, to that lady," (smiling and looking at Agatha).

"'Tis not worth it," replied Mr. Milson, "but if you wish it, and Miss Belmont will not be offended –"

"Surely not," answered Agatha. "The subject of the muse is generally as much a creature of the imagination as the muse herself; and if we were not previously informed that the picture was taken for me, no one would, I dare say, discover the likeness."

Mrs. Milson then took out of her pocketbook, and read the poem she mentioned, and of which the following is a copy:

O that I were a sylph to fly
Through the light air my Love to shield!
To hover near that speaking eye,
Where all thy spotless soul's reveal'd!

Unseen – unfelt – to touch that cheek,
And press those lips of vermeil hue,
Or in thy polished temples seek
The veins of soft, celestial blue!

My task, delighted, it should be,
With light and viewless wing to screen
The fierce sun's scorching rays from thee,
Or the cold blasts of winter keen;

To fan, with humid breath, the flowers,
And bid their sweets for thee exhale;
To shelter from destructive showers,
Thy soft auric'la's dusty veil:

To tend the rosebud's verdant womb,
And bid the imprison'd sweets expand,
Or guard the rich plum's purple bloom,
Till gathered by that loveliest hand;

To watch whene'er thy mind should yield
To downy sleep's resistless sway,
By potent spells that sleep to shield,
From each dark phantom of dismay;

While every dream of gay delight,
Should to thy happy pillow fly,
With fairy scenes sweet sounds unite,
Till every sense was ecstasy!

Yet when I gaz'd upon that face,
All memory but of that were o'er;
I could, as now, but view each grace,
Then sigh – and tremble – and adore!

When Mr. and Mrs. Milson were gone, Mrs. Herbert was called out of the room, and Agatha remained alone with Hammond. After a silence of some minutes during which she appeared lost in thought, "Hammond," said Agatha, "Mr. and Mrs. Milson are happy."

"They are," replied Hammond, "perfectly so."

"And yet," rejoined Agatha, "she was not the first object of his attachment. He is happy – would it not therefore have been weaker indeed if he had sacrificed his comfort to the romantic idea of marrying only the woman he could not marry? O Hammond! Shall I speak it? I have often thought what this day has confirmed. You are formed for domestic happiness; formed to make happy, and supremely so, the woman, whomever she be, that you marry. My doom is fixed – irrevocably fixed! Yet deny me not the blessing of exulting in your felicity. Heaven may call me hence to join my parents even now perhaps at rest forever. Let me not leave you comfortless! Let me enjoy the sweet, and the consolatory reflection, that when I am gone, there are others to attach you to life, and render existence a blessing! Others yet dearer – whose filial cares shall lighten the evils of life, and in the season of decrepitude support and cherish you till with pious hand they close your eyes in the last awful scene. And even then you shall not all die. Your virtues shall live in the remembrance of your children; while their piety, the fruit of your precepts and example, shall bid your name be referred even to after ages; and ascending as incense to Heaven, increase (if it admit of increase) your happiness in the abodes of bliss. You are silent my friend. I will not pursue the subject now," perceiving Hammond too deeply affected for utterance, "but reflect upon what I have said in your cooler moments; and if you have seen a woman whom, besides your Agatha, you can perfectly esteem –"

Mrs. Herbert now entered, and ignorant of what had passed, entered with an air of vivacity; but observing the countenances of Agatha and Hammond, her feeling heart instantly caught the alarm, and though fearful of renewing their distress by enquiring the cause, she checked her gaiety in a moment, and with a voice and manner of the most soothing tenderness, endeavoured by gentle degrees to dissipate the cloud that hung on the brow of her friends.

During the remainder of the evening, Hammond was silent, thoughtful, and dejected. Agatha assumed a vivacity – but it evidently was assumed; her tremulous voice betrayed the agitation she strove to stifle; and when she smiled, the tears sometimes forced their way in spite of every effort to suppress them.

At night Mrs. Herbert attended Agatha to her room, and speaking with the utmost tenderness, "Shall I, or shall I not," she said, "ask the cause of the uneasiness too apparent on my entrance this evening? But if the enquiry pain you or renew a distressing subject, do not answer it. Yet surely nothing that I, in many of my heedless humours, have said, has hurt either you or Hammond? I would rather tie my tongue for a twelvemonth than give a moment's pain to either."

"Far from it, my dear friend," said Agatha, "your charming vivacity delights but never distresses me. The cause was totally different. One day, perhaps, you will know what passed – at present, I think I had rather not reveal it."

"Enough, my love," returned Mrs. Herbert, "I am perfectly satisfied. It was a wish to remove your uneasiness and not a childish curiosity that prompted the inquiry."

When Mrs. Herbert was gone, Agatha gave way to a flood of tears, which, on the stretch as her mind had been for some hours, was the greatest relief. Long as she had ceased to regard Hammond in any light but that of a friend, and long as she had been endeavouring to accustom her mind to the idea of his marrying another, she felt the trial more severe when it came to the point than the enthusiasm of her virtue had suffered her to expect. Yet the greater the pain she felt the stronger she believed the necessity of urging him thus to destroy both in himself and her every faint ray of hope, which love, in spite of reason, might unguardedly cherish. And shall I, she said, when Hammond may be the happiest of husbands and of fathers, and give and receive a thousand blessings unknown but in the sweet circle of domestic life, shall I wish to shut him out from these, because I cannot be the happy being that shares them with him? No! Perish the selfish thought! May he be happy! My heart shall break if it accede not to all that can make him so.

By degrees, Agatha, long accustomed to subdue her feelings, became more and more tranquil, and reconciled to the idea which she believed it her duty to cherish; but Hammond appeared at times absent and dejected, and studiously avoided giving her an opportunity of renewing the subject.

Chapter 6

After some weeks had thus passed, a messenger came from Mr. Ormistace who was in London on some pecuniary business, to desire Mrs. Herbert and (he hoped) Agatha and Hammond to attend him there, since he feared he should be detained longer than he had at first apprehended. As the finishing of Agatha's habitation had been unavoidably delayed, and as Mrs. Herbert assured her she might live with as much, and even more privacy in London than in the country, she consented to go; and Hammond, who had himself business there, gladly attended them. Mr. Ormistace had taken lodgings in Hollis Street for the time he remained in London, and to these Mrs. Herbert and Agatha went, Hammond taking others at a small distance from them.

As Agatha as well as Mrs. Herbert had frequently expressed to Hammond a wish to see Mrs. Ammerville, pleased with the description he had given of her, and considering her as instrumental in restoring him to his country, he called upon them one morning soon after their arrival in London, and entreated them to accompany him thither, assuring them, that though not apprised of their visit, she would receive with pleasure any friends he should introduce to her. The carriage was immediately ordered, and Mrs. Herbert and Agatha, who, to avoid particularity, concealed her dress as much as possible by a hat and long cloak, proceeded with Hammond to Mrs. Ammerville's in Bedford Square.

On delivering the name of Hammond, they were instantly shown into an elegant dressing room upstairs, where Mrs. Ammerville was at work engaged in conversation with Sister Agnes and Madame St. Clermont. Agatha flew to meet them, but overpowered by the sudden and violent emotions of her joy, sunk into a chair, incapable of utterance. Mrs. Ammerville ran for hartshorn, while the gentle Sister Agnes threw her arms round Agatha's neck and wept on her bosom, and Madame St. Clermont conjured her to compose her spirits in a voice and manner which showed that her own were little less agitated. When a flood of tears had somewhat relieved her, Agatha impatiently enquired, now of Sister Agnes, and now of Madame St. Clermont, what happy event had thus restored them to each other; and learned that Madame St. Clermont, whose sister was mother to Mrs. Ammerville, had, after her escape from France, retired to a convent in Spain, intending there to have passed the remainder of her life; but being advised on account of an illness, the consequence of the fatigue she had undergone, to try the efficacy of the

Bath waters, she had come to England with Sister Agnes, whom she had fortunately met in a cottage among the Pyrenean mountains, and who had accompanied her to Spain, and entered the convent with her.

On Agatha apologising to Mrs. Ammerville for the confusion and trouble she had occasioned, "I ought rather," Mrs. Ammerville replied, "to ask your excuse for my inadvertency in suffering you to have so abrupt and, to one of your sensibility it might have been, so dangerous a meeting with your friends; but when the servant told me, that Mr. Hammond and two ladies were below, it did not occur to me that one of them might be the Miss Belmont of whom I had so often heard, and who I knew had been placed under my aunt's protection. But let us be no longer an impediment to your pleasure. Friends so dear to each other, and so unfortunately separated, will have many things they are impatient to hear and communicate, which the presence of strangers to anyone of the party will prevent."

"Certainly," said Mrs. Herbert, "a circumstantial detail when anyone but those to whom we would particularly address it is in company, and where the eyes of all are of course fixed on the speaker, is painful and unpleasant to all parties."

Mrs. Ammerville now rose, and followed by Hammond and Mrs. Herbert, went into another apartment, leaving Madame St. Clermont, Agatha, and Sister Agnes, to recite, in the anxiously-impatient ear of friendship, all that had befallen them since their separation.

Before Agatha began her own long and melancholy narrative, she entreated Madame St. Clermont and Sister Agnes to inform her of the particulars of their escape.

"Mine," said Madame St. Clermont, "contained as few events as the nature of my situation would admit. Escaping before the mob returned, I was met by our venerable confessor at the distance of a mile from the convent. Anxious for the safety of his little flock, and aware of the impending storm, he had procured several disguises, which he had concealed in a hollow to which he led me, where leaving me immediately, he hastened to apprise others of the circumstance and conduct them to the spot, after which, he purposed to conceal himself in the house of a friend who had promised to favour his escape.

Putting on a peasant's habit, I pursued the road through Languedoc towards Spain; sometimes exciting suspicion, and being denied admission into the houses of those to whom I applied, and forced to wander whole nights through wilds and forests, at others received and accommodated with a bed, in return for the scanty pittance I ventured to offer; and now and then, though seldom, obtaining a horse or mule to take me part of my journey, and rest my weary limbs. At length, worn-out with fatigue, I stopped at a hut at the foot of one of the

Pyrenees, and too feeble to support myself, lay down at the door of it, expecting there to breathe my last. Though I heard voices within, I lay some hours before anyone perceived me; at length a woman espied me from a window. 'God help thee – what ails thee?' she said in a compassionate tone. I raised my head and endeavoured to reply, but was unable to speak. The woman then opened the door, and with the assistance of her husband and his father carried me into the house, and laid me on a pallet of straw. She then applied to her little stock of medicines, and giving me a cordial, bid me cheer up, for they would be very good to me. When I was sufficiently recovered to speak, I endeavoured to express my gratitude for this kindness to a stranger. 'A stranger!' said the woman, 'alas for thee, if in a strange land the more need thou hast of assistance! But I do no more to thee then I did to a sick goat last week, and God bless me and mine only as I do well by others be they who they will – Christians or creatures.' In short, my dear sister, I was treated, though with no more kindness than the sick goat, with all the attention their benevolent hearts could devise, nor was I suffered to think of quitting their hut till I was perfectly recovered, when the young man promised to be my guide through the mountains, and, if I wished it, to escort me into Spain.

The day was fixed and everything ready for my departure, and the good woman had just put up our little stock of provisions, when the door opened and a youth entered, followed by my beloved Sister Agnes. Imagine my transport on beholding her thus unexpectedly! Our kind guide set out with us the next morning, and conducted us safely through a great part of the Province of Arragon, not leaving us till we reached Saragossa, where a relation of my sister's husband resided. I made myself known to him, and having through his means made some amends to our generous conductor, proceeded with sister Agnes to my sister's, and from thence to a convent near her country residence. What followed you already know. I have been only two days in London, where my happiness in meeting one whom I ever regarded as a child is greater than I can find words to express.

"Heaven bless and reward those kind and hospitable cottagers!" said Agatha with fervour, when Madame St. Clermont had closed her narrative, "may no storms shake their hut from without, no calamity wreck its peace within! Virtue is never more strikingly interesting than when she appears under the coarse features of rustic simplicity – the child of nature rather than of education: or is it, that seeing her adorned with all her loveliest graces where we least expected to find them, our wonder increases our admiration? And now, my beloved Agnes," continued Agatha, "I wait with impatience to hear by what strange chance our hopes were frustrated and we lost each other in the general tumult, and what happy circumstance brought you to the friendly hut that sheltered Madame St. Clermont."

"How shall I tell my dearest Constance," said Sister Agnes, "how confess to her that a romantic and, in my case, I fear, a culpable weakness was the cause of our separation – the cause of the terror and misery you perhaps endured in consequence of it? O Constance! I had a miniature – a resemblance but too striking of my poor Dorville! It lay in my bosom, and was unto me as a daughter – no treasure on earth could have tempted me to part with this dear memento of happier days. Even when my mind was resigned, as I believed, to my fate, I would gaze on it – talk to it – bid the sainted spirit of him it resembled look down from Heaven, and witness my faithful affection to its earthly representative. The first and last object in every year I gazed upon it; the first and last words addressed to it. Was it shame for my weakness, or the romantic delight of preserving the dear remembrancer unknown to, unseen by any other, that induced me to conceal the circumstance from you, when I related, contrary to your prudent wishes, my past though still-surviving sorrows? But I know I did conceal it.

On the morning of the day in which we were forced to forsake the convent, I well remember talking to it both in the garden and in my cell. The ribbon by which it was suspended to my bosom, by some accident was broken; and the bell ringing for None, I left the picture, as I think, in my cell. In the alarm and terror that succeeded, my little treasure was for some hours forgotten; but recollecting it at the moment in which we were preparing to depart, I flew to my cell to secure it, at the instant I saw you enter yours. I searched for it in every part of my cell, but to no purpose. Imagining I might have dropped it in the garden, and that by some blest chance it might have escaped the ravagers, I ran thither to seek it. When I opened the door, I heard the mob shouting at a distance, and saw everyone flying from the convent. Still, however, I pursued my purpose, and ran to the garden. But my search there was equally fruitless. The shouts now advancing nearer, I returned to the convent for you – but you were gone. It grew darker every moment, a dead stillness reigned in the deserted walls – and everyone was fled. I ran to your cell, to my own, but all were alike deserted. In hopes of overtaking you, I determined to leave the convent without another moment's delay. As I passed through the door of the chapel, something caught hold of my gown. Almost losing my senses in my terror, I believed it was one of the mob, and not daring to speak, flew like lightning I knew not whither, till at last I stopped, breathless and faint, at the door of a cottage. An aged peasant brought a light, and looking at me, bid me fear nothing. Then speaking to his wife and children, they supported and led me into their house; and seeing me feeble and exhausted, the woman and her daughter undressed and put me to bed in a small back room, conjuring me, in a whisper, not to speak. The daughter soon after brought me refreshments, and sitting down by my bed side watched me during an hour with mute but tender attention. My kind nurse then asked me in a low voice if I had any further occasion for her; and on my assuring her that I had not, and beginning to express my gratitude, she gently put a finger to my lips and bidding me a good night left me.

The next morning she again attended me, and after assisting me to dress, silently brought my breakfast and placed it on a table before me; she then went out, shut the door gently, and locked it. I know not whether my astonishment or gratitude was predominant. The extreme silence and secrecy preserved around me, with the precaution of locking my door, once led me to suspect the sincerity of my entertainers, ignorant as I then was of the extreme hazard those incurred who ventured to give shelter to obnoxious or suspected persons. But the cruel doubt instantly vanished, and my heart as instantly reproached me for the ungenerous suggestion.

In some hours the old man came, and unlocked my door softly and again fastening it after him, sat down by me, and in a whisper assured me that I was now safe, for that he had everywhere spread the report of my death. 'You may therefore,' continued he, 'pursue your way without danger. You were seen to enter my house last night, but I have assured everyone I met that you died immediately afterwards, and that my son threw your body into the lake.' My astonishment was not lessened by this extraordinary assurance, and I was preparing to reply, when he made a sign to me to be silent, and continued, still in a whisper. 'Shame as it is to your countrymen, your benevolence has but drawn upon you the resentment of those whose prayers you merited, but who have long grudged you the possession of that wealth, the greatest part of which you bestowed in charity on them. But you shall not have it to say or think that all are ungrateful – the blessed Virgin forbid it. Your bounty in the time of need, your medicines and advice, saved the lives of my son and daughter, and though I and they were to perish for protecting you, we should think ourselves bound to do it. But my house must and will be blessed for having had an angel under its roof – the dear, the good Angel of Auvergne! My daughter shall furnish you with clothes to prevent your being known, and you shall set out at night on horseback, attended by my son, who would die to serve you: my wife has a daughter who is married to a goat-herd in the Pyrenees. You will be safe there till you can send to your friends wherever they are.'

Think what I felt on this discovery. Either from a slight resemblance which some have remarked in our persons, or from my having sometimes performed the office of her almoner, I found I was mistaken for my beloved Sister Constance, and had received the kind offices which were designed for her. You will imagine that I could not bear the idea of continuing the deception, and imposing on my generous preserver by personating my friend; my mind spurned the thought, however my safety might be endangered by the confession. Conjuring him therefore to suffer me to speak, I assured him that his gratitude had mistaken its object, that I was not the excellent nun who had deservedly been called the Angel of Auvergne. He heard me with evident surprise and regret, but made no reply; and going out immediately, locked the door as usual. I saw no one for several hours; at last the young woman entered, and setting a repast before me, made signs for me to partake of it. In a short time afterwards her father returned, and laid a paper on the table before me, making signs to me to read it. The contents were these:

I dare not speak to you. This house joins another whose inhabitants are democrats and my bitterest enemies: they wait but pretext to destroy me. When I ventured to converse with you this morning, I had watched, and knew they were absent from home. But even then I trembled while you spoke; for spies are everywhere, and the voice of a stranger might have been my ruin. Fear not but I will protect you, since Heaven has thrown you in my way, though you are not the Angel: your nobleness in confessing that you are not, entitles you to my care. My son shall go with you tonight; but do not speak to him till you are many miles from hence. Should you see the Angel, tell her, if she can come to me, I will preserve her, though at peril of my life. Tell her I pray for her night and morning. God preserve you likewise. Give this paper to my daughter to destroy before you go.

In the evening the disguise was brought to me. The tender-hearted girl wept as she assisted me to put it on; and whispering a blessing led me to her brother. He placed me on a horse, and walked himself by my side. During part of our tedious journey, I obliged him to mount the horse, while I walked; and when we were at a sufficient distance from Issoire to escape detection, we stopped some days to rest the faithful companion of our flight. Passing for a peasant and his sister, a tale the truth of which his appearance and conversation led no one to suspect, we were suffered to pass without molestation through the province of Languedoc, and pursuing our journey by easy stages, arrived happily at the place of our destination, which proved to be the very cottage that had given shelter to Madame St. Clermont. And now, my dearest Constance, I wait with anxiety and terror the recital of all that has befallen you. How will the distresses you may have endured reproach me as their cause, since my romantic folly occasioned our separation?"

"Let me conjure you to silence these self-reproaches, my beloved sister," said Agatha. "The awful volume of fate is concealed from our view; and who shall dare to say what would have been the consequences had the events been other than they have been? Our separation might be ordained for the wisest of purposes. The protectors each of us found might have been missed. Our steps would have been differently directed; and instead of the safety we presaged in each other's society, we might have been involved in distresses from which we might not at last have been thus happily extricated."

"Doubtless," said Madame St. Clermont, "the foresight of erring mortals cannot direct events so properly as they are disposed by the great Author and Disposer of all things. But your friendly endeavour to set the mind of Sister Agnes at ease, and to reconcile her to herself, does not exempt her from blame, who, in a moment on which her own and your safety depended, could forget a dear and deserving friend in her anxiety for an inanimate treasure – the picture of her lover! Forgive me, my dear Sister, I am not accustomed to conceal or gloss over my real sentiments. When our attachment to even an inanimate object becomes a passion, and is suffered to interfere with our duties, it is surely condemnable. Every weak, every idle indulgence should be nipped in the bud: if suffered to grow and flourish, its fruit is poison."

"Enough, my dear Madame St. Clermont," said Sister Agnes, "I feel and acknowledge my fault; and bless Heaven whose mercy has withheld the punishment it deserved."

Agatha now related the particulars of her escape from France, with the various incidents that delayed it. When she came to that part of her narrative which described the miserable death of Madame Dorville, Sister Agnes was for several minutes too deeply affected to bear the recital. "Gracious Heaven!" she at last exclaimed, "how just and awful are Thy judgments! Thus, then, perished the unhappy Madame Dorville: and with her perish every remains of my resentment! God of thy mercy hear her contrite prayers, and as her penitence was sincere, and her earthly sufferings great, avert the dreaded future, and receive her soul to mercy!"

When Sister Agnes was sufficiently composed, Agatha resumed her narrative. She concealed nothing from Madame St. Clermont and Sister Agnes; describing Hammond's unfortunate attachment, and her own sufferings in consequence of it, with her last painful endeavour to crush every delusive hope.

"Come to my bosom, my beloved, my more than ever beloved Sister," said Madame St. Clermont. "Nobly indeed have you sustained the conflict; and were you never to receive any other reward, the approbation of your own heart must in the end amply repay you. But imagine not, my sweet friend, that seeing you so constantly as I find Mr. Hammond does, he can love another. If you would accomplish this point, you must meet less frequently. Let the society of others become necessary, and it may possibly in time become dear to him. But why wish him to marry? Time and reason will doubtless destroy every weak hope that yet remains: why, therefore, give an unnecessary pang to your own generous heart, already too deeply a sufferer?"

"My dear Madame St. Clermont," said Agatha, "if my heart felt only friendship for Hammond, would it suffer a pang in seeing him in another's? And if it does yet inadvertently cherish an attachment more tender, ought it not to be surmounted? Am I not by my vows devoted to God alone?"

"Noble, excellent woman!" said Madame St. Clermont. "O, did the feeble slaves of passion witness your self-command, how would they blush at their own weakness, and spurning every propensity that oppose their duty, emulate in future your noble example: and to will sincerely, is to perform."

After some further conversation, Madame St. Clermont, Agatha, and Sister Agnes, returned to Mrs. Ammerville, Mrs. Herbert, and Hammond, whom they found now joined by Mr. Ammerville and Mr. Ormistace; Mrs. Ammerville having sent to the latter to request him to join the society of happy friends whom she could not consent to part with till the evening.

During the time Agatha and Mrs. Herbert remained in London, few days passed in which they did not see Mrs. Ammerville and her amiable guests. As they were going to Bedford Square one morning, they were stopped by a string of coaches, and before they were able to proceed, they saw a person go into a hatter's, whose singular dress and manner excited Mrs. Herbert's attention, not less than her face did that of Agatha, to whom every feature seemed familiar, though she in vain endeavoured to recollect where she had seen her. She had on a green riding habit, with few if any petticoats under it, a neckcloth in holes, and not of the cleanest, and a white riding hat, with a poppy coloured feather in it. Her hair was fashionably dressed, and her face highly rouged. They observed her in the shop, examining and trying on several hats; at last, coming to the door in one of them, she espied Agatha, whom she instantly recognised. Heedless of the attraction her singular appearance excited, she ran to the door of the coach, and putting her hand in at the window, rather seized than took hold of Agatha's. "My dear Constance!" she exclaimed, "do you not know me?"

"Sister Frances!" said Agatha, in astonishment.

"Even so, I assure you; though no longer Sister Frances, but Madame La Rive. I am married, my dear."

"Married?"

"O, yes, I told you I should be; and though I had not so many offers as I expected, I had one, which, you know, if you mean to accept it is as good as a hundred. Have you had many lovers?"

"I did not desire any."

"Poor thing! I pity you. I am very happy, I assure you. My husband, poor fellow, was obliged to fly his country almost as soon as we were married! We had not time to bring over even a change of linen with us. Since, however, by good luck we secured a little money, I mean to buy some; but I could not resist the temptation of buying a black hat first, they are so becoming – though our finances are rather low."

"And where is your husband?"

"At home – at our lodgings, and very poorly; he has never recovered his seasickness, I believe. He sits there, shivering over a little fire, with his red night cap on, no shirt, for it's gone to be washed – the most dismal figure you ever beheld. You would laugh to see him, poor creature! But I do assure you, that though he is not the handsomest man in the world, we are a very happy couple."

"Good God! And thus distressed!" said Agatha. "Sister Frances, your levity is shocking."

"Why now would fretting mend our situation? Nothing on earth but a convent could make me melancholy; and even that sometimes failed, as you have witnessed."

"And what means of subsistence have you?"

"We have not thought of it yet; what we brought is not all gone."

"Accept of this," said Agatha, offering her purse, "we were Sisters you know. But let me conjure you to purchase necessaries first. Have a physician to your husband if he is ill."

"Thank you," said Sister Frances, taking the purse, "you are a good creature! And I will do as you desire me. But a physician would do him no good in the world; for I don't believe he can take physic, unless it's palatable: I know I never could. But will you go and see him, since you are so good?"

As Agatha could not conveniently comply with her request that day, she took her direction, and promised to call the next.

"And pray," said Madame La Rive, "have you heard or seen anything of the rest of the sisterhood? I wonder where my good Lady Abbess is – whether she has relaxed from her severity of manners, and made some good man happy?"

"Far from it," replied Agatha, "she is the same estimable character she ever was."

"Fie! What reflection on me! And after all, what have I done wrong? I made you a promise that I would be married – and the promise of a truly good person is as sacred as their oath; and I could not, consistently with my conscience, have broken my word."

"But your vows, Sister Frances!"

"O, my vows were not more binding than the promise I made to you: not so much so, indeed; for that was voluntary, they were compulsory:

and which was made first, the promise or the vow, is of little importance. But where is Madame St. Clermont? Tell me, that I may avoid her – for I would not have one of her lectures for the world."

"She is in London."

"In London! O, Heavens!"

The carriage being now at liberty to proceed, Agatha took leave for the present of the thoughtless Sister Frances. When she came to Mrs. Ammerville's, she communicated to Madame St. Clermont her extraordinary interview with Sister Frances.

"Her levity," said Madame St. Clermont, "is incorrigible, and I always believed it so; but I did not imagine she seriously intended to marry; for I have known many a volatile character, whose moral and religious principles were as strict as those of the most serious and precise. Victim of a father's pride, she certainly deserves our pity; and it shall be my prayer that her crime may be forgiven."

"And mine," said Agatha, "while I will endeavour all in my power to serve her; and if there are any means by which her husband can maintain her, will enable him to pursue them."

The next morning Agatha and Mrs. Herbert went to Sister Frances's lodgings, and inquiring at the door of the house for a Madame La Rive, were shown into a dirty and half furnished apartment up two pair of stairs, in which sat Monsieur La Rive, exactly in the situation his wife had described, close to a miserable fire, in a red night-cap, a rusty black coat, buttoned close, and dirty white stockings; his coarse and irregular features rendered more disagreeable by the hollowness of his eyes, and the fallowness of his complexion.

"O, here you are!" said Madame La Rive; "Jeanbon, this is the good creature I told you of. And now, Constance, continued she laughing, is not he a deplorable figure? I would not desire a better subject for a caricature."

"My vife be fi gaie, fi vive," said Monsieur La Rive, "she be tres bonne compagnon!"

Alas, thought Agatha, a companion less diverting, and a friend more kind, would be far better in your situation.

"In consequence of what you said yesterday," said Madame La Rive, "I have been endeavouring to think of some means of support for us both, when our money is gone."

"I am happy to hear it," said Agatha, "and will gladly give you every assistance in my power."

"Why then, you know, the English are wondrous fond of sights – I was thinking of exhibiting Monsieur La Rive for a shilling a piece, under the name of the handsome Frenchman."

"O, no! – O, no, my dear!" replied Monsieur La Rive, understanding her seriously, "O que non – C'est me flatter trop. I have not de vanite to tink of dat. Mais, cependant, I vas de hansomest man in de Province if it vas not been for my face."

"True, very true, Jeanbon; 'tis a thousand pities your head is not off – that alone might, perhaps, make my fortune at Rome – a century ago I am sure it would, for it might very well have passed for John the Baptist's."

"Ah, c'est bien drole!" said Monsieur La Rive, smiling hideously, "My vife be tres amusante – elle a tant d'esprit!"

Agatha now enquired of Monsieur La Rive his former situation in life, and learned that he had been a painter of some eminence; but that having been employed by several of the French nobility, by whom he had been warmly patronised, he had become obnoxious to the then ruling powers, and was therefore compelled to quit his country.

After promising to assist him as far as lay in their power, Agatha and Mrs. Herbert rose to take their leave.

"Jeanbon!" said Madame La Rive. "Why don't you offer to hand the ladies up to their carriage? – Where is your French gallantry?"

"Sit still, Monsieur La Rive, I entreat you," said Agatha, seeing him feebly attempting to rise, "you are ill, and I would not disturb you on any account."

"Ah, c'est vrai," said Monsieur La Rive, "Je me porte mal – But I be gay, be happy – et voila tout!"

As soon as she returned home, Agatha, with the assistance of Mr. Ormistace, procured a nurse and an apothecary to attend Monsieur La Rive; and when he was sufficiently recovered to pursue his profession, Mr. Ormistace obtained him a promise of constant employment from the master of a print shop who had seen a specimen of his performance. Madame La Rive, from her natural talents in the same line, was soon capable of assisting her husband; and before Agatha left London, she had the satisfaction of seeing them placed above want, though the natural carelessness and improvidence of Madame La Rive effectually prevented their ever enjoying a competency, however successful in their profession.

During their continuance in London, Hammond and Mr. Ormistace made every possible enquiry concerning Sir Charles and Lady Belmont, but were unable to gain any information. It was certain they had never come to England; but they were probably yet alive, since, had they fallen the victims of popular fury, their deaths must have transpired. This hope, therefore, slender as it was, was now Agatha's sole dependence; and she eagerly clung to it as a refuge from despondency. "If they still live," she would say to herself, "we may meet – may yet be happy – many dear hours of comfort may yet be reserved for us – these dark clouds be at last dispersed, and the sunshine of peace gild the evening of their days."

Chapter 7

As soon as Mr. Ormistace had settled the business which brought him to London, he returned home with Mrs. Herbert, and Agatha, whose own house was now ready for her reception, went thither with Sister Agnes, whom she entreated to consider it as her future home. Mr. and Mrs. Ammerville accompanied Madame St. Clermont to Bath; her health, having already received a benefit from the change of climate, no longer requiring the attendance of Sister Agnes.

Agatha now determined, in pursuance of Madame St. Clermont's advice, to see Hammond less frequently, whatever pain she might feel from the privation of his society. One morning, therefore, as he walked with her and sister Agnes in the little garden adjoining her house, she made a sign to Sister Agnes to leave them.

"My dearest friend," said Agatha, when Sister Agnes was gone, "will I fear be hurt when I entreat that we may not meet so often. Attribute not the request to want of friendship or to an ingratitude how foreign to my heart – but reasons which I cannot explain, render it necessary."

"Enough Agatha," returned Hammond, "you was not satisfied till you had withdrawn your love, and stifled if not destroyed mine: our friendship must now be annihilated; till every link of the chain that attached me to you broken, you exult in your emancipation. Farewell, Agatha – once the mistress, since the friend of my heart – farewell! May you be happy though I am miserable."

"Witness Heaven," said Agatha, bursting into tears, "that life itself, and every blessing it can give me, is as nothing compared to your happiness! 'Tis that I seek, and therefore would –"

"Sever our friendship."

"No, far from it. Nor would the task be easily effected; it is not in the power of time or absence to destroy a friendship like ours."

It has severest virtue for its basis,
And such a friendship ends not, but with life.[40]

"And are we never to meet then?"

"Never! Heaven forbid. But let us meet less frequently. Hammond, is it possible you can indeed doubt my friendship?"

---

[40]Joseph Addison, *Cato*, act iii, sc 1.

"I do not, Agatha – my beloved Agatha, I do not doubt it. But some idle caprice, the suggestion of some slave of worldly prejudices, has occasioned us both this unnecessary pain."

"Hammond, we have before agreed that the world's good opinion is not to be despised. But, whatever are my reasons, which at some future period you will perhaps know, be assured the request (for I cannot call it a wish) springs solely from anxiety for your happiness, to which I would sacrifice my life were it necessary."

"My Agatha, I believe you from my soul. Forgive my impetuosity – I will be, will do all you desire."

When Agatha next saw Mrs. Herbert, she entreated her to endeavour, by those friendly attentions which a heart feeling as hers knew so well how to administer, to supply to Hammond the loss of the society of his other friend; Madame St. Clermont having advised, in order to destroy every possible remains of their former attachment, that their meetings should be less frequent.

"I will comply with your request, my dear," said Mrs. Herbert, "and that as well for Hammond's sake as yours: but the cause of these new measures is inexplicable to me. Your love has subsided into friendship; would you go farther? Would you tear even that up by the roots? Have a care, Agatha, or you will leave your own heart as well as his a desert."

"My dear Mrs. Herbert, you cannot be more sensible of the value of Hammond's friendship than I am."

"So I once thought – but of this I am sensible, I would not give him a moment's unnecessary pain."

"Nor I," said Agatha, sighing deeply, "his happiness is the end of all my wishes, the first blessing of my life – I wish but to witness that, and I shall sink into the grave in peace."

"There is a mystery in this, Agatha, which I would fain penetrate; but it mocks my boasted discernment. Madame St. Clermont cannot have advised – you cannot surely wish him to marry another? It is improbable – impossible to suppose –"

"Not unless he can love another; if he can, I would not for worlds be an obstacle to his wishes."

"O my Agatha! But what a stab that would give to your bosom!"

"Why so, my dearest Mrs. Herbert? Why should I, who professed to feel, who actually do feel no happiness superior to his, repine at seeing him a husband – a father – dispensing innumerable blessings to others, those blessings recoiling on himself?"

"Amazing excellence!" said Mrs. Herbert, "but do you think that Hammond can love another as he has loved you?"

"With as much truth, as much sincerity, though possibly with less enthusiasm. Can a heart generous and susceptible as Hammond's be ungrateful to the woman who shall make his happiness the study of her life? And who can marry Hammond, and not make it their study? Then must he not regard with exquisite tenderness her to whom he shall owe the endearing name of father?"

"My Agatha – say no more –" said Mrs. Herbert, endeavouring to suppress her tears, "What would I give there had been no obstacle to your union! You alone deserve him."

"That has long been out of the question, Emma: for a few weeks only I indulged the hope of being his, for years I have known it impossible; and it is on his happiness now that I build my own."

The conversation was then turned into another channel, and the subject was not for some time renewed.

Agatha and Sister Agnes now, retired from the world, and blest with the society of each other, found many comforts in their little dwelling, where the neatness and simple elegance that reigned everywhere bespoke the superior minds of its inhabitants. One room, comfortable to the life of piety they had embraced, was sacred to the offices of devotion, and was called the chapel; another was fitted up as a library – and here their mornings were generally passed. Small as was Agatha's income, the excellence of her economy enabled her to allot a part of it to charity; and in the luxury of dispensing blessings to others, her heart felt lightened of its own burdens.

When Agatha next saw Hammond, she observed with pleasure that his mind seemed tranquil, and his spirits no longer dejected. He conversed cheerfully on several subjects, spoke of the comfort he had received from the society of his other friends, and though he was absent at times, it did not appear the absence of a perturbed or melancholy mind.

Hammond soon after going into Wales with Mr. Ormistace and Mrs. Herbert, an interval of six weeks passed before he again saw Agatha. But the apparent tranquillity which she had observed with so much pleasure when they last met, was now fled – the change was too striking to escape her notice for a moment. His countenance was dejected; and when he attempted to smile, his gaiety was evidently forced.

"Nothing, I hope," said Agatha, with a voice of tender solicitude, "nothing has arrived to distress my dear friend?"

"Why should you imagine it?" replied Hammond confusedly.

"Your countenance, Hammond, speaks it but too plainly – I could not look at that without asking what had distressed you. It is the sacred province of friendship to share our sorrows as well as blessings. Tell me then what has happened. Are you unhappy?"

"I ought to be otherwise, my Agatha, for I have just enjoyed the transport of conferring bliss on others. St. Valorie's charming daughter is beloved by the son of a neighbouring farmer, a man of opulence and worth. On my giving her a few hundred pounds as a portion, the young man's father made no objection to the match; and I left them the happiest of beings."

"May such happiness be yours my Hammond! And may I, may your happy Agatha witness, and by witnessing share it!"

Hammond turned from her to conceal his agitation.

"Have you ever, my dearest friend, have you ever," pursued Agatha with sweetness, "reflected on what I once urged to you? Have you, indeed, seen a woman who could make your life happy?"

Hammond was silent.

"Speak Hammond, speak I conjure you. Open your whole heart to me, to your friend – the friend who looks up to you for all her happiness."

"Surely," said Hammond with fervour, "thou art an Angel and no woman."

"Not yet," said Agatha, sweetly smiling through the tears that glistened in her eyes, "but the time will come when I trust I shall be one, and looking down on you from the seats of ever-enduring bliss, shall behold you with pious steps treading the path that leads you to me – a husband – parent – while all the sacred duties of domestic life shall be your blessings here."

Agatha paused; but Hammond, too much affected for utterance, did not even attempt to reply.

"Speak then, my Hammond," resumed Agatha, "Is there a woman whom you could, whom you do love, her only, who is dead to you and all the world, out of the question? Speak – fear not to repose every thought on me. Is there?"

"My Agatha, had I never, perhaps, seen you –"

"You shall suppose you have not seen me; or if you have, must remember that I am no more; for, when I took my vows, I mystically renounced life itself. Tell me then whom, (your Agatha always out of the question) whom could you perfectly esteem – love?"

"If there is another, whose virtues claimed my perfect admiration, whose society I should relinquish with pain, whose sensibility and sweetness seemed the counterparts of yours, it is –" He hesitated.

"Mrs. Herbert?" said Agatha.

Hammond covered his face with his hands, in silent though extreme agitation.

"May blessings, innumerable blessings be your portion, my Hammond!" said Agatha, clasping her hands together with fervour, and raising her eyes to Heaven; "may no cares disturb, no sorrow embitter your moments,

Till evening comes at last, serene and mild,
When after the long vernal day of life,
Together freed your gentle spirits fly."[41]

Unable to bear a longer continuance of this affecting scene, she took Hammond's hand, and pressing it to her lips, uttered a scarcely articulate blessing, and left him.

Going into the library, she threw herself into a chair, where the cares of Sister Agnes with difficulty preserved her from fainting. When she was able to speak, she conjured Sister Agnes to go to Hammond; "but tell him not," continued Agatha, "if you value my peace, that you saw me thus agitated. Soothe him, comfort him – say I am returning to him – tell him anything but that I am unhappy."

"But I cannot, dare not, leave you thus," replied Sister Agnes.

"Yes, go, I charge you – I want nothing – I am better – call Martha then, but go to him."

Sister Agnes, though extremely unwilling to leave her, now called the servant, and went herself to Hammond.

She found him walking up and down the room, apparently struggling with his emotions.

"My dear friend has sent me to you," said Sister Agnes.

"And how is she?" said Hammond, starting, and seeming to awake as from a dream.

Sister Agnes knew not how to reply. At last, after some hesitation, she answered, that she was a good deal better.

"Better! Was she ill then? Good God!"

"No, but agitated a good deal – rather –"

"O, Agnes! I would die rather than give her pain – tell her so; and conjure never more to give a thought on the subject. Conjure her to make her own mind easy. Bid her be happy; for 'tis that alone can render me so."

Hammond now took his hat, and went out of the house. Sister Agnes immediately returned to Agatha, and found her greatly better than when she left her: she was talking to the servant with much assumed composure, and was giving directions for a medicine she had bid her prepare for a sick child. She desired the servant to leave them, and after assuring Sister Agnes that she was infinitely better, entreated her to dispense with her repeating the cause of her agitation for the present. "A few hours spent in reflection," said Agatha, "will I doubt not, enable me to relate everything that has passed without renewing my sufferings. I have long laboured to conquer myself; but mine is a stubborn heart, and harder to be subdued than I once imagined."

---

[41]James Thomson, Spring, from *The Seasons.*

In about an hour, she went to her pianoforte, and opening a volume of Handel's songs, accidentally turned to that delightful one in Jeptha,

Fare well thou busy world, where reign
Short hours of joy, and years of pain:
Brighter scenes I seek above,
In the realms of peace and love.[42]

Though her voice faltered frequently, she sung it with an enthusiasm which seemed to raise her above the world; and getting up from the instrument, "Yes, my Agnes," she exclaimed, "What is this gew-gaw life, what the perishable pleasures of a few short years, that we should thus 'disquiet ourselves in vain,' thus 'grasp a vain shadow,' when there are blessings in store for us hereafter, one hour instead of an eternity of which would be an ample recompense for every trial?"

In the evening, Agatha was sufficiently collected to relate to her sympathising friend the substance of her conversation with Hammond. Sister Agnes heard her with equal grief and astonishment, and repeating to her all that Hammond had said on his departure, conjured her to drop forever all ideas of a project, by which she would wound Hammond in the most tender part – in her comfort.

"Except during some painful moments, when the feelings of my heart strive to master my reason," replied Agatha, "I do, indeed, contemplate the idea of his marriage with pleasure. I love to build airy castles for his happiness. I love to imagine him possessed of all the felicity this world can bestow. And then, to enjoy the exulting thought, that to me, to my solicitude to see him blest he shall owe them; to think that my momentary anguish, the victory obtained over my rebellious heart, has given him these blessings! O Agnes, shall I not be rewarded, even here?"

"But my dear sister, can you imagine that Mrs. Herbert, your dear, your bosom friend, who loves you as I do, can marry Hammond, even though she loved him?"

"If I can persuade her that it will make me happy –"

"O Constance, but Mrs. Herbert has penetration – the tears of anguish cannot be concealed from her; she would discern your sorrow however thick the veil you cast over it?"

"But when I use no deceit, when I really feel what I profess?"

"It is not possible. Think you I could have borne that Dorville –"

"Our situations are totally different. In you, love was a duty; in me, it is a crime. Besides, the first lesson I was taught was to command myself; and born with feelings too acute it has been a severe one: but

---

[42]From the libretto to Handel's *Jeptha* based on Judges 11.

how have I triumphed when the victory has been at last obtained! My dearest Agnes, the approbation of our own heart is a jewel of inestimable value, a jewel that cannot be too dearly bought."

Agatha, conscious that she could write with a calmness which she should in vain endeavour to assume in conversation, wrote to Hammond to repeat her arguments. After dwelling on what she had formerly urged, "I will not," continued she, "deceive you by saying, that I have felt no pain, have endured no struggles, before I brought my mind to consent to, and even to wish your union with another; but, if I know my own heart, they are now at an end; and I contemplate the idea with the fond anxiety of a parent who looks forward to an event from which she expects the felicity of the child of her hopes."

Agatha received these lines in reply.

Can I, dare I believe you, my Agatha? I know the nobleness of your mind, I know it would spurn a falsehood – but do not deceive yourself? Think not that I can be happy if you are otherwise. Yet why do I say this? You know me, and know it is impossible; if it were not, should I deserve or possess the friendship of a mind as elevated as yours? Your persuasive eloquence drew from me a confession no one else should have extorted from me. O, examine your own heart, my Agatha; and do not bid it make a sacrifice, which, if such, would ruin my peace forever. Yet no – think of it no more. The dread that a secret grief might rankle in your heart would prove a canker worm to mine, and convert my promised blessings into torture.

Agatha wrote in answer.

I know my own heart, Hammond, and neither deceive you nor myself. I know I am preparing a triumph for myself, and I cannot relinquish the idea. May blessings be yours and Emma's portion, and they must be that of your Agatha.

She dispatched, at the same time, a messenger to Mrs. Herbert with the following lines.

My beloved friend,
Let me see you tomorrow. I have much to say to you – Hammond more than esteems – he loves you – I have drawn the dear confession from him. His heart is a treasure, Emma – surely you will not prize it the less for having been once in the possession of your friend? You are not insensible of Hammond's merit – reward it, therefore, I conjure you, and you will make me happy – happier than I dared hope to have been in this world.

Chapter 8

The next morning Mrs. Herbert and Hammond arrived nearly at the same minute. In compliance with Agatha's solicitations, they consented to pass the day with her, though embarrassment and uneasiness were evident in the countenances of both. Sister Agnes, trembling for her friend, and considering her present fortitude as the result of an effort too painful to be long sustained, betrayed continual apprehension and anxiety. Agatha, her mind elevated by the heroism of her virtue, was alone firm, collected, and serene. She endeavoured to dissipate the uneasiness of her friends. She started new subjects repeatedly; each of which was only supported by her own animated and pointed remarks. Mrs. Herbert's wonted vivacity was fled. If she caught Agatha's eye, her own filled with tears, and she was obliged to turn from her to conceal her emotions. Hammond was sometimes absent and thoughtful; at others, he watched every turn of Agatha's countenance with trembling anxiety, endeavouring, as it seemed, to trace if her serenity were real or assumed.

As evening advanced, the embarrassment of Hammond and Mrs. Herbert by degrees wore off; Agatha had not once, even by a hint, reverted to the subject on which she had written to them, and they began to hope she did not intend it. Mrs. Herbert's carriage arriving, she rose instantly to obey the summons, and Hammond, at the same moment, was preparing to depart, when Agatha caught hold of his arm, and addressing herself to him and Mrs. Herbert, "before you go," she said, "there is a question I wish to put to you both concerning the brother of one of my servants; and as there are various opinions on the case I wish to hear yours before I decide either way. A fortune considerable to persons in his station of life has been left to Martha's youngest brother by a distant relation. With this he proposes to purchase a little estate, and to reside upon it with his wife and family during the remainder of his life. But his elder brother, not having had equal good luck, is not of course able to purchase a farm; and the mother, whose darling he is, cannot bear that one son should buy an estate, and become a squire, as she calls it, while the other continues to labour for his support. The young man himself is, notwithstanding, desirous that his brother should employ his little wealth to the best possible advantage; and he is certainly right: do you not think so? Would he not be highly condemnable, should he, in compliance with his mother's narrow wishes, endeavour to impede his brother's advancement?"

"Certainly," replied Hammond, "there is not a doubt in the case."

"Ought we not," pursued Agatha, "to exult in another's enjoying a blessing though it may be out of our reach? Is it not natural to every generous mind? Do you not think so, Emma?"

Mrs. Herbert turned pale.

"My beloved friend's countenance tells me she penetrates the reference I would make," said Agatha. Then taking Mrs. Herbert's hand, "Here Hammond," she said, "first, and best-beloved of my heart, receive from me the dearest treasure in the world – the hand of the most estimable of women: her heart I am sure does not, and her lips must not, shall not, contradict my wishes."

Hammond was motionless with astonishment.

"Must I take yours too?" said Agatha to Hammond and with an animated smile. "Here then, my Emma, I join them – your Agatha, your happy Agatha unites the two beings dearest to her in the world. May every blessing be yours; and many, many years may Heaven spare me to witness them!"

"I cannot bear this," said Hammond, forcing himself from Agatha, and throwing himself into a chair.

Mrs. Herbert, too much affected to shed a tear, and incapable of utterance, was only preserved from fainting by the salts Sister Agnes held to her.

Agatha went first to one, then to the other of her friends, soothing each in their turn, while her own feelings seemed entirely obliterated and lost in theirs.

When Mrs. Herbert was somewhat recovered, "I will ask you, my dear friend," said Agatha, "one question, to which, by all the friendship that ever subsisted between us, I conjure you to answer me sincerely. Were I wholly out of the question, had there never existed such a being, or had we never met, would you, knowing Hammond's worth as you do, have rejected his proposals? Speak, Emma, and answer me sincerely. I may have been abrupt. The warmth of my feelings, my ardent wish to promote his happiness may have prompted me to give your hand where your whole heart could not be given, though of your perfect esteem for him, as a friend, I have long been convinced. As you wish to preserve my friendship, as you value my peace, I charge you answer me from your heart. Would you, I repeat it, have rejected him?"

"I know not," replied Mrs. Herbert, at last relieved by tears, "nor can I say, how, in different circumstances, I might have acted, or wished to act: but in the present, considering our friend as the plighted husband of another, (however fatally divided) that other the friend of my bosom –"

"Enough, my dearest Emma," interrupted Agatha; "that doubt satisfies me, and ought to do Hammond. Had I been a man, I should have made an admirable wooer, for I have penetration enough to spare her I loved the pain of a direct confession. Be not pained by my vivacity, for indeed and indeed, it is not feigned. I have just accomplished the darling wish of my heart, and ought I not to feel gay and happy? My trial is now at an end – I have nothing but comforts before me: a prospect illumined by the future happiness of you – of you – and of you, my Agnes; for will you not share my felicity? Will not you too exult when they are blest?"

Sister Agnes, who dreaded a continuance of this scene, and whom Agatha's vivacity, however natural it appeared, but alarmed the more, now with tears entreated her, for the sake of her friends, if not for her own, to drop this affecting subject.

"Yes; now, and forever, my sweet Agatha," said Mrs. Herbert.

A servant, at that instant, came to inform Mrs. Herbert that her carriage had been waiting some time.

"Not yet," said Agatha, as Mrs. Herbert offered to go, "I cannot part with you thus. Will you then force me to repeat my solicitations? Must I again take this dear reluctant hand? – Hammond – must I once more ask you to accept it?"

"O," said Hammond, taking Mrs. Herbert's hand, "with what gratitude should I receive it, did I not fear your own generous heart! No, Agatha, I repeat it – it is impossible."

"Hammond I scorn deceit – I am what I appear, feel what I profess to feel. My mind, long riveted to this idea, cannot relinquish it. But promise me – both promise me that you will, at least, reflect on what I have urged."

"I will," said Hammond, sighing deeply.

"And you, Emma?"

"I do – I will, thou Angel of a woman!"

Hammond and Mrs. Herbert now took leave of Agatha; Hammond, at Agatha's request, attending Mrs. Herbert home, as her spirits appeared too much agitated to be suffered to depart alone.

Sister Agnes, wished yet dreaded their departure, and who expected every moment to see Agatha fall prey to her exertions, watched her countenance with fearful anxiety; but she saw, with equal astonishment and satisfaction, that her spirits remained unaltered. She conversed with ease on different topics, and though a few minutes of absence sometimes intervened, she did not appear to struggle with any inward distress.

At night, however, she was unable to sleep; and in the morning was not entirely free from fever. Observing the alarm impressed on the countenance of Sister Agnes, she conjured her to calm her apprehensions. "It has been ever thus," she said, "the weakness of my frame was always incapable of supporting the exertions my situation required. But believe me when I assure you, that I am internally happy. My mind feels relieved from a weight that has long oppressed it."

Agatha, as she conversed with Sister Agnes, grew insensibly more and more tranquil, and before the evening was perfectly recovered: when a messenger coming from Mrs. Herbert and Hammond to enquire after her health, she was well enough to send them a written reply, assuring them of the tranquillity of her mind, and, in the most forcible manner, renewing her former entreaties.

The next day she neither saw nor heard from them, but on the day following she was surprised by a visit from Mr. Ormistace and Mr. Crawford.

"I come, my charming Miss Belmont," said Mr. Ormistace, "on a most extraordinary errand. Is it possible – tell me – do you desire that Hammond shall marry Emma? You, who I always believed attached to him from your very soul!"

"It is, indeed, true," said Agatha, somewhat agitated by the abruptness of the address, yet almost instantly recovering her composure. "I wish the happiness of Hammond and Mrs. Herbert, and therefore would –"

"Torture yourself! Put your own feelings on the rack!" interrupted Mr. Ormistace. "But no, Miss Belmont, angelic creature! No, it shall never be. If Emma dare to think of him, if Hammond dare indulge a hope –"

"Be calm, my good friend," said Mr. Crawford, observing Agatha terrified by his warmth and menaces. "We come to consult with this excellent young lady, to learn her real sentiments and feelings, and to convince her that the happiness of her friends cannot be purchased by her sufferings. Speak then, my dear Miss Belmont, you know the excellence of Mrs. Herbert's heart, and must be assured it cannot have built its felicity on ought that could shake or injure yours. Does not your heart give the lie to your tongue? Or rather, does not your magnanimity lead you to deceive yourself? Can you see, not merely without pain, but with pleasure, Mr. Hammond married to another?"

"Impossible!" said Mr. Ormistace. "Good God, Sir, she cannot! Can she endure to see the man she once loved (and if once, always, with a heart like hers) lavish upon another that tenderness, those attentions, which, but for the cursed superstition of her parents had been hers? It cannot, shall not be! She shall not, if she would, make herself miserable."

"Be calm, my dear Mr. Ormistace, I entreat you," said Agatha, "and suffer me to speak. What feelings are those which must induce me to oppose Mr. Hammond's marriage, if I did oppose it? Jealousy of his superior regard for another, and envy of that other's happiness? And do you imagine me capable of passions so odious? Or, if they had found a place in my breast, think you I would harbour and indulge them?

Besides, is it the duty of anyone to forego a benefit because it is out of the reach of another?"

"But where the heart is concerned, my dearest lady," said Mr. Crawford, "the case is widely different. We might not perhaps hold it condemnable to buy a tenement which our neighbour had not ready money to purchase, but we could not bear, because adverse circumstances have put it out of the power of our friend to marry, to unite ourselves to the object of his affections: this would be to wound him where all are vulnerable."

"Not if that friend were dead, Mr. Crawford," said Agatha, "and by the ceremony which took place at my profession, I am literally dead to the world."

"Cursed, cursed superstition!" said Mr. Ormistace.

"It is indeed astonishing," said Mr. Crawford, "that rational beings should ever have imagined, that to exclude themselves from the duties as well as the blessings of social life while in this world, would be the only method of ensuring salvation in the next. But it is a question we do not now come to discuss. You, my sweet young lady, have been a victim immolated at this barbarous shrine; and that you have, has cost many and many a tear to those who had seen you, and knew your virtues. But will you suffer me, once more, to repeat my question? Can you assure us that your former attachment to Mr. Hammond is so entirely subdued, that your heart actually wishes what your lips have declared?"

"Indeed, indeed it does," replied Agatha with firmness. "To Mr. Hammond I, perhaps, owe the preservation of my life: he did not hesitate to risk his own for me; and to see him rewarded as he deserves is the ultimate wish of my heart. Mrs. Herbert has every virtue that can adorn her sex; she does not, I am convinced, regard him with indifference; they must be happy, and I shall share every blessing that is reserved for them."

"Good God," said Mr. Ormistace, "you almost persuade me out of my reason."

"I would rather seek to convince it," said Agatha. "Be assured that what I urge is not the impulse of a hasty moment; it is the result of calm and deliberate reflection, seconded by an idea, perhaps the offspring of superstition, that I shall not long be an inhabitant of this world; and I would fain see Hammond happy before I die – would leave him some ministering friend to make his future days serene and blest. Do you then, my dear Mr. Ormistace, and you, Mr. Crawford, my other valued friend," pursued Agatha, offering a hand to each, "by your endeavours, reconcile Mrs. Herbert as well as Hammond to a lot that will, I am assured, make them happy; and which their generous fears for me can alone induce them to reject. Paint me to them, such as you have seen me, such as I am – tranquil and happy; with no cloud overshadowing the dear view before me – every tint in the delightful picture harmonised by the contemplation of their blessings."

"Wonderful woman!" cried Mr. Ormistace, the tears in his eyes, "every word you utter increases my astonishment. Where could you have learned this? Or are you really a being of a higher order?"

"From my cradle," replied Agatha, "I have been taught to regulate my feelings; it was the first lesson my mother, the first Miss Hammond inculcated; and from nature I learned, in common with you, and every other whose heart is not ignoble, that the happiness of others is our own."

"Heaven will in future reward you as you deserve," said Mr. Crawford. "No blessings this world has to bestow can do it."

After some conversation on other subjects, in which Agatha took a part with every appearance of ease and tranquility, Mr. Crawford and Mr. Ormistace took their leave, promising, in pursuance of Agatha's earnest entreaties, to promote a marriage which they now believed would be no less conducive to her happiness than to that of her friends.

Some months, however, passed, before Hammond and Mrs. Herbert, still doubtful of Agatha's real feelings, could be prevailed upon to yield to her entreaties. At length, convinced by her repeated assurances, that, far from distressing, it would in the end restore tranquillity to her mind, and that, from her generous desire to promote their happiness, it was become the first and darling wish of her heart, they yielded to her reiterated persuasions, and were married on the first of March 1792.

When the appointed day came, Sister Agnes, who had long dreaded its arrival, in spite of the fortitude Agatha had hitherto invariably displayed, watched every turn of her countenance with the most tender solicitude, and in her apprehensions for her beloved friend was herself in need of the consolation she wished to bestow. Agatha pressed her to her bosom – assured her that her fears were groundless – that she felt not only tranquil but happy. Yet when she essayed to employ herself as usual, she was incapable of fixing her attention. She opened a book, but shut it again, unable to read. A little stuff gown which she was making for a poor child, lay on the table. She took it up with intent to finish it, but the needle dropped from her fingers. When the clock struck twelve, she started from her seat, turned pale, and went out of the room. Sister Agnes, alarmed at her appearance and manner, followed her immediately. Agatha conjured her to suffer her to pass a few minutes alone. "It is now passed," she said, "the awful ceremony is over, and propitious be the event. I wish but on my knees to implore a blessing for them, and will return to you here."

Sister Agnes consented to leave her, though with reluctance; but alarmed at her not returning so soon as she had promised, she went to her room, and found her apparently lifeless on the floor, a paper lying near her, written, as it appeared, for the trying occasion.

Sister Agnes, in a terror that almost deprived her of reason, screamed and rang the bell for the servants; and by their efforts and assistance Agatha was at last recovered.

When Agatha had perfectly regained her senses, and the servants had left the room, she assured Sister Agnes that she was unable to account for the sudden privation of sense which had seized her. "Preparatory to this dear, though awful day," continued Agatha, "I had written some lines to invoke blessings on those I love, and, at the same time, to inspire me with fortitude and resignation, should my rebel heart refuse to rejoice when its day of trial came. I wished to read them when the hour of twelve was past, and they were indissolubly united, nor was I aware that I felt any violent emotions. I read, as I thought, with composure; but when I came to the words, "his wife," my heart turned cold – a faint sickness seized me, and I lost my recollection. Be not alarmed for me my beloved friend – it is over now. There lies the paper. Read it, my Agnes, but not to me – I am tranquil at present, and will not again agitate my spirits."

Sister Agnes took the paper, but fearing that her sympathising emotions might renew those of Agatha, promised to read it at a future opportunity. Following is a copy of the contents.

- - - - -

Lines to be read on the dearest yet most awful of days, at the hour of twelve.

Many and various are the sorrows of life. Some are fated to lament the loss of friends: some to struggle with the evils of penury and want; others to feel their bosoms rent by the sacrifices Virtue extracts: but thy blessing, O, Father of Mercies, is still left to sustain them; a Haven of Peace eternally open to all who seek and deserve to enter it!

Early did I become a Child of Affliction. Steep and rugged was the path given me to ascend; while Pleasure, under her fairest image, tempted me back; and pointing to the flower-strewn paths of domestic life bid me love, and be happy. But I turned from this sweet illusion, obeyed the monitress within me, was guiltless, and was happy. Thy blessing sustained me! O, withhold it not now.

Shower down blessings on Hammond and the Wife of his heart. Many and happy be the days of the years of their pilgrimage on earth; and if it be thy will, preserve me to witness and increase their felicity.

- - - - -

The soothing tenderness of Sister Agnes with Agatha's own heroic efforts very soon restored her former serenity; and she awaited with anxious impatience the day of Mr. and Mrs. Hammond's return from London, whither they had gone immediately on their marriage.

On the day of their return, Agatha, accompanied by Sister Agnes, hastened to welcome their arrival; and desirous that even her dress should bespeak her a sharer in their felicity, she laid aside her religious habit for that day, and wore a dress of muslin with coloured ornaments.

As she approached Hammond's house, and the idea of the different sensations with which she had once before entered and quitted it, struck her forcibly. She had then been received under its roof in the days of youthful delight, when no cares had corroded, no trials tortured her heart: it was the abode of friendship, peace, and pleasure. She left it, deprived forever of that friend, her heart yet bleeding for her loss, and, though unconscious of its feelings, too tenderly attached to another. That other she was now preparing to meet – to meet him, the husband of her dearest friend – married in pursuance of her wishes, her prayers.

Lost in reflection the chaise had stopped at the gate, before she was aware they were near the house. Hammond met her at the door; "My Agatha, this is kind, indeed," said Hammond noticing her dress, and immediately comprehending the delicate compliment.

"Nothing, my best friend," said Agatha, "ought on this dear occasion to wear the face of gloom. Where is my Emma, now, my dear Mrs. –" Hammond, she would have said, but her voice faltered. Recovering herself immediately, however, "surely," she continued, "she is well? Her impatience to see me cannot be less than mine to meet her."

At that minute Mrs. Hammond, who had been endeavouring to assume that courage to support the trying scene, ran into Agatha's arms, and letting her head fall on her bosom, gave way to a shower of tears.

"Let me kiss off these tears of friendship, my Emma," said Agatha with exquisite tenderness, "and endeavour to calm these dear agitated spirits. Hammond assist me to recover our Emma."

"Angelic Agatha!" said Hammond, raising his eyes to Heaven, his voice faltering with the emotions he felt. Then turning to Mrs. Hammond, and taking her hand. "Look up, my love," he said, "look up and witness the kindness of this best of friends – this angel – to whom we owe the life of felicity we enjoy."

"Forgive me, my sweet Agatha," said Mrs. Hammond, "that I cannot utter what my heart dictates; to your own I appeal – that only can tell you what I feel."

"Happy – happy may you ever be, my beloved Emma," said Agatha, with fervour, "happy as you deserve – as I wish you. We could, I know, dwell forever on the dear theme of our friendship – but it is too affecting to us all – my Agnes cannot bear it – we will quit this dearest subject then, but every other must be interesting to friends thus attached to each other."

Several months now glided on in uninterrupted tranquillity. Agatha, her trials over, participated all the blessings of her friends, and they with transport acknowledged that to her they owed them. Few days passed in which they did not meet; and occasionally joined by St. Valorie, whose amiable daughter had been some time married and enjoyed every prospect of continued happiness; sometimes by Mr. Crawford and his family, and very frequently by Mr. Ormistace, Agatha but for her apprehensions on account of her parents, would have believed her happiness perfect; at least as much so as there is reason to expect in a world where virtue is appointed to earn not to receive its reward.

Chapter 9

In little more than a year, Mrs. Hammond completed the felicity of her husband as well as of Agatha, by presenting to them twins – a lovely boy and girl. In these sweet infants Agatha seemed herself a mother. A thousand tender emotions before unknown to her now filled her heart. The value of her own life seemed enhanced; since with the exquisite feelings of a parent, she was anxious to preserve it for their sake; to witness their growth, their improvement; to trace the progress of their virtues, and assist in the delightful task of their culture.

As Agatha was one day contemplating the infant Emma as it lay asleep on her lap, a servant entered and informed her, that an old gentleman very remarkably dressed had asked to speak to his master, or if he was not at home to any of his friends. Agatha desired the servant to show him into the parlour; but how great was her astonishment and pleasure, when, in the face of the old gentleman she instantly recognised that of the good and venerable Father Albert. Giving the infant to its nurse, she flew to meet him while surprise and joy for some moments deprived her of speech.

"My dear daughter," said Father Albert, when the first emotions of delight were over, "I then see you happy; united to the man you loved – a wife and a mother. Imagine not that I am preparing to reproach you. God forbid! Your trial was a hard one; harder, perhaps, than human nature could sustain. But why this dress, when sharing the pleasures of the world?"

"No, my dear father," replied Agatha, "Heaven has given me courage to resist every temptation to violate my vows. That sweet infant, though mine in affection, has another mother."

"Amazement!" said Father Albert – "but Hammond, my other adopted child –"

"He is married at my earnest solicitations; and from his happiness and that of his estimable wife, I enjoy blessings that could not have been mine, had the sting of self-reproach once wounded my bosom. But how did you escape, my dear father? Satisfy my impatience. We feared – we lamented you as dead."

"My preservation was, indeed, wonderful," said Father Albert, "since my life was twice in imminent danger. My frequent visits to different towns to purchase provisions, had, as I imagine, been noticed; and on my return from one of them my steps were traced, I was pursued and seized at some distance from the cave. They believed me possessed of some hidden treasure, and on condition that I would lead them to the spot, and assist them in exploring every part of the recess I inhabited, they promised pardon, and possibly to set me at liberty. If, on the other hand, I refused to obey them, my life was to pay the forfeiture of my obstinacy."

"Just Heaven!" said Agatha, "and to preserve us –"

"They would not," replied Father Albert, "if their purposed treatment of me can be judged by that others have received, have performed their promise, though possibly they might not have ordered me to execution. I was taken to prison, and the gaoler received orders to put me to death during the night. But his wife, to whom, as she had lost her parents in her infancy, I had been a father and protector, prevailed upon him to suffer me to escape. Assured that I could confide in her fidelity, I informed her of your situation, and by my directions she went to the cave, being provided with a tale in case she had been discovered, but when I saw her afterwards, I learned that you and Hammond had escaped before she arrived to apprise you of your danger. Once more at liberty, I attempted to conceal myself from my persecutors, and became again an inhabitant of the forest; till at last, compelled by hunger I was necessitated to implore relief at the house of a peasant whom I believed a stranger to my person. He received me with pretended compassion; but while, by his orders, his wife prepared me an omelette, he went out of the house, and returned with a party of his neighbours to seize and conduct me to prison. Happily my person was not identified, but I was a priest, and that was a sufficient crime. I was conveyed to a prison some miles distant, and there the horrors I witnessed would exceed belief, were there not too, too many dreadful proofs of the reality of such scenes in my devoted country. The room in which I was confined had a small grated window that looked into a square stone court, in the centre of the building. Thither the prisoners were brought to be examined or massacred. At dead of night, I have heard the cells opened, the victims dragged to the court, and without the formality of a trial, or even a pretence of justice, there murdered: their dying groans yet resound in my ears. Fear sealed the lips of their relations and friends: an enquiry after those who were imprisoned proved to those who dare to make it, accessory to the PLOTS against LIBERTY and involved them in the same punishment. The nurse and infant son of the Marquis de Villarme were brought to the prison in which I was confined. The nurse was believed to have secreted some of her master's treasures, the infant was the son of a Noble! The woman after numberless interrogatories, was, at last, dismissed; the child died in prison. Two nights after this, a fire broke out in some part of the building, and in the general tumult I happily escaped.

Determined no longer to attempt to remain in France, I ventured during the night to apply to the good girl who had before favoured my escape from prison, and received from her a small supply of food. With this assistance, with what I occasionally received from some benevolent Lyonnaise, I reached Switzerland, where an English gentleman took me under his protection, and brought me with him to England. Learning that Mr. Hammond had likewise escaped to England, I enquired his abode; and, long accustomed to this mode of travelling, have come hither on foot."

Father Albert had just finished his recital, when Hammond entered, and after expressing his delight at meeting the venerable Father, entreated him to suffer him to return part of his obligations; and as he had been his guest in France, to consent to become his in England; and not merely a temporary but a constant one. Mrs. Hammond, who now entered the room, and to whom Hammond presented Father Albert as the preserver of his own and Agatha's life, joined her entreaties to his, while the good priest received their offers with tears of gratitude.

Agatha afterwards insisted on sharing with Hammond the pleasure and instruction of Father Albert's society; the venerable priest, therefore, sometimes a guest of one, sometimes of the other of his children, as he had been accustomed to call them, at once increased and shared the general felicity.

But this scene of happiness was soon to receive an alarming and dreadful interruption. Hammond, after an illness originating in a slight and accidental cold, had every appearance of an approaching consumption. His present dangerous symptoms, added to the benefit he had once before derived from its waters, induced his physicians to order him to Bristol immediately. Mrs. Hammond and Agatha, whose terror and distress he in vain endeavoured to lessen by making light of his complaints, and frequently concealing the pain he endured, attended him thither in a state of mind the anguish of which it is not possible to describe.

For a few weeks he appeared to receive benefit from the waters, and the wife and the friend whose existence seemed to depend on his, had began to flatter themselves with hopes of his recovery. But they were soon too fatally undeceived. The disorder advanced with rapid strides: and the Physicians, among whom was the excellent Dr. Harley, who with Sister Agnes had followed them to Bristol, confessed to his distracted friends, that there was no chance of his recovery.

Hammond himself had long been aware of his danger; and the countenances of those around him but too plainly proved the justice of his fears. "My Emma, my Agatha," he said, as he beheld them endeavouring to conceal their anguish from him, "deceive not me,

deceive not yourselves. I flattered you with hope while I had a glimmering of it myself – but it would now be barbarous, since it would but
render heavier the weight of the impending stroke when it shall at last
fall upon you. Support yourselves for the sake of each other, my beloved
friends – for the sake of our infants – I leave them yet two parents, two
excellent parents, who will train them up in the paths of virtue, and teach
them so to live that we shall hereafter meet them never to part. Consider,
my Emma, 'tis but a few short years, and we shall meet and enjoy an
Eternity of bliss together."

Mrs. Hammond, unable to bear this, caught hold of Hammond's
hand and with an appearance of distraction, and then screaming
violently, ran out of the room. Agatha, though too deeply a sufferer
herself, followed her, leaving Sister Agnes and Dr. Harley with
Hammond. She had before attributed the apparent illness of Mrs.
Hammond to that grief which preyed on her own frame; but she now
discovered, that, either occasioned or increased by the anguish of her
mind, she had a violent and alarming fever.

Agatha returned to Hammond, and sent Dr. Harley to Mrs.
Hammond; but who shall paint the misery of Agatha, when it was
pronounced that Mrs. Hammond was in extreme danger, while the
delirium which had seized her obliged her to be confined to her
apartment!

Agatha, at this awful crisis, seemed to be supported by that very
affection whence her sorrows sprang. While she was in the room with
Mrs. Hammond, or attending on her languid and almost dying husband,
she seemed to lose the remembrance of her sufferings in her endeavours
to soothe and ease theirs.

"My Agatha," said Hammond, calling her to his bedside one
morning, "I think my strength gradually forsakes me, but, at this minute,
like the departing taper I seem to feel a few flashes of momentary life.
Hard indeed have been thy trials, and this is more severe than all – God
give thee strength to survive it for the sake of my children; should they
lose their mother and thee, who shall protect and be a parent to them?"

"O Hammond!" replied Agatha, "bitter indeed as are the pangs of
surviving thee, I will pray for it, for thy sake. I have been accustomed to
sorrow, till this heart, though it feels it, heaven only knows how sensibly,
seems to have learned to support its attacks! Yet should this trial
overpower my strength, and should thy unhappy wife be taken from
them, there are many yet, bound to thee by every tier of gratitude and
friendship, that will be parents to thy children – St. Valorie – Israeli –
Father Albert –"

"True, O, true, my Agatha," said Hammond, "I have performed my
duty here, and how at this moment am I rewarded for it! 'The righteous

shall not be forsaken, nor his seed beg their bread.' No, I have acquired friends, who, when I am in the dust, shall revere my memory, and shelter my children. Agatha, my beloved Agatha, give me thy hand. 'O 'tis the only sting of death to part from those we love!' all else is nothing – death has no other terror. I go to rejoin my sister. Methinks I see her pure spirit hovering near me, and beckoning me to the regions of the blessed! My Agatha, if I have ever given a pang to thy generous heart, forgive me – I meant it not – dearer than life as you have ever been to me. And how at this awful minute do I bless you that you denied my wishes, that I have no crime, no vows violated for me to answer for. In one instance only I have deceived you: time or accident may perhaps reveal it; if they should, you will not love my memory the less, and will forgive the deception in favour of the motive. How little, at this moment, appears every earthly consideration, every pleasure of the world I am quitting."

At this minute, Mrs. Hammond, not to be restrained by the entreaties of her nurse, burst into the room. She ran to the bed where Hammond lay, and kneeling down by the side of it, snatched his hand. "This," she said looking wildly around her, "was Agatha's gift, and you cannot take it from me. I will follow thee to the grave. Think not I will bear the misery of surviving you – no, Hammond. Yet why should you die? You have not deserved it – you was so kind to everyone – sorrow fled at your approach. Everyone loved you. Why should you die then, Hammond?"

"My beloved Emma," said Hammond, "I consider it not as a punishment but rather as a blessing, that I am thus spared the anguish of surviving those I love. In friendship, in marriage, one must be the survivor – happy, happy those whom Heaven shall mercifully call for first! I die in youth, it is true, but not, I trust, young in virtue – I have run the race that was set before me, and I am bidden sooner than I looked for to receive an everlasting reward. Farewell, my Emma – my Agatha, farewell. God preserve and support ye both! I feel, even now, the hand of death, but it is sweet to be sustained by the presence of ye both; to gaze last on the objects dearest to my soul – a few fleeting years, and then, my Agatha –"

Then pressing her hand and Mrs. Hammond's at the same moment to his lips, his voice faltered – he attempted, but in vain, to speak again; and with a look of Christian resignation, expired without a groan.

St. Valorie, to whom an express had been sent informing him of Hammond's danger, now entered his chamber. Agatha's eyes were riveted on Hammond, while Mrs. Hammond was looking wildly around, in the returning delirium of her fever, not comprehending that he was dead.

"I come," said St. Valorie, as he entered, "to cheer my benefactor, and to recover him by the cares of friendship. Where is he?"

Agatha spoke not, but with her finger pointed to him.

"O scene of misery!" said St. Valorie, "beyond all I ever witnessed! And is it come to this? Is the dear, the generous Hammond, the friend of all, is he gone? So young too – it cannot, cannot be. Look up, Hammond – see St. Valorie – let the voice of him you preserved and supported call you back to life." Then sitting down on the bed, St. Valorie covered his face with his hands, in an agony of grief.

Mrs. Hammond was now forced from the room, but no entreaties could prevail on Agatha to leave it. "These minutes are precious," she said, "do not rob me of them. Look, Agnes, see how calm, how serene, how heavenly he looks – and is this death? Why would you force me from him? Let me prolong this last, last blessing! He seems not lost to me, while thus I can gaze upon his image: O, but the mind that informed it – the soul is gone forever. Yet whither fled? It was but now, he knew me, talked to me. Then whither is it gone? O, to be happy – and I will follow him. No, Hammond, they shall not force me to survive thee. And yet thy children – yes, I promised whilst yet thou couldst hear my voice, I promised to live for them."

By the tears of Sister Agnes and the prayers of Dr. Harley, Agatha was at last induced to leave the room. She then attempted to go to Mrs. Hammond's apartment, but was prevented, and taken to her own; and there she continued, during several hours, in a state of apparent insensibility, infinitely more alarming than the most violent expressions of grief.

Mrs. Hammond, overpowered by the shock she had sustained, and already weak from illness, survived her husband two days only. In the lucid interval that preceded her disillusion, Agatha, though bowed down by the weight of this second and little less heavy affliction, made her a promise not less solemn than she had made to Hammond, to use every means in her power to preserve her life for the sake of the sacred trust confided to her.

"Bless, bless you for that, for every other mark of inestimable kindness I have received from you, my Agatha," said Mrs. Hammond. "To you I have owed one year of perfect, unmixed happiness; and had my Hammond been spared to me, what a life of blessings had been ours! But he is gone, where even that happiness would appear faint and insipid, and where I shall soon meet him to share an Eternity of bliss. For you, my sweet friend, severe as is this trial, your piety and resignation will support you under it; and a few, few years and you shall join us."

Not to prolong this melancholy recital, Mrs. Hammond expired a few hours after this affecting scene, her last moments cheered by the recollection of past virtues, and the hope of future reward. Agatha kneeled down by her bedside, and raising her hands to Heaven, exclaimed, with a fervour which seemed to lose sight of this world, "may I die the death of the righteous, and may my latter end be like theirs!"

Agatha, with Sister Agnes and the infants Edward and Emma now quitted their melancholy lodgings, and returned to Agatha's house, leaving the heart-broken Mr. Ormistace, and St. Valorie to pay the last sad duties to the remains of the lamented pair.

On the stone that points out the remains of Mr. and Mrs. Hammond is engraven, "They were lovely in their lives, and in their death they were not divided," and on the stone a blank is left for the name of Agatha, whenever it shall please Heaven to call her to itself.

Chapter 10

While Agatha's sorrow was yet recent for this double stroke of distress, and ere the gentle hand of friendship had dried her tears, they were destined to flow from another and not less agonising source.

Mrs. Besford called upon her one morning, and taking out a letter, "O, my dear creature!" she said, "I have some news that I hope will reward you for all you have suffered; and therefore I would bring it myself. My sister (though I believe it was intended for my mother) has had a letter from Sir Charles Belmont."

"From my father!" said Agatha, her voice faltering as her mind fluctuated between the extremes of hope and fear. "He lives then?"

"He certainly was alive at the time he wrote that letter; it stands to reason, you know, that he must be. What he writes to my mother is nothing more than this."

Sir Charles Belmont requests the favour of Lady Milson to convey the enclosed to his unfortunate daughter, if ever she should reach England, and Lady Milson be able to discover her place of residence. Should certain information be received of her death, he entreats Lady Milson to open the packet, and apply the sum specified in it to charitable purposes.

Agatha took the letter, but her trembling hand had not the power to break the seal. Read it, my Agnes, she said, giving it to Sister Agnes, I cannot – I dare not.

Sister Agnes opened it, and as she glanced her eye over the first paragraph, Agnes saw her turn pale – "O, Agnes!" she cried, "my fears were just – they are ill – they are in danger."

"You have known many trials, my sister," said Agnes, "and have borne them all nobly."

"O, Agnes! Torture me not with suspense. They are in prison, in danger –"

"In imminent danger, my dearest friend."

"O, let me know the extent of my misery! Tell, tell me all. I am become familiar with distress, I have seen it under every dreadful shape."

"O, that the voice of friendship might speak comfort to you, my sweet sister!" said Agnes. "Remember I live but for you; and every pang you feel, shall more than share it. The danger you dreaded is past. Your excellent parents are happy."

"Surely, surely," said Agatha, "the measure of my sorrows is now full." Then resting her head on her hand, and fixing her eyes on the ground, she remained motionless and seemingly insensible.

"O dear!" said Mrs. Besford weeping bitterly, "how sorry I am! I thought to have given her comfort; and though my sister believed otherwise, I was almost certain Sir Charles was alive and well. However I can do no good, and so I will leave you – but I am very very sorry indeed."

When Mrs. Besford was gone, Sister Agnes endeavoured to rouse Agatha from her alarming insensibility; but though her tender cares at last succeeded, many days passed before she dared suffer her to read the fatal packet, breaking its contents to her by degrees, and as she found her able to bear the communication.

The following is a copy of the letter:

Arm yourself with fortitude, my beloved child. Before this can reach your hand, that of him that writes it will be cold and motionless forever. Your mother is already at peace; a few hours more, and I shall follow her. Hear the sad story of our fate: my end draws nigh, and I have not a moment to lose. On the very night in which we had appointed to fly from this barbarous country, our house was surrounded by armed ruffians. To obtain the respite of a few minutes we barred all the doors; and while I consulted with a faithful domestic on the steps we should take, your mother wrote a few trembling lines to inform you of our danger, and tying them to a little box of jewels, confided them to the care of one of the servants. Heaven knows if you ever received either! Jacques, the servant on whose zeal and fidelity we could most depend, was the companion of our flight. He had accidentally discovered a private door at the foot of the stairs which led to a subterraneous passage; and aware of the danger which threatened us, had concealed his discovery from everyone, till the moment in which it became necessary to have recourse to it. Jacques led the way, and we followed him with hasty and trembling steps. At the termination of the passage, which was half a quarter of a mile in length was a trap door lightly covered with earth. Through this door we entered the road; and putting out our light lest it should be espied from the house, and lead the mob to pursue us, wandered we knew not whither during the greatest part of the night. In the morning we found ourselves near a village about six miles from Issoire. As we had not had time to put on the disguises we had prepared, we did not venture to enter it, but turning to the right went into a small wood, which we knew to be little frequented, and in which we believed we might pass the day safely. Jacques, unknown to us, had brought a loaf with him; but it was with utmost difficulty that we prevailed on him to share it with us. At night we pursued our tedious journey, till your mother, sometimes supported by me, sometimes by Jacques, was so much exhausted by fatigue, that we were compelled to remain two days among the ruins of a chateau. Jacques in the meantime, went to a distant town to buy provisions for us, and was fortunate enough to purchase a mule of some travellers whom he overtook on the road. With this assistance we were enabled to pursue our journey. When we were, as we imagined, out of the reach of pursuit, and our persons no longer likely to be recognised, we proposed to remain at a cottage while Jacques returned for you. But the peasants, apprehensive for their own safety, should they entertain Nobles, as they said our appearance proved us to be, would not suffer us to remain with them; we were therefore obliged to continue our journey, till we should meet with someone kind enough to shelter us. At last to our equal surprise and comfort, we were met and accosted by a person in the garb of a shepherd, whom I instantly remembered to be the Baron de —— whom I had formerly known at Paris, and from whom, during my travels in the early part of my life, I had received many marks of friendship. He informed me that having lost his wife and only son some years previous to the Revolution, he had determined to retire from society; and that concealing his name and quality, he had since lived as a shepherd. His hut was many miles distant from any other dwelling; and this, added to the idea generally entertained among his neighbours, from his shunning as much as possible any intercourse with them, that his intellects were deranged, had enabled him to give shelter to many unfortunate Nobles who had been obliged to conceal themselves from popular fury, and whom he had discovered in his daily rambles. We remained at the Baron's cottage, while Jacques was dispatched to bring our beloved child and Sister Agnes to us. But alas, our faithful Jacques returned no more. What became of him we never heard; yet it is but too probable that his connection with us was discovered, and that his fidelity cost him his life. After remaining at the Baron's hospitable dwelling more than a fortnight, we were obliged to leave it; our residence there having been remarked by some casual visitors, from whom, though he invented a story which satisfied them at the time, he would have been in great danger had we continued longer with him.

Miserable on account of our separation from you, we once had thoughts of returning to Issoire, to take you from the convent; but the certainty of the danger to which we should by this means expose you as well as ourselves, deterred us from putting the rash scheme into execution. After taking leave of the Baron, we determined to continue our journey towards Bordeaux, and from thence to embark for England, whither we were assured you would follow us, whenever you should be compelled to forsake the convent. But we had not proceeded more than twelve miles after our departure from the Baron's when our mule dropped down and died. This loss was the more distressing, as there was little probability that we should have an opportunity of purchasing another; while my poor Agatha's inability to pursue our journey on foot, except by very short stages, would render it so tedious, that the money we had with us must be expended before we reached England. We had, however, no choice to make; and were obliged to travel on foot, without any attendant or guide, ignorant of the country through which we passed, and after losing ourselves in the trackless wilds of immense forests.

One fatal evening, passing near the skirts of a forest, I observed a man at some distance behind us, who appeared to be following and endeavouring to overtake us. Lady Belmont was leaning on my arm and at my entreaty attempting to quicken her pace, till, sick with fatigue, she stopped, confessing she could walk no farther. On our stopping, the man came up to us, and looking in my Agatha's face with an appearance of inquisitiveness, "My Lady seems fatigued," said he. "Alas, I am," said Lady Belmont. "Nature is quite worn out."

"My cottage is at hand," replied the man, "will you please to step into it, and rest you for the night?"

Countenances are sometimes deceitful, but there are features which cannot be mistaken; which, however hypocrisy may seek to mask with a smile, will betray the villain. The character of our pretended friend was but too visible, and I immediately rejected his offer, though with civility. On his repeating it more urgently, I replied, that I had relations at a neighbouring town to whom I had promised to return that night, and who would be alarmed at our absence; while your unhappy mother, in her present sufferings losing all sense of danger, supplicated me to grant his request. "Do try to prevail on my Lord, Madam," added the wretch, "but my house is always open to the weary traveller – I want no reward."

"God will give you one, good man," said Lady Belmont, affected by his pretended kindness. In vain I repeated the necessity of returning to our friends; the man was but the more urgent, and Lady Belmont joined her prayers to his. He then ran to the house, which, he said, was but a few paces distant, promising to return with his son who would assist in supporting the lady. The moment he had left us, I conjured Agatha to assume all the strength and courage possible, and to fly, while it was yet in our power, assuring her that we were betrayed. She attempted to walk, but overcome by fatigue and terror, fainted in my arms. The man returned in a few minutes in company with his son, whose appearance was that of a bravo. Convinced that resistance was now impossible, and might increase instead of averting our danger, I pretended to have yielded to his persuasions, and thanked him for his proffered assistance. They

helped me carry Lady Belmont into the house, in which we found an old woman and her daughter, the only other persons we saw. The old woman in a hoarse voice bid us welcome, and when Lady Belmont was recovered, brought a loaf and set before us, desiring us to sup with them. It now grew dark, and one small candle was lighted and put on the table. The old man then reminded his wife that she had forgotten the wine. She rose immediately, but as she was some time busied in preparing it, during which my host watched me with attention, apparently anxious that I should not observe her motions, I determined not to taste it; and on their offering it to me, declared, that neither my wife nor I ever drank wine of any kind, that water was our only beverage, and had been for years. They looked disappointed, but said nothing.

At night we were shown into a square room next to that where we had supped, in which was a bed with linen furniture, which the daughter very assiduously warmed for us, and then left us. I looked at the door, as we entered the chamber, and observed that it opened with an iron latch, and that there was no fastening on either side of it. By accident when we were packing up our plate and other valuables, I had put a piece of cord into my pocket; with this I tied the latch to the staple and afterwards took the further precaution of putting a penknife in such a manner into the staple, that every attempt to lift up the latch on the other side would be fruitless. I then examined the window, in hopes that, as the room was on a ground floor, it would be possible to escape from thence; but it was grated with iron bars placed so near to each other that scarcely a hand could have passed between them. The girl had left us part of a small candle, burned already so low that it could not last half an hour. Lady Belmont, by my advice, did not undress herself but lay down in her clothes; and exhausted by fatigue and pain, in spite of our danger which I did not attempt to conceal from her, dropped asleep. I now examined the room, and saw in one corner of it upon the floor, a small torn bit of fine lace, and near it some drops of blood which seemed to have been attempted to be scraped off with a knife. Examining the boards one by one, I observed that one of them as I stepped on it was looser than the rest, and on looking nearer, I saw an iron nail in the middle of it, higher and larger than was necessary to fasten the flooring. I took hold of it, and to my astonishment the board was lifted up immediately, and discovered a vault beneath it, the descent into which was by a rough ladder. I took the small remains of candle, carrying it with the utmost care lest it should go out before I returned, and descending the ladder, entered a place of horrors of which exceeded all that imagination can form. It had the appearance of the vault of a church, and contained the dead bodies of the murdered; one, a young man, appeared to be recently dead; his finger was cut off, probably to take a ring from it, but no other marks of violence were visible on the body: perhaps he had died by poison – by the preparation offered to us under the name of wine. I now heard something move behind me, and believing the assassins might have some other communication with this scene of horrors besides the trap door through which I entered it, I hastened to ascend the ladder to defend my beloved wife, or perish with her; but looking back, I found the noise proceeded from something underneath one of the bodies, and immediately afterwards I saw it was a huge rat whom the noise of my entrance had disturbed in his nocturnal feast. I once more, therefore, ventured to look around to discover if the vault had any opening by which we might escape; but finding none, returned without loss of time up the ladder, observing my light almost expiring. In order to prolong it for a few moments, I scraped the tallow that had fallen on the candlestick and put it near the wick. When I came into the chamber, I heard voices speaking in a whisper on the other side of the door, and perceived someone attempting to stir the latch. I awoke Lady Belmont, and conjured her to rise without delay, if she would save her life and mine; and when she had arisen from the bed, I drew my knife out of the staple, cut the cord with which I tied it, and, at the same instant, set fire to the curtains of the bed. The linen was in a blaze in a moment. Opening now the door, I screamed fire. The man and his son who were in the adjoining room, and saw the flames burst forth as a door opened, ran away in terror, calling to the women to save themselves while it was possible. Taking Lady Belmont's arm, I ran to the house door, and was unbarring it when the men returned. Save yourself, good people, I exclaimed, your house is in flames, save yourselves. Then passing through the door without interruption, we fled from the execrable spot. But the danger we believed at an end, still pursued us. My unhappy wife, too ill to continue our journey, was obliged to remain in the forest two days, supported only by wild fruits and herbs, and a loaf of coarse bread which I purchased for her from a beggar. At last, recovering her fatigue in some measure, we attempted to proceed, but had scarcely left the forest, when we were seized by the wretch from whose detestable habitation we had escaped, and other Officers of Justice, devoted, as it should seem, to him. "Those are they," he exclaimed on seeing us, "that is the Chevalier Belmont and his Lady from Issoire. I discovered them, and would have secured them for you, but they set fire to my house and escaped. Citizens, seize them – they are Aristocrats." We were bound and taken to prison, where we underwent an examination which proved the justice exercised in this country of Liberty. The officer asked me if I could deny that I was Sir Charles Belmont. I replied, that guilty of no crime, I did not wish to deny it. You are accused, pursued he, of distributing money among the inhabitants of

Issoire, through the hands of nuns, in order to spread fanaticism and tyranny. I answered, that pure charity, and no sinister motives had prompted my distributions; and that, with regard to the wretch at whose instigation and by whose orders I had been seized, were his character known, no charges he could bring against me would be thought to deserve credit, since he was an assassin – a murderer. I then declared, that I had seen the bodies of murdered persons in the vault under his house, and if suffered to do so, and that part of the building had escaped the flames, would conduct the officer to it, and make him an eye-witness to the truth of my assertions." "Do you hear citizens," said the wretch unmoved by the charge, "do you hear how aristocrats can lie, and how they would blacken every good patriot? Let him go to my house, and show you, if he can, the truth of a tittle of what he has the effrontery to say. But no, let him rather be imprisoned, and thus be condemned to expiate the atrocity of his guilt. Wretch! Aristocrat!" continued he, looking undauntedly in my face, "dare you prove your assertions?"

"I dare and will," I replied, "if suffered to do so."

"Come then, Citizens," said he, "let us go instantly; we will prove whether the word of an Aristocrat or a patriot is to be relied on."

"No, no," they all exclaimed in a breath, "we know you, you're a good patriot – let him be executed."

This part of my sentence was, however, agreed to be deferred, and I was ordered to be taken with my unhappy wife to a dungeon in the prison. The cell in which we were confined was damp, cold, and dark, and the provisions allowed us scarcely sufficient to support nature. To weep with each other, and pray for a happier fate to our beloved child, were our only comforts: the present was miserable, the future hopeless, and memory reverting to past blessings, but increased our torture. Death would have been welcome to us, could we have died together; but to survive each other was an agony we could not bear the thought of. During several months we were suffered to remain unnoticed, except by the gaoler who brought us our scanty supply of food, and who never spoke unless it were to revile us, and brand us with the name most odious in his estimation – Aristocrat. Yet even the little comfort we enjoyed was soon to be denied us. The barbarous Commandant of the prison, under a pretended charge of conspiracy, ordered us to be confined in separate cells. O, let your imagination paint our feelings at these dreadful moments, my child – yet rather, let it not paint them: the very thought is madness. It seemed now no crime to have lamented our fate while we were suffered to share it together; and what appeared a state of misery then, would have been happiness now. On our knees we implored our inhuman gaoler not to divide us; and declared, binding our asseverations with the most solemn oaths, that we had formed no plot, were guilty of no crime against the government or people; wishing but to linger out the last of our wretched days together. He was deaf to our entreaties, and my Agatha, the wife of my bosom, partner of my soul, was torn from my arms. It was in vain that I implored him to inform me from time to time if she yet lived; he exulted in and ridiculed my anguish, and, asking me if I imagined him a go-between in our plots, refused to give me any tidings of her.

One night as I conjectured near the hour of midnight, I heard a voice that seemed to be my Agatha's though changed by madness, singing wildly and talking alternately. On a sudden it ceased, and I heard loud and repeated screams. The dreadful thought struck me that they were murdering her; and frantic with terror and distress, I repeated her name, calling to her to answer me for mercy's sake, if she would save me from distraction. She seemed to have heard me, for immediately afterwards I could distinguish her repeating my name, and then singing as before. The certainty that she yet lived, after the horrid idea excited by her screams, was a consolation so great, that it destroyed for some minutes the sense of our past and present sufferings; yet when again my imagination beheld her the solitary inmate of a dungeon, bereft of reason, insulted perhaps by the wretch who guarded her, no friend near her whose soothing voice might calm her distracted mind, or give her comfort in her lucid intervals, my misery seemed more exquisite than ever, and with a fervour that I hope was no crime, I implored Heaven to take us both from a world of horrors.

The next morning I was surprised by observing that the person whose office it was to bring me my food was changed, and his place supplied by a young man whose countenance bore evident marks of a gentle and compassionate heart. I ventured to address him, and to implore that, if it were in his power, he would obtain permission for me to be confined in the same cell with a female prisoner who was my wife, and whom her distresses, added to her separation from me, had driven out of her senses. He appeared to sympathise in my affliction, and promised to obtain permission of the new Commandant of the prison to grant my request, if it was possible. He informed me that all those who had last had charge of the prisoners had been executed under suspicion of their having suffered some of them to escape. Then bidding me be comforted, and assuring me he would do all in his power to render my confinement easy, he left me.

In about an hour he returned, leading with him your dear and unhappy mother. But O, my child, how was she changed! Every trace of her former beauty was gone. Her eyes, wild and glassy, seemed to turn upon the objects around her without beholding them. She did not know me; and when flying to her, I offered to press her to my heart, she repulsed me with horror; and turning to the young man, bid him save her from the wretch that murdered first her child, and then her husband. And yet, continued she, still addressing herself to him, that child was such a jewel, that nothing less than a mother's insatiate cruelty could have devoted her to death. She was so good, so gentle, so kind to all – nay, the very murderers themselves kissed the cold stones she kneeled on. But it was a vow that did it all; and all our past and present sorrows come to this.

And then I was disobedient – that's yet another – but my husband, my poor husband – if he was here I should know him, I think I should – because you know – No – now 'tis all gone again. Then putting her hand to her forehead, she seemed to have lost the little recollection she had the minute before. The young man wiped away the tears that trickled down his cheeks, and telling me that he would try to get a doctor for the poor lady, left us, and barred the door. I endeavoured in vain to make my Agatha recollect me – I seemed an object of horror and aversion to her, and for three days that she remained in this distracted state, I was the most miserable of beings. The young man, whose heart seemed ill-suited to his situation, informed me with much regret, that he could obtain no advice for the lady, and that he had nearly involved himself in danger by desiring it. I conjured him to be careful of his own safety, and not to hazard his life for those, the term of whose existence will be short, and their sorrows soon at an end.

By degrees my Agatha's senses returned; but remembering the aversion with which she had beheld me, she hourly implored forgiveness for it of Heaven and of me as of a crime that lay heavy at her heart. In vain did I endeavour to reconcile her to herself; in vain assured her that she was innocent of any intentional unkindness, that it was usual in all whose illness had given a temporary disorder to the brain, to regard with dislike those they held dearest in health: nothing could efface this painful impression. But her fine faculties were never absolutely perfect. A melancholy succeeded her distraction, and preying on her frame, took her from me, it is now two months since. The impossibility of procuring medicines to assuage the pain she suffered, was an aggravation of my distress. I will not describe our parting scene – your heart could not support it – I will only say, that your name, and a blessing on it, were the very last words she uttered. Her lifeless body was suffered to remain two days in my cell. Two days, my child, did I spend in prayer over her remains – in holding her clay cold hand between mine in kissing the ring that had in happier days united us. I cut off a lock of her hair – I have since worn it at my heart – I send it to you – relic how precious!

When they came to take her from me, I conjured that she might have a Christian burial. But my request was scoffed at, and I was told that *death was Eternal Sleep! Eternal may it be to them whose crimes make that sleep desirable! For us, who look to be heirs of everlasting Bliss, the idea of annihilation is dreadful. No! I know that my Redeemer liveth, and though after this life worms destroy my body, yet in my flesh shall I see God. Then shall be brought to pass the saying that is written, Death is swallowed up in Victory. O Death, where is thy sting? O grave, where is thy victory?*[43]

My minutes are now few. I am sentenced to execution, after an examination similar to that of my entrance into the prison. But armed by the truths of Christianity, I heard my sentence without dismay, and shall go with pious transport, not to Eternal Sleep but to Eternal Happiness!

Should this ever reach your hands, my dear, my beloved child, let not your spirits sink under its affliction for our sorrows. Remember they will then be passed, and we shall be happy.

When the troubles in this wretched country began, I placed ten thousand pounds in the English funds, through the means of Messrs Simpson and Watford, Bankers, at Exeter, to whom I gave a letter of Attorney for the purpose, and, through whose means you will duly receive it. This is all I have left to bequeath to you.

The charitable person who sends this bids me be brief.

Farewell, my Agatha, my beloved child, farewell – but not forever – farewell till in the Regions of the Blessed we inherit fullness of joy and pleasure for evermore.

Charles Belmont

At the end of this was written in another hand:

The person who at the hazard of his life ventures to send this Packet, informs the daughter of the unfortunate Chevalier Belmont, that her father expired under the axe of the guillotine, this morning at the hour of Eleven. He met his fate with fortitude and pious resignation.

Many months passed before Agatha recovered the shock she sustained on reading this pathetic narrative: but hers was the sorrow of a gentle spirit; it was plaintive rather than passionate; and though deeply-rooted, calm and resigned. In the soothing cares of Sister Agnes she found relief; and with the meekness of a Christian, she sought instead of spurning comfort. She had, besides, long placed her affections on another and a better world.

Some months after this fatal letter arrived, she sent for the young man from whom she had received the small fortune on which she had

---

[43]I Corinthians 15, verses 14-15.

hitherto lived, to insist upon his accepting the sum his property had induced him to bring to her, and which, as no mention was made of it in her father's letter, she was assured he did not intend to receive.

On her urging his acceptance of it, Mr. Smith at last acknowledged, that the story was a fiction, invented by Mr. Hammond, who wished to spare her the pain of knowing herself indebted to others for support: that Mr. Ormistace was a party in the deceit, Mr. Hammond being under a necessity of disclosing the affair to him, in order to prevent his enquiries leading to suspicion of the truth, and that he promised to keep the secret on condition of being allowed to add five hundred pounds to the intended sum.

Agatha deeply affected by this new instance of Hammond's delicate generosity, could only reply to Mr. Smith by her tears. This, therefore, was the discovery to which Hammond alluded in his last moments, and renewing with it the recollection of that dreadful day, it was long before she recovered the patient resignation she had began to feel.

But time, friendship, and religion 'with healing on its wings,' have at last, in some measure, restored her tranquillity. She has instituted a school for orphans near her habitation; which she daily visits and inspects. She has another little society of widows, pensioned by her bounty; besides it innumerable other occasional charities, to which she liberally contributes. Her mind will sometimes revert to scenes past never to return; but she endeavours to chase the painful remembrance, nor suffers herself to indulge in the luxury of sorrow; and blessed with the friendship of the tender and affectionate Sister Agnes; with the maternal regard of Madame St. Clermont, who has promised never again to leave her; blessed with the pious precepts of the kind Father Albert, with the friendship and society of the amiable though eccentric Mr. Ormistace, by whom she is rather idolised than loved, and that of Mr. Crawford and his estimable family; blessed with the prayers of the poor, and the esteem of all; enjoying the smiles of the infants Edward and Emma, who already begin to lisp their gratitude to their more than mother; and, above all, blest with a spotless and self-approving heart, she leads a life of peaceful resignation here, in the firm hope and assurance of Eternal Happiness hereafter.

"Write, my friend," said Agatha to the author of this work, "write my melancholy story, and, since you wish it, publish it to the world. If it teach the young, that the conquest of ourselves, arduous as it appears, is generally obtainable, and often rewarded in that very attainment; if it teach them and all, that there are few trials, however severe, but may be supported with the aid of religion and a conscience clear of reproach; if it teach this – your Agatha will not have lived, she will not have suffered in vain."

FINIS.

Subscribers

Norbert Besch	Udolpho Press
Vesselin Budakov	University of Sofia, Bulgaria
Bernadette Collins	Birmingham
Garry Faux	Birmingham
Helen Fensterheim	London
Margarita Georgieva	Université de Nice, Antipolis, Nice, France
Sarah Gordon	Birmingham
Philip Goss	Douglas, Isle of Man
Charles Goss	Birmingham
Margaret Griffiths	Meriden
Isobel Grundy	Oxford
Thomas Huggenschmidt	Füsson, Germany
Stephen Jackson	Solihull
Felicity James	University of Leicester
Eleri Jones	Birmingham
Amy Lloyd	Shirley, Solihull
Tessa Lowe	Sutton Coldfield
Ian McMillan, poet	Barnsley
Fred Potts	Weta Films, New Zealand/Alaska
David Ravenscroft	Birmingham
Dan Rodger	Birmingham
Malcolm Speake	Birmingham
Kamil Szul	Birmingham
Dominik Szul	Birmingham
Mark Vanner	Birmingham
Tim Yates	Birmingham
University of Alberta	Canada

Lightning Source UK Ltd.
Milton Keynes UK
26 July 2010

157456UK00001B/54/P